TALES OF THE APT

Volume II
A Time For Grief

Tales of the Apt
(NewCon Press)

Spoils of War (2016)
A Time for Grief (2017)
A Love of Distant Shores (2017) (forthcoming)
Tales of the Apt 4 (2018) (forthcoming)

The Shadows of the Apt
(Tor UK)

Empire in Black and Gold (2008)
Dragonfly Falling (2009)
Blood of the Mantis (2009)
Salute the Dark (2010)
The Scarab Path (2010)
The Sea Watch (2011)
Heirs of the Blade (2011)
The Air War (2012)
War Master's Gate (2013)
Seal of the Worm (2014)

TALES OF THE APT

Volume II
A Time for Grief

Adrian Tchaikovsky

NewCon Press
England

First edition, published in the UK April 2017 by
NewCon Press
41, Wheatsheaf Road,
Alconbury Weston,
Cambs,
PE28 4LF

NCP121 Hardback
NCP122 Softback

10 9 8 7 6 5 4 3 2 1

ISBN: 978-1-910935-45-3 (hardback)
ISBN: 978-1-910935-46-0 (softback)

Cover art by Jon Sullivan
Editorial meddling by Ian Whates
Interior layout by Storm Constantine
Cover layout by Andy Bigwood

Contents

1. Introduction   7
2. Loyalties   9
3. Bones   35
4. Queen of the Night   53
5. Fallen Heroes   79
6. The Price of Salt   99
7. The Naturalist   129
8. The Last Ironclad   141
9. Alicaea's Children   175
10. A Time for Grief   195
11. The Peacemongers   223

Author's Forward:
Stories of the Peace

Spoils of War, Newcon's first volume of kinden stories, was indeed mostly about the war – specifically the Twelve-year War that ended shortly before (the second chapter, anyway, of) *Empire in Black and Gold* took up the tale. The stories were presented in the order, roughly, that they occurred, and the offerings in this volume follow suit, meaning that (as the subsequent fighting between the Empire and the Lowlands is covered in the novels themselves) these stories are mostly about the peace. Peace in the world of the kinden has a set of problems all its own, and the characters in these stories are fighting for their lives no less than the soldiers and refugees of the last. Their enemies are harder to kill than the warriors of the Black and Gold: poverty, inequality, prejudice and personal demons pose as much a threat as the criminal gangs of Helleron or the ancient magics of the Moths. There are also a couple of stories about how remarkably dangerous it is to be an academic in the world of the kinden, no matter how abstract the field, and the last story sees a return to the Commonweal to revisit the aftermath of the Twelve-year War, and of the *Shadows of the Apt* novels.

Because these stories take place from before *Empire in Black and Gold* all the way to after *Seal of the Worm*, there are some spoilers, as the events of the novels inevitably impact on and get referred to in the stories here. The rough timeline is:

- *Spoils of War*
- 'Loyalty' through to 'The Naturalist' in this volume.
- *Empire in Black and Gold* through to *Salute the Dark*
- 'The Last Ironclad' through to 'A Time for Grief' in this volume.
- *The Scarab Path* through to *Seal of the Worm*.
- 'The Peacemongers' in this volume.

Whether that matters is, of course, at the reader's discretion.

Adrian Tchaikovsky,
Leeds, January 2017

Loyalties

It happened when Balkus was playing cards: just a touch, a murmur in his head, but he jerked to his feet by instinct — to attention, nearly — upsetting the table with a heedless knee, to the complaints of his fellows. Artice, the little Fly-kinden woman, was in the air instantly with a speed that belied her age.

"What? What is it?" she demanded. The other two players, a couple of trail-dusty Beetle artificers, scowled at the pair of them, but as Balkus was the biggest man there by some margin they set to picking up the cards and the coins without calling him on it.

"Nothing..." Balkus said at last, but only after a minute of silence with his head cocked to one side, a man listening for a far-off horn to call him to battle. "I'm tired of this game. You hold my stake."

The taverna was a temporary little affair, part of a seasonal tradertown that piled itself together like driftwood each summer within sight of the walls of Tark. The Ants of Tark had plenty of money, and their city was a good place to acquire or be rid of any kind of human merchandise. Between the limitless appetites of the Spiderlands to the south, the factories of Helleron to the north, and the Empire's hungers to the north-east, the Tarkesh did well enough out of other peoples' misery.

Balkus stalked away from the gaming table. Artice was a little old thing, but she had a stern haughtiness to her, as befitted the majordomo of a Spider-kinden Arista. The Fly woman would be able to look after herself, and if not there were a dozen bronze-skinned Kessen Ants sitting in shouting distance who had pledged their swords to Artice's mistress, just as Balkus had. He passed them on the way out: they ignored him and he ignored them. Even though they were all exiles from the city-states that had birthed them, there was no love lost between Ants of disparate heritage.

Balkus had been a man of Sarn once. He had that city's light brown skin and straight black hair, quite different from the worn-bronze hues of the Kessen men, or the fish-belly paleness of Tark, His chief distinguishing feature was his height. Ant-kinden were seldom much over five foot eight, but Balkus was a big, broad-shouldered man, over six foot and brawny with it.

It had been a good eight years since he had turned his back on his home, choosing a life of solitude and silence over the constant mental buzz of an Ant-kinden community. He had heard others say how quiet his home was: how the natives went about their errands without greetings or farewells or excuses. Sarn was more open to outsiders than most, but foreigners still had an uneasy time of it, surrounded by all that quietly busy silence.

A lot they know, Balkus told himself. If you were born to it, the city was full of noise, only the noise was all in your head. That mindlink, that universal Art of the Ant, meant that everyone was talking to everyone *all the time*, constantly passing on knowledge, orders, gossip and speculation, reaffirming the boundaries between *us* and *them*.

It had been a long time since Balkus' head had played host to any thoughts save his own. But just then, just as he looked over his cards, there had come a touch of it, a whisper. His own people were near, there was no other possibility.

They've come for me. He was, he realised, keeping his own thoughts close, lest the least whiff of them let his former compatriots trace his whereabouts. He cast about, inside his head, hunting for that elusive trace.

There. Just a twitch of them, but he had the sense of at least two, probably three. It had been a long time since Balkus packed his bags, shouldered his army-issue nailbow, and turned his back on his ancestry. Since that day he had taken care to ply his mercenary trade up and down the Silk Road, far from the haunts of his people. In his imagination he had made a deal with them: *I won't rub your nose in the fact of my desertion, and you'll forget I was ever born.* Now it seemed that their memories were better than he'd thought.

The tradertown was a ragged, jumbled affair of shacks and tents congregating about a Tarkesh customs post and a spring of fresh water. Tark itself had a foreigners' quarter, but the Ant-kinden were not welcoming hosts and most merchant visitors preferred to spend as little time within their walls as possible. One never knew when the militia would suddenly decide to make an example of some luckless outsider, just to keep the rest in line. Balkus passed down the narrow, cluttered alleys of the place, surprisingly quiet for such a big man despite the hauberk of good Helleron mail he wore. His nailbow, a bulky, gleaming monster of a weapon loaded with a magazine of ten firepowder-charged bolts, hung from its strap, a comforting weight, but it would be sword work tonight, if they'd come for him. This was private business and no sense alerting all the camp.

Well, almost private. The tradertown was crammed full of visitors and their wares: Scorpions from the deserts to the east, Beetles from Helleron, Spiders and Fly-kinden from the south. Everywhere men and women were making deals, playing games, selling each other drink, singing and brawling in ways that would have horrified the Tarkesh, or Balkus' own people for that matter. He stalked between them, eyes skipping from face to face, looking for people who looked just like him.

And close. If their mind-speech was bleeding into his head then they couldn't be far.

...Tarkesh will...

He stopped. There it was: a voice in his mind as though the speaker was whispering in his ear. His hand was at his sword-hilt as he edged along the wall of a lop-sided hut, listening to the raucous babble from within, merchants betting and boasting and toasting their rivals' downfall. Someone had stoked up a fire out front, and amongst the huddle of figures warming themselves Balkus saw *them*.

Up to that point it could have been other renegades, just a pack of sell-swords that had cut their way loose from familial ties. When he saw them he knew, though, recalling his first difficult year away from the all-pervasive company of his fellows. There were three of them and they stood close together, angled away from each other to be ready for attack from all sides. *Straight out of the city gates to here,* Balkus thought, watching one of them talk to a tall Scorpion-kinden. They were all stocky, brown, their faces as similar to one another's, and to his, as siblings.

He considered his own recent career. Before hiring on with the Spider Arista, Giselle of the Artkaetien, he had been a month in Helleron, settling disputes in the fief wars. Before that he had been bodyguarding a slaver out in the Dryclaw, at one of the Scorpions' great trading and fighting assemblies. Hunters from home would have been led a merry chase, perhaps a fatal one. *There's not a chance that they could have made a line straight for me. Even I don't know where I'm going to be, half the time.*

He felt something leach from him, at the thought that he might not have to turn kinslayer yet. Whether the feeling was disappointment or relief he did not bother to analyse.

He watched and waited, whilst the other Sarnesh concluded their business. Instead of following them off, he made a count of twenty and sat down at the fire beside the Scorpion. The man – no, now he looked closer, the woman – was even taller than he was, and as broad across. She had curved blades of bone arcing over thumb and forefinger and her jaw was a nightmare of jutting teeth. In the firelight her waxy, pale skin was faintly luminous.

"Drink?" Balkus held out a jar to her and she took it without question, first sniffing and then swigging. She was wearing a motley of Spider silks badly tailored to fit, but he saw she had chainmail beneath it. A merchant adventurer, then, no doubt peddling the loot from wherever she had traded or raided most recently.

"You've lost your little friends?" she asked him. Her small eyes glinted with humour.

"I don't do clever or subtle," Balkus said frankly. "I'll give you money if you tell me what they want, and more money if you make sure word of me doesn't reach them. Fair?"

"Show me 'money'."

He held out a hand that mingled Helleron and Imperial coin.

She nodded happily. "The innocents want to attack Tark."

It was not what he had expected and his face must have communicated this, because she laughed at him.

"There is one of their own – one of your own, no? Or perhaps not. One of their own, then. The Tarkesh have him. The children want to see if he can come out to play. I think their captured friend will have company soon."

Balkus smiled. "None of my business then," he said. "Not my problem."

"It's good that a man knows his business," said the Scorpion woman, accepting his bounty with a clink of coin. "May yours be sweet, friend."

"And yours."

Balkus set off back for Artice, finding that she had inexplicably lost

12

his stake, but on her own account had fleeced the other players unmercifully. It was turning out to be an expensive night.

"I thought there was trouble, but it was nothing," he reported the next day.

Giselle, youngest daughter of the Aristoi family Arkaetien, nodded. "Well that's good. I do find trouble so bothersome." Her stance and manner was every inch the spoiled child, save for the twinkle in her eye that let him in on her self-mockery. "Artice thinks that matters amongst the Tarkesh will be sufficiently advanced that we should try a sally at their gates."

"An attack, Lady," said Aulus, the leader of her Kessen bodyguards, "only defenders make sallies." The man instantly and obviously wished he hadn't spoken.

"What a shame," Giselle mused. "A perfectly lovely word shackled by military convention." She smiled at Balkus again. "But we have business in Tark, O cadre of mine. There's a caravan of these merchant types heading off there at midday. Artice will make sure everything is ready for us to take our place with it."

Which meant that Artice would be giving the orders, and the old Fly woman had a tongue like a rapier. Balkus decided this militated his giving his news now, so that the Kessen contingent could do the heavy work.

"Lady," he said, and immediately had Giselle's wide-eyed attention again.

"See to it, Artice," the Spider said, dismissing the Fly and the rest of her retinue with a wave of one slim hand. They shuffled out of her tent, a gorgeous thing of red and gold silk, leaving Giselle sitting cross-legged on her cushions and looking up at Balkus as though he was an entertaining private tutor.

The renegade Sarnesh lowered himself into a soldierly crouch, trying not to meet that blisteringly innocent gaze. He had worked for more than one Aristoi in the past, but they had all been cynical old hands at the game, with plots and stratagems at their finger-ends, not one of their words or expressions serving as a clue to the next. This Arkaetien commission was different. Giselle was young. Oh, Spiders always looked young, and always elegant and beautiful too, but Balkus reckoned Giselle was no more than sixteen, and on her first piece of official house business. She looked at everything not only as though it was utterly novel, but as though she found it delightful. She smiled a lot, and she even smiled at Balkus. When he dared look back at her, he saw infinite reserves of faith in his experience of the world.

Even Spiders have to start somewhere, he considered. The problem was that he strongly suspected that a lot of them never quite made it to their majority. Spider Aristoi played for the highest stakes, always. They had no place for the clumsy or the witless, or even the naive.

"Lady..." he started.

"Please Balkus, I do keep asking you to call me Giselle," she said. "I know Artice calls me 'Lady', but she was my nurse and from her, believe me, it's anything but a term of respect. So, was this nothing you discovered last night more of a something after all?"

"No, not that, L- G-" Wrong-footed, he forced himself to a compromise. "Lady Giselle." Merriment was dancing all over her face, but he pressed on gamely. "I have to be blunt. I think you've been set up for a fall. I think someone back home has it in for you."

Instantly she was serious. "But what do you mean?"

"Your family, the Arkaetien – you have rivals there?"

"What would life be without rivals?" It was a Spider truism, but he saw from her expression that it was also true, and that she did.

"Lady Giselle, you're being sent into Tark, which believe me is far from the friendliest Ant city-state, and your retinue is a dozen Kessen mercenaries, led by loud-mouth Aulus, and me, probably the only rogue Sarnesh they could find at short notice. If there'd been a fugitive criminal from Vek, no doubt he'd be along for the ride as well. This is not good company to go into Tark with. Ants hate Ants."

She nodded, frowning, a woman barely more than a child pretending to sagacity. "My aunt told me that it was time to learn about the Ant-kinden," she told him.

"Well you might learn more than you want, is what I'm saying."

"Do you suggest Artice and I go through their gates alone?" she asked him.

"Seriously," he told her, "if it weren't that you'd have to try and manage the goods alone, I'd say yes."

She regarded him for a moment, and then smiled, radiant. "I do not deserve this care, Balkus, but I am touched, truly."

"Just my job, is all."

"But you have not called me 'Lady' through all your advice." She leant forward and caught his hand before he could draw it back. Her own were tiny in comparison, exquisitely clean. "I have faith in you, Balkus. I trust to your ability to protect me. I must, what else have I? After all, you have been into Tark before, have you not?"

"Three times," he said, aware he was not strengthening his case, but wanting to show off anyway. "I'll wager Aulus and his lot haven't."

"Then you and Artice will have to keen them in hand, Balkus." Abruply she was sitting back, arms clasped about herself. "You may be right, for all that. I am far from the best-loved of my family and they may have planned this adventure to be the end of me." Her use of the childish term for the mercantile business they were about was wounding. "Still," she told him, all resolve now, "what else is there? And if I return, the matter accomplished despite it all, then perhaps I may find more acceptance there. I have seen the poor wretches forced from their families, trying to live as Aristoi in far cities, in darned robes. I would rather try against all the odds, and fail if I must. You Ant-kinden understand dying in battle, don't you? Well this is my battle."

"We understand it's better to live," Balkus muttered, but her fragile bravery had cut him, in places that he had thought too well armoured for it. That and the soft, fleeting touch of her hand, the slightly awestruck way she looked at him, had sparked all manner of thoughts unfitting for a mercenary to harbour for his employer. *Well just maybe we will get through Tark,* he decided, *and give the cursed Arkaetien something to chew on.*

Giselle travelled in style: A low, flat-backed beetle painted in gold and red and purple bore her howdah, with Artice sitting behind the beast's head to keep it steady. The Kessen marched uncomplainingly behind, and Balkus fit in wherever he wanted, ranging ahead and back and keeping an eye out.

This time he spotted them before his mind caught the echoes of their speech: the three Sarnesh, cloaked, walking in a defensible little clump between wagons and automotives. Of course his three countrymen were headed to Tark as well, for their rescue or whatever it was that they planned.

He considered ignoring them, but he reckoned that they would have noticed him before the caravan struck Tark in any case, whether by spotting his face or feeling his mind. *Best to bring matters to a head then.* He placed himself ahead of the tireless insect, in Giselle's view, his nailbow tilted over one shoulder.

It took only a moment, although he had not sent any intentional thought their way. Then all three were glaring at him, stopped in their tracks and expecting him to stop and await their confrontation. He walked straight by them, and they were put to an undignified scrabble to keep level with him. Their eyes were raw hatred: two men and a woman who could be his brothers, his sister.

Renegade, came the thought in his head, and *Traitor, Deserter,* from the others.

And what about yourselves? he sent back, sublimely unconcerned. *Sarnesh secret service, are you? Doing a good job. Took me almost two seconds to spot you.* It was a good thought, actually. If they were agents of the city, they were lamentably bad at it. They were as out-of-place and clumsy as he had been when he first fled Sarn.

You are Balkus, one of them came out with, which surprised him, although he kept his face and tread even.

Didn't realise the old place missed me so much, he said.

The weapon you stole is worth more, the woman spat. He was starting to match voices to faces now.

Well you can tell them back in Sarn that I'm keeping it in good order. Don't make me demonstrate just how good, he told them, waiting for the predictable response. There were swords out on the instant, three short military blades clearing their scabbards. Balkus himself just regarded them, hearing the comforting sound of the Kessen drawing their own weapons, and knew that each of the Sarnesh would have a crossbow trained on them.

"Is there some difficulty, Balkus?" As the beetle was reined to a halt, Giselle parted her curtains and looked out. Her imperious gaze passed over the belligerent Sarnesh trio and made them shuffle their feet, abruptly ridiculous.

"Just giving some fellow countrymen directions, Lady Giselle," he replied easily. "They're a long way from home, see, and they don't know how things work around here."

Traitor, just you wait, one of the men hissed in his mind.

This isn't the field of battle, you pack of clowns, Balkus sent back contemptuously. *This is real life. Anyone here, anyone in Tark, could be on my side. You have only each other. How you expect to spring this mate of yours, I'll never know.* Even before they could respond he put in, *And yes, I know all about that. I may or may not tell the Tarkesh, depending. Now clear off or, I swear, I'll have you sold to Tark as privy-cleaners. This is* my *playground, children, not yours.*

He could feel their bitterness and frustration in the space between all four of their minds, but also their fear, their uncertainty. He had it absolutely right. They were far beyond anything they knew and he was cruel to taunt them, but he found he enjoyed doing so a great deal and regretted none of it. They slunk off towards the caravan's rear in a welter of half-formed threats and Artice started the beast of burden up with a flick of reins.

Aulus the Kessen picked up his pace to get within ten feet of Balkus, about the closest he ever cared to come. "They going to be a problem?" he grunted.

"If they are, we'll kill them." Balkus told the man. He caught a glimpse of Giselle's expression as she let the howdah's curtain fall, and it as much as said, 'My hero'. He considered how he had looked, standing there, facing off three armed Ants without even reaching for his sword, and had to conclude that he had been pretty heroic, at that.

It was late in the day before they reached the Tarkesh walls, and the gates had closed already, working less to a timetable and more to the Tarkesh's wish to make all foreign visitors understand just who was in command. Magically, the tradertown reassembled itself in all its shabby glories around the gate. There would be a very different mood tonight, though, with none of the liberties of earlier. The Tarkesh liked order and quiet, as did all Ant-kinden, and there would be a detachment of soldiers amongst the traders, enforcing laws and, no doubt, taking bribes. It was not that the Tarkesh were corruptible. Their duty to their city was ironclad. Any bribes would find their way to the city's coffers, and the Tarkesh Royal Court would decide what preferential treatment, if any, would result.

Balkus found that, like it or not, he was keeping an eye on the other Sarnesh. It was always possible that they would have a go at killing him, for no other reason than that he had walked away from what they held so dear. Artice had criticised him about bringing trouble down on her mistress.

"The opposite," he had told the Fly. "They'd have known I was there soon enough, and then they'd start thinking about how to get me. Facing them down, showing them I'm not alone here, should make them think twice." The old woman knew enough about Ants to see the sense in that.

He kept his mind open after that, once Giselle's tent was set. Whilst Aulus and his soldiers jostled elbows to give their employer appropriate space amongst the traders and the travellers, Balkus patrolled, loaded nailbow slung ready to hand, and felt for the echoes of three Sarnesh inexperienced at hiding their thoughts.

Sure enough, he sensed them whilst a few turns away from Giselle's tent. He took quick stock of his surroundings, choosing as his battlefield the space outside the camp of a Beetle merchant, some prosperous Helleron man with beasts and stock aplenty, and guards to match.

The three Sarnesh were doing their absolute best to be stealthy, creeping up on him from three directions with not even a clink of armour, but they were far from home and from the things they knew. They could not help sending one another constant thoughts of reassurance and coordination, and he felt the echo of them, enough to know exactly where they were. They had never had to fight Ants of their own city before, whereas renegades like Balkus learned to shield their minds.

He turned on his heel, the nailbow levelled, stepping back until he knew he could have shot all three through the canvas they were using as cover. *Come on out*, he sent to them. *You're so bad at this I'm amazed you're still alive.*

They came out with drawn blades, moving for him swiftly even as he brought the nailbow up.

The nailbow had been the key, of course: a man with a nailbow on your doorstep attracts attention. The merchant's guards, all Beetle-kinden mercenaries, were bundling out of the man's tent even as Balkus prepared to shoot: four men with crossbows directed at the would-be combatants, and a couple at the back who had been caught off-guard and were frantically tensioning the strings on their own weapons.

"Hold!" the Beetle merchant himself shouted out. To his credit he had a weighty mace in his hand and a leather cuirass beneath his open robe. "You take your stupidity elsewhere!"

The Sarnesh had stopped, bewildered at the response, scowling at the crossbows. Balkus rested his nailbow on his shoulder, a comfortingly familiar burden.

The Beetle glowered at all concerned, including the slackest of his guards. "I'll have the lot of you Ant bastards shot before you bring the Tarkesh down on us, or d'you think they wouldn't care, that you're brawling at their gates? They won't care whether I'm involved either, before they confiscate my stock and haul me off to their cells, so I'll forestall the matter by presenting them with some dead Sarnesh and see if that makes them any happier."

"I was just walking," Balkus said mildly, looking only at the Sarnesh.

"Well you go walk somewhere else," the Beetle spat. "I don't care if they're rogues and you're a loyalist, or the other way round, or what. You just take your trouble away from my door."

"Actually I'm signed on with the Arkaetien," Balkus said nonchalently.

The Spider house was name enough to conjure with that there was a distinct shifting of attention amongst the guards, crossbows inching over towards the three Sarnesh loyalists.

You see, you know nothing, Balkus told them. *Trouble me or my employer again and you're dead. And if anything should happen to befall me, don't think you won't be the very first that my employer and her Tarkesh friends, will come looking for. Don't make me prove it. Now go.*

Their exchange was silent to the Beetles, who only saw the three Ants twitch, teeth baring in impotent fury, then slink off like whipped beasts, sheathing their blades.

That night Giselle wanted to talk to him. Lounging on her cushions, sipping carefully at a bowl of mulled wine, she asked, "Was it hard to leave your home?"

He wondered if she was considering her own options if this venture failed. "Hard? No. It was going to happen sooner or later. I didn't fit in." Under her bright gaze he continued, "Most places you can rub along, if you're odd, but with them – with my people – they'll make you fit or force you out, one or the other."

"But your family, your city... They say Ants are so very close. How did you manage alone?"

"So close? Too close, like lodging ten to a room, which I've also done and I can't recommend it. No privacy, not a moment to yourself, everyone always knowing your business. Oh I won't say it wasn't hard, to make my own way, but I'd have run mad, otherwise. There was just no place for me there the way I was, the way I am."

"But even now, with those you just met?"

Balkus shrugged. "There's like a list engraved in the minds of every Sarnesh, a list of those that have left their posts. Renegades like me get hunted down a lot." He was trying on an air of rugged unconcern which he felt was going down well. "That's why I came out east. Not far enough, obviously. But they're not here for me. They're after some clown the Tarkesh have got hold of, here for a rescue. They'll get themselves killed and that's an end to it. If they try me again, I'll cut their throats."

She sipped at her wine again and he thought she looked concerned for him. "But are they not your kin, even so?" she enquired. "Would you truly see them dead, cast them off?"

Balkus wondered again if it were really his family she was thinking of, or her own. "Oh, Lady Giselle," he told her, heartfelt, "if they could do it without endangering their mission, they'd make a corpse of me. That loyalty, that binds an Ant to his city, when it breaks, it breaks with sharp edges. Just knowing they're out there, I feel hate for them, I feel I need to empty their veins before I'm truly safe. If I wasn't bound to you, we'd be hunting each other with drawn blades in the dark, right now."

She stared at him, one hand to her mouth, the cooling wine forgotten. "Then I'm glad my aunt hired you," she said, almost a whisper.

The Tarkesh opened their gates at dawn, with sufficient of their soldiers in attendance to suggest they expected an invasion. Each merchant and traveller was examined and questioned. Some, without obvious pattern, were turned away. Inching towards the gates, Balkus exchanged glances with Aulus of Kes. If trouble was in Giselle's future then trying to get a dozen foreign Ant-kinden into Tark was a gift of an opportunity for it.

Behind them, down the line, Balkus could see the three Sarnesh, cloaked like murderers, petitioning merchants up and down, trying to secure some manner of patronage that would get them through the gate. Apparently they had grasped the idea that to walk through as free Sarnesh would do nothing but get them killed or get them the cell next to whoever they were seeking to liberate. Once again he wondered that his old home had no better agents to send out than these three, if this prisoner was important enough to warrant the attempt.

Then the gate was looming and he braced himself for the Arkaetien family's apparent attempt to strip itself of an unnecessary heir. *When it kicks off,* he told himself, *up onto the animal, let Aulus' lads draw blade and then it's her ladyship over my shoulder and I'm out of here.* After a thoughtful moment he added, *and hope they're rotten shots,* because a fair few of the Tarkesh had crossbow bolts to the string.

Artice was already at the gate, though, and talking nineteen to the dozen, gesticulating at the gaily-coloured howdah, the stoic Kessen mercenaries. The Tarkesh were saying little back, but no doubt the words were running backwards and forwards across the city, from head to head. As Balkus and the rest drew closer, he heard a little of the Fly woman's speech, all full of the flower of the Arkaetien, the honour of service to such a noble line, so that any Ant of a lesser city than Tark would surely cast aside their bonds of patriotic loyalty for the chance of such a cause. It was a good line, Balkus had to admit, and he could see money changing hands too, a sign of value the Arkaetien continued to place on the friendship of the Ants of Tark. By the time Balkus himself reached the gate the regard the guards gave him had gone from open loathing to amused contempt, which might hurt feelings but got surprisingly few people killed.

In a flurry of wings Artice resumed her seat before the howdah, but she leant down to Balkus long enough to say, "Looks like I'm good at more than taking your money, eh?"

The business that the Arkaetien had sent Giselle to Tark after was a little forced recruitment. Tark was always a grand market for slaves. The Tarkesh themselves were keen slavers, more than most Ant-kinden and a great deal more than Balkus' Sarnesh kin, who had given up the trade. The city was conveniently situated for easy travel up the Silk Road from the Spiderlands for buyers like Giselle, easier still for the Scorpion-kinden who came out of the Dryclaw with their wretched strings of captives. Helleron factory-owners came down to buy up cheap labour, who they would set free under a crushing burden of debt to be their slaves in all but name. In recent years there were even the helmed, arrogant Slave Corps of the Wasp Empire, who rode in with the Scorpion caravans, eager to feed their great nation's inexhaustible hunger for human blood and sweat. It was a grim trade, and Balkus still found the thought of it distasteful, but a mercenary could not be too choosy and Spider-kinden paid better than anyone.

First they went to the Arkaetien's townhouse in the Foreigner's Quarter, which was as stark as any Ant-kinden hostelry on the outside but hung with silks and tapestries within, strung with brass lamps and gaudy with frescos. While Aulus and his men installed themselves, Giselle decided that she would go and see what the market had to offer, taking Balkus and Artice as her escort. Aulus wanted to send some of his men but she pointed out that, under the heavy hand of Ant law, there would be little enough trouble from outsiders. If the Tarkesh themselves took exception to her, Aulus' little band would be of no use whatsoever.

The stock on display was a mixture, more quantity than quality. True there was a fair selection of skilled Beetles and Fly-kinden, mostly debtors from Helleron or Merro or arrests from Tark's own Foreigner's Quarter. There were enough Scorpion-kinden there to lower prices, losers in the clan struggles of the Dryclaw, but Giselle looked over them carefully, obviously considering bidding for a lot. Scorpions were popular slaves in the Spiderlands: give them work to do that required casual violence and they were more eager than freemen of any other kinden.

There were Wasp Slave-corps soldiers selling, which was new to Balkus. It looked as though their colossal war against the northern Commonweal had finally produced an excess crop, for there were Dragonfly and Grasshopper-kinden slaves aplenty, and even a few Mantids bound and shackled, destined for deaths in some fighting pit. Giselle paused near one, watching the sharp-featured woman spit and snarl, arm-spines flexing against her bonds.

Beyond the Commonweal imports were the pens of children, another bumper crop. Child slaves were not the most lucrative, but they sold to certain discerning markets, the kindest of which was to guilds of professional slave trainers who would teach them skills and sell them at a profit. Other fates awaited the less lucky.

Beyond them there was a great morass of those who had nothing to recommend them save a full complement of limbs. A rabble brought in by slavers of all kinds, here were captives from Scorpion raids, luckless imperial deserters, the wretched poor sold by their creditors, fugitives from Spiderlands politics. Balkus looked over them with as dispassionate an eye as he could. They were held crammed together, not worth any space in which to display the talents they did not have. They stank, and flies hovered and buzzed about them in clouds. Balkus glanced at Giselle and thought he saw her flinch from this morass of failed humanity. *Not lost to the Spiderlands yet,* he thought, and then he spotted his mark.

Amongst this assembly of the hopeless he would have missed the man, save for the feel of his mind: a solitary Sarnesh Ant, his face swollen and mottled with bruising, stuffed into a cage with a dozen other captives. The only Sarnesh there, though: Balkus knew it just by casting his thoughts out. The man, therefore, that the three clowns were here for.

That made him frown: if this man was important enough to warrant a rescue, why would the Tarkesh sell him on as a slave? If he was a spy, an agent, then surely they would have tortured him out of his wits and then disposed of him. *Unless they don't know who he is.* But that didn't sit right. Something was missing from the picture.

He met the imprisoned Ant's gaze, and heard in his mind a spitting noise. It was all the captive would spare for him.

By that time Giselle was done. Abruptly she turned from the ranks of cages, the assembled stock in trade of the Tarkesh slave markets. "Enough," she said, her voice tight. "I've seen enough."

Of course she had lived with slaves all her life, but house slaves to the Aristoi lived lives that middling merchants of Helleron might envy, surrounded by wealth and privilege and beauty, and lowly only in that their masters and mistresses were so lofty. Balkus knew that there were fleshpits like this in the Spiderlands, that there were slaves sent to die in mines, in sport-fights, in factories, but the Aristoi did not need to see such things in person. They had other slaves who deal with the unpleasantness for them. What was slavery for, but to add so many levels between the great ones and the harsh realities of life? Giselle hid her thoughts well, barely letting them spill out on her face at all, but Balkus was sure that this was her first introduction to the true foundations of her culture.

He took her arm and led her from the place, feeling the captured

Sarnesh thinking hate at the back of his head all the way.

That night Giselle asked for him again, in her rooms at the Arkaetien townhouse. When he entered, Artice was just lighting the last of a scattering of candles that filled the air with a subtle, dreamy scent. The Fly gave him a disdainful look before retreating from the chamber, drawing the curtain across the doorway.

"Lady Giselle?" Balkus asked. She looked uncertain, withdrawn, sitting cross-legged on her bed.

"I wanted someone to drink with me," she told him solemnly. "I feel I have learnt a great deal here in Tark, even on my first day. Back home I would have cousins, peers, to confer with, entertainers and servants to take my mind from troubling thoughts. Here I have Artice, and I have you. Drink with me, Balkus."

There were two bowls and a couple of full jars on the floor, and she slipped down from the bed to them, deftly pouring out two measures. Balkus stood just inside the doorway, awkwardly, and Giselle rose lithely to her feet, a bowl in each hand and not a drop spilled. After that it would have been a discourtesy not to take one from her and drain it. The wine was thick, sweet, mingled with honeydew and cinnamon, a good deal finer than the best draft his purse had ever bought.

She had a hand to her mouth, failing to hide a smile. "Is that how soldiers drink?" she asked him. He saw belatedly that she had politely sipped at hers.

"I'm not a soldier any more, Lady Giselle," he said. The aftertaste of the wine was warm and rich enough that he could not help glancing at the jar, and Giselle sat gracefully straight down with the elegance of her kinden, not even an arm to steady herself.

"Sit, Balkus. If you're not a soldier then you needn't be on parade." Her look at him was all mischief. "Unless you'd prefer that." As he began to lower himself she sighed with mock-exasperation. "At least take off your armour!"

"My armour?"

"I promise I won't attack you, Balkus, and I doubt the Tarkesh will choose tonight to declare war on the Arkaetien," she told him.

Feeling foolish, he reached for the buckles at his side, and she said, "Aulus' men have mail that fastens at the back. Why not you, Balkus?"

"Aulus has the mail his city issued him with. In an Ant city there's always another man to tie your shoelaces for you. I had to get by alone." He reached for the buckles once more but she had sprung up again, seeing a new game.

"Let me! I want to see if I can do it."

"Ah…"

"No, I insist," she said sternly, and a moment later was virtually in his armpit, working at the clasps and no doubt ruining the nails that Artice carefully painted each morning.

"Lady Giselle, I'm not sure this is right," Balkus said, feeling one buckle surrender to her fumbling. She giggled, slipping round his back as she pulled at the next, making him turn round and round as she fought with the straps. "Look, it doesn't…" he started, and, "Not like that…" as she yanked it tighter by mistake, but she would not give in, and he ended up holding his arms patiently over his head until, more by luck than judgment, she had the mail undone all down one side, and he shrugged it off. She stared wide-eyed at his stained, stitched arming jacket.

"You have armour *under* your armour!" she declared. "Is there another layer beneath that? Is there actually a man in there at all?" She reached for the nearest clasp and he took her wrist, more forcefully than he had meant.

"This isn't right," he told her. "You're my employer."

She put a hand about his, holding his grip closed. For a moment she said nothing, seeming to steel herself. "I don't want to be your employer, not tonight."

"Then what do you want?" he asked slowly, suspiciously.

"I want to learn about Ant-kinden, as I was told." She brought her lips to her trapped wrist and kissed his fingers lightly.

"I don't…"

"Do you want me to dismiss you, just for this night, and re-engage you in the morning? Would I have to go that far, to strip you of your hired man's propriety?" she asked. Her free hand touched his cheek, flinching a moment at the coarse stubble. "It's lonely, amongst the Aristoi."

Slowly he released her arm. *This is a test, a trap, a something.* Her waist was nearly slender enough for him to close his hands about it. Her expression was all things: fear, eagerness, breathless excitement, the rich girl playing in the gutter, the child of deceit grasping for something solid.

He picked her up effortlessly, as though she weighed nothing, and laid her down on the bed.

Later that night, and feeling extremely full of himself, he wandered onto the streets of Tark. It was nothing he'd usually do, in a hostile Ant city-state, but just then he felt invulnerable, ready to take on the entire Tarkesh army. He strode through their streets as though he had just won them in a game of cards, and the Tarkesh watchmen stepped to one side without challenging him. He was surrounded by an aura of fortune and favour.

The very fine wine indeed had been freely flowing, leaving his head comfortably smoky, and he decided that the only thing for a good son of Sarn to do in these circumstances was go tell his kin how well he was doing. He meandered for the main gate, his mind fumbling into the ether for them. As he had suspected he found them as he reached the wall. They had been importuning merchants and travelers all day, and nobody had been fool enough to try and get them into the city.

What do you want, traitor? one of them hissed into his mind.

Oh well, if you're going to call me names, maybe you don't want my news, he sang out to them, leaning against the wall. The Tarkesh sentries eyed him suspiciously, in case he tried to open the gates to let in an invading army of three.

They did not answer that, and he felt their truculent silence like a physical thing, as gnarled and hard as a walnut shell inside his brain.

Don't be sore, he told them admonishingly. *I met your mate today, matey that you're after.*

He sensed them hurriedly conferring, and then: *He lives?*

Oh just, just about, last I saw. Tarkesh gave him a right going over, though. I hope you're not after him for his looks, is all I can say. Shame you can't get in, really. I don't think they were asking much for him. Just a handful of coin, and he's yours. Pity, really, how you're on the wrong side of the wall, and all.

They had no words for that, but a wave of loathing rolled over him, failing to pierce the armour of alcohol and satiation that he was encased in.

I mean, the more I think of you clowns, the gladder I am I went, he told them expansively. *Oh sure, it's not easy at first, the silence and all, but when I see the fools I left behind... Look at you! Sarn sent you to get matey there, did it?*

Royal Court gave you your top secret orders? 'You're the best we have, don't fail us!' Look at you! You utter bag of shambles, the lot of you. I'd not send you to get water from the well, let alone mount a rescue. Sarn must be on its last legs, is all I can say. I got out at the right time.

He waited for the arrows of their despite, but there was nothing, no insults, no taunts. Instead the timbre of their minds had changed to something less angry, more desperate, almost ashamed.

He frowned, trying to make sense of it. *What do you say to that, eh?* he assayed, hoping for a vitriolic comeback, but still they just drew into themselves, not even conferring. Their minds shrank from him, and he tried to think round it, to understand why.

Eh? he prodded again, but the fun was fast going out of it. Abruptly he felt the chill of the night air, sobriety leaching into him through his arming jacket, that was still open down one side.

They didn't send you, did they? he hazarded, and he knew, just from the change in the silence, that he was right.

They… The one word, from one of them, and the others trying to shut the speaker up, but she – Balkus guessed it was she, anyway – pressed on. *They will have sent us, if we retrieve him. If we go back to Sarn with him, then… how can they not acknowledge that it was Sarn's will?*

What bit deepest was that the words were forced from her not because she was justifying herself, but because she was defending the decisions of her city against his accusations of incompetence. Of course Sarn would not send three clueless fools to do its work.

And if you don't rescue him… He did not need to complete the thought. If Sarn had not sent them, then they were renegade, as renegade as he was. Maybe the city would take them back, if they returned as rescuing heroes. Otherwise, well, there was only one remedy for disobedience, as Balkus well knew.

I don't see what's so special about your mate in here, he grumbled, trying to recapture some of his earlier ire. *I mean, if he's so special, why* hasn't *Sarn sent some decent agents down here to get him. Why is it just you dumb bastards?*

They did not answer him, not directly, but in the echoes between them he caught the distant words, *Because we're his friends.*

The next day Giselle was out early, taking the Arkaetien purse to the markets to purchase her string of slaves to take back to the family. It was not that the Spiderlands was short of slaves, but the Spider Aristoi were fond of variety, and their constant aristocratic forays north allowed them to maintain their influence and prestige amongst the kinden of the Lowlands.

Her attitude to Balkus had been strange, but only in that it had not been awkward. She had smiled at him, a little shyly, but she had neither been overly familiar in front of the others nor stand-offish, just taking the whole thing in her stride. Balkus himself had been dreading either being dismissed, or being kept so close all day that he might as well have been on a leash. Spiders were an enlightened breed, he decided. *And tonight...*

At Giselle's command, Artice haggled with some of the Wasp Slave Corps until she was able to walk away with a string of dispirited Grasshoppers and Dragonflies for a good price. The Commonwealers were weary, footsore, ill-treated and far from home, and Balkus told himself that they would be better off as chattels of the Arkaetien than victims of the Wasp Empire. Then Giselle decided to get ambitious. She had Artice deal for the papers on a Mantis-kinden, not even a Commonwealer but one of the fanatics from Felyal, a shipwrecked pirate and as murderous a woman as Balkus had ever seen. Still, it would be a rare coup for Giselle to bring home one of those that had declared themselves her people's direst enemies. She was bidding against a couple of imperials, though, who no doubt wanted the belligerent Mantis for some blood sports of theirs, and sums of money were named back and forth as the subject of all this commerce raged and snarled.

Balkus had halfway hoped that the Wasps would have larger purses, but in the end Artice beat them down, and the Mantis, loaded with chains, was given into their care.

There was no question of keeping the spine-armed woman waiting around, and Giselle gave Balkus two of Aulus' men, and instructions to take her purchases to the townhouse, where the Mantis would be secured in one of the cellars and the rest held in the stables. Giselle herself would see how far her remaining coin would stretch, and return home with Aulus and the others later on.

Balkus had no faith in the Kessen, when it came to Giselle's safety. Two of them had already been arrested by the Tarkesh, beaten soundly and then released again without comment or charge, just on general principles. Still, a direct order was not something he felt like quibbling with, and so he gave Artice a meaningful *You look after her* look, and set off back.

Getting the Mantis into the cellar, even chained hand and foot, was like getting a two inch cork into a one inch bottle, and it seemed to take until past noon before the Felyen woman was finally locked out of sight. Balkus, scratched and bruised, felt that he had earned a break by then, and told the two Kessen to keep an eye on the rest of the merchandise while he hunted out some wine. They glowered at him, but they knew he was Giselle's favourite and so obeyed with poor grace.

Not long after that, to his relief, Giselle and the rest of her entourage returned, with another string of slaves stumbling in their wake. Whilst Aulus stowed them, she met Balkus in the courtyard, smiling brightly.

"It's done," she declared. "Tomorrow we head for home, and I shall bask in the adoration of my family." She said it with a self-mocking humour that Balkus liked. "Dear Balkus, I owe you a great deal. My family may have thought they were testing me, by hiring you to bring me into Tark, but their underestimated your experience." Heedless of Artice's stony face she leant into the big Ant, hands on his mailed chest. "I have a present for you."

"Not necessary, really," he muttered, but she was having none of it.

"Come with me to the stables," she told him. "Come and see."

He knew before he had gone a dozen paces. He felt the man's mind. No barriers of stone could sever the link of Art that bound all kindred Ants together.

"You didn't," Balkus said hoarsely.

Giselle turned, frowning for a moment, and then her face lit up. "Of course. Of course you know, You must feel his mind there. I did it, Balkus, just for you. A slave of your own. Think of it as a bonus if you must, O mercenary, though I'd rather you took it as a gift from me."

Hurrying now, Balkus marched into the stables, seeing all the slaves tied there, all the mournful Commonwealers, and the Beetles and Flies that Aulus had just brought in. In the midst of them all, like an island in a sea, was the Sarnesh, sitting with his back to the wall and his bruise-mottled head bowed. Still, even though the man's eyes were downcast, Balkus felt his mind glaring, thinking loathing at him with all the venom in the world.

And you're mine, Balkus told him. *She gave you to me, you surly bastard. How does that feel?* His heart was not quite in it, though.

Despair, a brief wave of it before the man clamped down on his thoughts. Balkus looked back to see Giselle still smiling, desperate for his approval, his nod.

"Thank you," he said heavily. He felt a little sick, in truth.

"Do anything you want with him. He's yours," she told him, certainly loud enough for the man to hear. "Kill him now, if you want. You could even torture him. You told me how much you hated your kin, how much they hate you. You could even sell him on, if you wanted. A life in the Empire or the plaything of Scorpion-kinden, whatever you think would be a fit punishment for his city casting you out."

She went inside then, leaving him staring at the bound Ant, his kin. Aulus and the Kessen guards were studying him thoughtfully, and he wondered what they would have done had Giselle presented them with a clutch of their former compatriots in lieu of wages.

He thought of the three failed rescuers, still waiting outside the city, too late now to go the easy way of simply purchasing their captured friend. What then? Would they trail Giselle all the way to Seldis? Would they try some doomed night assault against the Kessen crossbows? Would they end up themselves as slaves, the only way they could be reunited with their comrade? *Useless idiot children*, he told himself. *Coming out here, abandoning their city, and for what?*

It would be so easy to just cut the man's throat now, for what satisfaction it would bring him. Probably it would even be a kindness.

Balkus turned and stomped off.

Giselle had called for him that night, and they had drunk a little wine but not lain together. She had observed him, as he withdrew into a mind violated by that distant spark that was the prisoner's consciousness. His conversation had been halting, awkward, but she had seemed to understand.

That night he dreamt of Sarn for the first time in years. Sarn, that had birthed him and rejected him, the ill-fitting cog in its great machine, the mind that did not mesh. Balkus had lived in a dozen cities in the Lowlands and beyond, rubbing shoulders with twenty different kinden, and the one place he could not go was home.

That night he dreamt he returned to Sarn, but he was invulnerable, and they all feared him. He dragged the Sarnesh slave behind him, took him to the great commodities exchange on nineteenth and fourth street. He dreamt he saw the people of Sarn gather, wide-eyed and impotent, as Balkus took out his knife.

He dreamt of killing the Sarnesh slave. He stabbed and hacked at him, cutting his throat, opening his guts, he dug the man's eyes out, tore his tongue. He shot him down with an explosive glitter of nailbow bolts. He strangled him with bare hands. All the while the horrified populace watched on, powerless to prevent him enacting atrocity after atrocity on a man who never seemed to die.

"You see!" he shouted at them in his dream. "You can't save him! You're all cast out! You're all renegades now, because you couldn't save him!" The feeling, as he raved at them, as he browbeat them with his superiority, was as intensely sexual as his encounter with Giselle the previous night.

And the next morning, of course, they were ready to go: the servants of the house had Giselle's howdah, her beetle, and all the slaves assembled in the courtyard, even the double-chained Mantis. Balkus awoke to the clatter of armour as Aulus' people made ready.

He hurried down to join them, still buckling on his mail, arriving just in time to see Giselle ascend to her mount. The Sarnesh slave was a glowering, baleful presence behind Balkus' eyes. The dream returned to Balkus then, and he cuffed the slave viciously across the head with gauntleted hand, sending him reeling.

They reached the Tarkesh gate early enough that they could leave without much waiting, Artice smoothing the way out as she had the way in. Outside there was already a little tent-town of merchants who had come in too late the previous day to gain admittance. Slavers and provisioners, artificers, silk and spice dealers, they watched the progress of Giselle's entourage enviously, seeing those who had come through the Tarkesh mill unscathed and at a profit.

He felt them out there, of course, the three of them. They kept out of sight, but to Balkus the air stank of their frustrated rage and disappointment. Their comrade was tied on his own short line, close to the toiling beetle and within the cage of Aulus' guards. Worse, Balkus stood close by, nailbow on shoulder. The three would-be rescuers must have been plotting all night, back and forth and going mad with desperation. Here was the morning, though, and all their plans had come to naught. The best they could do was a suicide charge against Balkus and the Kessen.

He could sense them considering it, and he knew the slave was bitterly cautioning them against it. *Go home*, Balkus heard him tell them, but of course there was no going home for them. Without a rescue to turn their desertion into something more noble, they were cut loose. They would learn to live as Balkus lived, or they would die as their friend was doubtless going to die.

The dream in its entirety came back to Balkus then, all of it, all the blood and the triumph, the gloating and the satisfaction, all the way to the end of it.

At the dream's end, the Sarnesh, all the Sarnesh, had bowed to his logic. It was clear they were as cast-out as he, and so they left their city, each soldier and artisan, each merchant and bureaucrat. Even the queen and her tacticians had abandoned the Royal Court to trail off across the dusty farmland. Each one of them, from the lowliest to the greatest, was Balkus' equal in solitude, cut off from each other, cut off from home.

Balkus held himself steady, because he was *not* going to do it. He would rather knife the bastard now and let his body drag all the way to Seldis.

Because, of course, in the dream it had been no sop to his loneliness to know that they were all alone as well. Ten thousand lonely strangers in the world took the edge off his own abandonment not one bit.

He sensed eyes on him, not the eyes of his estranged kin, but eyes he knew well. *Oh preserve us from those who can see through us better than we see ourselves.*

His knife was in his hand, and he felt them twitch, the slave and the three freemen, not at the sight but at the feel of the hilt in Balkus' mind.

He did it before he could stop himself, ducking under the reach of his own best interests. The knife flashed, severing the slave's rope, and he gave the man a shove with his free hand that sent the wretch sprawling.

Aulus shouted something, but there must have been a counter-signal because, when the Sarnesh slave ran, no crossbow bolt found him, nobody gave chase.

This means nothing, traitor, came the clear words in Balkus' head. *You cannot buy your way back by these means.*

Shove your city up your arse, was his round reply, but his heart wasn't in it. The murderous part of him was filling him with sour, baffled hate. *He was ours! How could you let him go? He was our revenge against the whole sanctimonious pack of them.* His knife-hand shook.

He looked round and saw that Giselle was leaning out of the howdah, looking down on him. Her expression was cool, slightly amused, and he knew that she could see every bitter, self-loathing thought as though she, too, partook of the great Sarnesh mind.

"Careless, Balkus," she said lightly. "But how your people will rejoice, no doubt." Driving her own knife in, the kind never seen and never sheathed.

They sent her out to understand Ant-kinden, he thought bitterly, as he trudged on after the beetle before Aulus' mocking grin. *I reckon she's just about there.*

TALES OF THE APT

When I was about twelve or thirteen I had my first taste of role-playing games, a hobby still with me to this day. My first D&D character was, of course, a fighter named Balkus. As I was about twelve or thirteen, he was named "Balkus Slayer", leading to all manner of question as to what a Balkus was and how many he'd slain. Balkus, in the Shadows of the Apt, was originally just a bit-part player, one of the named members of Scuto's crew in Helleron. He went on to become something of the series' Wedge Antilles, never quite a lead, but always with a role to play. Here we see him before he hooks up with Scuto and starts to settle down.

Giselle obviously impresses her family well enough, because we see her later pushing the cause of the Arkaetien in occupied Solarno in *Seal of the Worm.* "Loyalties" also provides a pre-siege view of Tark, showing that just because they get invaded by the Wasp Empire, it doesn't mean they're the good guys.

Bones

Between the scarf and the hood, hardly anything of Elantris' face was exposed and still he was breathing grit, every blink grinding the stinging particles into his eyes so that he thought he would go blind before they reached Dust Port.

"Is this a sandstorm?" he demanded of the man in the locust's forward saddle, leaning forwards to yell in his ear.

"Sandstorm'd strip your flesh from your bones!" The rider's amusement was plain in his voice. "First time in these parts, then?"

"Domina Hastella never wanted to visit before," Elantris yelled. The man's back was offering no insights. "Which means you found something?"

Their locust dipped and dived, some current of desert air slipping out from beneath its wings. For a moment the pair of them could only cling on and let the labouring insect regain its hold on the element.

The rider cursed the beast, swatting at its antennae for emphasis. "Found lots of things," he called back. "But yes." When not proving a surprisingly able locust-wrangler, the man in the forward saddle was an academic, a Beetle-kinden named Fordyce Gracer, student of the buried past.

Elantris recalled waiting for Gracer in a shabby town of white-walled, flat-roofed buildings where south had been the desert, only the desert, like the edge of the world: vast, ground-down stretches of broken, rocky country standing barely proud of the sea of sand. If there was some habitable place on the far side of that barren ocean, nobody could swear to it. Even airships that had tried to brave the storms and the heat and the abrasive air had either come back in defeat or not at all. *Surely nothing of any value to man lies that way,* had been Elantris' only thought. And yet not true: here were Elantris and, on the locust ahead, his mistress Hastella, two Spider-kinden come all this way to inspect her family's investment.

"It didn't use to be like this," Gracer bellowed. He seemed to be guiding the locust lower, but the blowing sand kept Elantris from taking a look as he hunched in the Beetle-kinden's wind-shadow.

"Like what?" he managed.

"We've known for a while this wasn't always a desert. Sea was much closer, and we've found where rivers were. It was green, all this."

"So what happened?" To Elantris it sounded like something out of the old stories, that some ill-worded curse could parch a whole country to this death-by-dust.

"Time," was Gracer's curt reply. "Things change. You go digging around the place as much as I have, you realise that. But in this case it's a good thing. When the desert came, it buried a lot of fascinating stuff, and that stuff's still there. So long as it's out of the wind, you'd be amazed what secrets the desert keeps."

Then the locust had spread its legs, although its wings flung so much sand up that Elantris could not even see the ground. The insect came to a clumsy, skidding stop, hopped a few paces as though uncertain, then folded its wings primly.

"Welcome to Dust Port!" Gracer boomed. "Dig's just a little way on. You'll learn to love it, just like we have!"

A moment later the wind lulled, the dust swirling and sinking, revealing a camp of tents and slope-sided shacks ringing a stand of stunted trees that Elantris thought must be a watering hole. Gracer was waving at a train of animals winding its way in from the far side, half a dozen round-bodied beetles with ridged, black shells, laden with boxes and barrels but stepping lightly enough that Elantris guessed the containers were empty. A little logic suggested that the caravan had been sent to Dust Port from the dig site for supplies.

Elantris slipped sideways from his mount's rear saddle and reached the other locust just in time to help his mistress down. She was sufficiently swathed in silks that he had no clue to her mood, but then even her bare face was seldom a good guide to that. They were both Spider-kinden, but Hastella was pure Aristoi, a distant scion of the Aelvenita family that was paying for Gracer's research. Her Art always hid her true thoughts deep behind her customary mask of watchful patience.

So has he finally found something to repay the investment? Elantris wondered. *Or is it something else?* When Hastella had ordered him to arrange the journey she had not seemed keen, so much as resigned.

Elantris was just a humble secretary: letters, music and a little divination on the side. What would he know?

Gracer was heading off for the caravan. Beetles of his sort were tenacious, robust and found everywhere, just like the insects they drew their Art from. They got caught in Spiders' webs like any other prey, though, and now Gracer's little struggles had attracted the spinner's notice.

Hastella watched him go, then gestured imperiously for Elantris to follow her over to a ramshackle collection of wood that turned out to be a taverna. There, he procured some watered wine from the leathery-skinned Fly-kinden proprietor and brought it over hesitantly.

"This won't be up to much, Domina," he murmured. "I think it has sand in it."

She hooked her veil down so that he would receive the sharp edge of her expression. "If there's anything within ten miles that doesn't have sand in it, I'd be surprised." Still, she took the wine and downed it without a flinch, which was more than Elantris could manage.

He looked about the close, slope-ceilinged confines of the taverna's single room, the stifling air glittering with dust motes where the sun crept in. There were a couple of big Scorpion-kinden sitting in one corner: waxy-skinned, bald men with snaggling underbites and claws on their hands. A scarred Spider woman reclined nearby, wearing armour of silk and chitin, a rapier displayed prominently at her belt. Most of the rest of what passed for the taproom was taken up by a dust-caked party of Flies and Beetles and a single sullen-looking Ant-kinden, all glowering at Elantris when they caught him looking their way. In Dust Port you kept your curiosity to yourself.

"You think I'm mad, of course, to come out here," Hastella said softly.

He started guiltily. "I would never…"

"Gracer is quite the scholar, you know. He believes what he does is important. He's right, though perhaps not quite in the way he thinks."

"Mistress, forgive me, I don't even know what he does, what anyone could be doing out here."

"The past is a book, and knowledge is never wasted. A grand discovery – an ancient palace, a city from time before record lost to the sands – these things buy status and prestige: for him as a scholar, for me as his patroness, for the Aelvenita as my kin. And sometimes men like Gracer turns up something genuinely intriguing – some scrap of ancient ritual that might be put to use, some antique blade still sharp despite the ages… Knowledge is never wasted. But, like good wine, it is sometimes best kept to those who appreciate it. After all, Master Gracer would scrabble in the earth with or without the patronage of the Aristoi. Better that we pay for his hobby, just in case it profits us. Just in case he finds something remarkable…"

"Mistress, can I ask… what was it that drew you here, really? You wouldn't say…"

"No, I would not. Not back where the foolish lips of a secretary could spread the word." Her cold look did not endure, seeing his hurt expression. "Very well, Elantris, as we've arrived." She reached into one of her many pouches and produced a folded paper. "Feast your eyes."

For a long time he stared at the sketch there, turning it and turning it and trying to understand what he was looking at. In the end he was forced to confess his ignorance.

"It's a skull, Elantris. A drawing of a skull."

As though the sketch had been one of those trick images, abruptly he saw it, the line of the jaw, the eyesocket, the teeth… he had never seen such teeth. "A skull of *what?*" he asked.

"That's just it," Hastella confirmed. "Nobody knows." Her gaze might have been fixed on some image that existed only in her mind, but Elantris fancied that, while he studied the sketch, she had been staring at the two Scorpion-kinden, and that they had been looking back, yellow eyes fixed narrowly on the Spider Arista. *Brigands?* was Elantris's alarmed thought. Scorpions hereabouts were not noted for their genteel or law-abiding ways.

Interrupting his thoughts, Gracer ducked in, spotted them and ambled over, sketching a creditable bow before Hastella. "Domina, we're ready to head to the dig site. You may fly the last leg if you wish, but we have a howdah for you if you prefer a more comfortable ride on the beetles."

"So kind, Master Gracer, and I accept." She favoured him with one of her warmest smiles, the kind she reserved for truly useful underlings – and which Elantris himself saw precious few of.

Gracer's dig was out where the bones of the earth jagged up from the dusty ground, tiers of barren, red-rock uplands rising higher and higher until they broke free of the abrading hand of the sand to form the true mountains that spiked the horizon. It was stark, uninhabitable, malevolent country, and yet even here people lived. Riding atop one of the pack beetles, Elantris saw huddles of huts that must count as villages, corrals of animals.

"What do they raise here?" he asked Gracer.

"Crickets, beetles," the man explained. "The local varieties barely need to drink from one tenday to the next. The herders let them out before dawn, and their carapaces catch the dew like cups. If you know what you're doing you can fill your water-skin from them."

"And you say this place was once green!"

"Look ahead." Gracer's finger led his eyes along the stepped and broken terrain. "See the land dip there? follow the gully up – that was a river once. People lived here, many people. This land wasn't just good enough to keep them alive, it was good enough to fight over."

"How do you know?"

The Beetle-kinden's teeth flashed in his dark face. "Because of what we found, young Spider. Because of what brought your mistress here."

Monster bones? But it was plain that Gracer meant more than that.

The dig itself was a large tent backed onto a sheer rock face, surrounded by a collection of smaller shelters, all dust-coloured, patched canvas looking as though it had suffered there for decades rather than just under a year. The motley collection of people who came out to greet them had rather the same look. Elantris's image of academics was the elegant and sophisticated, debating some point of abstract interest in an Arista's parlour, not this pack of weathered, villainous men and women, their hardwearing clothes layered with dirt and their hands calloused from the spade and the pick.

Gracer was making introductions but the names passed Elantris by – even though he knew Hastella would recall every one. Instead he was just looking from face to face, wondering how one would separate a scholar from a fugitive killer just from the look. A half-dozen were Beetles like Gracer, stocky, dark and powerful, and there were a couple of Elantris's own kinden as well as three Flies and a lean Grasshopper woman employed to look after the locusts.

Elantris could see how such a team would function out here, the strengths each would bring. Every insect-kinden had its Art, the abilities it drew from its totem. The Flies would bring swift reflexes and the wings they could manifest on demand, able to scout the sands as swiftly as the saddled locusts. The Spiders drew on their archetype's patience and presence. The Beetles had their rugged endurance, and the Grasshopper must own that most ancient of Arts, able to speak with her kinden's beasts. Elantris watched her commune with them before walking off to their pen with the great creatures trailing meekly behind her. Without Art the merely inhospitable would have become uninhabitable.

Art aside, the barren surroundings and the looming rock face oppressed Elantris, loaded with an invisible threat that plucked at the edge of his mind. He felt as though some predator was laired there, crouched within those cliffs, having drawn the substance of the desert before it as a blind to entrap the incautiously venturesome. He glanced at Hastella, but her smooth composure admitted nothing of her thoughts.

And besides, this was one reason she kept him at her side, despite his more general failings. He had good eyes for the invisible, and what was history if not a great edifice of the unseen?

I shall have harsh dreams here.

He came back to himself because Gracer was guiding his mistress towards the largest tent, and presumably she had invited him to show her his finds, or else he was just too enthusiastic for propriety. Elantris followed hurriedly, catching the Beetle-kinden's words.

"We've dug a selection of trenches, and we hit stone everywhere: foundations, loose blocks, all of it worn by the sand but still recognisable as the work of human hands. No idea how far it extends – that would take far more labour than we have – but I think at least several hundred inhabitants, potentially well over a thousand."

"Where are these trenches?" Hastella asked him.

"We've marked locations and covered them, otherwise the sand will destroy anything we leave exposed. A day or so here and you'll feel the same way, Domina." A jovial chuckle. "However, in *here* we've exposed the entryway to a dwelling set into the cliff. The entrance had been carved into the rock and then choked with sand and rubble, maybe actively filled in. People knew there was something here, though. We came here following travellers' tales."

"What did they say?" Elantris blurted out. Gracer and Hastella stared at him and he coloured. "About this place? What did they say?"

Gracer shrugged. "Some nonsense. They're not fond of it. Who would be? Nothing but dust here now – not like it was all those years ago. Thousands of years, Domina, five, ten... I've never seen anything such as we've found here – what we're still finding here. It's from before any history, from before even stories." And, with that, Gracer stepped into the largest tent, forcing his two guests to follow.

Inside, the heat was stifling, as though the very gloom radiated it. The slope of the ground within was steep where Gracer's team had dug down to the level of the old, that point in the sands that history had sunk to. There, the shapes of the past emerged from the dry substrate like ships from fog, and Elantris saw the angled lines of walls that had been ground down to mere stubs, the scatter of fallen blocks, carven sides effaced, worn almost smooth. At the far end of the tent, lit up by twin lamps, was a gateway, a crack in the rock that had been widened into a low rectangle of darkness, flanked by uneven, lumpy columns or, no... Elantris recognized the contours: statues cut into the stone. There the swell of hips, there elbows, shoulders. Time had played the headsman, though: barely even a stump of neck was left,

"We've collected a lot of odd artifacts, potsherds and the like, all unfamiliar styles," Gracer explained. "But you probably want to see the guardians."

There were a handful of pits dug there, covered with sheets against the dust that still got in somehow, to hang in the air and prickle the throat and eyes. With a showman's flourish, Gracer drew the nearest one back, revealing –

For a moment Elantris was convinced he saw living flesh, movement, locking eyes with a fierce, ancestral glower, but there were only bones left of this ancient warrior. Bones, and the tools of his trade. An irregular lump of reddish corrosion was an axe-head, according to Gracer. A near-identical blot was a knife-blade. The armour had fared better, loose scales of chitin still scattered about the ribs, and curving pieces of some sort of helm placed reverently next to that yellowed skull.

"We've found more than twenty so far, buried before this gateway," Gracer explained, "and doubtless we've not found them all. Soldiers, guardians, sentries left to watch the threshold, interred with care and respect."

"What kinden?" Hastella asked him.

"Impossible to say." Gracer frowned, the dissatisfied academic. "You must know, from a skeleton alone the kinden is usually impossible to tell, unless Art has made modifications to the bone structure, like a Mantid's spines or a Scorpion-kinden's claws. The thing is, most of the old sites I've worked on, there's usually some fairly strong pictorial evidence to suggest who the locals were – statues of beetles, spiderweb motifs, those mantis-armed idol things you get. Go back a couple of thousand years and that's usually the principal decorative motif. Here – nothing of the sort, not on the stones, not the walls – it all seems to predate that period entirely. Our dead friends here had some personal effects, and we've found a pendant with what might be a bee insignia, and a shield that's been embossed with fighting crickets, but it's circumstantial… Who were they? We don't know. We also found the remains of some dead insects close by, again apparently buried with full honours – two fighting beetles, a scorpion, but again, it doesn't necessarily follow that the people here were any kinden we know today. But you didn't come all the way to our humble hole in the ground to see these dead fellows, Domina."

"Show me," she told him sharply, perhaps feeling that the Beetle-kinden was forgetting himself. Gracer bobbed, grinning, and headed for the doorway, snagging a lamp as he went and beckoning for them to follow.

Once inside, Hastella had gone still, so Elantris squirmed past, careful to avoid jostling her, and became so involved in proper decorum that he only saw the *thing* when he straightened up.

He let out a brief, strangled yelp and sat down hard, heart hammering as fast as beating wings. Gracer whooped, typical coarse Beetle, and even Hastella had a slight smile at his expense. Red-faced, Elantris picked himself up and backed away from the skeleton Gracer's people had assembled beyond the doorway.

They must have set this display up to impress the woman paying their wages. They had gone to some lengths to wire and strap the thing together, and had sunk bolts into that antique ceiling to suspend the thing. It was an impossible monster.

It was bones, just bones like the men outside, but no man this. It had been posed on its hind limbs, rearing up like a mantis, its forelegs – arms? – raised as if to strike down with their crescent claws. Its spine had been reconstructed into a sinuous curve, and Hastella's sketch had not done that head justice. Elantris looked up at it, that broad, heavy skull with jaws agape, baring its long, savage fangs.

The whole beast looked to be about the size of a man but ferocity dwelled in every bone of it, as though without the wire and the cord it would have lunged forwards to tear the throat out of any mere human.

"Is it a human of some unknown kinden, perhaps?" Hastella suggested, for there was little in the world that carried its bones on the inside, after all. There were humans, and there were a handful of species domesticated by them: goats, sheep. Nothing like this beast dwelled in the world any more, and for that Elantris was profoundly grateful.

"Probably not, Domina," Gracer told her. "The relative proportions of the limbs suggest that it went on all fours, and the skull... my anatomist tells me that it has a lot of attachment points for muscle – not a bite you'd want to get in the way of – but a far smaller brain-space than ours... It's something new, Domina."

"But this reconstruction, it's speculative," she offered.

"Ah, well, no." Gracer had that smug look universal to academics with the answers "The skeleton was found not quite in this, ah, dramatic pose, but still complete – tucked just around the doorframe. There wasn't much interpretation required. If you would wish to take it back, Domina, as a gift from us in appreciation for your support, it would make quite the conversation piece, perhaps?"

He was being too familiar again, but Hastella seemed content to let him get away with it. "Show me more," she directed.

The next chamber was a great, long hall, and for a moment Elantris had to stop, swaying, his eyes bustling with shadow movement that had not been cast by Gracer's lamp: hurried flight, the thrust of spears, a tide of furious darkness, the silhouettes of monsters. His ears rang with distant howls and screeches, hideous and alien.

He realised the hand on his shoulder was his mistress's, and bowed hurriedly. "Forgive me."

She was studying him, though, and he understood unhappily: *So, she brought me here for my eyes, then.* He had medicines for when the seeing dreams became too insistent, but if dreams were why Hastella wanted him here then he would have to forego the cure and suffer.

The floor here was littered with stone, irregular forms that eventually resolved themselves into the broken fragments of statues. Once he had understood that, Elantris felt he progressed through a stone abattoir. Everywhere he looked there were broken arms, legs, sundered torsos.

"No heads," he said, before he could stop himself. The other two looked back at him.

"Very good," Gracer said. "Yes, this isn't just wear and tear, and our dead lads out there weren't just taking a nap. There's holes in some of the skulls and shields, broken bones. They died defending this place, I reckon, and whoever got in here, they weren't gentle with the fixtures. We guess this walk we're on was lined with these statues, and they all got knocked over, and someone took care to hack off every head and cart them off."

"But why?"

"Symbolic, probably. Ritual purposes." Gracer shrugged. "My best guess."

At the end of the hall was another low, rubble-choked entryway, and a handful of Gracer's people were working at it, shifting the stones and setting in wooden props. "Ceiling came down here," the Beetle explained. "And that *was* just time did it, I think. We're almost through, though. Seeing as you're here, I was going to get my crew to go all night, and maybe in the morning we'll all get to see what's in there.

No! The thought struck Elantris without warning. *I don't want to know.* But he said nothing. Of course he said nothing.

"A perfect idea, Master Gracer," Hastella said warmly. "So good to find a man of your profession who understands proper showmanship. Perhaps, after my tent has been pitched, you might join me for a little wine, and we can discuss what else I may be able to provide for you and your team."

Hastella's tent was a grand affair, overshadowing the little billets of the scholars. Elantris got a separate chamber to himself, metaphorically if not literally sleeping at the feet of his mistress. He had thought she would want him to wait on her while she and Gracer talked, but she had sent him off around dusk, and he understood why. It was not that she cared about privacy, but that she wanted him to dream.

The temperature had fallen as soon as the sun crossed the horizon, and yet the day's heat still seemed to linger feverishly in Elantris, leaving him alternately shivering and sweating, fighting with his hammock, staving off the night as long as he could while the murmur of Hastella and Gracer's voices washed over him like waves.

He was standing before that crude opening again, in his dreaming. In the dark of the desert he could not see the restored heads of the statues flanking it, but he felt their stone gaze upon him.

He did not want to go in, and for a moment he felt that he did not have to, that he could still walk away and let the past keep its secrets. Then there was a rushing from all sides, and shadows were streaming past him, of men, of beasts, and he was carried helplessly with them.

He was racing down that hall, seeing the great flood of bladed darkness course on either side of him. He wanted to fight, to resist it, but he could not: he was a part of it, and it a part of him. He was responsible for what the darkness did.

Ahead, the monster reared, bones at first but then clad in a ripple of fur and flesh. He saw those claws strike, the savage jaws bite down, flinging fragments of the dark on all sides. Then it was not a monster but a man in a monster's skin, face loud with loathing and hatred. There were many men, many monsters, creatures of the absurd, of the horrific: long-necked things with cleaving beaks; snarl-muzzled grey nightmares that coursed in seething packs; branch-horned, plunging things that used their antlers like lances. And the darkness was torn and savaged and brutalized by the monstrous host, but gathered itself and came again, pulling Elantris like a tide, forcing him into the jaws of the fiends to be torn and clawed and run through, over and over.

He awoke, crying and flailing and finally falling from his hammock completely – a real, physical pain to drag him from the morass of his nightmares. Looking up, he saw Hastella standing over him. How long had she been watching?

It was dawn already, the first threat of the desert sun just clawing at the eastern horizon outside the tent. "Tell me," Hastella said, and he did, all he could remember, a jumbled, near-incoherent rant of a story, and yet she listened all through.

Gracer had been optimistic, and his ragged band was still trying to safely clear to the next chamber through most of that day, leaving Elantris nothing to do save kick his heels and steal bowls of wine when he thought Hastella was not looking. He wanted rid of this haunted place. Every instinct told him to cling to his ignorance.

At the last, close to dusk, Gracer came, with much apologetic scraping, to say that they were ready, now, to break through. The delay had plainly dented his confidence as, even as they passed down the hall of broken statues, he was insisting that they might find nothing of great import. Now the moment came, he was abruptly nervous that he might run out of material.

His entire team were standing there, shovels and picks and props in hand. Elantris squinted through that dark straight-walled aperture, seeing that there was a space beyond it but nothing more.

Like looking into a grave.

As thoughts went, he could have wished for something more uplifting.

"Olisse, you go first with the lantern," Gracer told a Fly-kinden woman. She nodded curtly and hunched down, shining the lamp through. She was just a little thing, like all her kind, barely reaching Elantris's waist. If the ceiling ahead was unsafe her reflexes, and the Art of her wings, would give her a fair chance to get clear.

She slipped under the lintel, barely having to duck, and the darkness within flurried back from her. Elantris shuddered, remembering his dream.

There was a long moment of silence, in which they could see the light within waxing and waning as Olisse moved about. Then: "Chief, you'd better get in here," came the Fly's hushed voice.

"We're all coming in," Gracer decided.

"Chief —" Elantris heard the Fly say, but Gracer was already hunkering down to duck through the doorway, and Hastella was right on his heels.

"Founder's Mark!" Gracer swore, his voice almost reverent. The other scholars were staring at Elantris, plainly expecting him to be next after his mistress. With no other choice, he scrabbled into the next chamber.

It was carpeted with bones. The chamber was wide and deep — deeper than the lantern would reveal, and everywhere was a chaos of ancient skeletons, heaped and strewn and utterly intermingled. Some were plainly human, whilst others — larger, heavier, stranger — must be the remains of more monsters, so that Elantris wondered if this had been some den of theirs, and these multitudes their victims back in the dawn of time.

We are well rid of such horrors.

Olisse was hovering overhead with the lantern, unwilling to touch down. Hastella was impassive, but Gracer regarded the ossuary with wide eyes.

"I never saw anything like this," he murmured.

By now Elantris had seen that, like the statues, one thing was missing. There were no skulls in all that chaos of jumbled bone, neither human nor other.

"How far back does this go?" Gracer was asking, and Olisse glided forwards, thrusting the lamp out, then letting out a startled curse. She had found an end to the slew of bones, and it was marked by a pile of skulls that reached close to the ceiling. The lamplight touched on the sockets of men and of fiends, the bared teeth of both united in decapitation and death.

What came here and did such a thing? Elantris wondered. The contrast between the orderly burial of the guardians without and the mound of trophies within was jarring, and as much as he tried to convince himself that this could just be the respect that some ancient culture accorded its honoured dead, he could not make himself believe it.

"Well, obviously it's going to take a lot of study, to sort this out," muttered Gracer, the master of understatement. "It could have been… a number of things."

A massacre, say it, Elantris challenged the man silently. *A massacre of men. A massacre of monsters.*

The Fly came down gingerly beside that great monument of skulls, which towered over her. Some of the inhuman relics there had fanged jaws great enough to seize her entire body.

Elantris thought he saw it in the lanternlight then, even as Hastella was turning to go. Beyond that mound of grisly prizes, against the back of the cave wall: more skeletons, human skeletons, still intact and huddled together, and all of them as small as a Fly-kinden. Or a child.

Then his mistress was heading back for the surface, and he was hurrying after her, out into the gathering dusk.

She would not talk to him all evening, nor to Gracer, just sat in her tent and, perhaps, tried to come to terms with what she had seen. The scholars were uncertain what this meant. Gracer dragged Elantris off to their fire and plied him with questions he could not answer, angling for some insight into Hastella's mind. Elantris drank their wine and bore their inquisition because it kept him from sleep.

Even after the scholars had turned in, cramming themselves into their threadbare little tents, he loitered on, in the steadily deepening cold, staring at the canvas that hid that fatal doorway, mute witness to an atrocity ten thousand years old.

At the last, it was either drop on the chill sands or haul himself to his curtained-off corner of tent. When he had finally opted for the latter, he found Hastella still awake, staring at him as he entered. He could never read her eyes, even at the best of times. These were not the best of times.

In his dream the darkness was receding like a tide, leaving only bones in its wake. The monsters were all dead now, and so were the men who had stood by them. In his dream he watched each of their skeletons hauled up, clothed briefly in flesh in the moment that the blade came down, in the moment that the scissoring mandibles cut, then the head was free and the body was left where it fell. He was in amongst the darkness. The weight in his hands was the great head of a monster torn from its body by savage pincers, its mighty jaws gaping impotently, teeth helpless in the face of history. He placed it with the others, on that gathering pile, and did his best not to look beyond.

In his dream, he retreated down that hall and smashed the statues one by one, taking from those carven human shoulders the heads of monsters, the gods of a vanished people.

In his dream, he moved the stones to wall in that doorway in the cliff, blocking up his ears to the shrill cries of those they had left alive within. In his dream it was necessary. He had cast his lot, given his allegiance, and that made them his enemies in a war that only utter extermination could bring to a close.

In his dream, he buried his comrades and their beasts, those who had fallen in bringing this final conclusion to an ancient rivalry. He heaped earth on the shattered wing cases of beetles, the broken legs of spiders, the serrated mouthparts, the snapped antennae of those who had brought survival and victory to his ancestors.

He started from his dream to hear Hastella re-entering the tent, wondering blearily what she could have been doing. Had she been into the dig site again? Had she stood, staring mesmerised at that great trove of the fallen and the dismembered? Had she pieced together some story in her head to account for it all, and would that story resemble his dream?

She was a hard woman, honed like a knife by the politics of the Spiderlands, where to be weak was to fall, where emotion was leashed and used, and ran free only behind closed doors. Had she been shedding tears over that host of the unknowable dead? Had she been drinking in the tragedy of ages?

He thought not. A humble secretary he, but he knew her too well.

In the first grey of pre-dawn she had orders for Gracer. "I want all your team working double time in the new chamber," she told him. "I want a catalogue of everything you've found. This is the greatest historical discovery of our age, Master Gracer. You have two days to conduct an overview and provide me with a report I can take back with me."

Was it academic prestige or financial reward that glittered in the eyes of Fordyce Gracer? In any event he had his complement on the move before the sun cleared the horizon, filing into that darkness with their tools and their sketchboards and their lanterns, eagerly tossing theories back and forth.

Hastella watched them go with a proprietary air, standing under the canvas of the tent that shadowed the doorway. "Elantris," she said, when the last of them had gone in, "pack my possessions. We leave shortly."

He glanced at her, then at the gaping socket of the opening. "Mistress?"

Her expression did not invite further inquiry.

As he stepped out into the sun he saw that the camp had visitors.

A couple of the scholars had stayed at the fire, preparing food. They were dead – and soundlessly – before Elantris came out, and the newcomers were already heading his way. They were Scorpion-kinden, almost a score of them: huge, pale men and women in piecemeal armour, bearing spears and long-hafted axes, and with curving claws arching over their forefingers and thumbs. With them were a handful of their beasts, scuttling purposefully beside them, slung low to the ground beneath overarching stingers and raised claws, each held in tight control by a leash of Art.

The brigands from Dust Port! Elantris thought, stumbling back into the tent. "Mistress!" he got out.

"I gave you an instruction," she snapped at him. "Go to it."

The light went almost entirely as a bulky figure shouldered in behind him, a Scorpion-kinden man fully seven feet tall. His eyes sought out Hastella.

"Go about your work," she said quietly. For a moment Elantris thought she meant him, but the Scorpion was loping past them both, heading for that shadowed entrance, and his men and his animals were on his heels.

"I don't understand," Elantris heard himself say.

"I think you do," Hastella said softly. "I think you have seen something of the past here, what was done of necessity by those who came before us. We are the kinden, Elantris. We are the inheritors of the world, and that is the order of things. There is no sense confusing the academics with what might have been, or confounding them with what price we might have paid to ensure our survival. Such knowledge is not to be showered on the common herd."

"You knew..." Elantris whispered.

"Of course. Do you think this is the first such site? But such study is best undertaken covertly. Where men like Gracer are involved, there is only one way to guarantee secrecy."

There was a cry of alarm from within the cave, and then the screaming began. Elantris was trembling, staring into the beautiful, composed face of his mistress. She smiled slowly.

"I should have them kill you as well, I suppose, but you are a useful little tool, and I think I am fond of you. Now go and pack my bags, I'll have the mercenaries strike our tent."

He did so, numbly and, when he returned, the Scorpions were standing around Hastella respectfully – all so much bigger than she, and yet she dwarfed them with her presence and her Art, always the centre of her own web.

"I will send those I trust to further examine the site," she explained. "For now, block up this door. Let us seal away the monsters once again."

Too late, Elantris thought, watching them all, reliving the moments of his dream. *We are already outside.*

TALES OF THE APT

One of a couple of stories about the perils of academia, this follows on from a throwaway remark from Teornis in *The Sea Watch* where he refers to a similar archaeological site, and the bizarre horrors found there. This is one of the very few pieces of kinden writing where I go back to How It All Came About, a period the kinden themselves have no records of, and rediscovery of which, as shown here, is actively suppressed by those who understand the implications. Once, at the dawn of time, people went two ways, the kinden with their bond to the invertebrate world, and others, who were edged further and further out, driven to extinction initially by the rise of the giant insects, but finished off by the human hands of those who ensured their own survival by living in those insects' shadows.

And of course, for those who have read my *Echoes of the Fall* series, there are further conclusions to be drawn about how things fell out back then, and what happened next.

Queen of the Night

First off, I need to explain to you just what the Peachpit Street Merchant Company was all about. This was before the war, before the words 'merchant company' conjured up nothing but a pack of artisans crammed into ill-fitting armour and pretending to be soldiers. We were singers, actors and musicians. We were, for the most part, also tradesmen, shopkeepers and the like, but we were performers as well. We weren't exactly the Grand Siennis Ballet, but we had a determined little following from the residential and mercantile districts about Peachpit Street, and we would sometimes tour a few of the tributary villages around Collegium, when we had a particularly good show on our hands. Once every couple of years our producer would secure us a booking in Sarn, perhaps, and we'd travel by rail and stay at some barren little Ant-kinden hostelry and do a few nights up there in the foreigners' quarter, but we were a small company. Like any small company, though, we had big dreams.

It started with the Annual Company Assembly, where those of us highest up on the steps of art got together to see how much was in the money-jar and decide what we would do with it. Since Keyness Bounder became producer, this almost always meant him dictating to us: each year a bolder production, each year a new trick to draw in the punters. Keyness was not a shopkeeper or a craftsman. Keyness Bounder had trained at the Aristarta in Seldis, and was an actor and theatre manager the whole day long, and a remarkable proportion of our take went to keep him in fancy-edged robes and fortified wine. Two years ago his command had been Banxawl's *For the Love of Two Doctors*, with a real preserved cadaver from the College's medical wing, and last year Keyness had tried to top that with Lysarea's fiendish *Phaladris*, which some professionals would balk at, and our leading man risking his neck every night, leaping off the castle wall to his death whilst trying to hold a high note. Our success had been debatable, but Keyness Bounder was not in the least disheartened, and we could see in his face that he had something special for us this year.

I should say who counts as 'us', the leading lights of the company. There was Sheppa, the little Fly costumier, and Madame Graspin, who owned both the Masque theatre and the taverna it backed onto. There was Eswell Broadwright, our perennial leading lady, whose length of tooth had been noted last year when she played Cercera in *Phaladris*. There was a tedious old man who suffered under the moniker of Boswell Marwell and who, despite nothing about him being any more amusing than the name, generally scooped up any role with comic potential. He was a Master at the College, and so his continued involvement smoothed over a great deal of rough ground. Last, and least likely to have an opinion, was me, Miles Breakall. I don't act. By day I run a little repair workshop off Peachpit, and in the evenings I tend stage, paint scenery and keep the company's accounts.

Keyness Bounder leant back in his chair, there in the private room of the Other Masque taverna. "*Pathaea*," he said.

"*Pathaea?*" old Marwell scoffed. "That old rag? You could drive an automotive through the holes in that one."

"It's just dreadful," Eswell Broadwright agreed. "She's *so* insipid." As usual she was only interested in the quality of the female lead.

"Too short," Sheppa put in, concerned as usual with practicalities. "What do we double it with?"

"And besides," Marwell ground out, "You know our audiences. If they go to an opera called *Pathaea* they'll want someone called Pathaea, and she doesn't even feature in it."

"Yes she does," Bounder said, quietly but with enough confidence to catch the ear.

"I think you'll find…" said Marwell, working up to a good pontificate, but Bounder cut him off gleefully.

"There's a common misconception about the work, it's true. There are whole essays on how a composer like Scriatha could produce such a rotten apple amongst all her classics. When I was at the Aristarta, though, I heard differently. So this spring I went off to Merro to track down the rumours. Yes, the version that we see here is frankly terrible, but that's because it's *incomplete*. *Pathaea,* as Scriatha wrote it, is a beautifully-constructed full-length opera in the old style, and a few years ago some clever Fly-kinden transcribed a complete score in modern notation and I was able to secure a copy." He looked inordinately pleased with himself.

"And?" Marwell prompted. "Is it any good?"

"What about that miserable little wet Eriphe?" Eswell pressed. "Has she a single piece worth singing?"

"She does not," Bounder admitted. "However, as far as a rewarding role for you, my dear, who do you think Pathaea is?"

He had come prepared. He put three bundles of paper down on the table and let people paw over them. I peered over Sheppa's shoulder. The music was dense, the printing not of the best. Sheppa leafed through it until I saw the name 'Pathaea' feature in the lines.

Old Madame Graspin, our sour-faced landlady, made a "huh" sort of noise. "Good luck," she told Eswell flatly, singling out one page of music. My grasp of notation is only good enough to follow the passing of the bars, but the others stared and even Eswell herself looked a little shaken. Still, she tossed her head and declared, "It shall stretch me," in a fairly blithe tone of voice. As usual, there was no suggestion that she would actually have to do anything so coarse as *audition*.

With that agreed, and any other business taken care of, we retired to the public room of the Other Masque to drink to the coming season. A few of the company breezed in and were told about the play, and we all drank up enough enthusiasm that we were toasting each other and the company with Graspin's best wine. And, of course, we toasted Pathaea.

That was the first warning we had that we were about something particularly foolish. The Other Masque was only a few streets away from the College itself, but because of the theatre it had always catered to a mixed crowd. As long as I remember there was always a little coven of Moth-kinden that met there, who must have represented most of the Moths in Collegium. They came to the plays, as often as not, and so we got to know them, as much as Beetle-kinden can ever know a Moth. They were shabby, scruffy creatures, exiled or self-exiled, scratching out a living on the periphery of Collegium society and yet somehow never quite going away. There was Velvet Lise the procurer, and a man named Voadros who did conjuring tricks in the parlours of merchants for a living. There was old Doctor Nicrephos, who was a Master at the College but could not afford a robe without patches and darns. The man who came over to us, though, was Gravos, a small-time silk merchant and the most solvent of them. He didn't look happy.

"What are you blathering on about?" he demanded. He was tall for a Moth, all angles, with high cheekbones in his grey face. His eyes, blank white as Moth eyes always are, were narrowed.

"Our new production," Bounder toasted him, "the lovely *Pathaea*."

"You Beetles have no idea," Gravos said disgustedly. "Stick to what you know. Stick to Banxawl, or Latchey comedies. How about *A Master of two Servants?* It's been at least four years since you did that one."

"No no, you mistake us," Bounder insisted, solemnly drunk. "*Pathaea*. The full *Pathaea*, with added Pathaea."

It took a moment for the meaning to sink in, and Bounder had been loud enough that the other Moths had overheard as well. Then they were staring at him, eight white and featureless eyes locked onto Bounder's dark, wine-sweaty face. I thought they were angry, and then I thought they were about to burst into laughter, and then I realised that whatever they felt or thought, it wasn't something I had any easy name for.

"Whatever you say, Beetle," was all Gravos came out with, at last. "Be careful what you wish for."

"Full houses and full bowls," Bounder declared and dismissed it all from his mind, as did we all, but it came back to us in time, nonetheless.

A few tendays later we came to look over the score and cast the piece. We held a few desultory auditions, but we had done a lot of plays from around the time Scriatha was writing, and they all had the same kind of structure: there were lovers, there were villains, there were clowns and maids and supporting bit parts. We had a regular company and everyone had worn their own personal rut in the road of drama. In addition to that we had a few non-artistic considerations. For example, every few years we had to find a role for Madame Graspin, as a sop to the low rent we paid her, and then there was old Master Gafferow, our longtime and most generous patron, who would expect to see his son in some prominent and flattering role. Poor young Mosley Gafferow was a perfectly pleasant lad, and everyone was very fond of him, but no amount of coaching could much get past the fact that he was apparently made of wood. He could hold a tune well enough, certainly, but he couldn't *act*. Still, Eswell made no complaints. She had no fear of him ever stealing the audience's love from her, for all that they made an odd leading couple. One unkind critic had said, of *Phaladris*, that she hadn't realised that the title character was in love with his own mother.

The script was in a bit of a mess, Fly-kinden draftsmanship and printing presses being what they are, but Bounder had sketched out a cast list for us to mull over. Boswell Marwell harrumphed and grumphed over that, because the last item was "Chorus of Beetle Slaves" which he said was in bad taste.

"You can't judge everything by modern standards," Bounder told him genially. "A story set in Pathis-that-was is bound to have slaves. All our ancestors were slaves back then, remember?"

Marwell's dour expression suggested that, as the College Master, he was more used to giving than receiving lectures. Still, it was true enough that when our Collegium had been named Pathis, and when the Moth-kinden had been lords and ladies here, our forebears had presumably not had a good time of it. They taught that, a bit, but mostly they tended to start history off with the Revolution, and mumbled over the thousand years of servitude that preceded it. What did I care? I was an artificer. History before the machines came in was of limited interest to me.

The old *Pathaea* that we, and greater Collegium, was familiar with was mostly your standard love story, only with a number of difficult bits where there's no real sense to what's going on. A Spider lordling (Teranis, tenor) arrives in Pathis and is rescued by the servants of Pathaea, who is a Moth magician of some kind. She wants him to rescue her daughter from another magician (Sarostros, baritone). He runs into a Beetle-kinden clown (Prater, comic baritone) who is sent to the evil magician's lair to meet with the daughter (Eriphe, soprano). There are a series of escapades, and in the end Teranis is captured by Sarostros' Mantis-kinden servant (Menamon, bass). However, Sarostros dismisses Menamon and puts Teranis and Prater through a series of incomprehensible tests, which Prater fails in comic style. The last section is the most problematic one, because Eriphe tries to kill Sarostros for no reason, Menamon comes back from nowhere to fight Teranis, and then they all live happily every after except for the dead ones.

Well, that was the version that *we* knew.

The difference in Bounder's score was that Pathaea, who doesn't have the guts to show her face traditionally, actually turns up, adding a second and rather meatier soprano part to the proceedings. She only gets three scenes, mind, but when you stick her bits back in everything makes a vast amount more sense. It's Pathaea who gives Eriphe the knife to kill her rival (and former lover) Sarostros, and it's Pathaea who steals Menamon away into her own service and sets him on Teranis. At the very end there's a whole scene where she and Sarostros are having some kind of occult spat, and it's up to Eriphe to stab *her* to save the day, and her lover. She's the reason everything happens, you see, which is why the work was such a damp lamp after they took her out.

None of us asked *why* they took her out. We were all too sold on Bounder's idea.

In the middle, after handing out knives and bewitching Mantids, she has this piece to sing, what they call an aria. It was the one that Graspin had picked out earlier, and now Bounder was looking over it worriedly. "My dear," he murmured to Eswell, "whilst I have no worries whatsoever as to your ability…" but then he tailed off, seeing the look she was giving him. It was clear that, if the Peachpit Street Merchant Company was performing *Pathaea*, then so was Eswell Broadwright.

The rest of the parts were disposed of without much consultation of the company. Bounder would take Sarostros, and we would shoehorn poor wooden Mosley Gafferow into the Spider-kinden shoes of the Aristos Teranis because otherwise the rent wouldn't get paid. Boswell would take the clownish Prater, and drain the role of humour as a mosquito drains a man of blood. There was a bit of discussion about who, if Eswell was taking the plum title role, would actually do the miserable part of Eriphe, and it was agreed that it would be offered to one of our Fly-kinden, Fratte, who usually specialised in maids and understudies, because she had a pleasingly clear, high voice and because it was probably her turn. There were three Moth-kinden functionaries who were parcelled out to reliable third-stringers, and after some deliberation the role of Menamon the Mantis was given to a newcomer, a renegade Tarkesh Ant-kinden, because he was pale-skinned and quite lean, and it was felt he would look the part, whatever his voice was like. Also, as an Ant, we thought he would make the fight with Teranis look good even if Mosley Gafferow just stood there. How little we knew; how little we suspected.

We got most of the company together a tenday after, having

printed off enough scores for the leads. Everyone not cast got to be a Chorus of Beetle Slaves, and Sheppa the costumier was busy asking people to bring in any torn or damaged clothes to be converted into slavish rags. Eswell had decided that she would wear the gold dress that she had donned for *Lysperrae the Tyrant* five years ago, meaning that poor Sheppa would have to go shopping for several yards more of the expensive material. Meanwhile her numberless relatives discussed amongst themselves just what combination of pale make-up would give Bounder and the others a complexion even slightly approaching the grey of Moth-kinden.

Whilst everyone pored over the scores, and a couple of our regular musicians discussed what other instruments we'd need to hire in to do it justice, Eswell was backstage working ostentatiously on her big aria. It was, to be frank, something of a distraction. I wouldn't say anything against her voice. She had a fine timbre that would have cut wood at twenty paces, and normally she got the music to agree with her by sheer volume and force of personality. *Pathaea* was not behaving, though. Eswell stopped and started, started and stopped, breaking off mid-line, mid-note. The aria was an order of magnitude grander than anything she had attempted before, and the pitch! I don't know whether poor Eswell had ever got within reach of that top note on her best day. This didn't stop her battering away at it, though, and woe betide anyone who dared pass a comment. The rest of us got on with what we could, and Bounder called me over to discuss the staging.

"There are about six different locations," he told me, "so I want some flats on revolves. No long changes, we learned that one after *The Merchant of Merro*." He was right at that. By the time the Aristoi Palace at Seldis had made the stage, half the audience had gone.

"Also," Bounder went on, "I want something special for Pathaea's entrance. She's a Moth. She won't just stomp on. I want Eswell in the hoist, coming down from the rafters. It'll be magnificent."

"I'll reinforce the hoist," was all I said to that. Our Fly-kinden, Sheppa, quiet Fratte and a leery little man called Villo, were in barely-suppressed stitches of laughter at my elbow.

We had a good few tendays of rehearsals after that, mostly because Bounder was being uncharacteristically diplomatic and steering well clear of the problem areas – which meant anything involving Eswell.

She was always there, of course, at every rehearsal, whether she was called or not. She had commandeered the dressing room and, while everyone else slouched about the stalls, we could hear her warble and bleat through three walls. The other parts of the opera, mostly those parts that had survived into the standard version, were going quite smoothly. The three Moth-kinden functionaries had a tendancy to lark it up during their scenes, and the fact that one of them, Villo, was half the size of the other two, would cause comment on the night. Boswell declaimed and posed his way through his lines, demolishing two centuries of careful Spider-kinden humour, and put in a great deal of dragging business of his own over which he and Bounder almost came to blows. Mosley was dutiful, polite, punctual and utterly uninspired, and across from him, Fratte's Eriphe always looked as though she was about to cry. However, as Mosley was used to playing across from Eswell, at least he would have a leading lady more diminutive than he. The big surprise was our Menamon, the Ant in Mantids' clothing. He was called Rannus or Rannius or something, but by the time he got to us he was just Ran, and he was expressionless and quiet and very still, only the last of which is much use on stage. He was also the only Ant we had ever got at the company, and nobody quite knew what to expect. However, his voice, which had been a bit croaky on audition, filled out beautifully with a little instruction from Bounder, and he turned out to be quite the find.

Anyway, we were doing a scene from the first act when it happened: Marwell, as Prater, was droning and bumbling about in Sarostros' court, whilst Fratte did her best to look attentive, and one of our musicians sat with a harp waiting to pick out the skeleton of their duet. In the background we could hear, and manfully try to ignore, the strained blarts of Eswell trying to follow her aria those last few notes to where it was waiting for her on its lofty peak. She almost had it, that one time, or so my memory tells me, just teetering, tooth-jarringly a half-tone away. And then she screamed.

We thought it was frustration first. The action on stage stopped and Villo and Sheppa looked up from their cardgame offstage left, but then she was still screaming, over and over, shrieking out for someone to *"get away!"*

I remember Ran had his wooden sword in hand, and he just vaulted the stage and was gone backstage before anyone else could move. Then we were all piling after him, getting in each other's way, tripping each other and stepping on the drapes until we exploded into the dressing room and found her.

Ran had arrived, like a proper hero, and not known what to do with her. She was huddled in one corner, her hands over her face, cringing away from... Well, away from nothing, really. There was nothing there but the dressing mirror. It was a big old piece, that mirror, Spider-kinden work, that had been there since long before the Peachpit Street Merchant Company ever took up residence, before Madame Graspin inherited the building, before anyone could remember. It was tarnished and dark these days, but it was enormous, one of those amazing works of skill that even modern-day artificers find it had to duplicate. Bounder was kneeling by Eswell, doing his best to console her, but she was still shrieking, not so loud, but too garbled and panicky to make much sense of what she was saying. Only one thing was clear, though. She had seen something in the mirror. She had seen something that had completely broken her. She was highly-strung, our Eswell, but she was strong, too. She was used to driving her ambitions through any number of reasonable objections. There wasn't one of us that didn't glance, at least once, at that old mirror, even Bounder, although he thought nobody saw him. It showed us nothing but us, and that dimly. There were a lot of shadows in that old mirror, that was all.

After a few days Bounder called the cast and crew together. Eswell, he explained, had gone to stay with relatives outside the city, a bit of country air. She was feeling much better, he assured us. Artistic temperament, he said, just a little too highly strung, working too hard, and we'd all heard how she was getting frustrated at the role. Hardly surprising that she had a bit of an off day. Bounder smiled and jollied us along, and most people went along with it. I didn't, so much. I'd seen her before she left for her family estates. Better, yes, but she wasn't the same. I tried to talk to her, maybe even to get her to stay on, but she was having none of it. Just as her carriage pulled off, Eswell hissed at me, "I saw *her*."

But it didn't matter what I thought. What mattered was that we were short a Pathaea.

We held auditions, then. There was nobody in the cast who could have carried off the role, certainly not poor Fratte. However, most of the other merchant companies in the city had wind of what we were doing and the chance to be the first ever Pathaea in Collegium was extremely attractive. Bounder put the word out, and next evening we had twenty would-be Pathaeas lined up at the Masque waiting to do their stuff. Not one of them had seen the piece, of course, and Bounder was taking no chances this time. With Eswell no longer in a position to squat on the role, he was determined to get someone worthy of it. He really could be a mercenary bastard, when the mood was on him. Anyway, it was *that* aria he handed out to the hopefuls, and I think at least one in three just gave up when they saw it.

The rest gave it their best. Beetle-kinden, Flies, a few Ant maidens even, they came and launched themselves at those cascades of notes with all the furious attack of the Wasp-kinden light airborne. The Flies were best, overall, because their soprano was a half-octave higher than anyone else's, but the aria defeated them all in the end, broke them like wreckers' rocks. There were a few strained voices in the city the next day, I can tell you. They came and squeaked at us, and then they left. Most of the time Keyness Bounder didn't even have to tell them that they weren't what we were looking for.

He was getting desperate, I knew him well enough to tell that. He staked his reputation on every piece we performed, and *Phaladris* had left him on the back foot already. If he couldn't get a Pathaea for his *Pathaea*, what a fool he would look. As the evening drew to a close he was muttering about sending to Seldis, to Siennis even. I wish he had.

And then *she* came in, stepped in out of the dark without a word or a nod to anyone. It was near midnight then, but she didn't ask if she was late, or whether we'd cast the role, she just stood in front of Bounder with her hands behind her back and waited.

Moth-kinden, she was: a slight, small woman with that dusky grey skin, those blank eyes. Her dark hair was gathered up at the nape of her neck, and she wore a drab, mottled robe. Most of her looked young, except for a certain tension about the face, a certain implication of the hardship of ages, but then with some of those old races it's hard to put a sum of years on them.

We had never had a Moth-kinden on stage at Peachpit Street. In the audience, certainly, but not in the company. We were a little provincial operation, and our attempts to perpetrate art were mediocre even by Collegium's standards, let alone those of a race that traditionally jeered at everything we did. Still, here she was and, after blinking at her foolishly for a moment, Bounder passed her the score.

She didn't take it, and she waved our harpist to silence when he started to pluck a string. She stood there, her arms at her sides now, small grey hands curled half-closed. It was impossible to tell what she was looking at.

And she *sang*. Hammer and tongs, how she sang! Pitch perfect, word perfect, but that was secondary. She sang the words as if everyone else had just been trained crickets chirping them. She sang them with meaning, with a thousand years of history that we couldn't guess at. Her voice soared and spun, like a fish in a stream, like a glitter of dragonflies, vaulting and dancing up, leaping the falls of notes until she found that elusive high point, that single clear tone that nobody else had quite been able to reach, that note that I have never, ever heard in any other work.

I felt my heart and lungs, my stomach and all the guts of me, resound, reverberate with the music she made. When her voice leapt, I leapt with it, inside. Her voice left an unfamiliar taste in my mouth, sent ghosts of wild thoughts flitting in my mind, like dreams forgotten on waking. I was gripping Bounder's hand and he was gripping Sheppa's, and the three of us had eyes – no, ears! – for nothing but her. She showed us what we were, really: a pack of Beetle-kinden trying to put on a two-hundred year-old Spider opera about a six-hundred year-old Moth-kinden city, a world we were unqualified to know anything about, and yet, with her giving voice to all of that, we knew we would make it. *Pathaea* would happen. More, it would be a show the like of which Collegium had never seen.

And when she stopped, when the last sound of her had rung away, we stood and applauded her, applauded her for sheer gratitude, not that we had our Pathaea, though surely we had, but that she had given that to us. If she had asked something of us just then, whether it was to fight a duel or travel to the Commonweal or slap the Spider ambassador, we'd have done it, all three of us.

"Orillaea," she said, when Bounder regained the self-possession to ask after her name, and she asked when the next rehearsal would be, cool as you like. Nobody actually told her she had the role. Nobody needed to.

The three of us retired to the private room of the Other Masque, which old Madam Graspin had left open for us despite the hour. It took a long time, and several bowls of wine, before any of us said anything. Eventually Sheppa started, "It's their Art, you know. All the Bad-Old-Days kinden. Spiders are the same. Look at you, talk to you, and their Art's in your head, making you want to do what they ask. It's like breathing to them. They don't even realise they're doing it."

"It's more than that," Bounder declared. From his tone he had obviously been thinking hard. "It's Aptitude. You know, the Moths, the Spiders, all of them? Can't fiddle a door-handle, can't load a crossbow. I remember when I was at the Aristarta, in Seldis. Not a locked door in the place, not a latch, just curtains and curtains and open doorways. Their minds work differently to ours. They can't see what we can, they can't understand it. And yet, and yet... Scriatha was Inapt. Without the new edition we wouldn't even be able to read her notation. I thought that would be the only difficulty but... There's something more, something in the music itself. Just in that role, in Pathaea's grand aria, there's something that *we* can't see, and just as Scriatha couldn't have picked a lock, so we can't sing her music as she intended." He grinned a little wildly. "But we don't have to, because we have the beautiful Orillaea to sing it for us, and we're going to be the most famous merchant company in the city!"

Rehearsals picked up in a couple of days. Everyone was very curious about our newcomer, and at first she steered well clear of all of them, hardly deigning to speak to them, only heeding Bounder's direction, and that barely. She came on and she sang, faultlessly, without book, and the rest of the time she might as well have thought us all slaves or savages.

But you can't live amongst a troupe of performers like that for long. It was the Fly-kinden that wore her down, mostly. Sheppa had to measure her for costume, of course, and the bustling host of Sheppa's female relatives, without number or limit it always seemed to me, treated her as if she was royalty, doting on her every need. She, in turn, began to treat them as if they were servants − I won't say slaves, that would be unfair − and they didn't seem to mind. I did, but then she never so much as looked at me, so there we are. One of the only times I ever ran into her face to face was for one rehearsal where someone had shut her out − not locked, just shut, but Bounder was right about that – and I went over to answer her quiet knock. She brushed past me as though I was beneath contempt, and I found I much preferred being out of her notice.

Once Sheppa and her people had broken the ice there were various other overtures. Madame Graspin brought her hot drinks, which she took without any more thanks than a curt nod. Boswell Marwell tried to show off by reciting a piece of poetry full of classical allusions, stentorian and over-enunciated, and the politely incredulous smile that established itself on her face, despite her best efforts, went a long way towards endearing her to the rest of the cast. Shortly after that, poor Mosley Gafferow began to hang about her.

He was an odd one, Mosley. Solid wood, like I say, but that doesn't mean he was stupid. He had good prospects in his father's export trade, and he was extremely marriage-worthy, worth a few thousand Centrals a month once his dad shuffled off. He wasn't bad to look at, either, just a bit bland, a bit stout, with his hairline a bit high. He was a lump: a personable, amiable lump.

The lump had got a new idea into his head, though, which was a rare event in itself. The lump had decided that he rather liked Orillaea. He would sit near her, when they were not on stage. He would smile and screw up his courage, consult his notes and then make strained pleasantries, offer halting compliments, try to strike up a conversation like someone trying to strike sparks from pumice. It was all his idea, certainly. His father would have slapped some sense into him, had he known. No itinerant Moth chanteuse was going to seduce his son, he'd have said, but he never knew, and I suspect he wasn't the type to notice a change in his offspring. Mosley, to Old Man Gafferow, was just as much a part of the business as the goodwill and the stock, and would be invested and borrowed against like everything else.

At first, Orillaea ignored him, and everyone assumed that was that. What you must remember, though, is just how dull a lump Mosley was. There was no room in that solid oak skull for doubt. He kept on with his faltering praise, his strangled observations. Throughout the tendays of our rehearsals he would always find a place to sit near her, would bring her little treats to eat, or once a book, a very old book of poetry. He even sang better when she was in the auditorium than when she was out of earshot, although the difference was very slight. She held him off as long as she could, with her indifference, but we could see the cracks start.

Eventually his plodding campaign bore some minute fruit. She would look at him when he spoke. She would eat a honey-pastry when he offered it. She took the book, though it's anyone's guess whether she actually ever read it. Towards the performance date, when Bounder was throwing daily tantrums at how unready we were, she would let him feed her, hand to lips, and once she held his hand. I don't think she was remotely attracted to him. We're all lumbering oafs to the Moths, for all that we oafs run the world now. He confused her, though, with his blundering kindnesses. She didn't know what to do with him. The odd thing was, I felt at the time that the last thing holding out in her was a kind of guilt: that by then she had realised just what an adoring fool Mosley was, and she was holding him at arm's length because otherwise she would hurt him: he the moth, and she the flame.

Bounder, as I say, was incandescent with rage at least once each day, but never with her. After all, everyone else had to rehearse. *She* knew it all already. She had come to us fully formed, and everyone assumed that she had played the role somewhere out east, somewhere in the Spiderlands, where the true *Pathaea* was still routinely done. I wonder now, myself, but enough of that. I can't prove anything, nor even quite believe what I might suspect. She was ready, as I say, and everyone else was shown up as the awful amateur hams they were. She made everyone in the company work, I'll give her that. By the time of the opening night there wasn't a voice, an actor, a chorus member, a musician, who wasn't giving their best ever performance. I'm still not saying that they were good, mind. Marwell was still as funny as losing a foot, and Mosley, for all his ardour and passion, was still more the province of the carpenter than the physician, but everyone was better than they had ever been.

I, on the other hand, had precious little to do. I had taken apart and reassembled the clockwork beneath the stage, tested out the winding engine and replaced the spring. The rotating flats were moving as smooth as oiled silk and, as for the rest of it, well, there wasn't much for me to do. For the first time ever nobody seemed to need a prompt and, as for the hoist that I had lovingly reinforced in anticipation of its labouring under Eswell's weighty talent, well… I had explained to Orillaea, another of my rare meetings with her, about Bounder's plans for her entrance. She laughed at me. It was such a disdainful laugh it rendered me speechless.

"If he wants me to enter from above," she said, "he has only to ask," and in the next moment she had spread her gleaming wings, darkly shimmering fans that glimmered and faded in the air around her, drawn from nowhere by her Art. I shrugged and conceded that my poor clumsy hoist would not be needed.

In the last tenday before the show we had a few warnings, none of which we heeded. One of Sheppa's cousins broke an ankle when something startled her on the stairs – and you're right, *I've* never heard of a Fly-kinden breaking an ankle before either. Another time, our Ant-kinden, Ran, got spooked by something and missed an entrance, and we wasted an entire hour whilst he hunted about behind the scenes for a quarry he would never name. A bottle of Madame Graspin's wine, left backstage, turned out to contain something so smokily, headily intoxicating that the entire chorus ended up coming on three scenes early and singing... something, some song not in that opera nor any other I ever heard, but at the time it sent shivers down my spine. Even Keyness Bounder himself was not immune to this spate of strangeness, but went through three evenings where he called everyone the wrong name, mostly names of people he had known at the Aristarta, all except for Orillaea. He had only called her one thing from the start.

'Pathaea,' of course.

But then, when you get close to the first night, there's always a certain air of energy and panic that makes odd things happen. Theatre isn't an artificer's game. You can't measure it and you can't properly control it. Nobody was about to admit that something unusual was going on.

The night before the show I got in early, as I always do, to make sure everything was in place. It's an engineer's neatness, to count off the props and the flats and all the raw materials of theatre, but it's saved us from ruin before. When I arrived at the Masque, however, I found a lean Moth-kinden man waiting for me. It was the silk-merchant, Gravos, who greeted me solemnly as I unlocked.

He asked me how rehearsals were going, and I said fine. I asked him if he was coming to see us, and he told me he'd already reserved a seat for tomorrow night. I wanted to go in and began counting things but it was clear he had more to say.

"How is Pathaea?" he said, and it was a strange thing: when

Bounder said the name, you always knew whether he meant the opera, or the character, or whether he was talking to Orillaea direct. He had distinct ways of saying it, depending. The way Gravos said 'Pathaea' wasn't any of those. It was odd enough that it stopped me halfway through the door, looking back over my shoulder and frowning at him.

I said nothing useful, and so he said, in his soft Moth-voice, "You Beetles love to play with things you don't understand," which was rich from a man who couldn't have turned the key in the lock or done double-entry book-keeping.

"What about Pathaea?" I asked, somewhat belligerently, trying to match the way he had said it.

"Pathaea of Pathis, greatest of her generation, ruler of this city, Queen of the Night," said Gravos, and there was reverence and a little fear in his voice.

"Is that the first night or the last night," I said, trying to make light.

"*That* work, in *this* city," he murmured. "Scriatha never dreamed that your people would do such a thing, and still she put down her pen for three years, after completing the piece. She had to empty her head of the dreams, the images, the sendings of Pathaea that cluttered her mind like old furniture." Gravos could normally be relied on to talk like a merchant, not a mystic, but there was something eating away at him, forcing him to it. When I turned away he actually grasped at my tunic.

"They called her the Queen of the Night," he told me, hoarsely. I just shrugged, and politely removed his hand, and went into the dark theatre. It was probably less than a minute I spent fumbling for the ignition on the gas lamps, but it seemed like whole years of my life, I can tell you. You see, that's another thing about the old Inapt people. Spiders, Mantids, even Fly-kinden, who have a bit of both ways, they see well in the dark. Moths, I'm told, see better in the dark than the day. Me, I need light, and so do almost all my folk. We're daytime people, just like the Ants and, until I got those lamps burning, I had all the old night terrors of my kinden dancing up and down my spine.

We had a full house for the first night. The Masque wasn't a large theatre but it had been a long old time since we'd packed them aisle to aisle, I can tell you. Word had got around, of course: the rediscovered opera, the mysterious Moth-kinden lead. We were turning them away at the door. Keyness Bounder was already planning the tour: not just Sarn this time but Helleron, Seldis, Merro, who knew where else? We were about to put the Peachpit Street Merchant Company on the map.

Everyone there, I reckoned, had seen *Pathaea* at least once before, or the emasculated version that normally hobbled onto the boards. They were waiting for the changes, the differences. We had a select audience out there, educated and sophisticated: College Masters, merchant magnates, the idle wealthy, our favoured regulars, and of course the Moth-kinden. All that little coven who gathered in the Other Masque were there, on that first night, and Gravos amongst them.

Well, it all started off without a raised eyebrow. Mosley Gafferow, dressed, as best Sheppa could manage, as a Spider-kinden Aristos, arrived in old Pathis to be menaced by Ran's Mantis-kinden, looking convincingly lean and deadly. The Spider is knocked out, the Mantis is driven off, and Teranis, still clearly poor old wooden Mosley, wakes to meet the clown Prater and a selection of Moth-kinden magicians, who first punish Prater, and then tell Teranis that they are the servants of Pathaea.

Then, with the name, Orillaea stepped on stage and you could feel the audience's mood change. Sheppa's costuming had done the woman proud. She was got up in a robe of black and silver that caught the lights like a dozen constellations of stars, and her grey skin – her face, her arms and one bare shoulder – were startlingly pale above it. When she sang it felt as though not just the audience went quiet to hear her. It was as though something else, something old and vast and forgotten that could not hear poor Mosley's voice, or Marwell's, was awoken and paying heed. The moment took me in too. I was supposed to be following the score but I forgot and I just listened when she started to sing.

Pathaea has barely five minutes on stage in the first act, but once she had been and gone the play was different. We were inspired. Bounder, as Sarostros, was menacing and smooth and crammed with secrets and power, which was, let me tell you, entirely different to the vainglory he'd been playing it with during rehearsals. Ran stood there in his green arming jacket, with wooden spines buckled to his forearms, and radiated calm murder. Fratte, usually so colourless on stage that you could see through her, mustered a little borrowed fire when told that Teranis would be coming to rescue her. Marwell was funny. Boswell Marwell got a laugh from the audience, free and without being prompted by some friend of his in the second row. History in the making, I assure you.

The first act tripped brightly to its conclusion: Eriphe and Teranis, the lovers, meet and are captured by Sarostros. Menamon the Mantis is disgraced and cast out. Sarostros sets the lovers and the slave Prater a series of tests to prove their passion. The curtain came down to applause that was more astonished than anything else. I half expected someone to come backstage and demand to know what we'd done with the real Peachpit Street Company.

The break between acts is usually an excuse for all manner of gabble and babble amongst the cast, but everyone was quiet that night – not subdued, just quiet. They didn't want to break whatever spell had been cast on them. I dropped in to give Bounder my nod and let him know all was well, and I took a moment to look at them: I remember thinking that, of our regulars, only Marwell was actually playing his own kinden, and he was playing at slavery. The others, Flies and Beetles and the Ant, were dressed up as people from a vanished world, people whose kinden had lost their way in history: I remember Bounder and Fratte and Villo all greyed up, and Mosley powdered practically white and, beyond them, beyond the trumpery, the slender Orillaea, sitting silent at the far end of the dressing room, the thing itself that they were all imitating. Perhaps her blind-looking eyes were fixed on the tarnish-webbed mirror, perhaps not.

Then we were on again, and the big moment was coming up.

Bounder, as Sarostros, outlined the tests he was going to set the lovers, and here is where the usual plot falls apart, because nothing anyone does for the next twenty minutes makes much sense. We had Scriatha's true script, though, and we had Orillaea. The audience's intake of breath when she made her appearance was audible even backstage. She sang, giving Eriphe the knife to stab Sarostros. She sang, playing with Menamon's loyalties and luring him to her side, and then she *sang*. Her voice, already by far the best thing anyone had heard all night, slipped free of the constraints of propriety and lifted and lifted, circling about the flame of that impossible top note. She sang the piece that had broken Eswell Broadwright, the piece that had been cut, ruthlessly cut, by those who had first brought Scriatha's great work to Collegium, and when she touched that fatal note, something *changed*.

What was supposed to happen, after that, is that she and Sarostros have a duel of what is supposed to be magic, but is just singing, of course, and Menamon and Teranis have a duel in the more conventional sense, and Prater the clown, who's failed the tests, is despairing of ever achieving his freedom, and it's up to poor Eriphe to jump up and dispatch her mother, Pathaea the Queen of the Night, back to the darkness and save the day for everyone. That's what the score says. It's almost what happened. I'm not entirely sure what the audience thought they were seeing. I've never dared ask anyone. I've certainly never dared ask Gravos or anyone of his sly, secretive kinden, but only for fear that I might, for once, get a straight answer.

There was a brief space after that aria where she was offstage, and Bounder put the lovers through their paces, and they pass and stupid Prater fails, and it was as though a storm, a real thunder-and-lightning storm was about to break. The air was crackling with leashed rage. I could see Bounder's eyes very wide as he swept about the stage, his manner, his very stance belonging to another man of another age. Mosley and Fratte clung together convincingly, the lovers convinced that at any moment this man, this Moth sorcerer, would part them forever. I remember old Marwell sitting in the middle of the stage, his seamed face a picture of misery, and I thought that it was not just Boswell Marwell trying for the tragic. There was a thousand years of slavery in that look, the face of an underclass, of a man whose fate is to be nothing but a toy for his betters, to live or die, prosper or fail, by their arbitrary word. I looked up from that ghastly visage, and I swear that Bounder's eyes, Sarostros' eyes, were blank white.

Then she came on again for her showdown with her rival magician: Pathaea, Queen of the Night, and all the gaslamps in the house guttered out, and yet it was not dark. There was light, a purplish light fit for funerals, and it came from Orillaea. No, I will be honest. It came from Pathaea, walking in majesty, the greatest noble lady of old Pathis come home after so many centuries.

It all went wrong then, which meant it all happened according to the script. She sang at Bounder, and he sang back, and they fought. They fought in song, and I cannot say it clearer than that. It was all beyond me, beyond my understanding, but the length of the stage bent and bowed between them, the very air clenched and strained to the sound of their voices, pummelling and twisting as they sang magic at it. There was nothing of Keyness Bounder in Sarostros' face now, no admission that he had ever been a Beetle-kinden actor-manager with grandiose ideas, and as for *her*, well, she was just as she always had been, and that was bad enough.

And in the middle of the stage, the other fight, because Ran was trying to kill Mosley Gafferow.

In all my remembrances, I reserve a special place for that Ant, Ran. In his swift, sharp movements, as he flung about the gleaming rapier that his wooden sword had somehow become, there were a multitude of different expressions trying to get out. Firstly he was trying to kill Mosley as a Mantis-kinden kills, all, that perfect poise and balance, all that sheer unadulterated lust for blood that they seem to reek of. And yet, in the grip of whatever hold Pathaea had on him, he was trying to kill Mosley as an Ant-kinden. Like all Ants, he had trained in arms back in his city, and I could see a lot of that in the quick, brutal economy of motion, the guarded lunges and thrusts that would better fit a man with a shortsword and shield. In harness with those two conflicting killers there was Ran the actor, because part of him was still forcing his actions into the choreography of the stage fight that he had drilled into Mosley over the course of months, and finally, mark you, finally there was Ran the human being, Ran the citizen of Collegium, and he was doing his absolute cursed best to rein in his traitor limbs, to hobble himself, to do anything, in short, except kill Mosley Gafferow: four men fighting in the same body at cross purposes: Ran, whatever his full name was, was a hero as far as I'm concerned.

And what of Mosley? Was the wooden man about to become splinters? Ran would have killed him, despite everything, had the boy not pulled something special out. As I watched, I saw a change come over him. It was not anything given to him by Pathaea, that I'll swear. It was just Mosley, solid, even-tempered Mosley, in real danger and left to his own devices. I saw an expression, a real expression come over that lumpen face, and a passion in his movements that nobody could have guessed at. As Ran drove at him, all that chaotic wrestling of intermingled desires, he fought. He was not Teranis defending himself from Menamon in a two-centuries-old opera, he was Mosley fighting for his life, and it brought out something in him, some animation and life, that never truly went away.

Well, that was going to be it for me. I was well and truly out of my depth, and I wanted out, I'm not ashamed to admit. I deserted my post. Having seen all that going on, I ran for the backstage door and threw it open, meaning to come back in the morning when life was comprehensible again.

I cannot vouch for what I saw, beyond that open door. I can only say what I remember, even though I doubt my own mind when I recall it.

I saw the College, true, just as one might expect, because those white-stone buildings are very old indeed, but most of the rest was gone. All the residential tenements, the three- and four-storey places, gone. The row of little workshops where I had my living, gone. I could see clear down to the market, but the market was not the close clutter of stalls I knew, but a grander open space with something like a stage in the centre, and the people –

They were Beetle-kinden, for the most part, men and women and children, but they were not my people. My people never walked with such sloped shoulders. My people never looked solely at the ground or at their feet. My people never spoke in such mumbled whispers or flinched at a loud sound. My people would never have carried the chairs of their masters through the streets of their city, or stepped aside humbly to let a grey-skinned, white-eyed lord stride past, or cringe from a sharp-featured Mantis warrior as though none would decry the spilling of their blood.

And I saw the night. Of course it was night, it was supposed to be night – but not *this* night. Night in Collegium is not dark. The streets are picked out by the warmth of gaslamps, and each home has a cheery hearth ablaze, the firelight leaking past the shutters. The doorways of tavernas and hostelries stand open, spilling out golden welcome to passers-by. Collegium nights hold the dark at bay. This was not the night I knew. No gaslamps, no cheer. The silent city, the labouring masses, the august, blank-eyed lords and ladies, were lit only by the sparks of torches and by the vast, impartial face of the moon that bathed the city in cold, dispassionate fire. It was the old night of Pathis, lost these five hundred years. It was the night that *she* was queen of.

I retreated back into what passed for the familiarity of the theatre. I closed the door and forced myself not to think about what I might just have seen, and I found my way back to my station offstage.

It was all as before, but more so. The air was so taut between Pathaea and Sarastros that it seemed to be about to tear in half, and what would come through such a rip was anyone's guess. Ran had forced Mosley upstage as far as he would go. Their rapiers flickered and danced, but it was clear that there were few moves left, and none of them choreographed. It was all about to fall apart.

Something was supposed to happen, I knew. This terrible, drawn-out moment was wrong. Something should have broken it, rather than allowing it to stretch and twist out like this, rather than allowing Pathaea's world, that centuries gone tyranny, an opening in which to reach forward across all the years. What, though? What was missing?

I was an idiot, of course. The answer was in the score, right before me. What happened was that Eriphe, in her one worthwhile moment of the whole opera, confronts Pathaea, breaking her concentration and allowing Sarostros to banish her. Our Eriphe was the Fly-kinden Fratte, though, and she was cowering at the side of the stage, her head wrapped in her arms, utterly incapable of doing anything but denying all that was going on around her. There's a mis-casting in every show, in my experience, and faced with everything she knew being turned inside out and upside-down, the poor girl had resorted to blotting it all out. She would be no use at all. Which left me, to my certain knowledge, and I had better act fast.

I first reached for a hammer with half a mind to just rush out on stage and have at Pathaea myself, strike a blow for freedom. It wasn't going to happen. Partly because I was stage crew, and going out before the audience was absolutely out of the question, but rather more because of Pathaea herself. Awe and dark splendour radiated off her in waves. I knew that I could never get close to do her harm without falling under her influence, without reverting to being a slave, as my ancestors had been her slaves. There was nothing I could do to stop her. Her influence was laid like heavy chains on me, ready to stop me raising a hand against her.

I saw Ran's blade raised, shining in that unnatural light.

There was something that Pathaea had not thought of. She had not thought of it because she could not think of it. My hand jumped of its own accord and found the levers for the hoist.

The hoist was not needed, of course. When Pathaea had made her first grand entrance she had floated down on wings of Art. The hoist had rested, unused, since the evening I spent strengthening it for use with Eswell, before she came face to face with Pathaea in the mirror.

I had been simulating Eswell's bulk as best I could, back then. I had fitted the harness about the biggest sandbag we had.

I heard the mad ratcheting sound of clockwork abruptly let fly without anything to stop it, three dozen gears suddenly going at top speed. I saw Pathaea's grey, beautiful face tilt up, and there was no comprehension in her face, no acknowledgement of what she was seeing.

And after all, it's something that every stage manager wants to do to an actor once in their lives.

I cannot swear as to my accuracy. It didn't really matter. Her concentration broke when the harnessed sandbag struck the stage, shivering the boards into pieces. Everything snapped back. Ran's sword was wood and Bounder's eyes had pupils, and the chorus, oblivious as always, launched spontaneously and raggedly into their end-piece, celebrating the union of the various sets of lovers, whilst the leads stumbled dazedly about stage in the pitch dark and I fiddled desperately to re-fire the gaslamps.

Of Orillaea, there was no sign. To this day I do not know whether there was ever such a person as Orillaea, whether there was anything else there but *her*.

There was no second night. It was not for want of audience, but we had no Pathaea and, even if some miraculous replacement had walked off the next boat, nobody felt that they wanted to return to Scriatha's great masterpiece just yet. Also the stage had suffered considerable damage from a falling sandbag, and it would be a tenday before I had it repaired. The financial loss to the company was devastating. Had it not been for Old Man Gafferow we would have ceased to be. As it was, he seemed to take the new, more motivated Mosley as just rewards for his patronage. Certainly the lad started to take a more active interest in the family business – in everything, for that matter – than he ever had before. Still, there were times, once or twice, when I saw a thoughtful look come to him, and I knew who he was thinking of. I think he'd have had her back if he could, despite it all.

The only person I ever tried to talk with about the events of that night was Ran, because I thought he'd understand. He just shook his head, though. Perhaps if I'd been an Ant-kinden too, perhaps if he and I could have spoken inside our heads with the clarity of their Art, then we would have come to an understanding. He was a good man, Ran, and a good actor. He gave the company a few memorable supporting roles, certainly. He died in the siege, they tell me. I was too busy with the artillery to see it happen.

And Keyness Bounder? His reputation was in a constant state of flux, afterwards. He was clown or genius depending on who you spoke to. There was a motion to have him fired, because of the money, and he only just clung onto his job with the company. You would have thought he was ruined, that he would have left for Helleron to set up a new company there.

But then, if you thought that, you didn't know Keyness Bounder. Next spring, before the season started, I ran into him in the Other Masque. He was sharing a bottle of some kind of clear spirits with a lean, sharp-faced woman whose forearms bristled with hooked spines.

"Ah, Miles," he addressed me happily when I came in. "I have the very thing for this year's production. How long has it been since we did a Mantis tragedy? Now Akkestrae here's been showing me just that. The only problem is, to do it properly apparently there has to be some kind of fight to the death..."

TALES OF THE APT

An outbreak of amateur dramatics while I was at university has left me with a lasting joy in writing about theatrical types – see Albaris in 'Alicaea's Children' later in this collection, or alternatively the two linked (non-kinden) stories 'The Roar of the Crowd' (in my collection *Feast and Famine*) and 'Dress Rehearsal' (in the anthology *Now We Are Ten*). My theatrical stories are also, always, something of an homage to one of my favourite authors, Peter S. Beagle, who always takes such joy in the topic.

Pathaea, the opera, is of course Mozart's *The Magic Flute*, that surreal, magical and masonic wonder, cut slightly to suit the kinden's cloth. It fits remarkably well.

Miles' brief glimpse is the only sight we have of Pathis, the city that became Collegium, back in its heyday – however accurate that glimpse might be.

The bit-part character of Akkestrae is, by *War Master's Gate*, leading an exiled population of Felyen Mantids in Collegium as they fight against the advance of the Wasp and Spider forces.

Finally, I just want to shout out to one line towards the end: Miles, of Ran, saying "He died in the siege, they tell me. I was too busy with the artillery to see it happen." That's the Vekken siege in *Dragonfly Falling*, and when I re-read this story (written some considerable time ago) it stopped me in my tracks, because when the Collegiates fight in the novels, it is always as civilians repurposed into soldiers, and that seems to be better encapsulated in those two sentences, about the fates of two amateur thespians when the war came, than anywhere else.

Fallen Heroes

The glass was so smudged and dusty that only a poor kind of light came through it, but the fly thought it was enough. It buzzed and battered, skating first one way and then back along the filthy pane. The greater world was out there, as the wan light told it, so it made its mindless bid for freedom over and over and over.

That's our totem, thought Bello hollowly. *My people, my race. That's our totem.* The machines in the factory next door thundered and crashed in a rhythm he knew by heart now, as he sat by the window with a score of other skinny little youths, waiting for the call.

The fly had stopped, walking up the glass bemusedly. It cleaned its face and Bello could almost read the insect's tiny mind as it thought, *Well if I got in, I can get out.* That was why flies were better than wasps or beetles. Wasps would just batter at the window until they fell and died. Flies would get the point, eventually. They would go and find another way out.

So why can't we? The Fly-kinden, Bello's diminutive people, and here they were behind glass, battering away, toil without end.

He thought about his father, coming back from the factory, jostled by a crowd of bigger men and women. His father with his shoulders bowed, balding head down, parcelled in his long coat. Old Frenno trudged the four hundred yards back home every evening and never thought to fly. The Ancestor's Art that gave his people shimmering wings, and the sky, had shrivelled in him. His feet never left the ground.

Trapped behind the glass, in Helleron. Helleron, city of opportunity. The Beetle-kinden that owned Helleron, each stone and soul of it, never turned anybody away. The factories were hungry mouths. They chewed up labour, ground it down to grit. There was a place for every newcomer in Helleron, and it was at the bottom. The magnates who owned the factories and the tenements and the big houses on the hill were all locals, but the grist of their mills came from all the people of the Lowlands. The little Fly-kinden were everywhere, running errands, serving food, crawling beneath machines to free them, adding a little blood to make the engines of commerce run smoothly.

The fat, brown-skinned Beetle man who was Bello's employer stomped in, staring at his charges. "Bello! Jons Prater, Lock House in Porter Square, quick as you like." Bello jumped up automatically as his name was called, almost ripped the letter from the big man's hand and was off out of the door. The Ancestor Art swelled in him, and he felt the twitch of his shoulderblades as his wings formed, shimmering and half-seen, and then he was airborne. Below him Helleron spread on all sides like a great stain, smogging the air with the smoke of its factories. There were some parts of the industrial district so thick with it that the air was impassable, poisonous. Bello had lived here all his life, and been running messages since his wings came at nine. Outside of the city the Messengers' Guild still held sway with its guarantees of quality and service. Inside there were plenty who did not want to pay their prices. Men like Bello's employer were swift to spot a market.

Bello raced at rooftop height, unravelling his mind's map of the city for the short road to Porter Square. It would be easy, winging across the sky's wide bowl, to take this for freedom. The rush of his wings spoke to him of his people's own warrens far south of here and all the glorious clear air in between. He was still behind the glass, though. He would give Jons Prater the message and take his money, and then he would be back, waiting with the other youths for the next job. His speed was not dedication, but knowing he would get no pay if he was late. He was thirteen years old and he had a reputation to keep up.

There were raised voices when he got home. It was an hour after dark and he was wretchedly tired, but he made the effort anyway, flitting from landing to landing without touching the steps in between. All around him the tenement creaked and grumbled with the lives of the cursed people who had no place better to live. He heard a dozen arguments and a fight through the thin walls. On the fourth floor he heard his father's voice: raised, but not shouting. His father never shouted any more. He could manage only a whining complaint that held the seeds of its own defeat. Bello stopped, not wanting to go in. He felt pressure like a hand on his shoulders, pushing him down, keeping him down. Beyond the day's long, tired haul he recognised it as despair. *Battering against the glass.* He sat on the top step and rubbed at his eyes. He would do what he always did. He would wait out here until it was done.

The stairs creaked on the flight above and he looked up quickly. There was only one person who lived over Bello's family. The man was a local celebrity of sorts. He, of them all, lived here because he chose, not because he must. He said it kept him closer to his clients. Holden, the pugilist: if he'd ever had a first name, nobody remembered it. He was just Holden, with the scarred face and the leather coat that didn't-quite-hide his shortswords. He was Beetle-kinden, with their squat, solid build, but he was lean and balanced with it. For all he towered over Bello's three-foot height he had a cocky grace unusual for his people.

As he passed the landing he ruffled Bello's hair. The Fly youth mustered a smile for him. "You off to work, Master Holden?"

"Always, son." The fighter paused, rolled his shoulders to loosen them. "Some fellow in the Gladhander fief's getting too big for himself, needs a taking down."

Bello followed the news of the fiefs, Helleron's criminal gangs, as avidly as all his fellows. Men like Holden were the heroes, the free spirits, who passed through their lives. The simple news that Holden was off to pull the Gladhanders' noses sent a vicarious thrill through Bello. He would surely lie awake tonight, imagining the man in chases down alleys, fights on the rooftops, stealthy stalking through the halls of his enemies.

"Good luck, Master Holden!" Bello said.

"Ain't no such thing as luck, son. Skill's all," Holden told him, setting off down the stairs. "Remember that, boy, and you can't go far wrong." As he went, Bello heard the door open and realised his father's voice had ceased its sad tirade.

The long-faced old Beetle-kinden man who came past on the stairs was the landlord's agent, who Bello had known and disliked all his life. He had become a symbol of the family's hopelessness and lack of prospects. He turned up every month for his money, and Bello's father would scrape together what they had, and sometimes it was enough, and sometimes it was short. If it was short then the man would be back within the tenday: slow, mournful, patient, three times the size of Bello's father, insistent. He always got his due eventually. By some grotesque chance he was called Joyless Bidewell. He carried the weight of the name like a sack of coal.

Bello went in before the door closed. His nose told him it was the remains of yesterday's thin vegetable stew his mother would be serving. His father was at his customary place already, cross-legged on the floor before the low table. He looked at Bello without expression until the boy had handed over the half-dozen bits he had made that day. It was not any threat of retribution that made him part with the money, but the crippling knowledge that there would be none. His father would not even rise to a confrontation with his own son.

"Saw Bidewell on the landing," he said, sitting opposite his father. "What's he want now? Rent day was last tenday."

Bello's father's haunted eyes flicked up to his wife, kneeling at the fireplace and spooning out the stew. He said nothing. He never did. He just locked his troubles up where they could be neither goaded nor charmed from him.

They preferred Bello to stay indoors after dark but lately he could not bear to. Tonight, with the unspoken *something* hanging in the air between his parents, he was out of the door the moment he had finished his meal. There were a dozen Fly-kinden families in the tenement, more next door. They did not mix with other races but they formed a little community of their own. Bello would go and find his peers, and scrap and gossip and boast about imagined connections with the fiefs and the street-fighters. His nodding acquaintance with Holden was hard currency far more than the ceramic chips he was paid in, that were good no further than Helleron's outlying buildings.

He almost ran into the man sitting on the stairs before he could stop, his wings flaring awkwardly at short notice, carrying him in a great leap over the obstacle's head. He landed in a stumble, catching himself with another ghostly flash of his Art. At first he thought it was some tramp off the streets who had come in from the weather. Then he saw it was Joyless Bidewell himself. The Beetle-kinden man was staring at him with that lined face of his. His creased lips moved. Bello hesitated, torn between rushing off and the prodigy of this man, the Big Man of their tenement for all he was some bigger man's agent, sitting on the steps like a drunk.

"Master Bidewell?" he said eventually. Politeness to the Beetle-kinden, to their faces, had been slapped into him.

Joyless Bidewell frowned, obviously not placing him, then: "You're Frenno's boy, no?" When Bello nodded the big man sighed, gathered his coat closer about him. "Well, I'm sorry, boy," he said. He sounded as tired as Bello's father, as tired as Bello himself had been when he came home.

"Sorry what? What's going on?" Bello demanded. "Tell me. Please."

Bidewell glanced up, up towards Bello's apartment. He shrugged. "Rent's going up, boy. Quite a step up."

"What?"

"Not my fault. Not my doing. Been all day telling people like your folks that they can't afford to live here anymore." He shrugged. "Nothing I can do." There must have been something in Bello's face that showed more fire than his father's, for the old Beetle levered himself to his feet. "Two day ago, boy, this street changed hands. The Firecaller fief's here now, kicked the House of Maynard out. Firecallers want more cut than old Maynard ever did. Nobody going to pay that 'cept for all you folks who live here. My boss sure ain't."

"Then... don't pay," said Bello, knowing as he did that it was stupid.

"Don't call'em Firecallers for nothing," Bidewell mumbled. He pushed past Bello, shaking his head.

Bello had not gone to his friends. They would have to brag the night through without him. He had sat on the steps where Bidewell had sat, and thought. In his mind the image of a fly battering at the glass came again and again. *So go around. Find another way.* Bidewell was nobody. Take him away and another servant would fill his shoes. Bidewell's faceless master, some factor of a city magnate, was so far away that to beg of him would be like pleading with the sun. Bello's parents and their neighbours would be kicked out and moved on. There would be some worse place awaiting them, and then some worse place again. Perhaps they would share a room with another family. Two other families. Already the room they had was only half of one, split down the middle to fit more families in. Everyone knew the Fly-kinden, the little people, needed hardly any space to live in.

But we were born to have the sky. The Beetles, clumsy and industrious and bound to the earth, did not see it that way.

There was only one way to push, and he had only one means of putting the pressure on.

There was a taverna seven streets away in the big Gold Boys fief where the fighters met. The Gold Boys had been around forever. They were comfortable, pally with the guard and the magnates, paying all the right people. They ran entertainments: brothels, gambling houses, illegal fights. It was the high end of the fief culture and it gave them an oft-pawned respectability. The Taverna Marlus had become the fashionable place for the well-to-do to gawp at the lowly-but-brutal. Thrills for the one, money for the other. Marlus and the Gold Boys did well out of it.

There were always a gaggle of youths hanging about the doorway. They were a mixture of Fly-kinden and Beetles, half-breeds and a few others. Bello was not one of them and, if he gave them the chance, they would have knocked him down a few times. His wings flung him straight past them, through the open door to skid on the rugs of the floor.

"Out, you!" bellowed Marlus. The proprietor was a pitch-skinned Ant-kinden man, playing dice with some of his richer patrons. He stood, scowling. The sword at his belt, no less than the crossbow above the bar, reminded everyone of his boast to be a renegade soldier from a distant city-state.

"Here to see Holden!" Bello gasped out, looking frantically around to find the man. For a swooping moment he could not see him, anticipating a hasty ejection and a kicking from the locals. Then he saw the Beetle-kinden fighter at one of the tables, nodding at Marlus. The Ant narrowed his eyes but sat back down.

"You got a message for me, Bello?" Holden asked. The Fly youth looked at him seriously. This was the part that he had not rehearsed.

"I need to talk to you," he said. Holden was sharing a table with two other Beetle-kinden brawlers, and they were already smirking. Bello pressed on. "It's really important. Please, Master Holden."

"*Master* Holden," one of the others snickered.

Holden grimaced and stood up, stretching. "Ignore them, boy. They're just jealous because they haven't pissed off the Gladhanders like I just did." Holden's drinking fellows looked a step more threadbare than he was.

"Right, be quick," the fighter said, when he got Bello out of obvious earshot. "I'm looking to pick up another job this evening." He did not say it, but he might as well have done: being seen talking to a ragged Fly-kinden youth would not help his reputation.

"I want to hire you," Bello got out, before his nerve could fail him.

"Yeah?" Holden grinned at him, delighted. "With what, Bello?"

Bello reached into his pockets and brought out a handful. Most of it was ceramic bits, but there were a few silver Standards in there. It was all the money that Bello had ever kept back from his parents, all the money he had kept secret and hidden for the right moment. This had to be the moment, and the money had to be enough. "They're going to throw us out. They're putting the rent up," he blurted out. "You must have heard."

"So put this towards the rent," Holden said reasonably.

"But what about next month? And what if they put it up again?" Bello asked. "I need to hire you to fight the Firecallers, Master Holden. Because then it'll be done, and we can go back to the way things were."

Holden's face had soured when the Firecallers were mentioned. He closed Bello's hands over the money. "Listen, boy," he said, "two things." Sympathy twisted at his scars. "One: the Firecallers are on the up. They're doing well these days. I'd charge a lot to start spiking their engines. Two: what you've just showed me is less than what I charge to meet with people, let alone actually draw a sword for them."

He let that sink in, giving Bello time to consider it. In Bello's head the fly was walking up the pane, trying to work out why it could not get out this way.

"Anyone around here's going to be the same," Holden said. "Marlus' place is for the doing-wells." He grimaced. "Course, there are other places. Someone might be desperate enough for rep to take on the Firecallers."

Bello stared at him desperately. Holden scowled. "The world isn't fair. Know it and move on. You don't want to get mixed in this."

"What am I supposed to do?" Bello asked him. "Please, Master Holden. I have to find *someone*. At least tell me where to look."

"Listen boy, you want to go to these kind of places, it's on your head. They ain't safe, not any way." The fighter sighed. "But I can tell you, if you want it."

Holden's first recommendation was a gambling house on the riverfront. Helleron's river trade was halfway to nothing since they put the railroad in. What had been rich men's warehouses and offices were fallen into rot and ruin, and all kinds of vermin had moved in. The place had no name but there was a picture of a scorpion painted crude and yellow above the door, just like Holden had said. Nobody stopped Bello going in.

The first two bravos he tried to speak to, a Beetle and some kind of halfbreed, just cuffed him away. The second one had struck hard enough to knock him to the floor. He righted himself with a flick of his wings. He found a third. She was a lean, elegant Spider-kinden woman, slumming it or down on her luck. There had been gems in her rapier hilt but the sockets were empty now. When he told her what he wanted she nodded to one of the house staff and took Bello aside into a little room.

"Let's see your money," she said, and he showed it to her, all two handfuls of it.

She laughed. She laughed for a long time, having seen that, and something went out of her. "You little idiot," she said, when she could. "I was going to rob you, you fool. Kill you, most likely." She said it quite merrily. "Not for that, though. I don't soil my blades for potsherds and tin-tacky. *Hire* me? You couldn't hire a man to drink with you for that."

Bello found, in the face of her laughter, that he was shaking. She was two feet taller than him, armed and a professional, but he had to hold himself back from doing something rash.

"But," he said through clenched teeth, "I need –"

She shook her head. "You're mad," she told him. "Mind you, I value that. Look, I've a man you can go to. Don't tell him I sent you, It won't help your case. I just happen to know he's down at Scaggle's tonight after a job."

There were lower dives than the scorpion-fronted gambling den. Scaggle's was one of them. It was further down the river, built under a bridge so that there were water-marks halfway up the stone steps. Scaggle was a Beetle-kinden crone, burly and round-shouldered. She was all the staff she needed, all the guards too. Even as Bello came up the steps he had to flit aside as she hurled a drunk down onto them, careless of whether he hit rock or water. She squinted at Bello, then hulked back inside.

It was very dark in there. The place was little more than a cave. Fly-kinden eyes were good, though. Bello could pick out a dozen men sitting about five tables, lit only by wan candlelight. They were Beetles and halfbreeds, save for one. That one was the man Bello had come here to find.

He was as outlandish as anyone Bello had seen: tall and straight and fair, with sharply-pointed features and skin that was very pale. He wore an arming jacket secured with an elaborate pin. He looked as though he had stepped out of another world, or a story.

He eyed Bello narrowly as the boy approached him, saying nothing. When he raised his earthenware mug to drink Bello saw flexing spines jutting from his forearm.

He made neither invitation nor dismissal. It was left to Bello to say, "Excuse me, you are Master Tisamon?"

A nod, only. Bello forced himself on before he dried. "I need to hire you, Master."

The man Tisamon's mouth quirked at that and he put his mug down. "Do you know why I come here?" he asked. His voice was dry and sharp as the rest of him.

Bello shook his head.

"I come here because people hiring men like me do not," Tisamon finished.

"I need to hire you," Bello repeated.

"Go away."

"I can't. I won't."

Abruptly Tisamon was standing and Bello felt as though he'd swallowed his heart. There had been no transition between ease and edge. The latter had always been there, just out of sight. There was a metal gauntlet on the man's right hand, ending in a two-foot blade jutting from the fingers.

"Please…," Bello said, through a throat gone dry.

"Can I help you?" Tisamon asked, but he was looking over Bello's head. Not wanting to take his eyes off the man, Bello forced himself to crane back. There were three newcomers there, burly Beetle men squinting in the gloom.

"Don't want to disturb you, chief," said one of them. "Just need a word with the little fellow here."

Bello choked, flinched back from them. "Who are you?" he demanded.

"We're the fellows you're walking out of here with," said their leader. "You'll excuse us, chief, won't you?"

"Certainly," Tisamon said, relaxing back, only it wasn't relaxing. Bello saw the edge there still, though the Beetles missed it. "When I've finished speaking with my client, that is."

There was a moment with the Beetles exchanging glances, and Tisamon smiling urbanely at them.

"Now listen, chief," their leader started, and one of the others snapped out, "Look, this ain't nothing to do with you. We're taking the Fly-boy."

He grabbed Bello by the shoulder, surprisingly swift.

Tisamon *moved*. Bello saw nothing of it. As soon as he could he dived beneath the table, and the fact that the hand came with him and the man stayed where he was didn't register.

There was a lot of noise, tables being kicked over, shouts from the other patrons. Then there was surprisingly little noise. Bello put his head over the tabletop. Tisamon was standing, a dark, narrow shape. The three thugs were down and still. There was remarkably little blood and already old Mother Scaggle was hunching forward, gnarled hands reaching for rings and purses. Tisamon nodded at her and, when she was done, he hauled the bodies out, one by one, turfing them into the river. Bello saw then another virtue he looked for in his drinking haunts.

When he came back there was no blood on him, and the metal gauntlet had gone away. He resumed his seat, resumed his drink. "Come out, boy," he said.

When Bello did he found himself being scrutinised, as of doubtful goods. "You're no rich man's brat," Tisamon said. "So why do the Firecallers want you?"

"Firecallers?" Bello looked back at the river, that had borne the dead men away without complaint. "I... was going to hire you to fight them."

"Is that so? I'm not your first choice though. Who else have you tried?" Tisamon asked. Seeing Bello's expression he nodded. "Someone worked out that there was money in letting the Firecallers know about you." He was smiling now, although it was not a pleasant smile. "What have you got against the Firecallers?"

"They want to throw my parents onto the street," Bello said.

Tisamon shrugged, the spines flexing on his arms. "You're the second man to try to hire me against the Firecallers. I turned him down as well." As Bello sagged, the Mantis's smile became sharper. "I appear to be involved now. So let's go visit my other patron, shall we?"

Bello sat in a small cellar, watching Tisamon talk with a huge, fat Beetle. The fat man was robed in straining white like a scholar, sitting back in a big, stuffed chair. There was a man on either side. One had a crossbow and the other something Bello thought was a Waster, broad barrelled and gaping. From what he'd heard about the firepowder weapons, the blast of metal scrap would be quite enough to rip both him and Tisamon apart.

Tisamon was unconcerned, despite the fact that both weapons were levelled at him. All he said was, "Is this what passes for your welcome?"

"When a hired killer who's turned you down suddenly wants to talk, you get suspicious," the fat man said. "Now what the deal, Mantis?"

"I've changed my mind," Tisamon said easily, and the negotiations started. Bello sat in the corner, watching the light of the single lantern above gutter on their features. The fat man played lordly unconcern but there was a tremor behind it. Only when they had left did Bello realise he had been Maynard, of the House of Maynard, the fief whose borders the Firecallers were eroding.

"What happens now?" Bello asked.

"Time passes," Tisamon told him. Outside, in the House of Maynard fief, there was a dawn-edge to the eastern sky. He found it impossible to believe that it had all been one night.

"Go home," Tisamon said.

Bello goggled at him. "But, Master Tisamon, they're looking for me!"

Tisamon shrugged. "We cannot change that."

The fly battered against the glass, unable to believe it was not free. Bello grasped for an idea, and caught it.

It was an awkward breakfast. Little was said. Had there been an alternative, or had Bello's father been the man for it, he would had refused. Instead he shuffled aside, slope-shouldered, and a curdled look on him, when Bello brought his new friend home.

"Been people looking for you," he muttered. His stare at Tisamon lumped the Mantis in with those 'people'. "Been causing trouble?"

"Some," Bello said, torn between showing Tisamon a happy family and showing off. The fighter stooped in, giving each parent a brisk nod. Bello thought his mother would protest, but the Fly-kinden had their hospitality like everyone else. She went reluctantly to their unwanted guest, staring straight ahead at his belt, not up at his face.

"Will you sit down, Master?" she said. "Please, take your place."

It would be a comic scene to any of the larger kinden: Tisamon crouched at one edge of that low table, all elbows and knees and lowered head, filling far too much of the room. For a Fly-kinden it was an intrusion. A man like Tisamon, even had he not been what he was, could have broken them and taken what he wanted. He did not acknowledge it, nor did he find any humour in it. He took the meagre bread and cheese that Bello's mother offered with quiet thanks, not refusing out of charity nor demanding more. It took Bello all the meal to work out what was so strange about him.

"Master Tisamon," he said, afterwards. "Where are you from?"

"Far, far away," Tisamon said. He was sitting with his back against one wall, beside the window and looking at the door. "Far away and long ago," he murmured.

"I've never met a Mantis-kinden before."

"If you're lucky you'll never meet one again. We're a cursed breed," Tisamon said.

"How long have you been in Helleron, Master?" Bello finally got to his point.

"Ten years, more. You stop counting." The narrow eyes were watching him, waiting, but Bello did not say it. *You do not fit here*, he thought. *Not here in this room, but all the same, not anywhere else near here.* Tisamon's alienation was so great that he seemed to leave no tracks, to not touch the grime of Helleron at all. He was no more out of place dining with Fly-kinden than he was drinking at Scaggles.

"Why… did you come here, Master?" Bello asked, wondering if he was being too bold.

"A mistake, a long time ago," Tisamon said softly.

And you have stayed here ever since, Bello thought. *Another fly under glass.*

A messenger met them on the stairs just as Bello was hurrying off to work. His father was a floor below them, clumping and clumping, and did not stop when the Fly-kinden girl hailed Tisamon.

She passed him a folded note, hanging in the air all the while with her wings a blur. Tisamon glanced at it once.

"Agreed," he said, and she took that as her answer and flew off. She had been a cleaner and more respectable specimen of Bello's profession than he ever usually saw.

"What is agreed, Master?" he asked.

"You must know how the fiefs of Helleron resolve their differences," Tisamon said. "Or the chief and most formal way."

"A challenge?"

"The House of Maynard have laid a challenge," Tisamon confirmed. "The Firecallers are more than happy to accept. They have more coin than the Maynards and they can find a better champion. So the logic goes." His earlier melancholy was evaporating and Bello saw it was the thought of the fight that did it.

"Who will be their champion?"

"We shall find out tonight. The Golden Square shall host the fight, so that there might be a little money won and lost outside the main dispute." Tisamon's smile became sharper. "I would imagine that some fighter you tried to hire may have won himself the Firecaller's patronage with a story of your misdemeanours, child."

Bello had given that some thought. "It will be the Spider," he said.

Tisamon went very still, and Bello saw with a start that his bladed gauntlet was on his hand. "Spider-kinden?" he asked softly.

"A woman," the boy stammered. "She…" She had said not to say it.

"She pointed you in my direction, did she?" Tisamon was very still. "If it was some jest of hers, she shall not be laughing hereafter. Not if she is champion for the Firecallers."

"Master, what –?"

"Oh we hate them, and it is an old blood hate," Tisamon whispered. He was like another man, in that moment, with the weight of centuries dragging at him. "We kill them when we can. Though they laugh at us and call us savages, yet they do not think of us without a chill. I shall be glad, tonight, if it is a Spider-kinden they have chosen."

His face was a stranger's face, a face not to be met with on a dark street.

Bello could not concentrate at work. He only flew two errands, let the others pick up the slack. There was no shortage of volunteers. Everyone had a family trying to make ends meet. The broad, squat Beetle did not care who got paid, so long as the job was done. What he did mind was his boys distracting one another and chattering too much while they waited. Bello felt the weight of his hand at least twice when telling his fellows that he would be watching a real challenge fight tonight, that he was specially invited. It beat being on talking terms with Holden. It made him a celebrity.

He did not think about the Firecallers, about what they would do with him if they caught him. They would not move until the fight's end, Tisamon had told him. It was bad etiquette.

And if he loses?

He did not think about it.

The Golden Square had once lived up to the name, but not in living memory. It had been a theatre, hosting bawdy comedies for the artisan classes. Now it was a makeshift arena. The management let the place out to any local gangs who had a score to settle, and didn't charge. The bookmaker's takings more than covered costs and it kept the place independent of the fiefs, more or less. It had been on House of Maynard turf until recently but the tide had carried the Firecallers' borders past it.

Some half-dozen of the Maynard men turned up, led by a grim-looking Ant-kinden woman with a shaved head. It was no secret that if the challenge match went against them, so would a great deal else. They dressed drab, keeping the white-patterned bracers that told of their allegiance hidden under long sleeves. In contrast, the score and a half of Firecallers were rowdy and boisterous and wore their red silk scarves with fierce pride. Maynard himself had not shown but the leader of the Firecallers, a broad-shouldered halfbreed, was holding court at one end of the sand.

Bello's nerve nearly failed him three times before he managed to approach the place. There were all manner of toughs knocking shoulders outside it, from fief soldiers to the local labour and tradesmen here for a flutter. In the end he waited for his moment and just darted in, pitching over their heads and dropping into the doorway with, for once, the poise of an acrobat.

"Very adept," said a familiar voice from behind the door. He looked round, but it was a moment before he found Tisamon standing there. "You're a good flyer. Perhaps you should try the Guild. You're of an age to train."

Bello blinked at him. It was strange to face this well-travelled veteran and know something as second nature that the man had no idea of. "The Guildhouse here's a closed shop, Master. Unless you're sponsored, you don't get in. Nobody's going to sponsor me."

"The Messengers keep other houses in other cities," Tisamon said, but then looked away as the bald Ant-kinden woman came over.

"With you standing by the door, Mantis, it looks like you're going to run," she said. Tisamon stared at her coldly but she faced up to him without a blink. "What? We're all bug-food if you take your leave, man. Anyway, they're asking for you. We're about to settle this."

Tisamon nodded. "Keep an eye on this boy here, Clavia. Don't keep him with you, but I want him unharmed when this is done."

The Ant-kinden, Clavia, frowned, but Tisamon waved her objections away. "Call it a condition of my employment."

"Rack you, Mantis-man," she spat, but she was nodding. "I swear, if you foul the works here, I'll kill you myself."

She stalked off to her fellows, who had a good view of the sand. Bello wanted to go with them but then saw why not. *So I am not caught, if this goes badly.* He glanced up at Tisamon. *Does he fear he'll lose, or that the Firecallers won't accept his win?*

The fighter was making his way after Clavia, and Bello was about to find a place when someone said, "Oy," softly behind him. With a sudden stab of fear he turned, but then grinned to see a familiar face.

"Master Holden!"

"You're up late, boy." Holden's smile was barely there. "I see you got involved anyway. I tried to warn you. It's hard to make an honest living in this town, but you should at least give it a try."

"I've not joined a fief yet, Master," Bello said. "I just…"

Holden shook his head. "We all have to pay the rent," he said sadly.

"Even you?" Somehow Bello had never thought of old Joyless Bidewell making the extra climb to Holden's rooms above. "But you're doing-well. You said so."

"It's a close neighbour to doing-badly. They live on the same street." Holden tousled Bello's hair. "Now you've got this far, now you see all these men, these criminals, making more money in a night than you get in a month, you'll see things in a different way. You'll be a fief-soldier soon enough, working from the ground up. It's a shame, but you're not the first."

"Master Holden –" He wanted to say that his ambition was to be a freelancer, a duellist, like Tisamon or Holden himself. It was not a job for a Fly-kinden, though, not the biggest and hardest Fly-kinden there ever was.

"Go find yourself a seat," the Beetle said to him, and passed on through the crowd.

Bello looked around, and saw that there were at least a dozen Fly-kinden in the rafters, finding niches where they could enjoy a unique viewpoint. Some were wearing Firecaller scarves but he found just then he wanted to watch the fight more than he feared them. He let his wings take him up to a beam and sat there, his legs dangling. He felt the eyes of Clavia on him as he flew.

The sand, where the fighters would square off, was nothing much. It was just a strip about twenty feet long, five feet wide. In the fiefs they liked their fights close and bloody. At one end the Firecaller leadership sat enthroned. At the other end were Clavia and her few minions. Along each side, close enough that a missed stroke could clip them, were the gamblers, the drinkers and the fight-enthusiasts who had come to make a night of it.

Tisamon stepped down before the Maynard men. He cut an odd, stark figure in green arming jacket and gold broach, his folding-blade gauntlet on his hand and his arm-spines jutting. The crowd went quiet, and Bello heard the Mantis's name passing amongst them.

A Beetle-kinden man strode out before the Firecallers and it was a second before Bello cried out in protest, voice high above the mumble of the crowd. They looked, they all looked up to see him: skinny little Fly-kinden child with his mouth open and his face gone white. He had eyes only for one, though: Holden, with a Firecaller scarf about his neck. Holden, looking up at him briefly, face resigned.

We all have to pay the rent. It's a shame, but you're not the first. Bello felt numb. The crowd had already laughed him off. Only Holden spared him another glance. He was dressed in armour of hard leather: cuirass, pauldrons, kilt, bracers and greaves. The crowd went quiet again as he took his swords from their scabbards in a long practiced motion, holding them almost crossed before him.

Tisamon had dropped into his stance the moment the steel was drawn, his claw hooked back, one open hand thrust forward. He was quite still, waiting for Holden to come to him. For a long time neither man moved. The crowd, instead of more restless, became more and more involved, feeling the tension between the two pull taut.

Holden let out a shout and was at the other man, cutting at his ready hand, thrusting past at his chest. Tisamon shrugged aside from the lunge, beat the cut away with his palm and was past Holden in a moment. They were left at opposite ends of the sand, no blood drawn. There had not even been the sound of steel on steel.

Holden, with the burning gaze of the House of Maynard on his back, approached again. This time he changed his stance, one blade high and one low. He thrust with both, then cut out and wide to stop Tisamon getting past him again. The Mantis stepped in after the cut, the spines of his offhand slamming through Holden's shoulder armour but not biting deep. Bello heard the Beetle-kinden hiss. The shortswords drove in whilst Tisamon was close, trying to catch him. Again the other man was gone when they arrived. Holden was strong, and he was quick for a big man, but he could not pin his enemy down. Tisamon danced him from one end of the sand to the other in a space designed to force a bloody confrontation.

They paused, the length of the sand between them. Holden had been doing most of the work but his people were an enduring lot. Neither man was breathing hard. There was something about his stance, though, that Bello saw: something about Tisamon's too. It was as though the two of them were party to a secret that nobody else watching had understood. In seeing it, Bello saw the secret too, became an initiate into that tiny mystery.

They closed again and this time Holden held nothing back. His swords slammed at Tisamon from all angles, drove him before them like a leaf in a storm. There was a rapid patter of metal as Tisamon's claw came in at last, moving like a living thing, gathering Holden's blades and casting them like chaff. Tisamon struck with his off hand, the spines scoring across the other man's face, and as Holden cried out, he died. The claw made its first strike, a swift dart of silver between Holden's neck and shoulder, and he died. Bello felt the stab of it, even though his champion had won.

There was a lot of quiet, as the spectators passed back over those last moments, reconstructing them. Then the crowd, the idle punters, began to clap and cheer, and the lucky ones started to call in their creditors. Tisamon remained quite still, though, the dead man's blood on his blade, and his eyes on the Firecallers. All the Maynard men had drawn knives or swords.

Tisamon had made sure he was at the far end of the sand, closest to the Firecaller chief. There was a lot said in his stare about the cost of forcing the issue. Every man in a red scarf was waiting for the word.

The Firecallers left. Their leader stood up, face like thunder, and walked out without a backward glance, and the scarves followed him, as swiftly as they could. The turf war with the House of Maynard was not done, but they had lost face, lost the challenge. The streets they had wagered had gone back to the Maynard, who would be able to muster a few more allies with this victory. Things had changed between them.

There was another duel on tonight. People were getting drinks and food in for it. Tisamon went to Clavia and her people and Bello saw money change hands. He dropped from the rafters down to the sand, ignoring the looks he got at this breach of etiquette. and knelt by Holden's body. The man had sold him out, it seemed certain. He had taken the part of the Firecallers. He had betrayed all the people he shared the tenement with. He had been the brightest part of Bello's life.

Tisamon was leaving, pausing in the doorway to look back. Bello approached him hesitantly.

"Do you... want your money?" he asked.

"Hold it for me," Tisamon told him. He was swift and deadly, but he was not Holden, who had lived on the floor above and died on the sand below.

But Holden was gone, and Tisamon was going. "Please, Master Tisamon- Can't I..."

The fighter stopped. "Find other heroes than men like us, Fly-child. We do not last."

"But what can I do now?"

Tisamon weighed him with the same stare that had quelled the Firecallers, and gave his judgment, spoke the death sentence.

"Go home, boy. It's over. Go home and be thankful you still have one."

TALES OF THE APT

Just as *Spoils of War* dealt with war stories, this collection is mostly stories about the peace, and what goes wrong with that. Helleron looms large in several of them, always as a backdrop to social injustice, poverty and misery. The war machine of the Empire and the ancient magics of the Moths are by no means the sole founts of evil in the world of the kinden. Greed, corruption, prejudice and class boundaries can accomplish a great deal without ever drawing a sword.

This was the first piece of SotA short fiction I ever wrote, followed soon after by 'Ironclads', 'Spoils of War' and 'The Dreams of Averis' (all reprinted in *Spoils of War*). These stories set the tone for most of my kinden shorts – the opportunity to go to places and times the narrative couldn't. In this case, it was an opportunity to flesh out the career of Tisamon that took place between the first and second chapters of *Empire in Black and Gold*.

The surprising thing is that I appear to have written a Western: poor and needy are under threat, go seek out violent outsider who comes in to save the town without ever becoming part of it. It's a role that fits Tisamon rather well.

The Price of Salt

Trailing little dust, four riders were making the best time they could over the scrubby ground, pushing their mounts to greater speed and then reining them in when the terrain broke up. Here in the northern Commonweal the rolling hills of the wealthier principalities gave ground to the southernmost extremities of the great steppes, which ever gave the Commonweal a northern border defined not by barriers but by sheer atrophying distance. The Monarch's claim to the land grew less and less relevant as the traveller progressed, until not a soul would profess to know of the Commonweal's master, or even the Commonweal itself.

The riders had, until relatively recently, gone as far north as they cared to in the business of tracking down a fugitive, which hunt had ended successfully for all but their target. The seedy trading town in which they had cornered their quarry was still comfortably within the Monarch's domain, contained within the concentric circles of province and principality. Whilst the riders themselves were not exactly handfast friends with the Commonweal's laws, still they preferred to stay where they knew which rules they were breaking.

Fiol had been the town's name, and Fiol's Headman was a man of flexible attitudes. All were welcome in the caravanserai that domianted the town, which the Headman's family had owned since before recorded time, and there the emissaries of princes rubbed shoulders with bandits and fugitives and herdsmen from the steppe. The native Dragonfly-kinden of Fiol were at times outnumbered by the surly, belligerent or secretive outsiders who came there to barter.

The Headman had a similarly enlightened attitude to justice and law. Whilst he maintained a small clan of Mantis-kinden to serve as his sharp right arm when heads needed to be broken, he did not stand in the way of small scale personal vengeance, such as trackers chasing a bounty or the incursions of the Monarch's Mercers. Hence the four hunters had located their target in the caravanserei and the man's supper had been ended by a swift and fatal case of arrow poisoning.

The quarry had in life been Corde Liantes, who had capped a long career as a robber by murdering a farmhand who challenged him. The farmhand, Liantes had subsequently discovered, had been the nephew of a prince-minor living with the farmer's family under the bonds of kin-obligation. Corde had fled and the prince had promised a fine reward for proof of his demise.

Looking at Corde's body lying amongst the detritus of his supper, his sword half clear of its sheath and a long-shafted arrow through his chest, the hunters were faced with a problem. Corde Liantes had been a good runner. The hunt had been on for over three tendays, the distance back to the promised reward was long, and the only proof they had of their deed rested in the fixedly-startled face attached to the front of Corde's head.

If any enterprising Fly-kinden had flitted low over the riders, as they rushed north of Fiol now, they would have caught the tail-ends of a bitter conversation amongst the riders.

"It's not Corde I mind, it's the salt," The voice of the hindmost was a cultured drawl utterly belied by the man's squat, muscled frame and jutting lower jaw. A Scorpion-kinden, he was the worst rider of all of them and seemed hunchbacked at first, until closer inspection revealed the powerful segmented shape that clung to his back, sting-tipped tail coiled tenderly about his waist. "That's just unnecessary expense, and no wonder. We must be five hundred miles from the sea, out here." This was Barad Ygor, who hailed from very distant points south indeed. His clinging companion went by the name of Scutts.

"What's the sea got to do with it?" This from a solidly-built Wasp-kinden by the name of Mordrec. His presence here, in that part of the Commonweal that the imperial invasion had not reached, showed him as a renegade.

"Salt comes from the sea," Barad Ygor maintained.

"It does not."

"I assure you it does."

"I know thousands of slaves in Imperial salt mines who'd disagree," the Wasp shot back.

"Will you two give it a rest?" a third man spoke up, his voice suggesting that he was the sort of leader whose granted authority came and went like the weather. He was a Dragonfly-kinden whose grim face spoke of hardships and desperate deeds: Dal Arche, veteran, occasional tracker of fugitives and, more and more these days, outright brigand. His authority over his fellows had kept the four of them together for many months now, and common interest and a lack of options were slowly being reinforced by the first shackles of mutual loyalty. However, this was not his finest hour, and his captaincy over the others was at something of a low ebb.

"Speaks the man who got us into this," Mordrec accused him.

"Quite," Ygor agreed. "Who was it that was supposed to be looking after all that salt, eh?"

"And Corde's cursed *head*," the Wasp added heatedly.

"Forget the head. The salt was worth more." Ygor had paid for the salt out of his own pocket and was feeling particularly stung.

It was a poor business, Dal Arche had to admit, albeit only to himself. The four of them had killed Corde. They had decapitated the body to secure a more portable proof of the act. Ygor had, it was to be admitted, laid out a fair amount in barter and Imperial coin to secure sufficient salt to preserve the grisly thing, which he had then attended to, claiming that only the Scorpion-kinden ever understood how to preserve dead flesh properly. As their nominal leader, Dal Arche had taken custody of the head, safely within a waxed oilcloth bag.

And he had lost it. Or rather, it had been taken from him. The full details of that were not something he had shared with his fellows. All they needed to know was that a Dragonfly-kinden thief, a girl of barely twenty years, had wormed her way into their room at the caravanserai, taken the head and ridden off north with it, thus making herself the latest target of the hunting party.

Why the girl wanted a salted head in a bag had Dal Arche baffled. There had been a smaller pouch beside it which contained a handful of Imperial silver and a single lozenge of ancient Commonweal gold, but that she had left. Only Corde's head had been worth the theft. The only possible explanation he could think of was that she was some relative of Corde, and that she was aiming to repatriate the man's head with the rest of his clan, but Corde had run a long way from his usual haunts to get to Fiol. Nothing that Dal had heard along the way suggested the man was running *to* anything, as opposed to just *from*.

"Enough," he snapped at his comrades. "We're gaining on the bitch. Let that be enough. After all, you used enough damn salt. Corde will keep."

The fourth member of their party was a lean, careful Grasshopper-kinden man, another Commonwealer by birth like Dal, yet another imperial deserter like Mordrec. His name was Soul Je and he said nothing, but his watchful eyes were always at the horizon.

At the back of each of their minds was the uneasy thought that, in going north from Fiol, they were falling down that gradient of uncertainty, from clear Commonweal territory into the vast wild unknown of the steppe.

They had already left all the decent farming land behind, but they passed herders' huts, and saw flocks of goats dotting the dun of the higher ground like grey clouds, and the shiny brown backs of oil-beetles herding at their erratic stop-start pace across the lower. When they found a local who was willing to stand by while four armed men rode up, Dal Arche asked about their quarry. The people who made that place their home were Grasshopper-kinden mostly: gaunt, brown specimens of the breed, leathered by sun and wind and weather. Their manner was strange and unsettling. It was clear they had seen the woman pass, but they would barely admit as much. They obviously did not want to talk to four such dangerous rogues, and yet something compelled them.

"You should turn back," one said, "the hunt is not worth it." There was a shifty, guilty look to him. He would say little more, and he did not even seem to recognise the silver coin that Dal offered. Only when Ygor cocked his crossbow and threatened to put a bolt through the carapace of one of the man's beasts did the local admit that yes, yes a young Dragonfly maid had ridden that way. Yes, there was a Dragonfly village (he had heard) north of here, after Stae and then De Estre. But no. No and no again: they should not follow. Nothing good would come of it.

Dal glanced at his fellows, seeing disdain for the superstitious on Mordrec's face and disdain for the rustic on Ygor's. Only Soul Je looked thoughtful. He was a close-mouthed man, Soul Je, a consummate master of the longbow beyond even Dal's own exacting standards, whose conversation was only for the hunter's or the archer's art, but now he looked unhappy.

"There is something..." he murmured, so quiet that only Dal caught it, and Soul would neither repeat the words nor elaborate on them.

The hard, cold earth of the nascent steppe was not a tracker's friend, but their quarry was pressing her mount hard and making no attempt to hide her trail. When they were sure of their road they pushed their horses hoping to make up time. When the ground grew rockier and their path uncertain they would slow again, losing what they had fought for. Then, on the second day, the uneven ground gave up a village that was set into a deep cut dug into the side of a hill. There was a pallisade and pens for livestock, and Dal estimated that there might be as many as seventy living there, adults and children. More Grasshopper-kinden, the hunters saw as they approached.

"Feed for the horses if they have any," Mordrec suggested. "Provisions for us."

A dozen of the villagers, men and women, had come to the broad gap in the pallisade that served as a gate. Some held spears, others cudgels; the general sense of them was not hostile but frightened.

Soul dismounted first, his strung longbow dangling in one hand. He had the other hand held up, open and empty, a gesture of peace recognised everywhere except the Empire. Still, Dal knew he could get an arrow moving from that bow with unearthly speed if necessary. The other two stayed mounted, Ygor with a bolt at the ready, and Mordrec with the blocky weight of his nailbow resting on his shoulder, although it was likely the locals would not even recognise the weapon for what it was. Dal took a deep breath and slung himself off the saddle, approaching the welcoming party. *Definitely scared*, he saw. He felt as though a harsh word would spook and scatter them. *And yet not scared of me.* He wondered if there was some greater brigand stalking these barren lands.

"We wish to trade for food, for ourselves and the horses," he announced.

"We have nothing," one of the Grasshopper-kinden stated flatly. Dal frowned. There was a bustle of activity in the village's enclosure behind the welcoming party. He had a glimpse of children being hurried away, some of them crying out. Some of the huts were secured, as though to keep something dangerous in, or out. Fully half the villagers seemed to be lost in a frenzy of preparation for the worst of worsts, and yet the rest were just standing about, their faces slack as though they were simple-minded.

Is it a plague of some kind? he wondered, but what he was seeing did not match any preparations for pestilence that he had ever seen.

The pens were empty, he saw. Had their animals died of the sickness? They none of them seemed as starved as that would suggest, nor so well fed that they had slaughtered them. He tried to remember if he and his fellows had passed a lot of unattended animals, and guessed that perhaps they had. *Let them go? Why would they just let them go?*

"We're looking for a Dragonfly-kinden woman," he announced to them. "She would have ridden through here perhaps a day ahead of us, perhaps less."

"Go back," said the village's spokesman, as though he had not heard. "Please, leave here. This place is not for you."

"They're protecting her," Mordrec accused and, although it was not what Dal believed, it seemed a useful line to take.

"My friends are angry men, tell us or I'll not be answerable for them," he barked out. Soul had an arrow to the string now, waiting for the word.

There was a strange, bright look in the spokesman's eye that put Dal Arche in mind of a fever victim. Some of the men and women with him were shaking ever so slightly.

"Take what you wish, if you are desperate men," the spokesman told him bleakly. "We have little: we have only our thought and our peace. Take, and we shall not stop you."

Something was going on here that Dal decided he wanted nothing to do with. He was just on the point of letting his wings flick him up to the saddle when one of the other villagers pointed: north.

"A Dragonfly woman passed. She is not far ahead of you," the woman intoned. "She goes to her doom. You also, if you follow her."

"Thank you," said Dal without much courtesy, and the four of them set off without delay.

"Folks around here are mad," was Ygor's pragmatic assessment.

"We should turn back."

They reined their mounts in: the words were Soul Je's.

"Don't tell me all that mumbo-jumbo got to you," Mordrec demanded.

Dal Arche wisely remained silent. It had got to *him*, certainly, but he was their leader and to turn back would be to shake their faith in him. Still, he found himself hoping that Soul would make a good case.

"You don't feel it," Soul stated. "I feel it. This is a bad time to be out on the Steppe. Madness..."

They stared at him.

"Soul," said Ygor at last. "You're not Steppe Grasshopper. You're from Sa, which is miles away from here and under the black and gold. What do you know about it? The amount I spent on that salt, we're catching the little bitch and stringing her up by her toes, right?"

Soul said nothing.

"If you want to turn back, turn back," Dal told him, seeing that Mordrec and the Scorpion were both for pressing on. The lean Grasshopper-kinden just shook his head and kicked his horse onwards.

Dal pulled away from the other two until he was riding close by. "What 'madness'?" he demanded.

"There will be a grand moon soon," Soul Je stated flatly.

"What...? So there's a full moon, so what?"

"Not full, *grand*," the Grasshopper corrected him. "A once-in-a-century moon. A lunatic moon."

"So what? You were here a hundred years ago, were you? You're looking well for it."

"I've never been to the steppes before, Dala," Soul said quietly, sounding as though all this unaccustomed talking was wearing him out. "There are stories, though. You know my kinden. We're a peaceful people, left to our own devices."

"You're the most bloody-minded Grasshopper I knew," Dal confirmed.

Soul winced. "I can feel it, Dal. There's something in the air, in the earth. The mystics amongst my people have always held that the moon is the enemy of peace of mind. When there is a grand moon then perhaps one or two of a town may go mad with it, and have to be held for their own good, but it is easy to escape the moon in a town, in a city. Out here... They live in tents here, under the sky... the tribes of my kinden – but they're not my kinden, no, though you'd not tell us apart by looking. Only when the grand moon is above us would you know, and then it's too late. We must be swift, Dal, double our pace and hope the horses can take it. Before the grand moon comes we must be heading back south."

Dal glanced back at their companions, knowing that they both hailed from homes where this kind of talk would be laughed out of doors.

They passed an old man next, digging a hole with remarkable energy, long Grasshopper limbs plying his spade to lever the earth aside. He had a satchel on the ground beside him that looked crammed with books and scrolls.

"Why bury your learning, old father?" Dal asked him.

"What good will it do me now?" the ancient replied wearily. His hands trembled as they rested on his spade, but not with his years. Dal guided his horse away a little, possessed by the strangest idea that the aged scholar was suppressing the urge to attack him.

Before dusk there was another village, and this clearly built for defence. The outer walls were sloped inwards, with slits cut in them for the defenders to shoot out and up at attackers. At the top the wall-builders, in a sudden change of heart, had thrown out a jagged profusion of spikes and sharpened canes so that anyone scaling the steep incline of the wall would find themselves facing a bristling fence of spines. Individual huts would be tucked under the slanted walls, and in the centre of the compound stood a squat tower, broad-based and rising to a narrow crown that was likewise ringed with wooden teeth. Dal had heard that the steppe was dotted with little fortified communities like this, but that the great majority of the steppelanders were nomads, moving with their herds, meeting, warring, raiding, but mostly simply following patterns as ancient as memory about the appallingly unbounded expanse of the steppe.

"Maybe she's gone to ground there," Mordrec suggested.

"Let's get closer and see if they shoot arrows at us," was Ygor's plan. A closer approach showed them the place was abandoned. The gates were thrown open, the solid metal-shod bar lying in the dust between them. The four riders rode in cautiously, awaiting an ambush, but there was no sign of a single living soul.

"She's hiding here," Ygor decided, slouching off his mount. Scutts uncoiled from about him, dropping to the ground and flexing her claws and sting, stretching just as a human might after a long and uncomfortable journey. Then the great bronze-hued scorpion was rattling off, scenting for any trace of the living.

Dal glanced about him, looking for damage, signs of violence. The individual huts were just goathide over cane frames backed onto the shadowing wall, and he kicked off from his saddle to touch down before one. With a dagger drawn, he pulled aside the flap. Inside there was a rug laid out, and on the rug a few bowls. One was still half-full of some kind of mash that enterprising weevils had discovered and were working their way through. There had been a rack hanging from the sloping back wall, but the clay pots that had been kept there were all smashed on the ground, their burdens of herbs and dried plants ground underfoot.

In another hut he found the ashes of a fire still warm, and shreds of a Dragonfly-made silk robe someone had razored into ribbons.

Outside, Ygor had found some bodies.

There were probably five of them but it was hard to tell, because they had been hacked into scattered pieces, and because every one of the victims had been no more than a babe in arms. There was no sign of any mother or father who had fallen defending them, only the meagre scraps of former humanity that scavenging ants were already attending to. The savagery of the act was such that the four hunters, none of them with a clean conscience, were silenced for quite some time.

They left the village. Nobody there would be answering any questions. Heading north, soon they were certain of the trail again, though profoundly less certain of the land around them. That they were beyond the Monarch's civilizing influence seemed undeniable.

It was cold out on the steppe and the wind had picked up, forcing them to raise hoods and scarves against dust that cut like ice shards. Soul Je was shivering more than the chill could account for.

The wretched girl's trail led on, and now there was a third village ahead, to the same defensible plan as the last.

"Ride!" shouted Mordrec suddenly, spurring his mount on. Dal tugged his hood aside to look about, and saw that the pale ground half a mile east was darkened with a host of people: an army for sure. He saw no formations, no engines of war or clumsy flying machines, but his mind was briefly thrown back through the years, to when he stood within a mob of hungry, frightened Commonweal spearmen watching the Imperial lines break into a thunderous and unstoppable advance. He knew well just how quickly a body of men like that could cover ground, if they were trained and ready for it, and soon he was outpacing Mordrec, praying that all four of them would make the walls, and that the village was as abandoned as the last.

The gate was shut, he saw. He was about to wheel his horse and try for a straight run west when, to his surprise, the portal opened smoothly as though there were allies within who had been waiting all this time for him.

He had a moment to think, then, knowing that the others would follow his lead. It could be a trap, but he had his shortbow strung and to hand, and he could loose from horseback or from the air without difficulty. The others would all be ready for a fight, and he had no idea whether the force out on the plains had cavalry or airborne forces.

Putting an arrow to the string he rode straight through the gates, standing in the saddle ready to fly or shoot. Mordrec followed with his nailbow over his shoulder, and Ygor had eschewed his crossbow for a short-hafted lance yanked from its saddle-holster. At the rear Soul Je simply rode, and did not look back.

An expectant ring of villagers met them, Dragonfly-kinden all. Most were armed. slings, shortbows and spears all in evidence. There was no threat, though. Instead they actually seemed *pleased* to see the hunting party. They were a determined looking lot: herders and farmers, their beasts penned up between their huts and vocal in their complaints about it. The villagers wore clothes of a steppe cut: heavy cloaks lined with felt, moth-fur trimmings to their clothes, broad-brimmed hats secured at the chin and tall boots of goatskin reinforced by plates of beetle-shell. Dal had stood with people like these in the war: he had seen them ordered from their land by headmen and princes, given spears and slung together and placed in the way of the Empire, while the nobles and their retainers stood behind them, with bows and swords and armour. Not that he could fault the nobles' courage, in the end, but if they had been so driven to get themselves killed it seemed poor grace to drag so many poor frightened farmers and herders and artisans with them into the bloodshed.

The gate was closed behind them, but still there was no sense of a trap, at least not a simple trap.

"We're looking for a..." Mordrec's voice died out. "Just what is going on?"

The villagers had been staring mostly at Dal, clearly the leader, and at Ygor, patently the ugliest. Now they marked the other two newcomers. Soul they regarded with wide eyes, edging away from him, though never giving him the excuse of directing a spear his way. Mordrec, though... Mordrec they seemed to view with awe, whispering and staring, pointing him out to their children.

And at last Dal saw her, standing in the second rank with a shortbow slung over one shoulder: the headhunter girl who had robbed them in Fiol. She was a slender thing, hair cut short, wearing a banded chitin and leather cuirass beneath her long coat. Her gaze was clear and challenging, just as it had been in Fiol, which was, indirectly, what had led to all of this mess.

"Right," said Dal Arche, and swung off his mount. "You, give back what you've taken and we'll be on our way."

The bulk of the villagers were uncertain about this and it was clear that, while the thief had apparently told them to expect visitors, she had not told them why.

"You'll never find it," the girl declared. "In three days you can have it."

"Now, if you please," Dal pressed. This was going to get awkward, he knew, mostly because he hadn't exactly been wholly honest with his fellows either.

"It's buried. Only I know where," she stated. "Three days."

"Oh, what is going on?" Ygor demanded.

Dal looked from the wildly hopeful stares of the villagers to the increasingly suspicious ones of his friends. "You, into one of these huts," he told the girl. "We talk."

"Now wait –" Mordrec started.

"Give me two minutes," Dal asked.

The Wasp scowled, an expression that softened slightly when one of the locals came forth with a goatskin of something to wash the dust from his throat.

Dal pushed into the nearest slant-walled dwelling, and the girl followed him. He glared murder at her. "All right you, Alle or Elle or whatever your damned name is –"

"Lirien Aell," she said sweetly.

"What's going on?"

"I brought you here to help my people, Dal Arche. I've never been a thief, but it was the only way I knew you'd come with me."

"I have no interest in helping your poxy people," he growled. "You'll hand over the head and then we're off."

"I won't." She folded her arms again. She was filled to the top of her head with righteous defiance, like a child wearing her mother's overlarge clothes. "It's well hidden. You'll never find it unless I lead you to it."

"You're assuming that we won't just get that information from you one finger at a time," Dal told her darkly.

"You're not the torturing type. You talked a lot about yourself in Fiol, before you bedded me."

It was not that she was beautiful, certainly. At best, properly cleaned up, she might qualify as pleasing. It had been that impudent, insolent look, though, that had caught his eye and led inexorably to the two of them finding his bunk at the Caravanserai He had never quite been able to resist a woman like that. And it was true, perhaps he did talk too much. A part of him that still suffered some dregs of guilt over the life he had taken up still wanted to give her the chance to turn him down. He had guessed that she might ask for money. That she would abscond with a severed and salted head had not occurred to him.

"Maybe not," he allowed. "I wouldn't go so far for any of my companions, though, and I wouldn't bet that I could stop them."

She went pale at that. "It's too late for them now. They'll have to protect the village. I never heard of a Scorpion-kinden that could fly, and probably your Grasshopper can't either."

"Protect the village from who?"

"Dala!" It was Mordrec's voice. "Get out here now!"

He swore and bundled out of the hut. Mordrec was atop the wall, scanning the horizon, and now he dropped down. "That mob's on the move," he reported. "Hundreds of them, looks like. They were fighting each other a moment ago. Now they look as if they're forming up."

"Who's out there?" Dal demanded, of the village in general.

"My people are out there." The voice was cracked with age. The crowd parted to let a rake-thin Grasshopper-kinden totter forwards. She had most of her weight on a cane, which barely bent beneath it, and her long face was a nest of wrinkles. She was perhaps the oldest living human being Dal Arche had ever seen.

"And they're after you?" Ygor pressed, trying to wrestle the situation into something they could all understand.

"He knows." The ancient jabbed a finger at Soul Je. "The grand moon is upon us. The time of the Locust is here."

"What's she talking about, Soul?" Dal prompted, but Soul Je said nothing, long arms wrapped about himself and head bowed.

"*Someone* tell me what's going on," Mordrec asked almost plaintively.

"You have come to save us," Lirien Aell told him.

"I've bloody not."

"Our seers knew the Time of the Locust was near, and they divined that, if I rode to Fiol, I would find the help we needed. You are that help. You, especially."

Mordrec was backing away from the girl as though she was infected with a contagious disease. "What, now?"

"Why, you are a Wasp-kinden. Everyone here has heard of the Wasp-kinden. Everyone knows the Wasps *never* lose a battle."

Mordrec's expression was a mix of incredulity, despair and pride perhaps never before seen by mortal man.

"They're coming!" someone shouted, and one of the villagers pointed at Soul Je, demanding, "What about him? Take his bow from him!"

"You can try," drawled Ygor, hefting his crossbow.

"He'll be fine," Dal snapped. "You're fine, right, Soul?"

The Grasshopper nodded. His gaunt face looked strained.

Then the enemy was upon them. The first Dal heard of it was a weird ululating howl that seemed to spring up all around them, a maniac shrieking and hollering that made his skin crawl. The villagers were instantly taking to the air, flitting to the walls. On the inside edge of the canted palisades there were ledges joined into place, ready for spearmen or archers to crouch in partial concealment. There were arrowslits cut into the wood as well, and Ygor was already at one, peering through with his crossbow at the ready. Dal kicked off from the ground and took wing to the crenulations, drawing back his bowstring.

They were not soldiers or warriors of any kind. He stared at the onrushing enemy, arrow forgotten. The majority of the host beyond the walls had not even moved, in fact, but a couple of dozen of them had broken away to storm the walls. They were Grasshopper-kinden, all of them: men and women, some only children, others well past middle years. About one in four had a real weapon: a spear, a Dragonfly-made sword or the chain of wooden pieces the Grasshoppers called a 'broken rod'. The rest had clubs, staves, animal goads. Some were unarmed, although their Art had given them vicious spurs on their heels that Dal knew to be wary of. There were almost no bows, he noted, and only a few slings. They were not soldiers. They were not even a levy such as he had known in the war. They were a rabble.

But they were mad, virtually frothing at the mouth. There were far too few in that initial rush to take the village but they cared nothing for the odds. A few fell to sporadic arrow-shot from those villagers who owned bows, but the hunters themselves just stared, waiting for the charge to lose momentum and the attackers to realise that they must turn back or die.

The front-runners leapt, their Art taking them in great arcing bounds to crash against the walls, clinging and scrabbling upwards. One, jumping later, landed right before Dal Arche, raising aloft a stick set with jagged flints. She was a grey-haired woman, someone's mother, someone's grandmother, but her face was twisted into something other than human, teeth bared and eyes great circles of white about tiny pupils. Dal shot her through the chest, releasing the string by sheer instinct, and she fell howling away. All around him the attacking maniacs were throwing themselves onto spears, hurtling in impossible dives through the air, snarling and smashing at anything within reach. One of the defenders had his arm broken, the stave coming down so hard that it splintered in two. Another attacker cleared the wall entire and landed within the compound. At Ygor's unspoken prompting, Scutts rushed forwards and lanced the intruder's leg with her sting, retreating hastily from the Grasshopper's thrashing stick. The attacker ran on, though, charging the nearest Dragonfly defenders, shrieking like no living thing Dal had ever heard. After a few wild blows the poison began to work and the wretched creature fell to its knees, but even then its screaming continued until someone put a spear through it.

It, thought Dal numbly. *It* had been a man, but after that display of insanity he found *it* easier to work with.

He sent a shaft into the ribs of another man as the starved-looking creature slammed into the palisade. Even as he did so the attack was over. Some wounded were still keening and kicking at the wall's base, the rest were dead. There were no runners, none whose nerve had broken.

Dal looked out at the greater host. To his surprise they were eddying away, beginning to swirl and flow across the plains, perhaps in search of easier game.

"Well that's that," he announced with false bravado.

"Can we have our head back, please?" Ygor added hopefully.

"Look again, southerners," came Lirien Aell's impalcable reply. "Look to the west."

With a sinking heart, Dal skipped over to the narrow top of the central tower. There was a second host, at least as large as the first. It darkened the land, hundreds of running bodies, surely the same breed of gibbering lunatics in the guise of Grasshopper-kinden. If they kept their pace they would strike the village before nightfall, whilst the existing madmen were not going far. Feeling disproportionately tired, Dal slid down to the ground.

"You." He singled out the ancient Grasshopper woman. "Who are they? What is this?"

"They will stop at nothing," the old woman replied in a sing-song voice. "They will consume everything in their path and destroy what they cannot consume. They will eat raw flesh. Now they are weak and divided, but tonight and for some nights to come there will be the grand moon. They will find new Art within themselves. They will become strong. They will become swift. Their skin will be tough like armour. Worst of all, their minds will grow together, each sharing the thoughts of all the others, but as each one has the Locust Madness, then madness is all that they can share. They will know only the need to destroy all who are not like them, everything of beauty, every living thing save those who can run with the Madness."

"Even their own infants," Dal Arche finished for her sickly.

"Yes," she said simply, and in that one word there was a shadow casting back many years.

They could hear the weird howling and jabbering now, as the fresh horde neared them. There were plenty of the locals aloft and keeping watch, and none had warned of an attack yet. Dal glanced at the sky, seeing that they had perhaps a few hours before dusk.

"What are our options?" he asked of his fellows in a low voice.

"Run for it and risk it?" Mordrec suggested, not sounding overly convinced.

"Fight," put forth Ygor. The old woman's words had him rattled.

"Soul?" Dal prompted.

Their Grasshopper-kinden was crouched on his haunches, one hand tracing symbols in the dust. "I can feel it, Dala," he said softly.

"Just whispers, like dead leaves brushing against the inside of my head. The Locust mind is forming."

"Are you... going to be all right?" asked Dal gently, because he did not have it in him to ask, *Are you going to turn into a madman and force us to kill you?*

"Well I suppose I'll have to be," the Grasshopper replied, with an empty and despairing smile.

Dal Arche clapped him on the shoulder, not knowing what more to say. He nodded at Mordrec. "I didn't hear that thing going off in the fight."

Mordrec cradled his nailbow protectively. "Jammed, didn't it. I'll have it ready for tonight. Ask the locals for more arrows, Dal. It won't help me or Ygor, but there are thousands of the bastards out there."

There was another shout of warning just then but, when Dal's wings had taken him up he saw that there were only three attackers, a doomed trio hurling themselves at the walls. The situation did not seem to merit his intervention. Instead, he went in search of Lirien Aell.

"You," he told her, "are madder than they are."

She had been going through a stack of short, rough-made arrows, checking the chitin-shard fletchings of each one. Now she looked up, wordless.

"*This* is the salvation of your people? Two imperial deserters, a Scorpion animal-trainer and me?"

"And what are you, Arche?" was her solemn question.

"I'm someone who'd be briganding right now if Corde's head didn't have such a fine price on it," he told her roughly. "And however fine that price is, I don't appreciate your efforts to make it more than it's worth."

"If I'd found Mercers, I'd have found a way to bring them. If some noble lord had been breaking his fast in Fiol I'd have gulled him into coming here somehow. Soldiers, Weaponsmasters, heroes, I'd have reeled each of them in one way or another. But I found you, you and your fellows. Should I regret it so much?" The look she gave him was abruptly twinkling with mockery, despite everything.

"Don't give me that," but he said it gently. After all, the situation was bad enough and there was no way out of the trap. No need to put knives at his own back.

The moon was up even as the sun set. Dal couldn't have said

whether it was a *grand* moon but it was certainly a big old full one. He knew that seers and mystics endowed the moon with all manner of significance that the layman could not understand. He had even heard of a man cursed by a Moth-kinden Skryre, who had to be locked in the cellar each time the moon was full to keep his family safe from him. *Perhaps that was just a touch of the Locust Madness,* he wondered, because the moon was certainly doing its work on the seething host beyond the walls. They were calling and dancing, swirling in weird, chaotic patterns, leaping and springing high into the air, working themselves into a frenzy. Within the greater mob, currents and whirlpools of movement surged; never one acting alone but entire groups suddenly going through the same meaningless flurry of motion. The effect was one of superficial chaos guided by an invisible order.

"So." Mordrec was abruptly beside him at the wall's top, landing heavily in a flurry of wings and then wavering for a moment before he caught his balance. "You slept with her."

Dal started. "What? Just *now?* With all this going on?"

"Back in Fiol. You know what I mean. And you told her about Corde's cursed head, and she nicked it and lammed off while you were snoring."

After a pause Dal Arche shrugged. "Maybe."

"Remind me again why we do what you say?" Mordrec pressed.

The Dragonfly-kinden turned and looked at him, eyebrows raised. "I don't know, Mord. I've never known. Maybe you should tell me."

The yammering and yelling from the mob outside was getting louder, and the two hunters watched the great host surge and swirl and gather itself.

"They're coming in!" Dal shouted, a moment before some of the village's own lookouts gave the same warning. A moment later everyone was scrambling to find a vantage point, to shoot from or to set a spear against the charge.

If the attackers had truly possessed the linked minds of Ant-kinden it would have been over very quickly indeed. Whatever communal spirit had burrowed into the the fanatic Grasshopper-kinden, though, it had neither any grasp of tactics nor even an ability to respond to the defence. The crazed madmen swarmed forth as though a single order had been called, several hundred of them on the attack at the same instant without a moment's hesitation, but there was no plan to it. They simply hurled themselves at the walls in blind, raging fury, tearing at wood and flesh with equal fervour, heedless of any danger. The rest of the mob swirled and danced but seemed not to know that an attack was even underway.

Still, the old woman had been right: the quiet calm of the steppe-folk had been burned away by some new fire. They were swift and savage, limbs bursting with Art-fuelled strength that leaked out in a berserk frenzy. Dal Arche had learned in the war just how little swift and savage was worth without an organising mind behind it, though. The attacking horde made no attempt to hide from arrow-shot, leapt onto spears, pounded at the walls or the huts inside when armed enemies were all about them. They died screaming but their screams were not of pain or fear. Even their faces seemed to have changed, their eyes bulbous and wide, their lips peeled back from huge, square teeth.

They got over the wall several times, for all the defenders could do to stop them. Not only were their leaps greater and greater, until several cleared the wall cleanly in one bound, but, as they neared, almost one in three was suddenly airborne, clumsy and reeling on unaccustomed Art wings. Dal knew that a very few Grasshopper-kinden could fly, though he had never met one who could. Suddenly the gift had been sprinkled liberally over the mass of their enemies and, within moments, the sky was full of them, blundering into one another, wheeling wildly, crashing down on the wall or the ground, clinging dazedly to the central wooden tower until they had almost covered it. They seemed to have almost no control of their flight but spun and gyred in random arcs above, or dropped spontaneously from the sky. At least a score must have killed themselves coming down, falling from a height or impaled on the spiked posts of the palisade. For the rest, and for those hopping and crawling up the wall, it was a bloody business to keep them off. If those who got within the compound had turned their attention to the defenders then all would have been lost, but instead they ran mad, slashing at the goatskin sides of the huts or rushing for the animals. There was a fire lit before the squat tower's gate, and several of the intruders blundered into it, seeming not to realise they were burning. Nothing had halted the attack, not the death toll, not even the explosive roar of Mordrec's firepowder-charged nailbow as it ripped into their close-packed ranks. Only when the very last attacker was dead was there quiet. Not one of the others out on the plain had lifted a finger to aid their comrades. The killing frenzy had yet to touch them and, until it did, they milled and danced and howled but did not attack.

Seven of the defenders were killed, plus an old man and two children found by one of the rampaging Grasshoppers. Dal had no intention of counting the bodies of the enemy fallen. He could barely bring himself to dub them 'enemy'. He knew Grasshopper-kinden: they were a humble, introspective people by nature, fond of music and philosophy. They had made poor and reluctant soldiers when the Wasps had invaded the Commonweal but nonetheless they had carried spears for their overlords alongside Dragonfly-kinden yeomen such as Dal Arche had been, and they had died just as readily. Some hideous spirit of chaos and death had come to possess the wretched creatures outside. They had been robbed of their minds and their peace and driven to kill themselves on the spears of their neighbours.

"They will come again, later this night. More of them," Lirien Aell told him. She handed him a fistful of arrows, most still dark with blood. The nimblest of the villagers were over the wall even now, within plain sight of the enemy swarm, retrieving as many shafts as they could.

"How long is this going on for? Tomorrow? Tomorrow night? Longer?"

She shrugged. "How long's a grand moon, Arche?"

He frowned. "Did that old Grasshopper witch survive all that? She'll know."

The old woman was still with them, just. She was shivering and shuddering, hugging her knees to her chin.

"How long will this grand moon last?" Dal demanded.

"The moon..." the old woman wheezed, "the moon is just a moon, just a full moon. The madness starts with the moon, the moon does not end the madness."

Dal felt his stomach sink. "Then... how do we stop this? There are thousands of them out there. We can't stop them forever, even for very long. There have to just... burn themselves out eventually, go back to normal, please?" He had not intended that pleading tone, but he had suddenly seen his future as nothing but acts of killing and dying interlocked so closely that there was no space between them.

"You do not understand. Listen, listen. There are many kinden on the steppes," the old woman told them, forcing the words out. "Cicada, Dragonfly, Roach-kinden, but most of all there are my people. We have many tribes. We roam the steppe in our thousands, in our tens of thousands, increasing and increasing, many and many, until there are *too* many. Then the full moon will be a grand moon. Then the Locust Madness comes, and we run mad and destroy all we have, and we *kill* and *kill*," her withered hands made jabbing motions at each other, "and we die and die. We dash ourselves against stones. We drive ourselves onto our neighbours' blades. We fight and dance and run until we starve or drop from weariness. Until at the last there are no longer too many of us, and the Locust time is passed, until it comes again. Perhaps tomorrow, perhaps the night after, perhaps in a tenday, who can say?"

"Not in a tenday," said Dal. "We won't last a tenday."

"They say that a thousand years ago there was a warlord who could somehow control the madness, and who led a thousand thousand warriors south to the Commonweal," Lirien murmured.

"Oh yes? And how did that end?"

"The Monarch stood before them and dispersed them with the light of purity," she recalled, "or that's how the story goes."

"Oh, right. Well if we see anyone in an enormous glowing crown we'll know we're saved, then."

The midnight assault was worse. There seemed to be no end to the howling throng, until the spikes that lined the walls were clogged with bodies or simply snapped away by the unrelenting weight, until the defenders' spears were wrenched from their hands by the flesh of their enemies. At one point it seemed that the swarming Grasshopper-kinden would overwhelm a section of the wall entirely and simply bury the defenders alive with the weight of their numbers. Then Mordrec opened up with the nailbow, emptying his magazines ten bolts at a time, ripping the tide apart even as it rose above the wall. The moment was saved, and Mordrec resorted to sword and sting, having used every bolt he owned.

Another eighteen of the villagers did not survive, a further handful were wounded beyond being able to hold the walls. That the number of wounded was so low was mostly to do with the savagery of the enemy: any who fell into their hands were torn apart, disjointed and partitioned and then the pieces set upon in a cannibalistic frenzy. The ravening feeders were easy prey, not even stopping to defend themselves from swords and knives.

The attack seemed to go on forever, until all sense of reality had fled and the grand moon shone ogrishly down onto a nightmare, the palisaded village surrounded by a twitching carpet of the dead and drying whilst the insane host leapt and flew and crawled on every side.

And then there were no more, and the dawn light revealed an expectant host still milling on the plain, seeming not in the least diminished, as though all those bodies had simply risen from the earth like a fungus.

Dal Arche's chitin tab, that saved his fingers from the bite of the bowstring, was worn through and ready to crack, so he was improvising another out of a scrap of goatskin. He had snapped two strings in the fight and loosed every arrow he had got his hands on, and here came Aell with another fistful. She had been beside him for much of the fight, a keen shot herself, and now she looked grey and worn down, stumbling with fatigue.

"Get some sleep," he advised her.

"You get some sleep," she rejoined.

"When I've done this, I will. How many can fit into the tower?"

The village's central tower had so far hosted only the old, the children, the badly wounded, and even they had made use of the arrowslits, or simply stabbed at the invaders when they had come to rest against the tower's raked sides. Dal doubted that the whole village would have been able to get inside it before the grand moon came, but as of now the 'whole village' had a notably smaller headcount.

"Will it come to that?" she asked, seeing immediately where he was going with the thought.

"If this kicks off again today or tonight then yes, it will. I don't know how we held this place last night. I'm not sure we really did, it's just that we managed to kill every one of them who got over the walls."

"There isn't room in the tower for us all," she told him.

He looked at her bleakly. "There will be. Or there will come a point where those that *can* get inside will have to, and those that *can't...*"

"I don't accept that," she stated flatly.

"Well, girl, you are very plainly too used to getting your own way," he told her. "You dragged us here from Fiol, and it's good odds you've got us all killed, but if they keep coming like they have been doing then nothing's going to save your pisspot of a village." He said the words without acrimony or any intent to hurt. He was too tired to be anything other than philosophical about his impending demise.

"You, they will kill. Your Scorpion and the Wasp, if even the imperial army cannot triumph here. Your other friend I'm not so sure about."

"What are you talking about?"

"His quiver's full. He's not shot a shaft all night."

Dal didn't like the sound of that at all but he kept his face neutral. "You go sleep, girl," he growled at her, but when she had gone he sought out Soul Je.

The Grasshopper-kinden was crouched atop the tower, staring out at his maddened kin. Dal let his wings carry him up until he could alight beside the man.

"Still with us, then," he observed, aware that the words could be read in two very different ways.

Soul looked up at him, his long face taut with strain. "Don't press me, Dala," he said, his voice little more than a rasp.

"Is it because they're your people, that you won't fight?" As a man who wouldn't hesitate to shoot down another Dragonfly, the concept was a novel one to Dal.

"They're not my people," Soul said, and his voice was still low and controlled, so pointedly devoid of emotion that it unnerved Dal more than shouting. "They were. Perhaps they will be. I haven't fought because I don't want to *become* one of their people. I can hear them, Dala. They're singing in my head. There's a chorus of maniacs ten thousand strong who want me to be one of them. It would be easy. All I'd have to do is let go. If I'd have been born here, lived here, I'd be one of them already. I'm clinging to all I've seen of the world, to stave them off."

"You hold on tight then," Dal told him, trying to keep his voice comforting though his skin crawled with the other man's words.

"No guilt, Dala," Soul said. "No blame. No cares. Can princes and empires promise so much?"

"Soul..."

"I'm fighting it. I'm fighting to master it. I'm not one of them. I'm not a steppeman. I'm not Locust-kinden. I'm a Grasshopper from Sa. But there are so many voices... The old woman died."

"She did?"

"The madness took her at last, and she died. She was too old for it. Her heart, perhaps." Soul shrugged. "Sleep, Dala. You look like you need it."

"And you?"

"I'm not tired. Not even slightly."

Outside beyond the wall the host continued their ceaseless dancing and chanting.

Nightfall found everyone tensely waiting for the attack, the air cleared by the imminence of the next wave of Locusts. Dal Arche had already locked horns with some of the villagers earlier when he had told them to release their livestock. Aell had supported him and the entire village had nearly come to blows. In the end it had not been about whether the livestock would be taken by hunting spiders or centipedes, nor about whether the howling host outside would kill the beasts, but about the implication: *we cannot hold the outer wall.* It was a fact that stared them all in the face but many of them would not see it, for all that it was pointed out to them again and again. In the end the village's goats and beetles were shooed out of the main gate to take their chances, as were the hunters' horses. That way some of them might escape and be recoverable later. Trapped in their pens they would be slaughtered when the attackers finally came over the wall in force.

And when that happened... everyone knew what they would have to do, and that there would be many who would not make it into the tower.

Now they waited, whilst the horde beyond the wall danced its spiral dances and lifted its voice in wordless song. Dal had given the enemy as close an inspection as he dared and seen that there were plenty who had fallen from thirst or exhaustion, and been trampled beneath the pounding feet of the others. *But how many? How many is too many?*

Mordrec had spent the day laboriously casting new nailbow bolts from whatever metal was to hand, enough to burn through all the firepowder he had left. Ygor had been cutting at arrow-flights so they would fit his crossbow.

Soul had sat atop the tower and stared at his kin, his mad and savage kin.

There had been an unlooked-for respite. Cloud had eaten the moon and the crowd gathered all about had become quieter, and for two dark hours it had seemed as though a bloodless dawn was a realistic proposition. Then the moon had fought its way clear and from every side a weird high shriek had arisen, and then the host was upon them.

Dal Arche was unsure how many of them there were. It may have been all of them. The front-runners died almost instantly, men, women, children and all, the first few flights of arrows unable to miss the close-packed tide. Then the sky was full of them, leaping and flying, and each defender tracked an individual targets across the face of the moon.

Dal could see almost immediately that the defence would not hold this time. The defenders' losses, their fatigue and their dwindling hope had taken too much of a toll. A score of the attackers were within the wall almost immediately and every fighter who abandoned the walls to bring them down left a door open for more. The villagers began dying – falling, it seemed, not to the weapons of the foe so much as to their sheer fury.

Aell had been given a snail-shell horn and a place atop the tower. She was to blow it when a retreat to the tower was inevitable, or when attrition made it possible, whichever happened first. When the call came, shockingly soon into the attack, Dal Arche had no idea which it was.

The plan had been that certain picked villagers would throw open the doors and hold them whilst everyone else did their best to funnel in. Most of those so chosen were either unable to reach the gates or already slain and the doors were pushed open from within. The oldest of the village children stood shoulder to shoulder with their grandfathers and great-grandmothers, armed with spears and sticks and knives, to hold the way for their families.

Dal swore and kicked off from the wall-top. Immediately he was amidst the floundering, confused mass of the enemy fliers, and he left a bloody trail through them with his knife, cutting several out of the sky as they were swung about by their own unfamiliar wings. Then he reached the tower door, finding Ygor already there with Scutts at his feet. The Scorpion-kinden had his lance held in both clawed fists and was wielding it like a battleaxe, slashing with its broad-bladed head. The villagers were fighting their way inside in twos and threes, but as each abandoned the defence, the press of enemy on the remainder grew greater, and then unstoppable, and in an instant the wall was blotted by swarming bodies and the enemy were at the tower.

Mordrec appeared, dropping from the sky at Dal Arche's feet with a bloody scalp, but still fumbling to bring his nailbow up. Dal himself was searching for Aell, who had been atop the tower. Ygor was shouting something, but all words were being swallowed and chewed beyond recognition by the yammering of the horde.

There was Aell, in a moment's glimpse between bodies, falling from the sky, her wings dancing her out of the way of a swung staff, only ten feet away from the tower door, but there were so many attackers in her way...

Dal made no definite decision but he was gone from Ygor's side, wings throwing him in a somersault through the cluttered air. Halfway down he rammed one of the Grasshoppers bodily, falling to the ground in a tangle of limbs with all the breath knocked from him. Still he had the presence of mind to jam his knife home into his enemy. A moment later something heavy was brought down hard onto his leg and he yelled in pain. His wings flared, clawing for the sky, but a hand dragged at his ankle. He killed the woman who was clutching at him, then lost his knife in another. In a second he was on his feet, surrounded, then his battered leg gave way.

Lirien Aell stooped on him, lashing about herself with a short-bladed sword. She was shouting for him to get up – he could see her lips moving but barely hear a word. In a moment she had an arm about him and was half-dragging, half-throwing him at the tower. It was no good: they were surrounded. They were only still alive because most of the frenzied attackers about them had not realised that there were victims within arm's reach.

Dal was never sure whether he caught a glimpse of the tower gateway then, or whether the shout somehow cut through the chaos to reach his ears. He did not so much hear the cry as reconstruct it in his imagination, but he was collapsing down, dragging Aell down with him. The shout was "drop-*drop!*" and it was a cry the hunters used amongst themselves, and Mordrec most of all.

The nailbow hammered, the bolts zipping through the crowd, meant to puncture armour and barely slowing as they lashed through flesh. It was as though an invisible scythe cleared the way to the gate as Mordrec emptied one magazine of ten, and then got five shots into the next before one of his home-cast bolts jammed in the breach. With a supreme effort Dal flew for the gate. If Aell had not been on her feet then he could not have dragged her but, as it was, she outstripped him there.

They closed the gates practically on Dal Arche's heels. They were the last, and only Mordrec and Ygor's intervention had kept the tower open that long.

Dal looked from face to face until he found the absence.

"Where's Soul?" he demanded.

"Still up top last anyone saw," Ygor reported grimly. "He didn't come down when the horn went."

Dal found an arrowslit and stared out at the frenzied host that was busy destroying everything that they could find. There was a thunderous drumming all around them as the swarming Locust-kinden clawed and kicked at the tower itself, smacked down against it with blundering wings, clung to it and to each other, in mindless bewilderment, then launched away for more pointless circling in the cluttered sky.

"Count up arrows," he shouted over the roar.

They had twenty-seven shafts left between them all. Mordrec had a few shots left but his nailbow was being uncooperative about the jammed bolt and there was no space for him to dismantle it.

"What about you?" Dal asked Ygor.

"Precisely one bolt left," the Scorpion told him, "but it's my lucky one."

Dal took a glance through the arrowslit. "How lucky?" he asked.

Barad Ygor crouched to let Scutts clamber up him, letting his pet take her accustomed place coiled about him, with her claws clasped above his collarbones. They were nearly shoulder-to-shoulder within the tower, the old, the children and the surviving defenders all crammed in together, and getting a large venomous animal out from underfoot could only help.

"We can kill a few more of them," Dal mused. "More will die of other causes, the longer this goes on. We have some food in here." Nobody could hear him over the noise. *How many do we have to kill? How many are dying elsewhere? When will the Locust Madness release its hold?*

Aell was beside him and he put an arm about her, letting her lean into him. His eyes never left the narrow slice of chaos that was his window on the world.

She must have felt him twitch, as though he had been shot.

He saw Soul Je.

The Grasshopper-kinden was standing in the midst of the frenzy, the one still point. Dal had heard stories of the damned: that people who died badly and in bad places could be cursed to stay there in spirit, tormented and tormenting and unable to escape. Soul Je could have modelled for such lost spirits. There was a look in his face that Dal had seen once or twice in the war, on the faces of men who had, by their great courage and conviction, led thousands of their own people to futile deaths.

Soul's hollow eyes sought out the tower. He could not have spotted Dal Arche within the darkness behind the arrowslit but there was a shock of contact even so. For a moment the flurrying savagery of the attackers came between them, and when Dal could see his friend again, Soul had his bow up, arrow nocked and the string drawn back. Another interruption: Dal did not see the arrow fly, instead there was a second shaft to the string. The clambering whirling mass of the Locusts crossed back and forth, giving only brief still images of Soul Je: draw, nock, nock, loose, draw, until his quiver was empty. Then Soul had taken up a spear and, blank-faced, got to work. He passed through the whooping hordes and was not marked by them. They took him in as one of their own, danced with him, whirled about him. He stalked and stabbed and they took no steps to fend him off as he left a trail of the dying in his wake. Without emotion, falling into a dreadful rhythm, Soul Je set about killing his kinsfolk.

When his spear broke he found another one, and then another after that. He was a man possessed, as all of the Grasshoppers were out there, but he sat in the saddle of the thing that possessed him. He bound it with iron and held to it. Not a moment's anger crossed his face: not rage, not fear, nor pity nor joy. The emotions that would have cracked his mind open to the Locust were banished to the furthest reaches of his mind. He was calm, killing calm. After a while Dal could no longer watch.

The siege of the Locusts lasted almost until dawn. They kept flocking to the village, over and over. Grey-faced and haggard, Soul Je was waiting for them with his spear. When at last the chanting and whooping grew faint, when the first light touched the eastern sky, it took eight men to force the doors open against the weight of bodies.

Out beyond the walls the host was already half-gone, the remainder dispersing. Huddled groups of Grasshopper-kinden were departing, seeking across the vast steppe for some sign of the places they had known. They had slain their neighbours, they had uprooted and destroyed their own lives, they had slain their own children. A generation of the steppe-kinden had been purged in blood and would live under the shadow of horror and guilt, victims of their own atrocities, resuming their nomadic lives and running from the memory of the Locust Madness. Those that remained did so for one reason only: to search over the faces of the slain.

And in a hundred years, or two hundred, when their numbers had recovered, it would happen again.

Not one of the villagers suggested retaliation or revenge: as well call for revenge against a storm, against starvation or a harsh winter. Only victims were left, on all sides.

Soul did not want to talk about it. Soul would never talk about it. He took what happened to him and locked it away behind his taciturn manner and, for their part, none of his companions felt particularly keen to press him on the subject.

The survivors of the village were gathering what little had been spared: foodstocks, possessions, anything portable. Others were flying out and seeking to reclaim any surviving livestock. Nobody had openly made the decision but they all knew that the village was finished. There was too much destroyed, too little food left. The sheer weight of the dead would defy disposal, and the numbers inside were dwarfed by the corpses beyond the walls, all of those who had fallen simply to fatigue and thirst. The villagers would seek a life to the south, hoping to find some land to farm or a community to take them in.

Later, Dal would hear that the steppe had suffered a year of pestilence and then, the year after, the barren, dry land was ablaze with verdant life, a once-in-a-century explosion of green, flowers and plants never seen in living memory, rooted in the decay of dead flesh, watered in blood. For years to come the grazing land would be lush and rich, and people would begin to migrate north to take advantage of it. When he was told that he would stop listening and walk away.

For now, Mordrec and Ygor prodded him into pulling Aell from the salvage work.

"You have something that belongs to us," Dal reminded her.

She stared blankly at the three of them for a moment until incredulous understanding dawned. "The *head?*"

"*Someone* might as well clear some profit from this bloody business," Mordrec grumbled. "Come on girl, give it up."

After a moment's further staring she shrugged and located a broken piece of wood that would serve as a shovel. While her people scavenged through the wreckage of their lives she took the hunters outside the sagging walls, spent a moment getting her bearings, and began to dig.

She had not buried Corde very deeply and, under other circumstances, Dal reckoned they could have found the wretched trophy themselves in time, had there not been an army of marauding madmen on the loose.

"Here," Aell declared, and hoisted the sack from the shallow hole, trailing ribbons of sandy earth.

Trailing more than earth. They stared, seeing the scissored hole in the oilcloth, hearing the patter of hard bodies. Beetles spilled from the gap, the furry-bodied black kind they called escarrabins: burying beetles.

"No way!" Ygor objected and snatched the sack from Aell. Furiously he emptied out its contents, scattering beetles in all directions. Even in that moment Dal found himself thinking how much happy work those same beetles had ahead of them, how they would prosper from the misery and madness of others.

Corde's face, that was worth so much, was mostly gone now. The escarrabins had done their diligent work in the name of preserving their own next generation.

"It's impossible," Mordrec spat, aghast. "Salt meat? Beetles that eat *salt* meat? Who ever heard of that?"

Aell backed off as the three of them contemplated a suddenly impoverished future, standing like mourners about a miniature open grave. Their fourth, Soul Je, watched them from just outside the village wall, bow slung and desperate to be gone from this cursed place.

"Salt," Mordrec complained again, and Dal knew that it was not the loss of the bounty he was trying to rationalise, but all that they had been through in the last few days. "Beetles that eat *salt.*"

At the very last, Ygor gave a huge sigh, watching the busy insects scurry in all directions, some even venturing into the shadow of Scutts' claws.

"Well, I don't suppose I can blame them," the Scorpion declared, reaching down to touch his pet's arched stinger affectionately. "It *was* cursed expensive salt, after all."

So this is the sort of thing Dal Arche and company got up to between the events of 'An Old Man in a Harsh Season' (in *Spoils of War*) and the open banditry they have descended into by *Heirs of the Blade*. This is also a story that fulfills one of my own aims in writing these short pieces, in that it expands the world beyond the known maps. What's north of the Commonweal? Now we know.

There is a cost to being one of the kinden – the bond with the invertebrate world that confers Art and, in the older days, protection from the emergent giant insects, sometimes results in too much of the insect bleeding through. In some kinden that means disfigurement: the spines of a Thorn Bug, the teeth and claws of a Scorpion. In others, such as the placid Grasshopper-kinden, it can mean something else. Just as their totem swarms in response to the pressure of population, switching from solitary to gregarious and proverbially destructive, so the same transformation can come to them. If Mosquito-kinden are the kinden's vampires, so the Locusts are their werewolf myth, slaves to the violent madness of the moon.

The Naturalist

The smell was a thin acid reek even from the top of the stairs: the biting, chemical scent of the preservatives. Kaelia paused to steel herself, knowing that it would be far worse below in Dinsawl's workroom. For perhaps a minute and a half she would be all but unable to breathe, until the smell had bludgeoned her nose into insensibility. The only consolation was that the place would smell a good deal worse *without* the preservative: better the chemicals than the overwhelming perfume of massed decay.

She still found it hard to believe that the man would voluntarily subject himself to this nasal assault on a daily basis, but then it was a Spider-kinden article of faith that their senses were keener and more refined than most other kinden. Perhaps to Dinsawl it was all just a minor unpleasantness. Certainly the city of Collegium had always seemed unnecessarily pungent in the long, hot summers, especially on days like this when barely a breeze came in off the sea to relieve the stagnant air.

Mustering all the fortitude she possessed, she began her journey into the darkness. That was how she thought about it, anyway. In truth the cellars of the Great College were cheerily lit with some manner of artificial fire that the Beetles had devised, tame little sunbeams locked behind glass. Most of the College's cellars were appendices to the library or the museum wings, crammed with stacks of books and documents in various stages of cataloging, or cluttered with potsherds, old armour and the varnished shells of long-dead animals. This particular warren, however, was reserved for areas of study like Dinsawl's, which profited from being kept cool.

In fact, on blistering days such as this, she was surprised that more of the locals weren't down in the cold rooms, but then again perhaps their noses weren't as unfeeling as all that and the stench below had proved the worse evil than the heat above.

Certain artificers kept cold rooms for their studies, arcane matters of mechanics that required constant cooling. However, most of the rooms here were set aside for dissections. More than once Kaelia had come down to visit Dinsawl and, glancing through an open door, seen a Beetle-kinden lecturer guiding his class through the mysteries of the human digestive system, enough to put anyone off their lunch. These days she had taught herself not to be so curious.

The welcome chill seeped out of the cold rooms into the corridor. Combined with the slightly unreal effect of the unwavering artificial light it always reminded Kaelia of the old stories: the kingdom beneath the earth where all manner of ancient evils had been sealed by the great magics, and how some bold woman would inevitably be put to find a way in and rescue her beloved. The thought made her smile. *I'm a bit past that, I fear.*

She had asked Dinsawl once how they made it cold down here. He had given her some rambling explanation of pipes within the walls, and pumps, and some way that the clever Beetles had devised of turning water into ice. She had understood not one word of it, but her word-perfect transcript had winged its way back home to someone with enough of a purse to hire up some Beetle engineers, and now the summer palaces of a half-dozen Aristoi houses enjoyed a reprieve from the season's excesses without even having to endure Dinsawl's smell.

She had with her two goblets, together with a bottle of wine from the far, far Deluciel vineyards, which she knew travelled very comfortably indeed and which Dinsawl was extremely partial to. As she neared the man's room, letting the stinking air wash past her until her nose grew numb to it, she rang the brass rim of a goblet from the stone-clad wall to let her host know she was approaching. A moment later a tousled head poked itself out from his doorway, not Dinsawl's but that of his assistant, a young Beetle-kinden woman called Limer Steadry.

Steadry retreated inside to report their visitor's identity, and Kaelia swaggered in, bracing herself for the sight of Dinsawl's workroom which always seemed to her as though someone had let off some Beetle-kinden explosive in a taxidermist's.

The study of the natural world was by no means a great preoccupation of the Beetle-kinden, coming far behind history, artifice and social philosophy. The Beetles, or at least those of Collegium itself, preferred to live their lives without any particularly close contact with the animal world, save those parts of it that might contribute, on a day-to-day basis, to their diet. However, it was unavoidable that, given the number of enquiring minds the College hosted, some number of them would turn to matters of natural history and, being Collegiate Beetles, that they would divide themselves into opposing schools of thought.

By far the more fashionable kind of naturalist was the Observationalist, as Kaelia understood the terminology. Observationalists held that the true study of animals was that of their behaviour. There were various sub-divisions of Observationalist, she had been told. The most fervent applied themselves in the field, travelling great distances to sketch and study the objects of their admiration. Those lacking either the funds or the courage for such sport would arrange for isolated creatures to be brought to them, to be prodded, poked, tested and occasionally released onto Collegium's streets by pranking students. Still more Observationalists paid pittance amounts for the unreliable accounts of travellers, and based their academic studies upon those. Dinsawl had noted with waspish humour that, as the latter two wastrel breeds spent far more time at the College than the former diligent one, and therefore had more influence, the entire Observationalist credo was based on error and hearsay and it was no wonder that the science of natural history was in its current parlous state.

Dinsawl was an Anatomist, a little-regarded subset of naturalist. His claim was that true knowledge of the animal world could only be had by cutting it into as many small pieces as possible, or so Kaelia had surmised. Recent rumours, admittedly, had stung her into a keener appreciation of what he had meant.

"My dear Master Dinsawl," she declared, setting down her wine and goblets. She had known Dinsawl for more than a year now but the contents of his workroom still gave her a shudder of discomfort. The cold walls were lined with sturdy shelves, and the shelves themselves bore a regiment of clear jars, some as small as her thumb, others bigger than her head. Beneath the lowest shelves were reinforced tanks, their thick glass warped and cloudy enough to obscure their contents. Each held a specimen and some held several. There were so many dead creatures arrayed in their ranks about the room that Kaelia sometimes had trouble believing that any live ones were left beyond it.

In a single glance she took in mantids, scorpions, a dozen different kinds of beetles, a lacewing, five small ants arranged in size from an inch to a foot long, a harvestman with its dot of a body caged by the delicate lace of its half-folded legs, earwigs and millipedes and the sad, drowned bodies of butterflies. They hung suspended in their preservative solution, buoyed up enough by the thick liquid that a single leg-tip at the jar's base would suffice to support the entire cadaver's weight. If someone walked too close to a wall, the slight vibrations of their footsteps would cause each captive to stir minutely, their compound eyes seeming to search the room for their tormentor. Despite this, for Kaelia the most upsetting quality to this necrotic menagerie was the way the preservative itself had leached the colour from each captive, bleaching them a uniform pallid white like fishbellies. It was as though Dinsawl had somehow discovered a lightless reach of the deep dark, one that housed an entire mirror bestiary echoing all the forms of the daylit world but that had never seen the sun.

But she had visited here plenty of times and, although her imagination occasionally twitched, she could recline amongst these pickled prisoners with equanimity.

Master Archer Dinsawl – Collegium's pre-eminent Anatomist natural historian, for whatever that was worth -- turned from his workbench and beamed at her. His parents had been somewhat optimistic with his warlike monicker. Kaelia had never seen a man less likely to take up the bow. Dinsawl was a broad-bodied man who gave the impression that, just as he spent his days in the disassembling of animals, some greater scholar had somehow assembled him from parts intended for very different men. He had the heavy, stocky torso of a wrestler, out of proportion to all the rest of him. A scrawny neck thrust his head awkwardly forwards from between his shoulders and his arms and legs were surprisingly thin. Countless days of bending close to his specimens, making delicate incisions and dissections, had given him a hunched pose, his knees always slightly bent, his arms held with the elbows crooked out and his large, long-fingered hands close to his chest. His face was pleasantly regular, mahogany dark and bespectacled. He was somewhere in his late middle years, but these Beetle-kinden always looked older than they really were, to Spider eyes.

Not for the first time she failed to suppress the image of Dinsawl, after his eventual demise, being interred floating in an enormous bell jar, preserved for all eternity until one of his successors should come to dissect him.

To his eyes she would look younger than her true age, although she had her ritual of morning cosmetics to thank for that. Still, by the best outward appearance the two of them were a close enough match, two scholars who had applied themselves sufficiently to their disciplines that the prime of their lives had passed by unnoticed.

"My dear Mistress Kaelia, once again you grace us with your company. We are very lucky, Steadry, aren't we?" Dinsawl exclaimed.

His assistant made some muted affirmation. That Kaelia had brought only two goblets yet again was no doubt a bitter pill.

Dinsawl was already washing his hands, his half-attacked specimen abandoned on the work-bench. Kaelia saw that it was a whip-scorpion, its pinned-out legs spanning almost two feet across. For a moment her imagination rebelled, conjuring the image of a pet her family had doted on, when she had been young. *This squeamishness is unfit for someone of your profession*, she reminded herself sternly.

"Now, to what do we owe the considerable pleasure? What brings a distinguished lecturer in fine arts to my humble workshop?" Dinsawl enquired. He stripped off his stained tan smock to reveal paler woollen robes, the sleeves rolled up at the elbow. Spending so much time down here, he was one of the few people in Collegium who kept a cold-weather wardrobe. He was also one of the few Beetles who had mastered unfailing and effortless good manners, which made up somewhat for the preservative's pervading odour.

"You have been down here for a good tenday without coming up for air, Master Dinsawl," Kaelia chided him. "Some of your colleagues thought that you might have died." *And pickled yourself*, came the immediate thought, and she clamped down upon it.

"Alive, alive and well, Mistress Kaelia." He had a remarkably warm smile and she returned it easily. "However, you dissemble. I'll wager my colleagues have a little more than that to say about me?" His bantering tone could not keep the hope out entirely. A little-marked man toiling in a little-regarded field, he was desperate for recognition.

"Perhaps I've heard something. You have made some great discovery, down here amongst the dead?"

"The dead, yes," he confirmed happily. "You can watch a cricket chirp all day long, yes indeed, but you can't know *how* it chirps until you look within it."

"At which point it will never chirp again," she noted sadly. "However, there are always more crickets, I suppose."

"You are, as ever, correct. And correct, in equal magnitude, when you speak of a great discovery. I am at the point of organising my proofs and setting it down. A small matter, to the greater flow of humanity, but a punch in the eye, if I might use the somewhat violent image, for the Observationalists. Yes, we shall see a swell of followers for the Anatomist cause when I present my paper."

"Why, Master Dinsawl," she told him, "I have every respect for your devotion, but your opponents will still say that to know a thing best you must know how it moves, how it acts, its society and work. Surely knowing how to take one apart, they will say, is no great matter. Not that I agree, necessarily, but you know what they will say." She measured out a little wine into each goblet.

"Let them say it. I will rock the foundations of their science."

"You have learnt, perhaps, to put your subjects back together and restore them to life?" she needled gently, with a brief sad thought of the piecemeal whip-scorpion.

He chuckled at that. "To listen to our medical anatomists, they are within reach of doing the same for a human cadaver on any given day. No, I have humbler ambitions. A matter of classification is all." He picked up on her expression immediately and, even as he accepted the goblet from her, was waving his free hand in admonition.

"I know, I know, but it's *important*, my dear. Just as you and yours must needs group your art into schools and styles and whatnot, so it is that we naturalists, all of us, are united in our belief that there is an order to the natural world. There are similarities and differences to animals that divide and subdivide them into nations and tribes and families. There is a cartography of the animal world, my dear, and where to draw the borders is a matter of constant debate." He smiled, all pomp abruptly banished. "We have so little, Mistress Kaelia. Allow us our tiny battles."

"Well, well," she said, managing a laugh. "I suppose I shall permit them. So, you are about to marshal your troops and redraw some boundaries, are you?"

"Indeed I am, and in a manner that will make the Observationalists tear up their maps, and no mistake," he assured her. "You may not be aware, but for some time now there have been a few grander divisions that all naturalists have accepted." He had adopted a self-consciously bombastic tone now, playing the academic grandee. "Here we have the nation of true insects, and somewhat distant is the nation of spiders, here the undiscovered country of centipedes and millipedes and other things whose parts vex the Anatomist, initially in their proliferation and subsequently in their tedious uniformity. More distant still, offshore we might say, are the kingdoms of the marine insects, the lobsters and gribbles and what have you. A naturalist, I assure you, would take no issue with any of this, yes?"

"Ah... yes?" she echoed, making plain her uncertainty.

"Ah, *today*, yes! Tomorrow, no! I am changing the boundaries, as of this moment. Or as of whenever I finish my paper, anyway. The Observationalists are wrong. The Anatomists shall rub their noses in it. True science triumphs over myth yet again. I present to you the humble scorpion."

He indicated one of his jars in which a ghost-white example of the breed hung, claws-down, its tail coiled forever in useless threat.

"A dead scorpion?" she exclaimed. "Why Master Dinsawl, you spoil me." Within, her sense of unease stirred.

"I have dissassembled some two score of scorpions of all kinds, these last few months," he explained to her. "I have anatomised them, by word and by picture, every part of them."

"Surely deserving of some kind of award in itself," she jibed.

"Ah, but wait. Spiders, also, I have had spread on my table." The look he gave her was perfection, academic detachment almost but not entirely hiding a precisely calculated leer. "Silk-spiders, jumping spiders, hunting spiders, recluses, orb webs, widows, quite the variety. They have been reduced to their component segments. They have no secrets from me."

She refilled the goblets carefully. "And...?"

"It is a simple thing, my dear – for an Anatomist. A scholar could Observe all he wanted, and it would avail him nothing. I redraw the boundaries. Scorpions are spiders, or the other way around."

Kaelia blinked at him. "But Master Dinsawl, scorpions are land-lobsters, surely. They have ten limbs and pincers. Or else they are some other thing entirely. What else has a sting like a scorpion, after all?"

"No, no no," Dinsawl fussed, obviously delighted to be able to expound. "Superficial, my dear. An Observationalist argument."

"Master Dinsawl, how can it be superficial? Lobsters have claws, scorpions have claws, spiders... not so much." She managed a jovial look, imitating snapping pincers with her fingers.

"But they are not claws, my dear. Rather call them *teeth*. I can show you the most carefully annotated diagrams to support it. The claws of a lobster are arms and hands, but a scorpion is a more inventive fellow. He has made his mandibles into a new set of arms. A lobster has ten limbs, a scorpion only eight and a great deal of dental cutlery. However, his more regular teeth tell a clear story, to those who have the wit to read it. The fangs of a spider, you see, are the veritable siblings of the fangs of the scorpion, or of our poor friend the whip-scorpion whom you found me interrogating. An Anatomist values such similarities, for they show us where the true borders should be drawn."

"You are certain of this, are you?" Kaelia asked. "Surely your opponents will have a dozen arguments, all equally persuasive to the general herd of academia?"

"I think not," he said, with quiet satisfaction. "Raise the barricades as they may, my proofs shall batter them down. A new dawn, my dear, a new dawn."

She swilled the wine in her glass distractedly. "Master Dinsawl, have you considered that this news may prove... unpopular? I don't mean with the Observationalists, I think we can take that as a given. I mean to a wider audience."

"I wouldn't have thought a wider audience would much care, much as I'd have it otherwise," he said glumly. "No, I'll carve my tiny fiefdom in the halls of naturalism and let the rest of the College do what they will."

"I'm not even thinking of the College as such," she said, picking her way carefully. "Master Dinsawl, have you met many Scorpion-kinden?"

"Not in person, not this far west, but I'm appraised of them," he replied.

"You would characterise them as...?"

"Oh, barbarous louts, the lot of them," he agreed. "Thugs, raiders, slavers, exponents of brute force over all else, yes, I know."

She remained still, watching, waiting for him to meet her half way.

"Bah!" he exclaimed. "Really, my dear, I'm not talking about *kinden*.

Kinden have nothing to do with it. By *anatomical* rights our nation shares a border with the principality of goats and sheep!"

"Yes, I understand that, *but...*" Her level stare secured his full attention. "Most people do not see the world as an Anatomist does, Master Dinsawl. You are Beetle-kinden and you cannot divorce yourself from those beetles up on your shelves. The Mantis-kinden hold their beasts in high regard. We see these creatures as reflections of us. The Ant-kinden see their herds working strong and hard and with a single mind, and they see these qualities mirrored in themselves. The Fly-kinden see a bluebottle dart and dance in the air, and know it as one of their own. When some Collegium malcontent wishes to satirise his betters then I'll give you good odds he represents them in his pamphlets as the animal their kinden takes its name from. Our very Art is imitation of these species that you so easily pick apart. A spider is patient, elegant and ingenious, a weaver of beauty. A scorpion is a brutal hunter, savage in sting and claw. The Scorpion-kinden are the same and what does it matter who gave the bad name to which? It is enough that when you say the word 'scorpion,' that image will come to mind whether you speak of beast or man. A spider is not a scorpion, just as a Spider is not a Scorpion." Her emphasis made the different meanings clear.

He waved his hands irritably. "No, no, this is *science*. I am Beetle-kinden. I am not *a beetle*, to crawl on the ground or push a heavy load. That there is a link between my kinden and the insect is undeniable, for the Art is there to prove it, but that is a talent that we, as humans, have learned, which is why we are masters of the natural world and not the other way round. The fact remains that beetles are animals, and subject to science. The fact remains that scorpions and spiders are close neighbours within the same nation of animals. The truth is the truth, my dear. It's not *political*."

She took a deep breath, feeling the last sense of the chemical air rasp at the back of her throat. "No doubt you're right, Master Dinsawl, but I do hope that you know what you're doing."

Afterwards she was more affected than she had thought. Standing in that odious workroom, with a thousand glassy witnesses, she felt as unhappy as she had ever been since childhood.

She carefully retrieved the goblet from where Dinsawl had dropped it, tipping the bottle so it spilled half its contents over the floor.

There was a slight shifting from Limer Steadry, who was staring wide-eyed at her master's body. "What... what will happen now?"

"I would like to think that his colleagues will institute a respectable period of mourning," stated Kaelia sombrely. "However your kinden never did know how to mourn and he never had the recognition he deserved, and so more likely they'll just send him to the earth with as little accolade as they think they can get away with."

"No but... they'll know," Steadry said awkwardly. "A murder..."

"Murder? Nonsense," Kaelia snapped. "After all, hasn't he been convinced that he had some great discovery for tendays? And now it's come to nothing, he's a broken man. Small wonder that, when your back was turned, he mixed himself a special bottle of wine and ensured his own demise. Poor Archer Dinsawl. If there's any justice some of his colleagues may at least feel ashamed of the way that they snubbed him."

"You speak as if you liked him," Steadry accused her.

Kaelia met the young Beetle woman's gaze without flinching. "I liked him more than any other Beetle I ever met. He was good company. He had that worst of flaws, though, slightly less rare in your kinden than any other: he was too fond of truth. Nothing good ever comes of that."

Steadry visibly forced herself to stand over the body. "The poison. They'll ask where he got it."

"Hardly," Kaelia corrected her. "What else would the man use, in his most desperate hour, but his own beloved preservative? Remarkable, how something brewed to maintain dead flesh should be anathema to the living. I suggest you come in and discover the body by the next bell, having begun to wonder why he had not sought you out before."

Steadry's mouth was opening and closing, but she was sharp enough to catch the purse that Kaelia threw her.

"Don't draw attention to yourself in the spending of it," the Spider warned her.

"What... what happens to me now?" asked the Beetle woman faintly.

"You're a bright girl. You've proved as much by your diligence in keeping me appraised of Dinsawl's progress. I imagine that your career will advance shortly. You will find some patron or other within the

College suddenly takes an interest in you. At some point in time, perhaps tomorrow, perhaps next year, a colleague of mine will make herself known to you. You will start to report to them, and do what they say. If you decide that anyone else needs to know what has happened here then your career as an academic is likely to be cut very short."

"But you... You're just leaving me?"

"I am leaving all of Collegium," Kaelia stated. She looked back at the corpse, the one dead thing in the room that time would have a natural hold on. "I have done a cruel, wrong thing, and it has cut me deeper than you can know, and I need to return to my own people to regain my perspective."

Her sense of bitter misery stayed with her as she climbed up from the cellars, and only grew as she left the College itself. Seven years ago another Beetle naturalist had made the same discovery as poor Dinsawl, but that man had possessed the acumen to bring the news secretly to the Spider-kinden Aristoi. He had been well rewarded for his discretion, and the shameful conspiracy of natural history had remained a secret. Ever since then, however, one Spider house or another had maintained a spy in the College, and now their caution had proved justified.

But Kaelia knew that all she had bought, with his life, was another turn of the hourglass. The discovery would get out eventually, some other academic springing on the world before anyone could dissuade him, and then... the way that others looked at the Spider-kinden would be forever tarnished, by a small but intolerable degree, all her work would be undone, and poor Archer Dinsawl would still be dead.

TALES OF THE APT

Sometimes it's not about the great sweep of armies, but the tiny obsessions of unregarded academics. The Spider-kinden (a) know more than they let on; and (b) are very concerned with image. Enough so that they are willing to murder to preserve it, as here and as in 'Bones' earlier. This is an odd little story, almost entirely divorced from the events of the series but giving a view of the kinden's world not seen elsewhere, a small and private struggle for dominance, And of course I come back to this story to edit it for the collection and consider the references to "the kingdom beneath the earth where all manner of ancient evils had been sealed by the great magics" and try to remember just how much of *Seal of the Worm* had actually come together by this point, or whether the line is pure serendipity.

The Last Ironclad

Varmen awoke to the burnt-sugar smell that was Tallius taking his Medicine. He lay in bed for as long as he could force himself to, trying to recapture sleep. The world could only be staved off for so long, though. The coarse, lumpy straw mattress beneath him, the sour rotting reek that was the constant tenant of every room in the tenement, the thunder of the factory machines from the thrown-open window, all of it ganged up on him, hauling him unwillingly into the bitter present.

"Bit early, isn't it?" he croaked.

"Says you."

Varmen opened his eyes to see his roommate drop a flaming sugar crystal into the bowl before him, which promptly caught fire. There was a comical moment of fumbling before Tallius dumped in a tumbler of water to put it out, and then downed the bowl in three gagging gulps. Medicine, they called it: some sort of honey spirits with anise and wormwood, and an acquired taste that, once acquired, tended to persist.

Tallius, who only a moment before had been pale and sweating with the sheer rigour of being awake, sober and in Helleron, shuddered and then sighed greatly. Tranquillity took up a brief lease of his face, due to be evicted once the man's cravings began to gnaw at him again.

Speaking of which. Varmen's mouth felt as if it were lined with wood dust, and there was a steady beat in his head that could have been set to music. *Going to need some medicine of my own to get going this morning.* He was aware that, when he had come here two months ago, he had promised to himself that he would have sorted himself out by now – the past securely behind him and the present come to terms with. Certainly he would not end up like most of the other denizens of Huron Albrake's tenement, men and women like Tallius whose lives moved in smaller and smaller circles about the focus of their individual despairs: drink, women, gambling, violence in various combinations. No, no, Varmen would never descend to that level. After all, he had *been* someone. He remembered self-respect and pride.

Pride of the Sixth.

And he could not blame Helleron. He had heard from many quarters just how the city ground you down, chewed you up – how there was never enough work for all the bodies that crammed its streets. There had been work for Varmen – even good work at first – but the worm in the apple had been one he had brought himself. His despair, which he was circling ever more closely these days, was memory. The harsh grain spirits he favoured – still a step up from Tallius's Medicine – barely took the edge off.

Wedged between the folded, stained tunic he was using as a pillow and the big chest at the head of his bed, he kept a jar for just such emergencies. Clutching for it, he pulled out the cork with his teeth and upended it.

"Bit early, isn't it," drawled Tallius, because a bowl of Medicine gave him pretensions to wit.

Varmen would have riposted, but he was blinded by the disappointment of discovering that the jar was empty.

"Piss," he remarked.

"You shouldn't drink it then," Tallius smirked.

"Piss on you, too."

"I'm shocked." The death-pale colour of Tallius's skin made him look unwell, on the point of vomiting at any given moment, but it was normal for a Tarkesh Ant. His was a simple enough story: whatever explosive moment of exile had catapulted him here from his city down the Silk Road had broken something within in – all those years of seamless, mind-linked *belonging* abruptly brought to an end – and now he was busy finding out what parts of an Ant-kinden mind were best soluble in alcohol.

Speaking of which...

Varmen sat up, which caused all manner of upset in both head and stomach. A certain number of the nagging pains suggested bruises rather than the direct gifts of the bottle. It seemed likely that he had been fighting last night. He could only hope that it had all been in good spirits. Surely, even within Helleron's infinite variety, there was nobody stupid enough to get a drunk Wasp good and mad.

One of these days I'm going to push it too far. One day soon. Fight the wrong man. Kill the wrong man. Or just piss someone off enough that a bunch of them jump me as I stagger back here. Fine way for a fighting man to go.

He had retained – or acquired – just enough self-knowledge to know that such a death would still be better than rotting in a stew of brawling, drink and degradation, night after night. And that he had probably already started hunting out opportunities to bring it about.

Pride of the Sixth. The thought, the words that had once meant so much, felt like being stabbed now. What would they think, his comrades in arms of yesteryear?

Nothing. Dead, the lot of them.

He lurched from his bed. His mouth tasted like a latrine and he suspected that the rest of him smelled like one, but there was no water. Time for a trek across three reeking streets to the public pump, if it was working. After that he would probably need a drink to steady his nerves, just a small one. Helleron was a harsh mistress, and a man could come to harm, facing her sober.

The cramped room he shared with Tallius was on the third floor of Albrake's tenement building – just below the little attic rooms reserved for Fly-kinden because anyone heavier would have come through Varmen's ceiling. There were whole districts of Helleron crammed with just such buildings, leaning out on either side of the narrow streets until the view out of one window became the view into someone else's, and daylight just a dream even at noontime. Helleron was renowned across the world as a city of artifice and machines and money, but really it was a city of people, hundreds of thousands all living elbow to elbow and one above another like some horrifying wood-cut puzzle. Surrounding Varmen's malodorous little jigsaw piece were the intersecting lives of factory workers, artificers, artisans, sweepers, cleaners, clerks and hoodlums whose sweat and blood greased the wheels of Helleron.

Of course, for those sunk as low as Varmen and Tallius, the only relationship they had with those wheels was to avoid being crushed by them, day in, day out. So it was that Varmen descended the narrow, groaning stairs of the tenement, already aware that his pockets seemed to have become magically denuded of money, only to run straight into Huron Albrake himself.

Varmen had known Rekef torturers and Imperial army generals, Consortium magnates and Dragonfly-kinden nobles. Never had he met another human being with the sheer intimidating presence of Huron Albrake. The Beetle man was twenty years Varmen's senior and about eighteen inches shorter, but he seemed to be made of something other than frail flesh and bone, something dense and indestructible. When he was in a room, even sitting quietly by himself, he was impossible to ignore, dragging the attention by dint of personal gravity. Unarmed, untrained and of an unwarlike kinden, he stood before Varmen with the self-assurance of an Emperor. For his part, Varmen would rather have crossed the real Emperor than Huron Albrake.

"Rent," the old man grunted. He was broad and stocky, going to fat a little about the waist, dark of skin and mostly bald but with a shock of grey moustache which was, Varmen sometimes theorised, the source of his power.

Varmen tried to pretend that he thought Huron was talking to someone else, and thus breeze out of the door unhindered, but a slight adjustment in the set of Huron's eyebrows stopped him cold.

"It's not rent day already, is it?" he managed weakly.

"No," the landlord told him. "Was rent day last tenday. Now you're two behind." Huron's secret weapon was not anything as trivial as anger or threats. No, he was *disappointed*, and that cut like a knife. The killing Art in Varmen's hands was nothing to it.

"I'll get the money," Varmen promised.

"Give you another three days," Huron Albrake stated, each word heavy with the implication that he was displaying unprecedented magnanimity. "Then you're out."

"I'll get the money, sir," repeated Varmen, almost out of the door.

"Wasp." A single word meaning, *Stop there, Wasp-kinden, remembrance of whose name is beneath me, for I am not finished with you.* Sure enough Varmen stopped.

Huron took a deep breath, contemplating him. "Don't think I don't know what you've got up there in that box of yours. I remember, from when you came in. Used to polish it then. No more, hm?"

Varmen, still caught mid-exit, stared at him.

"I know people," Huron continued implacably. "What you've got'd earn you a few months tenure, with the right buyer." His expression suggested that he was being very good to bring such an opportunity to Varmen's attention.

But: "No," said the Wasp-kinden. There were limits, and even the indomitable tide of Huron Albrake would break against those rocks. "Sorry, sir, but it's not for sale."

Albrake nodded philosophically, plainly believing that Varmen would come to his senses in three days.

"I'll get the money!" Varmen insisted, diving out of the door before he could be prevented by a further edict.

Money, however, was not to be easily gotten. Holding onto it in Helleron was like carrying water in a sieve at the best of times, with so many expenses and temptations at every corner, but Varmen had just about exhausted his means of acquiring it. When he had come to this city, after that final bitter parting of the ways with the Imperial army, he had done well for himself. He had skills and his kinden had a reputation, and Helleron had until recently been under the Imperial colours. There were plenty of Beetle-kinden magnates willing to pay good money for a Wasp bodyguard.

He had started working for a rich merchant, hired to watch the man's back, fend off unwanted advances and generally use his muscle and Art to emphasise his patron's wealth and power.

A few tendays later Varmen was a few rungs down the latter, standing security for an artificer with a workshop in one of the better parts of the city – watching for thieves and ensuring that nobody took the haggling that little bit too far. Varmen's employer was well-to-do and the job paid well and demanded little of him.

After that it was chucking out at a decent taverna, and after that it was chucking out at a brothel, and then a seedy chop house, and then another taverna of a decidedly poorer vintage. That finished with, he ended up strong-arming for one or other of the fiefs, Helleron's fiercely territorial gangs who were quickly repartitioning the more wretched areas of the city now that the Empire had gone.

Even in that, he had failed. In the end, not even criminals would employ him – or not for long and not twice.

It was his pride, he knew, but that was the one part of him *not* soluble in alcohol. Varmen had known triumph, and he had known adulation. He had been part of something the memory of which still caught in his throat. He had lived a life of meaning, the best of the best.

The pattern had been the same each time: a short period of good service before his vices got the better of him. The boredom and sheer pettiness of the work would drive him to start fights where no fights were needed, or distract him so that he failed to stop trouble that could easily have been warned off. Later on, there was the drink as well, exaggerating both ends of his scale of failure. In the end criminals and honest men looked for the same virtues in their followers, and Varmen could simply not lower himself to that menial level. His life had been too rich and full and he was all too aware of the man he had once been.

Whatever he had been, the man he now was needed money, both for rent and for drink. As he trudged through Helleron's dirty, jostling streets he tried to think who might be desperate enough to need his services. Was there some fief on the brink of extinction, for whom a renegade Wasp with a reputation for erratic violence could not possibly make matters worse? His grasp of local politics was fumbling, but he did not think so. The Empire had destroyed a lot of fiefs during its time of occupation. The survivors had been given plenty of space to expand into, and they were mostly staying out of each others' way.

In that case, was there some menial, dismal piece of labouring that could use an extra pair of hands? Surely someone wanted something heavy taking from one place to another, loading or unloading, work that even Varmen might be trusted with, at least by someone who did not know him very well. It would be hard, and he would be paid a pittance, but it would get a little coin into his purse.

It turned out that a taverna he had once worked for as enforcer was taking in a big shipment of barrels, and he arrived just when even a one-handed Fly-kinden might have made himself useful. The place was a nameless, woodwormed dive, cellar on cellar chewing into the ground beneath the city, the lowest ones half-drowned and only the highest one accessible by hoist. The proprietor was a bloated Beetle man named something like Mthl – Varmen had missed the name the first time and everyone slurred over it so effortlessly he had never been able to work out what it really was. Whatever his name, the man obviously retained some awkward sympathy for Varmen, who had lasted two tendays in his service. He kept the Wasp and a dozen other lowlifes slaving away until past noon, stowing the shipment in one of the deeper cellars, paid them all a decent handful of coin for their time, and stood them a drink as well.

"Got any more work?" Varmen asked him, sipping at the sour wine in his bowl and trying to make it last. His muscles were cramped and painful, stretched and tortured beyond what they had become used to.

"Rent day, is it?" Mthl asked with grim humour.

"Something like that." Varmen did not say just how many rent days had gone by unpaid. "Well?"

"Not me. Nothing more here." Mthl shrugged. He stared at Varmen for a while, plainly a man already regretting what he was about to say. "Still, a man like you could do well. Better money than shoving boxes. Better money than minding the door, too."

Varmen looked at him suspiciously. "What's that, then?" The wine was almost gone and he felt that Mthl's generosity would quickly follow it.

"Alester Tasky on the lookout again." Now Mthl wouldn't look at him.

Varmen put the bowl down, not hard, but the click of it made Mthl flinch. He said nothing.

"Well, you know," the taverner continued awkwardly. "Your kinden, you brought the business in. Seems like you'd be the man for it if anyone was. There's other takers. Fief soldiers, mercenaries, people who want the money." Although Varmen had said nothing, the taverner threw up his hands defensively. "What? Your people do it. Can you deny it? It's a Wasp thing that your lot left us with. What's wrong with that?"

"In the Empire it's for *slaves*," Varmen spat. "Slaves and prisoners."

"Right, well," Mthl turned his back, "you know what else is for them types? Getting food and board for free. The rest of us have to pay. You remember that."

Before the Empire took Helleron, Alester Tasky had run a theatre with rooms at the back where discerning members of the audience could get to meet the pretty young actors and actresses, with the meaning of "meet" scaling with the amount the patrons were willing to pay. The Three Figs fief had its hand in that business, and they had gone the way of so many gangs when the Empire had cleared out the city's underworld almost by rote, after it stepped in. The theatre had burned down and it had seemed that Tasky would go the way of all the detritus that the black and gold broom was sweeping out.

He was a true entrepreneur, however, a dandyish little Beetle man who wore Spider silks better than most, could talk with the wealthy or the wretched equally and had an eye for the main chance. If the Wasps were not fond of bawdy theatre, he had decided to give them what they did want.

There had always been a few underground blood-fighting pits in

Helleron – illegal, and yet a few of the great and good always did find that only real violence could reach their jaded hearts. Alester Tasky was the first Helleren native to set up such an enterprise openly, touting for Wasp custom and paying Wasp slavers to instruct him on how it was done. Even though the Empire would only be in the city a relatively short time, Imperial officers had sufficient gold in their purses – and favours to grant – that Tasky did very well out of it, and a dozen imitators had set up pits of their own, desperate to grab some piece of his success.

The Empire was gone from Helleron, of course, but some of the pits remained, Tasky's included. Death matches were frowned on, but the city had a taste for the sport now. Open contests might be to first blood or billed as trials of skill, but behind closed doors a great deal went on with the tacit knowledge of the city's magnates, who were often to be found in the best seats. Something in that explosive release of violence had found its mark in the souls of Helleron's merchant lords, as though the city's constant rote of consuming and wearing down its inhabitants had needed a new metaphor.

When Varmen approached the man, he did so with the unhappy knowledge that it was not a need for rent that drove him to it, but because Mthl's wine had done nothing but sharpen a thirst he did not have the coin to satisfy. After an hour of putting it off and wracking his parched brain for alternatives, he had gone to seek out Alester Tasky.

Tasky was sitting at his private table in the taproom that fronted his fighting pit, armies of coin arrayed in rank and file before him as he made complex entries in a ledger. He wore a long padded tunic of pale blue silk over an under-robe of patterned red, all Spider-made and garish, but he had a Spider's own self-possessed confidence that most of his kinden lacked. Whatever he chose to wear was the fashion, as long as he wore it.

He had a twinkle in his eye as he glanced up at Varmen. He was no young man, not anymore, but he seemed to have rented a youth's expressions, all cheek and cheer set into age-worn features that cosmetics had smoothed over and rejuvenated. Everything seemed to amuse him, but Varmen most of all. This was not their first meeting.

Varmen loathed the very idea of pit-fighting – as a participant, anyway. What he had said to Mthl was the truth: it was a profession for slaves and criminals back home. Although there were professional free gladiators, they were almost always men to whom life had no better cards to deal, crippled by debt or dubious loyalties. Their hard-won celebrity lasted only until the moment they missed a parry. For a soldier of the Imperial armies it was a demeaning life. For a man who had been the pride and joy of the Black and Gold, it was unthinkable.

Varmen had fought in Alester Tasky's pit three times before. He had stopped because he had better prospects, and because Tasky had started making demands that Varmen did not want to stoop to.

"Well, hello there, soldier," Tasky said, sending a startlingly white grin Varmen's way. One of his girls glided past and left a bowl of wine in front of him, and he squeezed her thigh, a stockman checking the quality of the meat. He must have seen Varmen's eyes drawn more by the drink than the girl, because his grin broadened, and he pushed the bowl around the table's edge, skirting the formations of profit. "What chance seeing you here, eh? You're looking for work, I'd guess."

Varmen's pride held for the moment, although the bowl was calling softly to him. "I'll fight for you. I hear you've some matches need filling."

"A spectacle," Tasky announced, waving a hand expansively. "Something special. I've a private party who don't just want the usual dross."

"I'll fight for you," the Wasp repeated. "For the right price." His hands' patience had been exhausted and they got the wine bowl to his mouth without consent. He acquiesced to their demands with good grace seeing, reflected in Tasky's eyes, all the many steps he had descended to come this far. The man kept himself informed. No doubt he knew Varmen's recent dismal history like he knew his own ledgers, to the last decimal point.

"I can use you," Tasky confirmed. His eyes found Varmen's gaze and held it. "One night only and I can find you twenty centrals. Settle your rent and more, eh? But you've got to *wear* it."

Varmen's stare was bleak. "No."

"It won't work without. You think you're anything, just standing there in a loincloth? You think there aren't other Wasps in the city, men in better shape who'd fight for a quarter of the price. You know what makes you special. I pay for that, nothing else. And I'll have it, too."

"No."

Tasky shrugged, sublimely unconcerned. "You can fool yourself as long as you want. We both know how deep a hole you're in, and still digging. Come back when you're ready to stop wasting my time."

Varmen's fingers flexed, and for a moment he felt the killing Art warming his palms. *I am a soldier. No Beetle pimp talks to me like that. I should... I should...*

And perhaps, when he had first come to Helleron, self-respect still clinging to him despite all he had lost, he would have killed Tasky for that disrespect. He had fallen far since then, though, and Tasky knew it.

Varmen managed to get back to his lodgings without being collared by Huron Albrake again, choosing his moment to dodge up the stairs whilst the landlord was berating another tenant. The room upstairs was empty, Tallius having lurched off to whatever part of town had such a surfeit of charity that the inhabitants might spare him a few coins.

For a long while Varmen sat on his straw-stuffed mattress, listening to the low rhythms of Albrake's disappointed voice, and thinking about Alester Tasky and his offer. A lot of money, more than Varmen was ever likely to see by any other means, but he knew he would never take the man up. A step too far, was what Tasky was asking. There were some things that remained too pure to be sullied by his petty games.

Having reassured himself that he retained sufficient self-respect to turn the man down, Varmen knelt before the big chest he kept at the head of his bed. A ridiculous luxury, this: the second most expensive thing he owned, it would have paid the rent or bought several nights' worth of drinks if he had sold it. Locked inside, however, was his most expensive possession, his one remaining link to the man he had once been.

He opened the lock with the little bronze key he kept about his neck. No lock was thief-proof in Helleron, but Varmen had paid enough that nobody in this run-down neighbourhood would be likely to have the skills to overcome it. Full, the chest weighed so much that even a pair of diligent thieves would be unable to spirit it away without considerable noise and effort.

He lifted the lid.

His eyes were met by the glorious black and gold lustre of his breastplate, the enamel still holding a shine. He lifted it out, feasting his eyes on the articulated metal pieces beneath, like a miser gloating over his wealth. The armour was heavy, far more than any regular soldier ever had to bear, made for Varmen alone. He reached in and took out the closed helm, staring into the eyeslit as if he could see his younger self still in there.

Pride of the Sixth. The Sixth Army, that was, and truly he had been its pride. During the Twelve-year War against the Commonweal he and his compatriots had been the anchor of the Imperial lines, facing off the numberless hordes of the Dragonfly-kinden and their subjects, secure in their carapace of interlocking metal. Sentinels, they were called, a noble and an honourable tradition that long-predated the Empire, but that the Wasps had seized on and made their own. Whilst the chaos of battle whirled on both flanks and overhead, the Light Airborne trading blows with the Dragonfly nobility and the vast Commonweal levy pressing forward in undisciplined, spear-studded blocks, the Sentinels were the calm centre, unmoveable and untouchable.

All through the war, Varmen had stood in the front rank and fought for the Empire, and the cry of *"Pride of the Sixth!"* had struck terror into the hearts of his enemies. Even when the Sixth itself had suffered a crushing defeat, the worst reversal of the war, Varmen had survived it and lived to see the army reformed, victory against the Commonweal, and a new war start against the Lowlands.

He had been sent with the new Sixth to reinforce General Malkan's Seventh Army for the great push towards the Ant city of Sarn.

He had learned in one day that the world had moved on, that the grand and ancient tradition of the Sentinel, stretching back to the very Days of Lore, had come to an end, and nobody had told him.

He took up the breastplate, and his fingers traced the small, rough-edged hole to the lower right. Such a tiny imperfection in the beautiful, gleaming metal, to bring down a way of life.

He remembered: standing front and centre in the hastily-formed lines as the Sarnesh army rushed out of the pre-dawn grey. There had been soldiers still buckling his armour to him even as he hefted his sword and shield and waited for the clash. On either side the Imperial regular infantry – too heavily armoured to fly, and yet wearing less than half the weight of Varmen's metal skin – had strung out, levelling spears and crossbows and snapbows, and overhead the Airborne were taking to the sky. The air rang with relayed orders as General Malkan of the Seventh's glorious Winged Furies formed up his forces with creditable speed and clear-headedness.

To the Wasps, the battle was known as Malkan's Stand, but Varmen knew what the Lowlanders called it. For all that he still resented the general of the Seventh for overshadowing his beloved Sixth, the man deserved better than the legacy of "Malkan's Folly."

The Sarnesh had come in *en mass,* their heavy infantry to the front, supported by strung-out wings of snapbowmen – Sarnesh and Collegiate, Tseni and Tarkesh – and then a screening force of Mantis and Moth skirmishers to keep the Airborne off their flanks. The Wasps had greater numbers, but they were still forming up when the first shots were exchanged. More, the Ants were renowned close fighters, unmatched in discipline and coordination.

That was where Varmen's Sentinels would come in. Regular infantry seldom stood against Ants without support, but the Sentinels would provide that immovable object that even the Ant-kinden would break against, a rock and an inspiration, holding and holding until the Empire's superior numbers and mobility would tip the scales. It had worked before, and a half-dozen Ant cities flew the black and gold because of it.

Malkan's Stand had changed all that.

It was the snapbows. They had been an Imperial invention first, and had given Malkan victory over the Sarnesh at the Battle of the Rails the year before, but over winter the weapons had proliferated like mushrooms. Suddenly every Apt pair of hands had a snapbow pressed into them, and the Lowlanders had adapted to the new device's possibilities much faster than the Empire. The Airborne were clipped from the sky by the weapon's range and accuracy. The infantry, though they gave a good accounting of themselves, had been scythed down in their ranks.

And the Sentinels, who had clashed blade to blade with the Ant-kinden and held them without giving an inch, as good as their promise, as they always were... the Sentinels had died, reaped like corn.

Varmen fingered that single mute hole in his armour. He had not seen the man who had brought him low – some distant Ant or Beetle loading and loosing with automatic motions, seeking a new target as the bolt left his bow. The missile had struck through the enamelled steel of the breastplate, through the riveted chain beneath, then the padded jack under that, and then all the way through Varmen. Barely daunted, it had cut on through the padding and the mail again to knuckle a solid dent into his backplate. The miracle of it was that Varmen had survived.

That was always the last sworn duty of the Sentinels: *if all else goes awry, we will hold*. Many battles had been won because the Sentinels had delayed the enemy long enough for the Imperial forces to reform, even though it cost them their lives. No longer. A lifetime of training and practice, so as to make the heaviest armour like a second skin, so as to develop senses that could tell where the enemy was even through a helm that offered only the smallest slit on the world, and all of it wasted. What was the point of such a colossal investment when any Beetle shopkeeper with a snapbow could kill Sentinels for sport from a hundred yards?

He had known then what the Mantis-kinden had felt centuries before, when the Apt revolution had met their hard-won blade skills with massed crossbows and torn the world from their masters' grasp.

Of course, that had not been the utter annihilation of the Sixth and Seventh Armies. A camp of survivors had formed up, near Helleron as it happened, and the wounded Varmen had been brought there, last survivor of the Sentinels.

The Empire was in turmoil by then. The Emperor had been assassinated by a slave, and across the Wasps' domain ambitious city governors were clawing for independence. It had seemed the end of everything was just over the next hill. Lying on his sickbed, listening to the increasingly tense reports of the Sarnesh advance, beaten soldiers talking of last stands or furtive flight, Varmen had retained his confidence in the Imperial war machine. After all, even his own Sixth had taken a beating during the war with the Commonweal, but the Empire had survived, and thrived.

And then someone, some clerk from the Quartermasters' Corps, had finally found a moment for Varmen in his busy schedule. This had been as the Wasps were pulling out of Helleron as peaceably as they had been invited in, the camp packing itself up around them with a weary attempt at discipline.

"You'll have to report to one of the infantry captains, sergeant," the man had told him. "We're not sure who…" He stretched out a scroll in a vain attempt to bring order from the chaos of the insufficiently annotated. "Just find an infantry captain. They'll have to sort your assignment when we get to Asta." The man had looked harassed and

Adrian Tchaikovsky

worn, and he had come into the infirmary tent with a wincing limp that spoke of doing his part in the fighting. "You can walk?"

"Not sure I could do it in my armour, but yes."

"Ah, yes. You should return the mail to stores, of course."

Varmen's first thought had been, ridiculously, *It's not 'mail', it's plate. A quartermaster should know that,* but then his mind had caught up, and he had said, "Stores?"

For a moment the quartermaster had stared at him, then the man's lips had twitched – one more irritation for his overburdened life. "You were told your lot have been disbanded?"

"Well I'm the last Sentinel the Sixth has to offer, so –"

"No, no." As though Varmen was being deliberately aggravating. "The Sentinels, as a class. Imperial decree."

"Says who?" Varmen had sat up sharply, and damn the pain.

"The Empress." Spoken as to a slow child. "Who else? You see why, of course. I mean, what's the point of them now, hm?"

Me, Varmen had thought. *You mean, what's the point of me.*

Once the quartermaster had hurried off to his next task, Varmen had tried thinking slowly and pragmatically about the news that his life, and the lives of all his fallen friends, had been declared post facto obsolete. A life in the regular infantry might not be so bad, after all. He was a sergeant, he had prospects. The Empire would go on, even if there was now inexplicably an *Empress* giving the orders.

Pride of the Sixth. All those lost faces, all those battles standing front and centre, the years of training in armour that would bring a strong man to his knees. His life. His whole life.

That night he had discovered that he could indeed walk, although his armour had come with him on the back of a pack beetle that had no idea that it was about to become, firstly, a deserter from the Imperial army, and secondly, part-trade for a very well-made chest.

And this was what he was reduced to, now: Alester Tasky wanted him to don his mail again, but not for war, not for honour. For a show, a demeaning prostitution of what he had once been.

I might have no coin for rent, I might have no coin for drink, but not that. Not pissing on the memories of my comrades. I will not be a clown in Tasky's circus.

He blinked furiously at the mist of tears that crowded his vision, and his thirst laid a hand on his shoulder and suggested he should raise

154

a bowl to lost friends. It seemed a solid argument, although his stock of coin was much diminished from when Mthl had paid him, despite the free drinks he had cadged already that day. *The rent will have to wait. Drinking to the Pride of the Sixth is a solemn duty. Surely I can scare up some more coin after.*

Huron Albrake had retreated into one of the ground floor rooms, where Varmen happened to know his landlord exacted a very particular sort of rent from a young widow each tenday. The coast was clear for a quick getaway.

He almost walked on when someone whispered his name as he stepped out of the tenement. There were so few people in Helleron who both knew his name and meant him any good. When he glanced down an alley and saw Tallius crouching there, he came close to walking away all over again. The Ant was in a wretched state, though, and some misplaced pity dragged Varmen over to see what he wanted.

"Is Albrake... is he there? Is he waiting for me?" Tallius hissed.

"Why would he be waiting for you?" Varmen looked the man over critically. As an inveterate panhandler in the Lowlands' least charitable city, Tallius ran into the fists and boots of locals on a semi-regular basis, but it looked as though his most recent failed patron had been particularly irked, or Tallius had been particularly persistent. One eye was squeezed almost shut by swollen bruises and there was a crust of blood where a blow had split the skin over his cheekbone.

"Rent, got no rent," the Ant murmured, head swinging. "No bits for rent, no bits for drink. Varmen, Varmen, lend me –"

"Get lost." Spoken without acrimony but firmly. "You know I'm the same." Looking at the degenerate Tallius, though, Varmen knew that he was still a few rungs of the ladder up from where the Ant had gone. Bile squirmed in his stomach and tried to fight the words back, before spitting out, "Look at you! Your people are soldiers, warriors. Is there nothing left to you but this?"

Tallius actually snarled up at him, a grimace missing at least one tooth. "You don't know!" he got out. "You don't. You can't know what it's like, how quiet it is."

For a moment, the constant yammering and bustling of Helleron all around them, Varmen could not understand what he meant, but then he realised: for an Ant-kinden, any city not his own would be deathly silent, stripped of the constant inner voices of his kin.

There was a three-street fief named the Blackeners currently passing through that brief period between becoming aware of Varmen and losing patience with him, and he was able to hire himself out for them as extra muscle as they made to add a fourth street to their empire. What had promised to be a reasonably mindless scrap turned into a great deal of posturing and taunting, with nobody wanting to draw the first blood. If Varmen had been more sober then he would probably have touched off the fire himself, just through sheer irritable boredom. In the end he acquitted himself well enough simply by hanging about at the back and looking big and Wasp-like. He then had to haggle with the Blackeners' paymaster, which very nearly delivered all the violence that the actual stand-off had failed to. In the end that special magic, which the Wasp-kinden reputation brought to every place that had once been under their boot, paid off, and Varmen got a decent fistful of change out of the day.

Enough for the rent? Probably not. Enough to keep Albrake off his back for another tenday? Probably. Or he could start drinking it away and pissing it against a wall, in that order. He felt his desires teetering on the brink, now leaning towards responsibility, now towards oblivion. Treading a narrow line between them, he made his way back towards the tenement, interested in an almost academic way in how much of his hard-earned cash would remain in his possession by the time he arrived.

He had stopped counting coin by the time he finally made the tenement again, because a few bowls suggested to him that if he stopped looking into his purse he could pretend that the money was all there still. This left him feeling sufficiently buoyant that he forgot to look out for Huron Albrake and the landlord collared him as he was going up the stairs.

"Rent, Wasp," the Beetle stated, moustache bristling. "Come, now."

"Five days, you said," Varmen protested.

"I *said* three, and now I think I was too generous." Something in his stare made Varmen see himself as a stranger: some dirty, stinking hulk of a man, bloodshot-eyed, his tunic stained with spilt wine and old sweat. Viewing himself through Albrake's eyes, Varmen felt physically repulsed to be sharing a body with such a dissipated ruin.

"Even your friend the Ant can pay his rent," Albrake told him, "and he's nothing more than a cadaver the surgeons don't want yet.

"You…" The one word and its unspoken fellows encompassed all Varmen had been, and could have been.

Having lost all the borrowed wellbeing that a little wine had given him, Varmen stomped up the stairs, pieces of ill-made plan battering at each other inside his head, failing to make a whole.

He stopped. Something had happened to the room.

He had come to Helleron with a keen respect for the avarice of the mechanically-minded Beetle folk, and so he had invested all he could into that very fine chest. He had staked his pride that the lock would beat thieves, that the weight of the whole would break their backs before they could move it down the stairs. Any criminal with the resources to take from him what he had would, he had believed, have more lucrative nuts to shell elsewhere in the city.

The chest had been of sturdy wood, and iron-bound, but someone had literally torn it apart, wrenching at its strong substance until its various component pieces had simply parted company, the metal strips tailing off into jagged edges, the wood splintering. In the centre of the carnage lay the lock, its two sections still resolutely holding to one another.

The armour, all that weight of metal, was gone.

It took Varmen all of twenty seconds to reconstruct what must have happened, the only part of the mess that could be reconstructed. He wondered, then, if Albrake had intentionally been dropping a hint, back there on the stairs. What had he seen, that he had agreed to overlook in exchange for Tallius's rent money?

Ants were strong, of course, and their Art made them stronger, but Varmen had not even considered that sheer desperation would drive the dissolute and broken man to such a feat. The broken chest mutely proved him wrong.

Varmen knew all of Tallius's regular dives, each seedier than the last – the wretched, windowless haunts of the Medicine-eaters that had grown up to service the self-destructive vice. Most of them were run by men and women who styled themselves "doctor", because the Helleron vice trade always prided itself on its sense of humour.

He was relying on the Tallius he knew. Any reasonable man in possession of such a treasure would have made himself scarce – got out of town or at least changed district, lying low until Varmen had burnt out and fallen away. Tallius's life revolved around his single appetite, circling so close to the flame of his inevitable disintegration that he had only one thing on his mind. Actually planning ahead would be as alien to him as magic.

In Doctor Misa's, the third such dive he tried, he spotted Tallius' face floating in the gloom, lit by the uncertain glare of a burning sugar cube the man was about to drop into his Medicine.

Varmen had meant to shout the man's name, a civilized opener to the argument they were about to have, but what came out was a furious howl belonging to no man nor any beast man knew. Tallius stared up, the expression on his face everything Varmen could have wanted. The burning sugar dropped, and then a thin cloth of flames rushed across the tabletop as he dropped his precious Medicine, causing his fellow drinkers to swear and kick away.

"Where is my armour?" Varmen demanded, marching down on Tallius like a war automotive. Someone – probably the local chucker-out – tried to get in his way, and Varmen punched him hard enough to crack his jaw without even breaking stride. Spending a lifetime in so much steel gave a man a brutal all-purpose strength in every part of him.

Tallius, who by Art and heritage had already proved himself the stronger man, was gabbling and backing away, but Doctor Misa's was small and he had nowhere to go. He was saying something, over and over, but Varmen was too angry to decipher the words until he had the Ant lifted up by his tunic and rammed against a wall.

"I don't have it," was what he had been saying.

"You took it!" *Bang!* Against the wall again.

"I didn't –! I never –!" Because Tallius' failure to think things through had not even covered the fact that Varmen might actually *suspect* him. "I don't have it!"

And Varmen stopped, because he himself had not gone beyond this moment in his head: find Tallius, recover armour. But of *course* Tallius did not have it, because he had paid his rent to Huron Albrake, and where else had that money come from.

"Where," Varmen growled, "is my armour?" But already he could feel his tenuous control of the situation slipping from him.

Tallius's gaze slipped sideways, helpless as a man sliding from a ledge, and Varmen followed it, seeing the one person present who did not belong in Doctor Misa's. The man in Spider silks who sat at a table on his own, enjoying a bottle of wine that surely had not been sold to him there. Alester Tasky raised his bowl, his face creasing in that young man's congenial smile.

"You pissmongering *bastard*," Varmen hissed, and he could have meant Tallius or Tasky or both. He put the Ant down, though, setting him gently on his feet, and turned to the Beetle-kinden. "You put him up to this."

Tasky's expression radiated amused innocence. "My goodness, what a suspicious world you must live in."

"Give me my armour." Two steps more towards Tasky and looming, but the man was blithely unconcerned still.

"Of course. You know my price." Another sip of wine, but Varmen found that the drink had no hook in him just then.

And then Tallius came blundering back into that special proximity all Sentinels knew – just out of eyeshot and yet within sword-reach, leaping into Varmen's awareness as a potential threat. "I'm sorry," he was blubbering. "I had to – I needed – I'm sorry."

Varmen's hand splayed at him, his Art leaping eagerly to his will like a beast off the leash. The flash of gold fire illuminated the entire interior of Doctor Misa's, searing across all those dark-adapted eyes, and Tallius leapt backwards as though throwing himself into the wall once more for good measure. There was a charred hole under his ribs, crenelated with the burnt-hard edges of his innards.

Everyone there was frozen – staff and customers both. For just one moment the Black and Gold was over their city again and they remembered the curfews and the harsh justice and the soldiers on the streets.

Only Tasky was undismayed. The fight promoter leant back in his chair and he had an appreciative, even pleased expression on his face. "That's my boy," he said softly. "That's the man I want." As though the room was not still resounding to the echoes of murder. "Now come get your armour. You can walk away with it, and the money too, but you'll have to fight. I've a special little spectacle just waiting for your participation, Varmen. Come earn back your heritage." The smile deepened. "Before today I thought you might have forgotten it."

Tasky's regular fighting pit, where Varmen visited him previously, was for the public matches, where death was a regrettable accident rather than the main attraction. Varmen knew the other place, though. He had fought there twice, killed both times. Before Tallius that was all the killing he had done, in Helleron. People thought of Wasps as always on the point of murderous rampage, but anyone who grew up with harsh Imperial discipline learned to keep even a Wasp temper in check.

This part of the city was all factories – not the thunderous, machine-heavy haunts of the artificers, but cavernous buildings where hundreds of men and women were crammed shoulder to shoulder assembling pieces, stitching, carving, hammering, each one of them repeating forever one meaninglessly small part of a grander plan. The people who worked here earned just enough to pay for the privilege of living in their mean tenements, enough to keep their families just short of starving. They would never have enough to break free of Helleron's hungry jaws.

Some of the factories had a night shift, picking up each stitch and cog where the day workers left off, but others lived a curious double life. There were drinking and gambling dens that took from the workforce the money they made in daylight. There were fief headquarters where the criminals would meet and flaunt their ill-gotten gains. And there was Tasky's clandestine blood-fighting pit, in the extensive cellars of a place that by day paid the impoverished a pittance to make fine gloves for the wealthy.

Varmen turned up at a side-door, as he had in the past. Tasky, being a man of the theatre trade, did not approve of his patrons seeing the performers arrive. The neatly-dressed Fly-kinden woman who let him in was new – looking like a middle-aged shopkeeper's clerk save for the level and challenging way she met Varmen's eyes.

"I'm –" he started.

"I know who you are. Follow me, if you would."

She marched back inside, precise as a clock, leaving Varmen to shamble in her wake, like a great, decaying ship being pulled by an energetic little tug.

She headed downstairs immediately – the fighting trade did not touch on the daylight parts of the factory. The backstage quarters were just as cramped and dank as Varmen remembered, a warren of cellars subdivided into smaller rooms and tunnels, all lit by sullen gaslight. There were a handful of other staff on hand, none of whom spared Varmen more than a glance.

"I want my armour," he threw at the Fly woman's back.

"It's waiting for you," came her reply, almost contemptuously. "We all are."

He was expecting more games. He was not expecting the next thing to grace his eye to be the armour itself, still less that it should be half-tenanted.

They had left the chainmail off to spare the man some weight, an understandable mistake but a mistake nonetheless. The man suffering under that steel had about three-quarters of the outer shell on – and most of it cross-buckled or not buckled at all, so that entire plates just flapped and hung like washing.

"Get it off," the Fly snapped. "He's here."

"What?" came a voice from within the helm, hollow and exasperated. "Stenne –!"

"Just get it off him, you oafs," she ordered. Two Beetle men stepped forward to obey, but Varmen barrelled up and shouldered them aside, setting to the abused armour himself.

"Didn't think I'd show, is it?" he growled as he worked.

"My money was on you drinking yourself into a stupor for a tenday," the Fly woman, Stenne, agreed, not in the least penitent. "From what I hear that's your life in a nutshell."

"Is that so?" And Varmen realised, to his great surprise, that since killing Tallius he had not so much as thought about drink. The need to recover the armour had focused him in a way nothing had since leaving the army.

He dragged the helm roughly from its wearer's head and was surprised to see another Wasp-kinden, albeit a red-faced and sweating one. The man had close-cropped hair, and a scar on one cheek balanced the sting-burn on the other. Everything about him said 'failed soldier', an immediate kinship that made Varmen uncomfortable.

"You're the Sentinel, then?"

Varmen nodded, still working at reclaiming his armour, piece by piece.

"Glad you showed. Don't reckon I could have fought like this."

"Stupid to even try. They'd have killed you and danced on your corpse before you could take three steps," Varmen told him disgustedly. "What were you thinking?"

"That it's a better chance than being hung for theft, which is what

Tasky bought me out of," the other Wasp explained. "And just 'cos you're here doesn't mean I'm not fighting, just that I can fight without all *that*."

"Tell them how to put it on you," Stenne instructed, as soon as the other Wasp was suitably denuded. Varmen glowered at the two Beetles, but even if they were as hamfisted as they looked, the business would be easier with their help. "Deserter, are you?" he asked the other Wasp, as he donned his padded jack.

"And you're not?"

"The army deserted from me." Now Varmen was shrugging into his mail hauberk. "Varmen, former sergeant."

"Atric, soldier."

"And you're, what, the warm-up act? It's Wasp night at Tasky's arena?"

Atric's eyes flicked off in Stenne's direction.

"It's not all about you, Sentinel," she said caustically. "It's a special fight tonight – not just one-on-ones, but a nice group skirmish, something different for the punters. You get a team. Your own army, how about that?"

"That makes me one of your team," Atric added helpfully. The Beetles were crowding forwards with pieces of steel, and the Wasp took charge of fitting Varmen with them, one at a time. He was no Sentinel but at least he had worn armour in his time.

Varmen said nothing now save to instruct his impromptu helpers, but Stenne's words had started wheels turning in his mind, and they were grinding out no conclusions that he was happy with.

When they had him fully clad to his liking, Stenne let her wings carry her over to another door, low enough that Varmen and Atric would have to stoop through it.

"Come on," she told them flatly. "Come meet the rest of your team. The punters are already taking their seats."

"So what's the deal?" Varmen prompted, as he followed her.

"Live and get paid," she said unsympathetically.

There were another half-dozen Wasps awaiting them, all men, and all surely ex-army. Varmen had never seen a more wretched showing of his own kinden. Many were skinny and half-starved, and most bore old wounds. One man's right arm was a stump at the elbow. They were pale enough that he guessed they had been locked up for some time – *waiting for me, or at least my armour?* – and there was a flinching, cringing look about most of them. Men from whom the fight had been whipped, by either circumstance or the hand of other men. If Tasky wanted a tame Wasp army for his pit, then what else would he find? There were a fair few deserters hale and hearty and doing well for themselves in Helleron, but they would not have lowered themselves to dance to Tasky's tune. The only participants for this spectacle were those who had no choice in the matter.

Like me. But Varmen was more than these men. Even Atric the thief was something better. He wondered what miserable stories had dragged them to this turn, whether the war itself had brought them low or whether they were just further along his own road.

And they were all in uniform, that was the real tell-tale. It was a grotesque mish-mash of whatever surplus Tasky had been able to get his hands on, but Varmen saw Light Airborne cuirasses, and bits and pieces of infantry plate, an artificer's helm, a pilot's leather's. All of it black and gold, and the colours touched up from the dull and dented condition that Tasky must have acquired them in.

Varmen glanced at Atric. "What d'you reckon?"

The condemned Wasp was already shrugging into banded Airborne mail that was a little too large for him. "We're dead men."

It was a hard conclusion to argue with, informed not by the condition of their fellows but Varmen's whole sense of the story that Tasky was trying to tell with them. They were not just here as Wasps. They were here as the *Empire*, its conquering army that had only recently withdrawn from Helleron. Certainly this city had not suffered under the Black and Gold in the same way as the Empire's actual conquests had. The fighting in the streets had been against the criminal fiefs, penalties for breaking curfew had been non-fatal, and the great and good, at least, had retained the bulk of their property and privileges. The strange thing about the great and good, though, in Varmen's experience, was that the mightier they were, the more acutely they felt the loss of even a mote of their power.

No prizes for guessing what sort of a show Alester Tasky had arranged tonight, then.

"Fine, right," he stated flatly. "Whoever they throw at us, we sting the bastards down and piss on fair fights."

Atric jabbed an open hand out at him – it was such an unexpectedly aggressive gesture that Varmen had his shield up instantly, other hand reaching for his sword hilt. The man was not attacking him, though, he was displaying something.

"What's that?" Varmen demanded.

"I was a prisoner. We all were," Atric said simply. "They don't mess about, with our kinden. They know how dangerous we are. So they take steps." There was an ugly, lopsided brand across his palm, that some wit had decided to fashion to look like a big Helleron Central, the mostly-gold coins that were the Lowlands' favourite currency. A hand injury could stopper up a man's Art, Varmen knew. The idea of simply searing that characteristically Wasp-kinden ability out of someone was shocking to him.

"What about the rest of you?" he asked. Hands were lifted, presented to him in a manner that would have been taboo in any civilised Wasp place unless real harm was intended. Each one of them had received the same treatment.

But Varmen had thought about it now. "Right, now tell me the truth. How many of you *can* still sting. I'll bet it doesn't always take, and I'll bet you've been hiding it and biding your time, eh? Come one, some of you must have a little spark left in you." Into the cautious silence that followed he dropped, "Look, they're not going to be messing around. This is a death-match and we're set up to lose. Whatever you've got, we need it."

At the last, three of them kept their hands raised, fingers closed into a fist now. Varmen nodded, satisfied.

"Anyone from the Sixth here?" he asked them, and received shaken heads in response. "Typical, useless bastards. Seventh then, must be? Right. Well from now on, you're all Sixth Army, and I'm your sergeant, got that? Pride of the Sixth!"

There was precious little pride left there, it was plain to see. Even his best parade-ground bellow did little to stir the warrior in them. Still, he stared into each set of eyes, willing them to challenge him, to show some soldier spirit.

"You know what I am," he told them all. "You know this armour. You know what it makes me, and I'm the real thing. I'm your centre. I'm the solid heart of your line." For a moment, seeing those thin, pallid wretches, his own heart nearly broke. They were nothing but shadows of the men he had fought alongside. "I will stand. You know that. If they force you back, fall back on me. If I press forwards, follow into the gap I make. They will not stop me. They will not slow me. They will not make me retreat. I am the Sentinels, you understand." And it was true. He was all the Sentinels there would ever be. "You men with stings, you're on the flanks. The rest of you, just keep a line between you, so you can guard each other's flanks when they attack. A line with me at its centre, you see? And use your wings on the attack, if you can – quick in and out. You see?"

They saw. None of them was happy about it, but they saw.

Then the door was opened and Stenne was there again, with a handful of Tasky's men – not exactly guards, but they all had swords and a couple had crossbows – and Varmen understood that his doomed compatriots had been transformed since the Fly woman left, from prisoners into fighters, therefore to be handled with caution. It was more of an accolade than he reckoned they had earned, but he fully intended to make up the difference himself.

"It's all ready for you," she said, to Varmen in particular. When he met her gaze he saw a brief sliver of utter loathing and was surprised by it. Helleron was such a cosmopolitan city, whose factories and vice dens devoured all comers irrespective of kinden. He had grown out of the habit of being hated by most of the world for what he was. It was almost refreshing to be reminded.

"Let's go," he snapped, and shouldered past the men she had brought. They got out of his way quickly, too, and the other Wasps, the beaten and the lame, followed in his wake. The fighting pit was ahead, and he had his helm on before he reached it, sensing the opening out of the walls even though his vision was cut down to a slit, all the old skills coming back to him.

Tasky's pit was nothing the factory above ever laid claim to: he'd had it dug especially during the occupation to give the Empire what it wanted. It was intended for select audiences, and there were only two rows of seats up past the lip. In times past no doubt there had been army majors and Consortium captains rubbing shoulders with the Helleron magnates as men died for their sport. Now most of the seats were vacant, and a single knot of guests, perhaps twenty in all, sat and watched as the band of deserters stepped out onto the dirt below them. They were mostly men, just a couple of women, and they were all

Beetle-kinden and extremely well dressed. Tasky, normally the master of all he surveyed, hovered on the sidelines, eager to please. These were all Big Noises in the city, then, Varmen understood, patrons worthy of this investment, Helleron's little ruling clique of merchant lords.

His eyes met Tasky's as the promoter took a moment from bowing and scraping to regard his prize. The shock of contact was fiercer than it had been with Stenne. Tasky had always come across with such a suave charm, so utterly unconcerned about anything Varmen might have the power to do to him. The sheer confidence had armoured him in the world of Helleron society as much as Varmen's own steel had on his many battlefields. There had never been a sense of any passion below it.

In just that one moment, Varmen saw it – the thing that Stenne's look was merely the reflected radiance of. Possibly Tasky himself did not realise that his face could be read through that narrow visor. There had been real hate in that look, that Varmen had never suspected before. Tasky loathed him and wanted him dead, and in that moment the Wasp wondered whether that was not the point of this entire charade, with the wealthy patrons thrown in as an afterthought.

Why? But even though Helleron had barely suffered under its occupation, by Imperial standards, still the soldiers of the Empire were seldom polite house-guests. They had burned Tasky's theatre, after all, and perhaps this life of blood sports had not been the grand opportunity he made out, but an exigency forced on him by bitter chance. Perhaps there had been someone he had lost, some friend or relative, someone luckless enough to be in the wrong place at the wrong time, some girl who caught a soldier's eye, some boy who spilled the wrong man's drink.

Guess I'll never know.

Over the top of the pit, just below the feet of the spectators, they had strung a net. With so many kinden who could fly or climb or even just jump, containing the gladiators was always a worry for the discerning promoter. This left barely eight feet of clear space over the Wasps' heads. Nobody would be doing much flying, then – no more than a few short hops.

"My gracious friends!" Tasky called out. "You see before you the mighty forces of the Wasp Empire. Picture, if you will, the dry and rocky ground east of Sarn, where have come the invincible forces of

General Malkan of the Seventh Army. Never has the Lowlands seen such a grand army. The future of our world hangs in the very balance as the Black and Gold marches on!" He had a fine voice, truly theatrical, and it boomed about the enclosed space. "Behind them, their conquests," he went on, "heavy with their chains, and our own sweet Helleron amongst them. I take you back to the very fulcrum of history! On the one side, slavery, on the other, liberty."

Knowing how easily Helleron had capitulated and how well its people had been treated – better than they treated each other, for the most part – Varmen was almost moved to add his own coda. Instead he waited, watching the far doors as they swung open.

"But from the west another army is marching!" Tasky called out, almost shrill now. "Hear the sound of freedom in their tread! For here are the Sarnesh and their allies. Gracious guests, I give you Malkan's Folly!"

Varmen had already guessed it by then, but the name, the cruelty that history's winners had dealt to that one loser, stung him anyway. Then the Ants were entering the arena.

They were all professional fighting men, Varmen guessed – mercenaries probably – but Tasky had stage-managed their appearance as much as he had his Wasps. Varmen had keen memories of the Ants at Malkan's Stand, and they had not looked like this – oh, the same general picture, but a hundred little details awry. The mail of these soldiers was heavier, reinforced at the chest with a square panel. Their rectangular shields were bronze-faced rather than being all-steel, and their helms seemed both more restricting and less robust. With a start of intuition Varmen realised that these men and women were dressed according to some Beetle tradition. This was how Ants looked, in their picture books and their imaginations, and so Tasky had given them what they expected.

Varmen chalked up one small advantage – the enemy were in unfamiliar gear, just as his Wasps were.

There was one other major difference between these Ants and those at Malkan's Stand. Only a third of these were actually Sarnesh. Varmen wondered if most of the real veterans of that battle would think Tasky's display to be in bad taste, or whether the Sarnesh just didn't come to Helleron much these days, given the place's weathervane loyalties. He saw various skins across from him – fishbelly white like Tallius of Tark, the bronze of Kes, ruddy exiles from Maynes eager to give some Wasps a bloody nose, even a single coal-black Vekken a long way from home.

Oh Master Tasky, your reach might just have exceeded your grasp.

They were better equipped and in better shape than Varmen's vermin, but there was an insuperable gap separating them from the Ant military ideal.

"Remember your orders," he told his men, still wondering just when they had become *his* men. "Form up."

There was a comment from one of the patrons that might have been, "Get on with it, then," and Tasky shouted, "Fight! No quarter!"

The Ants began advancing immediately but, although they had made a battle-line, Varmen could sense the joins in it, all the weak places where Ants of one city rubbed against those of another. True, all of them came from cities that had reasons to hate the Empire, but their enmity for each other was centuries old, and the mind-linking Art that they relied on would only work with their kin.

The tiny few who still had their stings began loosing, maimed palms spitting golden fire at the Ants who took the brunt on their shields, not a man of them going down. They had no way to fight back at range, though, and so they hesitated for a moment, and then lumbered into the charge that Varmen knew they would have to make.

He wanted to say, "Remember your orders!" again, because this next move could go very badly for him if his men didn't, but instead what came out was, "Pride of the Sixth!"

Sentinels stood and held the line, everyone knew that, the Ants included. Those who had never trained under that weight of steel believed it was because they *couldn't* move with any useful speed.

Varmen moved. He *ran.*

He was slow for the first few steps, then his body remembered how to do it and he was bearing down on the Ant line faster than they were bringing it to him. On either side, his rabble of Wasp deserters were trying to follow him up – *if I press forwards, follow* – making Varmen the weighted point of an impromptu phalanx.

He aimed himself like a ballista bolt, and when he struck it was between the Sarnesh and the Kessen elements of the enemy. His sheer momentum, and their instant response of falling back on those they considered their *own*, burst their line asunder.

Then it was blade-work. Varmen himself just braced against his shield, letting their blows rain on it or bounce from his armour. A sword struck his helm hard enough to rattle his teeth. Another tried to ram at the seam between back- and breastplate on his open right side, but skittered off the steel without biting. One of Varmen's followers lunged forwards and bloodied the Ant that tried it, driving his sword over the man's shield and severing a handful of mail links.

Varmen's own blade lashed out. It was not the heavy piece he had favoured in the army, just a standard soldier's short blade, but he got it in the faces of the enemy, first to one side, then the other, keeping each little clique of Ants busy and getting himself in the middle of them, stopping them uniting.

If they'd been Sarnesh all, we'd be dead by now. Had the Ants been able to share their thoughts then they could never have been thrown off like this, but Tasky... Varmen suddenly wondered whether Tasky had gone for this mishmash for that very reason – a thirty second fight would hardly be entertaining for his guests.

Even so, the Ants were starting to turn the scales against him. The Vekken was dead – stung in the back with nobody to watch for him – and the Tarkesh had pulled back out of the fight to regroup. The Wasps were keeping themselves on the move, hopping in with brief flurries of their wings to strike a blow, then out again before the Ants could pin them down. To Varmen's left, half a dozen Sarnesh had already killed their share of Wasps and won themselves a clear space, shield linked with shield, and Varmen knew that the Tarkesh would come in to support them any moment, after which they could sweep the Wasps to the wall.

Atric and the bulk of the others were trying to bait the little knot of Kessen and Maynesh, keeping on the move, darting in and out, into the air for brief hops to keep out of reach, and Varmen hoped that they would be able to hold just a little longer.

He gathered himself, and struck the Sarnesh shields like a hammer.

The Ants were strong by Art and training, but Varmen was as powerful as a lifetime in heavy steel could make him, and he weighed almost as much as two of them. His only concession to his own survival was that he came in shield first.

He felt the thunderous impact of metal on metal, and for a moment he thought that they would stave him off. Then there was abruptly a chaos of fallen men in front of him, and he went down to one knee in a jarring clatter, hard enough that he felt an Ant's ribs cave beneath him. A blow came in on his shoulder, glancing from the pauldron and showing that at least one enemy was still on his feet. He swung out, all the old senses informing him, and felt the tip of his blade connect with mail.

Another Wasp dropped beside him, the one-armed man, scalp bloodied driving his blade like a dagger down at the fallen. Varmen lurched to his feet, and one of the enemy leapt on him, trying to bear him down. For a moment he felt himself going, but he rebounded from a Sarnesh trying to stand, then Varmen dropped his sword and took hold of the man that had jumped him, getting a blow into the man's chin with a mailed fist and catching the collar of his hauberk and hurling the Ant from him.

The one-armed man pressed a new sword into his hand immediately. Varmen took stock.

There were two Sarnesh retreating from him. The Kessen and Maynesh seemed to be down. There were a couple of Tarkesh hanging back as well.

Varmen had the one-armed man, and a single one of his stingers left in the fight. Atric and the rest had been cut down. Before they had fallen, though, they had fought like soldiers of the Empire once more. Tasky had thought he was getting tired, sad fugitives – he had bought in men who, in turning their backs on the army, had found that they had left the best part of themselves behind. It had taken this little fake war to bring them back to whom they had once been, and it had killed most of them too.

"Pride of the Sixth," he said, in the hollow quiet of his helm, and then, *"Pride of the Sixth!"* a battle cry to make even Ant-kinden flinch. So what if there was no Sixth now? While he stood, it still had its pride.

The Ants were almost to the wall, waiting, three men and a woman behind four big shields. They had eyes only for Varmen now, trying to read the future in that dark slot that was all they could see of his face.

The stingshot came in at a sharp angle, the Wasp choosing his moment and his target, so that the man in the middle went down with a scream and his head crackling into flame. Varmen had not so much as glanced at his ally, but he had been ready for the moment. At moments such as that, who needed a mindlink?

And he was in motion again, seeing the sole living Tarkesh spring aside from the other two Ants, abruptly wanting nothing to do with the fight. The one-armed Wasp's wings flared and cast him in a shallow arc that brought him and the Tarkesh Ant tumbling down together,

The two Sarnesh braced, and this time they were ready, skidding so that their back heels touched the wall but holding him off. A sword point missed his eyeslit by an inch and jarred his head back. Another cut beneath his shield and buckled the articulated tassets over his hip.

Stingshot exploded from one Ant's shield, and then the last Wasp had come to Varmen's aid, hooking a hand over the enemy's shield-rim and dragging it down. The Ant's sword struck home, opening the Wasp's throat, but Varmen's own blade was in motion, taking advantage of the opening, and he rammed it through the thin mail beneath the Ant's armpit and dragged it out before it could stick.

The other Sarnesh hacked at him, sword striking at the juncture between shoulder and neck, but Varmen's pauldrons had ridges to prevent just that, and the man's sword snapped off at the quillons.

Shame on you, Tasky, for buying cheap, and Varmen killed his enemy.

In the wake of that he expected more fighting, but the pit around him was very still. He swept his narrow slot of a view across the scene, finding not one other fighter standing, on either side. Here and there the wounded whimpered or cursed, or dragged themselves away from him, and he saw that, most likely, half the Ants would live, and perhaps two of his own.

He drew his helm off, starting to feel all the new bruises and aches he had just earned, and looked up at Tasky and his audience. The promoter himself looked as though he had died, all his debonair elegance drained from him, leaving only a Beetle wearing bad clothes badly, a clown capering before his betters. Varmen expected him to curse, to rage and bombast like a true man of the theatre, but something had happened to Alester Tasky during the course of the fight. Some memory, some old wound that Varmen would never know of, had aged him into a brittle, fragile thing. Stenne, beside him with her hand on his arm, seemed more a nurse than an employee.

Of the audience itself, the great and the good of Helleron looked as though they had seen better. A couple were discussing the merits of the fight, but the rest just looked on Varmen as though they were waiting for him to do something more entertaining than part lives from bodies.

Some looked bored.

Varmen shook his head, feeling as though he wanted to fly up there, hack open the net, run amok amongst those captains of industry to show them the true meaning of what they had just witnessed. In the end, though, the weight of his mail kept his feet on the ground.

"It's Malkan's *Stand*, not Malkan's *Folly*," he told them, hearing his own voice rough and cracked. "And you better bloody remember that when we come *back*."

It had been an empty threat, for him. There was no *we*. The Empire would retake Helleron with ease – and probably with consent – when the time came, but Varmen would not be with them. There was no place for a man in that armour under the Black and Gold any more.

He had paid off Huron Albrake, to the man's surprise, but only because he needed somewhere to sit and think. He could see the path he had been treading during his days in Helleron, and it was a downwards spiral that led where Tallius had gone. If he stayed here, he would be lost to the drink and the drudgery, and sooner or later he would pawn his prized armour for a bowl of wine, and that would be the end of him. Without his mail he was not the same man. Tallius had done him a service, forcing the knowledge on him while he was still able to act on it.

So he took the balance of Tasky's money and he purchased a little pack-beetle that could carry his armour, even though the creature seemed almost lost beneath it. He stood there, on the streets of Helleron, knowing that the Lowlands did not want him and the Empire was denied to him.

It did not matter. He only had one destination in mind, and it was easily realised.

Varmen was getting out.

If Dal Arche and co have maintained at least a flat trajectory from the straits they found themselves in, in the last collection, this is Varmen's nadir. Amongst all the losses of the war, his is a small and unexpected one: no more Sentinels. The technology of the Apt has outstripped them at last.

This, then, is the second Helleron story, the *contes cruels* of the kinden world. My inspiration, in creating that multi-stata world of penury and desperation, is less Villiers than Hugo and Gorky's *The Lower Depths*, which seems mighty grand for a story about people who can fly, but hopefully I have struck at least an echo in the tale of Tallius, Varmen, Tasky and the rest, all of them victims of the ever-hungry city.

Alicaea's Children

A month ago, the greatest professional challenge for Brandon Halfways had been getting from his lodgings to his office each morning without catching the eye of the landlord of either, both having a nasty tendency to lurk when the rent was overdue.

How life simplifies itself! Ever since he had crept home late one evening to find a family of Fly-kinden crammed into his digs, he counted himself a happier man. After all, sleeping in a cupboard in his own office meant no more tedious walking to work and, if it lends the environs a certain air of sweaty fug, he likes to think that's what his clients seek him out for.

Because, he knows, you already have to be half past desperate to want the services of a quisitor like Brandon Halfways. The sour smell of unwash that has begun to stalk his office in recent days is entirely in keeping with the reek of impoverished need that his clients bring with them.

He has lost track of the missing heirlooms that turn out to have been pawned, of the lost relatives already found in the river by the guard, of the bright futures that the city of Helleron has chewed up and spat out. These days, the only real service he feels he provides is to soften the blow.

A quisitor: finder of the missing, uncoverer of the hidden, follower of the fugitive. There's a good living to be made, if you have a reputation and a pedigree. Brandon has both, neither good. The pedigree is the sticking point. Few people like a halfbreed and nobody likes a half-Moth. What a combination! What is it that turns his clients' eyes away most? Is it the miscegenation that shows in his skin: the regular dark brown of his Beetle mother blotched and tarnished by his father's pale grey? Or is it simply his paternal link with the old days, the Moth days, when people believed any damned thing and nobody had heard of progress?

Brandon's remaining landlord has yet to resort to the crowbar, but if rent money doesn't feature in their mutual future that's likely to change. Brandon has clients, but all poorer than he is. What little they pay barely buys a meal while his creditors grow more numerous and more demanding.

Not for the first time he thinks about getting out. Collegium is easier on a halfbreed, they say, though probably not actually *easy*. He'd need money, though. He'd need to accumulate more than what he needs to live on, and not just piss it away.

The tiny window in his office lets in a single shaft of grimy sunlight. Brandon gets a lamp going, well aware that oil is another luxury. Helleron is a city of a thousand bright lights, the burning might of the Apt Beetle-kinden whose machines drive the mills of commerce and industry night and day. Where Brandon lives, all those lamps seem to cast nothing but shadows.

A man steps into his office, startling Brandon from his introspection: a stocky Beetle-kinden wearing a heavy coat, a broad-brimmed hat shadowing his face. He's a man trying to look rough, but Brandon sees that even the scuffed old clothes are well made and fit the man too neatly for cast-offs. Brandon smells money.

What the other man smells most is plainly Brandon. "You're the quisitor?"

Brandon nods cautiously, waiting to see which of his creditors the man has come from. The actual words surprise him: "I need your services."

Looking at him, the only logical thought is, *No, you don't. You want Parry on Feller Way, or you want those Ant-kinden brothers. You surely don't want me.*

What he says is, "Of course you do."

The atmosphere of the office plainly spurs his visitor to get to business quickly. "You find people," the man says, looming.

"It's been known. Sometimes I even get paid for it." Calm and collected, slightly detached, that's the quisitor way.

The Beetle tilts back his hat to get a better look at Brandon. "Find someone for me." There's a pouch in his hand and he empties it on the desk: a scattering of coin, at least four gold. "That's for expenses. Find her, and you'll get ten times that."

The professional thing is to nod, certainly not to choke over the money and then demand "Why me?"

"Because of your face."

The missing woman's name is Temasena. She is a guest of the city's elite.

"You're aware of our *guests* of course," the big man says. Brandon is. Everyone is. Not so long ago Helleron found itself within the curtilage of the Wasp Empire. At the end of the last war the Imperial tide ebbed away but nobody's under any illusions. The Wasps will be back, and everyone wants them to come as rich friends, not vengeful enemies.

One such *guest* is a Captain Kander, an officer in the Wasp Consortium. He's not exactly a big noise, but his superiors back home are. The Council are keen to keep him happy, and one obvious way of doing so is not having his wife vanish into the streets of Helleron.

"Why did he bring his wife?" is Brandon's question.

"Why do Wasps do anything?" The visitor doesn't seem to like the Empire much.

"Any leads? Helleron's a big city." That sounds more like the sort of thing that a quisitor's supposed to say.

"Unfortunately, yes. There's a fairly strong rumour about where the girl's gone. Word puts her near Winding Square, and on the Astos, and thence to…"

"The Alicaea," Brandon gives it the old name, also known as: "Alice Street."

"I knew you were the right man."

The old town. The Inapt quarter. Not a town, not even a quarter, but Brandon knows it: a dense tangle of streets in the pits of Helleron where the gaslight never quite reaches and the shadows never quite lift. Before the revolution, when the city was run by the Moths and their sham magic, that was their place of power. Now it's their place of degradation, their last shabby foothold within the city. "What are they saying?" he asks, not sure that he wants to hear the answer. *Dead? Or worse than dead?* There are consistent rumours about what the Inapt do, in the shadows, in the dark. Everyone hears them. Everyone knows someone who knew someone who had lost someone to their ancient, evil ways.

"I've sent people there. Nobody talks to the authorities." The big man shrugs, abandoning his pretence at rough-handed poverty. "But you've got their blood. Maybe they'll talk to you. What do you say?"

What Brandon thinks is, *I need the money*, but what he says is, "Yes."

It's true: Brandon has had cause to go as far as Alice Street before, but just because he and the Inapt are equally disliked by the Apt majority doesn't mean the Inapt like him. He's Apt himself, after all: a creature of light and progress and the *now*, rather than the threadbare old traditions that the Inapt cling to. And of course, they don't like halfbreeds any more than anyone else does.

He has a contact, though. And, if he's bare-pocket poor, then at least he's in good company. Nobody in Alice Street has money. The only living to be had there is the fickle patronage of the Apt, who count it daring to come there and laughingly have their fortunes told, or see an antique dance that always seems to leave someone naked at the end. The sullen truth is that all those ancient secrets boil down to nothing more than a nest of charlatans, burlesque shows and brothels.

Brandon seeks out the Theatre Hagarastos, looking for his actor contact, finding that he is too late.

"Show's closed." Hagarastos himself is a cadaverous Moth, grey skin creased as though he had spent a month folded in someone's pocket, white eyes stained yellow around the edges. He's rehearsing a troupe of dancers who are already three-quarters undressed when Brandon walks in. "Was doing well. Unpopular with the Lamps, though. They had a word. I know when to quit." *Lamps* meant the wider authority of Helleron. Artificial light symbolises the Apt and their revolution: Moths can see in the dark.

"So where's Albaris now?" Brandon presses. The dancers watch him cautiously. They're also Moths, of all ages from fourteen to forty, but they share the same jaded, world-worn expression. Nearby, a Fly-kinden man paints: *See the wonders of the ancient world: female votaries perform rites of forbidden magic!*

Brandon never knew his Moth father, but the whole business makes him inexpressibly sad.

Melancholy pays no bills, though. Albaris will be at the Taverna Semos if he's anywhere, says Hagarastos, and will Brandon kindly leave because they've a lot of rehearsing to do.

Albaris is a slight, pallid Spider-kinden, his careworn face knuckley as a puppet's. He's got up in a tattered robe stitched with coiling designs, having gone to the Semos to panhandle some coin with conjuring tricks, but the taverna is quiet. The whole of the Alicaea seems underpopulated, the moneyed clientele thin on the ground. By the time Brandon arrives, Albaris has spent his accumulated hoard on a shallow bowl of wine.

The look he turns on the quisitor is wary. Who knows if the halfbreed's errand isn't injurious to Albaris's health? The offer of another bowl of wine makes up for that, Brandon rationing out his expenses with a miser's hand. He waits until they have a table and then drops the missing woman's name into the conversation.

"Temasena," Albaris echoes hollowly. "Oh yes, just what we need. A Wasp girl goes missing and suddenly it's *us*." There are a hundred internecine rivalries down Alice Street, the feuding factions of a whole lost world compressed into a handful of rotting tenements. Against the wider city, though, it's *us* and *them*. "Probably she was never here, but suddenly it's the old story: someone gets lost and everyone's looking for dark rituals and bloody knives."

"I don't suppose…"

Albaris stops him with a hard stare that would have done justice to any magician of old. "Don't you finish that sentence," he snaps. "Don't you *dare*, Halfways." To Brandon's embarrassment the Spider hunches over his wine, almost in tears. "As if it wasn't hard enough, in this city. As if just *living* didn't take up all the strength we have. You think we take nice Apt girls for unspeakable rites? No, what we do, we get a good job, a decent role, and so what if it's sending up the Wasp Empire just a bit? And then the Lamps come and tell us, no, you're offending our *guests*. And so here I am, and I can't even make enough to buy bread because some stupid girl left her man and now people don't want to come here anymore." The wine bowl shakes and Albaris slams it defiantly down. "You want to know what happened to her? Well here in Alice Street we have our own people who find lost things. Go see one of them. I'll even give you an address. All the secrets of the world, for just a handful of coins."

The address is one of those crumbling tenements, where the old grey stone of some ancient palace has been divided and subdivided into dozens of little rooms, on top and underneath and behind each other, each a tiny Inapt kingdom. Here they live, the denizens of Alice Street: the Moths, the Spiders, the Commonweal war refugees, people whose lives fold each night to the length and breadth of a single straw mattress.

The building's manageress is another halfbreed, with an Ant's stocky frame and skin threaded with strands of light and dark. Brandon gives her the address and her surly manner changes immediately: servile, eager to help. "Yes, yes, you should have said. The seer, Madame Ellesthaen, yes. Follow, do."

Following, Brandon treads dingy, leaning corridors, picking his way by the light of windows either filthy or boarded-up. A flight of worn stairs takes him away even from that, descending through degrees of gloom until they stop at a door.

It's a fine door, perhaps original to the building: intricately worked stone turned into a study in shadow by the poor light. The manageress doesn't knock, hissing, "Madame, I have one who seeks your guidance."

There's a faint whisper from within that Brandon barely catches, and then the door swings open on utter nothing.

Brandon stares into the pitch dark, thinking of all those things that can happen to a man who walks into a lightless room and has not inherited the dark-piercing eyes of his Moth father. Suddenly Albaris's denials seem a lot less convincing.

"No light," the manageress whispers reverently. "Madame must have no light within her chambers. There are secrets there that would burn the eyes out of your Apt head." She retreats up the stairs.

"Speak, stranger." The voice is female, imperious, pitched to send a shiver through Brandon's body. It seems to issue out of a cavernous space, great vaulted halls consigned entirely to the dark.

"I..." He coughs. "I've been sent to look for someone. Someone lost. I'm told you might know something."

"No," comes the prompt answer. "I do not know *something*. I am the last and greatest of the true seers of this city. There is no limit to the things that I might know. If your offerings are acceptable to the invisible powers of the world, then perhaps what you seek can be uncovered."

For a moment, she has him, and his shrivelled little Apt soul trembles before the promise of ancient magic. Then he comes to his senses and recognizes the patter for what it is. Not so different to his own, save that it's pitched at a different market.

"Fine," he shrugs. "So what sort of offering do you have in mind?" He's just drawing his composure about himself again when she steps from the darkness. It seems to him that she comes from a great distance, far more than the building can contain, approaching as the one bright thing in all that pent-up night: an apparition out of time. She's a Moth, of course, grey-skinned and white-eyed, her dark hair held back by golden pins. She is young, starkly beautiful as a statue, and she wears a gown that gleams with the secret fires of silks, lined with bright bee-fur and cascading with iridescent butterfly scales, so that even the feeble light from the stairway cascades across her and is changed to strange hues. The darkness around her throngs with shapes never quite glimpsed, as if the reflected glory of her garment is cast back again by the riches of a vanished world: a throne, a carven chest, a suit of gilded mail...

Standing there, at the heart of this direly impoverished district, of all the filth and grime, the implied wealth in that one robe is obscene, compelling. Sorceress or not, *here* is power. Brandon comes perilously close to falling to his knees.

"Come," she tells him. "If you are to be a supplicant then you shall do this the right way, the old way." With that, she sweeps past him, gliding up the stairs with the manageress preceding her like a herald.

"In the Old Days," and the capital letters are right there in the way she says it, "this was a place of power. Supplicants came from across the Lowlands to seek the wisdom of the seers, and make offering in return." Madame Ellesthaen looks at Brandon coolly past the glittering collar of her gown, that seems to suck all the day into its darkly burning depths and turn the light out again, transformed and in her thrall. "This is where great Alicaea held court. Some say she still does." Uttering the name seems to momentarily draw the notice of every Inapt vagrant and panhandler in eyeshot.

Still: "It's a restaurant," Brandon gets out.

Her blank white eyes bore into him from her thin, grey, perfect face. "Be thankful that you may still make your offering here."

"I'm not sure I want the wisdom of the seers."

"Little halfbreed, of all the things *wanting* in you, wisdom is surely the greatest."

"You can tell me where the Wasp is?"

She moves past him towards the eatery's low door. "Make your offering, and hope Alicaea finds it acceptable. Or go, and remain forever ignorant."

Inside, it's maddeningly dim, and an arch, impassive Moth leads them to the last of a succession of close-walled booths. A single candle there casts a feeble light that shimmers across Ellesthaen like a miniature sunset and turns her featureless eyes into twin stars.

"Here it was that Alicaea sat, great lady of this city before it was ever known as Helleron." Her voice is soft and yet ponderous with import. "Alicaea, who is now only a fading echo to our new Apt masters. She, whose breath swayed armies, become nothing but a whisper in the dark. Here, she decided the fate of hundreds, told the futures of thousands. Here her spirit clings on, in this earth, in these shadows, on this street, that she may inhabit me and grant me the sight that you require."

One of the staff is near, kneeling at the table, and Brandon glances nervously at Ellesthaen who nods once. He passes over the coins: the sacred offering of a suitor to a queen amongst magi, hidden within the price of a meal.

The food, when it comes, is slender strips and snips of things, vegetables either near-raw or cooked into tastelessness. Everything is grey or white, and with no more flavour than colour to Brandon's robust Apt palate. While waiting for the meal he has set out the sordid, meagre details of Temasena's fate, and now he watches Ellesthaen meticulously clear her plate with the air of ritual, each morsel consumed to appease some hostile ghost.

He has a horrible sense of time wasting. Some primal part of him is still recovering from the sheer awe the woman engendered, but more practical elements are rising to the ascendant.

"So, wisdom," he prompts.

"Are you sure you wish that? It seldom brings happiness."

"Well, when you find something that does in this forsaken city, you let me know."

"Alicaea sees you, halfbreed. She knows you."

"I didn't come here to *ask* about me. I know me just fine." Abruptly his patience kicks him. "Listen, lady – you do your mystic act fine, but I was passed to you because you know things. Tell me it's the wisdom of Alice Street all you like, but just tell me: what happened to Temasena? Because, ugly as it is, it's going to get uglier round here if she doesn't surface."

Ellesthaen rises to her feet abruptly and he starts back. For a moment there is something more about her, the candle-light lending her a greater shadow than her slight frame can cast.

Then the waiter's at his elbow, passing him a folded slip of paper. A single line is written there that nearly pops Brandon's eyes out of his head.

"You... the, what...?" he manages as the seer scrutinises him coolly.

Temasena is with Councilman Scordrey in one of his townhouses. They are lovers.

"You can't just..." Brandon crumples the paper. "I can't... Proof, woman. I need proof. How did you find this out?"

Ellesthaen's expression is pure, refined disdain. "I did not 'find this out', halfbreed. It is the gift of Alicaea, borne on the shadows of her breath. There is no *proof.* Proof is for the Apt and their measuring and machines." She brushes past him, her gown smouldering with muted fire. "And do not come to our places and presume to judge our ways. Alicaea has weighed you. Be grateful she does not choose to truly open your eyes."

Several barbed comebacks occur to him, after he's well out of the Inapt Quarter and on his way back to the office. At the time he could no more have interrupted her exit than he could have arrested the moon.

Brandon sends word to his patron immediately, meeting the man in a taverna near his office and telling a pack of lies in which that one line of impossible revelation nestles like a pearl. Still got up as a well-do-to poor man, the client nods thoughtfully.

"I see," is all the man says at the end, rubbing at his chin. "And you can back this up, of course."

Brandon tries to look him in the eye. "It's not like I can go knock on Councilman Scordrey's door. But I thought maybe... if you had an in with the council... you could..."

The patron lets out one bleak bark of laughter. "Halfbreed, the name's Greenwise Artector. I'm *on* the council."

Brandon sits very still. Twelve men and a woman run Helleron, the richest and most entrenched of all the magnates. Dangerous people to share a room with, even more so to question.

Still: "So what were you expecting?"

Artector stares at his hands, disgruntled. "Something I could use. Something I could paste about the town: some fate for the woman that wouldn't stir up a mob." He cocks an eye at Brandon. "Maybe something that would help me get at the Wasps, if you want what's in it for me. Scordrey's well in with them, though. So far in that a jilted captain won't dislodge him, not without proof. Scordrey's star is up. Mine's not. I can't challenge him without more."

"So...?" Brandon presses.

If he's hoping for the money, he's disappointed. "You get me proof, you get paid," Artector murmurs. "Right now I've got nothing but some story from some halfbreed in a taverna." It's plain that he believes it, but nobody ever got rich by paying when they don't have to. "See you soon, Quisitor."

Left behind like driftwood, Brandon decides that expenses will stretch to wine, and another bowl after that seems only courteous, to toast the passing of his career. It's only with the third in front of him that Artector's loose words finally connect with something in his head.

Councilman Scordrey is topping the Wasp captain's wife. How the other half lives! Except the two sweethearts want some time to themselves, and even the most inattentive husband's liable to notice a prolonged absence of wife eventually.

So where do you go, to explain that absence? Alice Street. Those villainous Inapt and their wicked ways, after all. Everyone knows about it. Everyone gets very angry about it, now and then. And sometimes everyone decides to *do* something about it.

A mob, Artector had said: some fate that wouldn't stir up a mob.

Brandon stands suddenly, light-headed, and stumbles off back towards the Alicaea.

Brandon knows Helleron mobs. They're built of down-at-heels tradesmen, tramp artificers, factory labourers. Poor, honest people with poor, honest prejudices; people who hear from someone that some Apt girl's gone missing, and somehow find space in their grim lives to bring justice by way of violent persecution. Brandon's seen that human tide in motion before, unstoppable in its angry righteousness. And yet those downtrodden, vengeful, callous-handed men never turn that force of nature on those who deserve it. Their rough fists only beat on the doors of those who have even less than they. The true originators of their misery, men like Councilman Scordrey, sit far off in their drawing rooms and, tut over how dreadful it all is.

That is his plan when he sets off: he's going to turn the mob against the bearers of false witness. He's going to stand before that boiling riot of humanity and tell them they've been made fools of. At the start of his run, he's s a hero.

At the end, when he arrives wheezing onto Alice Street, he's barely a spectator.

The mob hasn't stirred itself yet. There's not nearly enough damage for that. This was a mere herald: a gang of Beetle-kinden apprentices who, outraged and drunk as evening drew on, descended on Alice Street and broke windows and gave the locals a kicking. There had been a dozen hurt, Albaris said. One old woman had died.

The Spider-kinden actor sits outside the broken front of the Semos, a patched cloak pulled taut about his bony shoulders. His eyes follow a pair of guardsmen who are cataloguing the mess without any suggestion that it's their problem. They work with brisk efficiency. They want out of the Alicaea before full nightfall.

"*Lamps,*" the Spider spits tiredly. "No justice for us. Nobody cares. Nobody helps." Within his version of events is the plain implication that he himself saw it all, and did nothing. "And you?"

Brandon tells him what Ellesthaen's tip-off said, where the truant Wasp girl has supposedly holed up after sparking the little rumour that set off this landslide.

"She must be laughing," whispers Albaris, and he shudders. "They'll be back. This was just the start. I've seen it before. Why won't you bastards just leave us alone?"

Brandon sighs. "I need to speak to the seer. I need to know where she got it from, her information."

"It was *magic*. She's a seer."

"Save it for the marks." Brandon stands, but Albaris tugs at his sleeve.

"Is there nothing stirring in you, halfbreed, that whispers 'magic'?

Even when you met the seer, nothing?"

Brandon thinks briefly of Ellesthaen's talk of Alicaea, lost lady of Helleron-that-was. He whips his sleeve free and moves on, Albaris trailing miserably behind.

The manageress meets then at the door, her face lopsided with bruising. "Madame is not taking visitors," she hisses, but Brandon pushes past her.

"I need to know how she knew," he insists, imagining the halfbreed woman and the Spider exchanging exasperated Inapt looks.

He had intended to storm down the stairs, but the descent is black as wells, the feeble lamplight from above barely lasting five steps, as though the primordial darkness of Ellesthaen's lair has roused for the night and is creeping up to feed. Brandon hesitates, and the manageress catches him up, remonstrating frantically.

He spoke no more than the truth, though. He needs to know. He needs his proof, his payment, his road out of Helleron.

He looks back, and the manageress flinches, her earlier beating robbing her of courage. Brandon pushes past, wrests a little oil lamp from the wall, and then heads back down the stairs.

"No!" the manageress shrieks. "The light – you must not!" but she doesn't dare try to stop him, not with the angry purpose thrumming through his frame. *Let's see it then,* he thinks. *Let's see your room of wonders, Madame. Let's see the hoarded wealth of days past that you keep down here, where nobody can see.*

He finds the fantastically carved door and puts a hand to it, calling out the seer's name. No response.

He rests a shoulder against the door and shoves, finding it unlocked, unlatched, swinging open so readily for him that he stumbles to his knees. Lantern held high, he feels like a tomb-robber, a thief of ancient places. He looks about him for the cavernous, windowless hall heaped with a magnate's ransom of antique treasures.

What draws his eyes most is the bucket.

It stands in the centre of the floor, a wooden pail of clouded water. Around it, the close, low-ceilinged walls of the small room are all amply lit by the feeble reach of the lamp. They are carved with the same abstract figures as the door, worn by the same lost ages. They are bare, though. The tapestries, the silks and cloth of gold fall away into the land of might-have-been when touched by his intruding light. The floor is plain stone, with a straw mattress in one corner covered by a woollen blanket, and what catches at him is how meticulously clean it all is, how carefully swept with that peculiar pride the very poor sometimes have.

Madame Ellesthaen is backed into a corner, a shaking hand up to block out the light. She wears only a shift and has been worked over more than the manageress, her delicate grey face blotched, one eye almost swollen shut. In the centre of the room, that magnificent gown hangs over the bucket, dripping dry. The image comes to him of the woman washing out the grime and bloodstains of her beating, trying to restore the magnificence of her sole claim to grandeur with desperate care. There is nothing else, no treasure of the ancient world. That one garment *is* Madame Ellesthaen, far more than the trembling woman trying to push her shoulder-blades into the stone at her back. He remembers the cost, then, of her inexplicable wisdom: an offering disguised as the price of a meal, that was really a meal disguised an offering. He recasts her thin face and slender frame from ethereal to half-starved.

Something breaks in him, and he realises that some part of him really had believed in the ancient glory of Alicaea. He feels the numb disappointment of the child who discovers how the trick is done. He's left only with a sick pity, and a biting sense of a grand injustice he cannot repair.

Albaris is sitting at the top of the stairs, waiting for him.

"She said the seer tried to turn the crowd away." The Spider jerks his head after the vanished manageress. "She had them, for a moment, then someone threw something and she flinched, and…" His real melancholy always looks put-on for comic effect. "How…?"

"Hurt," Brandon grunts, sitting down beside him. "And there's a mob gathering out there that'll make this little fracas look like chucking out time."

"Like you care."

Brandon, stares at the dying flame of the lamp, finding that he does. Perhaps his Inapt father's blood stirs in him at last. Perhaps he is touched by the memory of Ellesthaen's arch pride, that hollow eggshell over the depths of her circumstances. Perhaps he doesn't want to think of Scordrey and Temasena laughing over the news of riots and murder in the Alicaea.

"I care," he says, sounding surprised.

"The seeker of proof cares," comes that firm, soft voice. "So what now?"

They see Ellesthaen halfway up the stairs, the furthest extent of the lamplight playing on her face's new colours.

"Temasena's not coming out any time soon, not until it's too late," Brandon guesses. "Nobody's going to poke their nose into Scordrey's business to catch sight of her. Even that captain, her husband, won't push Scordrey, Artector as good as said. We can't beat the councilman. He's too big. And when the mob comes tomorrow, what do you have?"

"What the Inapt have always had," she whispers. "Smoke and mirrors."

"All the smoke and mirrors in the world won't save you from them," is Brandon's verdict. In fact there is only one thing that can defuse the mob.

Proof. Pure, simple proof. Or at least something that looks enough like it in a bad light.

The next day there is a new rumour abroad in the city. Just as the incensing news spread that poor Temasena went walking in the shadows of Alice Street and never returned, now people are saying that she's back, unharmed. In fact, the rumour persists, she is telling the world *precisely* what she thinks on a number of subjects, including the Wasp Empire, the city of Helleron and more.

Naturally, there's considerable resistance to this. Those Helleren from districts bordering the Alicaea have already stoked themselves up for a bit of vigilante arson. A lot of them storm over to dispel the inconvenient suggestion that their martyred victim is alive and well.

They find her at the Theatre Hagarastos, holding forth to a packed auditorium. The sight is so unexpected, so mesmerising, that they end up handing the old Moth their small change for the opportunity to hear Temasena the captain's wife hold forth.

She tells them a great deal during the hour that she's up on stage. She talks about their betters, their employers, their landlords. She regales them with the scandals she's seen as a guest of Helleron, the black comedy of affairs and furtive assignations, gluttonies and cruelties. She talks in pointed tones about Wasp men and their inadequacies. She parodies the manners of Helleron's council and other great men of the city, citing her personal experience of their failings.

She's funny. She's pithy. She plays them. The nascent mob listens, the thunderhead of its undirected ire slowly abandoning a clearing sky.

For all this was his idea, Brandon isn't sure how it's come to this. There is no way it should work. True, none of the audience has ever *seen* Temasena, and true, to a Beetle a lot of the paler kinden look quite similar, so that a slender Spider-kinden man can squeeze into a padded dress and burlesque a Wasp woman. Even made up, and even with a blonde wig, Albaris shouldn't be able to pull it off, though. He has the gaunt face and high forehead of a debauched philosopher. On that stage, however, Brandon has to concentrate to see the man behind the mimicry. He's never watched Albaris truly *act* before. Every gesture, every step and stance speaks of the female: a fierce, spiteful, funny, half-drunken woman that matches everyone's expectations of how a Wasp wife would be, if let off the leash. When Albaris laughs scornfully at some reported faux pas of Temasena's husband, and asks the world where the real men are, he could have his pick of his enraptured audience.

Albaris plays to packed houses for two more evenings, as fractured versions and variations of the story of Temasena radiate out through the city like cracking ice, from the mouths of the lowly to the ears of the great.

Brandon is on edge through each show, waiting for the endgame. After all, there are certain ears out there which must be burning with the lurid tales that Albaris tells through Temasena's purloined lips. There will be a reckoning. He's desperately counting on it being the Wasp woman herself whose indignation drives her to denounce the imposter and, incidentally, confirm her own continuing health. That is, after all, the plan.

Events do not quite run like that.

Brandon's place at the show is far left of the stage, sitting with his back to the proscenium and watching the audience. This last evening, someone taps his shoulder, making him start. He glances around, seeing nothing but shadow, then making out Ellesthaen's grey skin. She's foregone Alicaea's glorious robe: just a skinny Moth woman in a simple dress, and he hadn't realised that she was there.

"At the back," she murmurs, and he strains his eyes to see. She has to guide him until he catches that one pale face within the dark of the Helleron crowd. His heart clenches.

Captain Kander has come for his wife.

Brandon stands slowly and edges up the aisle, his eyes fixed on the man, expecting that the captain will just put out a hand and unleash the crackling fire of the dreaded Wasp sting. Kander just watches, as a Spider in drag impersonates his wife, and when Brandon is close enough to see the man's expression, he finds only a forlorn, lost misery there. Kander listens to himself, his Empire and his gender being lampooned, and his expression is one of utmost bereavement, a man who has loved well but not wisely. At no point does he ever appear to realise that the parody on the stage is not his wife, and he leaves before the show is done.

Brandon and Albaris retire to the dressing room afterwards, the Spider turning up the one murky lantern and then posing amidst the clutter of costumes with his hands demurely across his artificial bosom.

"I know, I know, it's appalling what one does for a living," he exalts.

"Your – her husband was in," Brandon tells him. "He was right there. He didn't know. How could he not know?"

Albaris' smile throngs with mischief and secrets. "Magic, darling."

Brandon rolls his eyes. "Oh, of course," but Albaris's face is abruptly serious.

"Magic, Halfways. Shadow and suggestion. It's the last true magic, but it's magic all the same. Because the shadows can hold anything."

"Oh, they can." The voice is sharp, weirdly familiar. From behind a rack of gauzy costumes steps a pale woman with fair hair. "So, my useless husband was in, was he? And did nothing? Craven bastard." She sounds irresistibly like Albaris had, in his act. "You like making fun, do you? Making me your laughing stock." She is between them and the door, a hand extended towards them, palm out ready to sting.

"You like having people avenge your supposed murder while you cosy up to a councilman?" Brandon asks her.

"I can live with it," she tells them. "Shame you can't say the same."

Albaris pulls his wig off slowly, looking twenty years older and a whole lot more male.

"You've taken your last bow, actor," the Wasp informs him, then, to Brandon: "Where do you fit in, anyway?"

"I'm his agent," he tells her smoothly. "We're thinking of touring the provinces. Come along. You could be his understudy."

For a moment Temasena chokes on his words, the sheer mad provocation of them freezing her in place, and then Brandon's mad plan to rush her is foiled when the lantern abruptly dies.

The room is plunged into darkness instantly, and Brandon drops for the floor as Temasena's sting spits twice, cauterizing the room in brief flashes, lighting her way to her victims.

After that second flare Brandon braces for the inevitable searing impact, but instead Temasena demands, "Who are you?"

Brandon lifts his head and sees a figure interposed between the Wasp and her prey. The lantern has resurrected itself, a fickle flame drowning in a swamp of wax, and the light falls on the shimmer of butterfly scales, on the bee fur and spider silk that comprise Ellesthaen's robe, the one she neglected to bring tonight.

The hairs stand up on Brandon's neck, and he hears the Moth proclaim, "I am the lady of this place, and you have brought harm to my children."

There's a trembling moment before Temasena remembers who she is and thrusts a hand out at Ellesthaen's face. "I've not even started," she snarls. "I'll go back to Scordrey and have them level every shack in this shithole, looking for me. I'll see every denizen of Alice Street sent to the Empire in chains, for daring to mock me." But her voice shakes, just a little, at this apparition.

"You will not," Ellesthaen pronounces, her voice resonant with ancient power. "You will go back to your own land and never trouble us again."

"And what if I don't?" And if Temasena's sting is locked within her hand for now, a prisoner of the glamour that Ellesthaen has woven about herself, that cannot last. She is building her courage back, and Brandon remembers that the Moth has tried to face down the crowd before, and how that turned out. Any moment, the Wasp will wrest herself free, and then Ellesthaen will die. He can see it in the narrowing of Temasena's eyes, the steadying of her hand.

But the Moth is possessed of infinite calm. "You spread the lie that you came to the shadows of my realm, and the shadows did terrible things to you," she whispers, and the dying lantern draws the darkness around her, layer upon layer. "If you do not quit my domain now, you shall have written your own end. I am Alicaea, and you are friendless in my place after nightfall. Another breath, and all the stories you have ever heard of the Inapt will be true."

What Temasena sees in Ellesthaen's face then, Brandon can never know, but the Moth takes a single step forwards, dragging the shadows along with the train of her robe, and the Wasp woman's eyes go horribly wide and she screams.

When Brandon and Albaris get back to the auditorium, Temasena has already fled into the street, and Ellesthaen sits there in her plain dress, bruised face mustering an expression of distant curiosity, answering no questions.

Temasena appears at her husband's lodgings the next morning, shivering and wild-eyed and demanding to return to the Empire. She's got some mad story about the Inapt terrors of Alice Street but the version of her disappearance that is told all over the city draws far more on Albaris's extemporisations than anything the real Temasena ever said.

A tenday later, a messenger passes by Brandon's office with Artector's money. There is no note of thanks but, folded at the bottom of the pouch, a letter of introduction to a certain statesman of Collegium, in case Brandon wishes to make a start there. How Artector knew of his plans, he could not say.

It would be easy, now, to pack his few belongings and buy a ticket to take him west, by rail, by airship, all the wonders of the Apt age at his disposal. He's not sure why he doesn't start out the moment the comforting weight of coin hits his hand.

Instead, he finds his feet turning him back towards Alice Street, with its ragged entertainments and its delusions of old grandeur, the blood of his Moth father singing a soft song in his veins. Somewhere in the shadows is a thin girl in a borrowed robe. Somewhere in the night is the terrifying, comforting presence that is Alicaea. Somewhere, the magic is still real.

Just as 'Fallen Heroes' was a kinden Western, here we have kinden Noir on the mean streets of Helleron. The idea of a kind of buddy cop team of Apt and Inapt, with the Inapt seer solving the crimes through divination and the Apt detective/policeman then having to justify the result by post-facto joining of the evidential dots is something I wanted to do for a long time, and perhaps Brandon and Ellesthaen will continue in partnership in later stories.

This is also a good look at how the world of the Inapt and their magic actually function in, literally, the shadow of the Apt, and it went to some dark places I wasn't necessarily planning at the start. There are a lot of historical echoes front and centre in the series, and the treatment received by the inhabitants of Alice Street, a ghetto in all but name, is familiar enough fare.

A Time for Grief

When she closed her eyes, she could see them: two men fighting, one shadow-dark, one bright like the sun.

They had brought her to this place. They talked to her, the old Roach man, his daughters, all the others who had survived. They had such enthusiasm, such plans. She looked through them. It was not the living she saw. Two men, sword against sword, dark and light. She sat in shadows, denied the sunlight that fed her, and had eyes only for her memories of when everything had gone wrong.

"Freedom!" Balkus announced, taking in the vista.

"Freedom from what? Hygiene?" Sperra asked him acidly.

"You don't get it." The big Ant-kinden looked out over the messy expanse of tents and shacks and lean-tos. "Look at them all. What've we got here? Tarkesh who don't want to go and put Tark back together; Spiders from Seldis and all that; we've got Mynans, we've got Solarnese, we've got about a dozen different flavours of escaped slave from the Empire. I mean, we've got Wasps, even, who skipped out on the black and gold."

"And how are you with that?" Sperra asked him. "I mean, killing Wasps has been your thing for quite a while."

Balkus considered the idea as though he were tasting a delicacy. "You know, I'm all right with it. They turn out to be spies, I'll gut 'em and string 'em up and bite their thumbs off, but if they just want out of the Empire, seems fair to me."

"'Bite their thumbs off?'" the Fly-kinden woman looked up at him with raised eyebrows.

Balkus shrugged. "I just thought I should have a thing, that I was known for. I'm an important man now. I led the Collegiate forces at Malkan's Folly."

"And that entitles you to bite people's thumbs off? You're going to sell that as a Collegiate tradition, are you?"

"All right, forget about that —"

"Only, that would really liven up their Assembly meetings."

"Look, I said —"

"I can just see Sten Maker using that as his closing argument on a shipping case."

"Enough, all right? Let's celebrate the founding of Princep Salma by finding somewhere to get drunk, shall we."

They wove off between the tents, losing themselves amidst the great bustle of destitute humanity.

"They're staking out some sort of foundations over there," observed Lucenta. "Looks like about a dozen people going at it." She sipped at her bowl and wrinkled her nose. "I see you've switched bottles on us again."

A handful of enterprising merchants had decided to import alcohol to the great camp that called itself Princep Salma. Most had already run dry through lack of forethought. One had met with an accident, after trying to set herself up as the chief publican for the entire mess. The accident came in the form of Garrerly Screwser, late of Collegium and then Helleron, who found such ambitions incompatable with his own.

Now he chuckled drily. "Just testing," he told Lucenta.

The Sarnesh Ant woman eyed him narrowly. "Testing my patience?"

"It's a matter of doctrine in Helleron and Collegium both, that Ant-kinden have no tongue for wine; serve them any old vinegar, they won't notice. How about you, Vekky?"

The third at the table was an Ant with skin like obsidian, thin-faced and sharp featured. Artescus of Vek looked on the Beetle man without much love, then peered into his own bowl. He shrugged.

"You see?" Garrerly observed. "It's only you Sarnesh who've developed half a sense of taste, and that's because you get the good stuff from Collegium."

Lucenta looked at him with that characteristic Ant-kinden absence of expression just long enough to make him shift on his stool, then shrugged. "Well I can tell. Go get us something the *hoi polloi* can't afford." The Spider-kinden phrase rolled off her tongue. For a daughter of Sarn, she was quite a sight. She eschewed the sombre colours and cuts of her home city; instead she was got up in Spider silks and

Collegiate linens, orange and grey with a green stone at her throat. The look would have been more flattering, she knew, if only the lines of her brigandine hadn't been bulking it out. But then, the nascent Princep Salma could be a dangerous place. A couple of Garrerly's rivals had discovered that already.

People came here because they were displaced, and were looking for a place. It seemed the whole Lowlands was buzzing with the news of it: a new city, built by the dispossessed for the dispossessed; a city of opportunity, where anyone could go to be free of tyranny and slavery. The war with the Empire had set hundreds, thousands, out on the road with no more than they could carry on their backs. Some had left homes in ruins, some had left behind chains and shackles. Others were just idealists. Lucenta thought that it was the idealists she found most ludicrous.

"You reckon this place will really last?" Lucenta asked, indicating the plot that was being delineated before their eyes.

"Ask our host." Artescus's voice was thin and dry, and he wore armour openly, a chain hauberk over a padded gambeson. The whole looked like more than his slender body could take, but to an Ant it was nothing remarkable.

Princep Salma had more than a dozen buildings up so far, spaced widely about the host of temporary shacks. They were mostly businesses, taking what little coin the destitute masses had in exchange for luxuries like food and clothes, the price of which kept rising. The remarkable thing was that when merchants tried to come in and sell at more reasonable prices, bad things happened. Lucenta knew that such bad things, and such rising prices, were both linked to Garrerly Screwser not getting his cut.

"Going to be a smithy," Garrerly announced as he returned with a couple of bottles. "Nails, tack, that sort of thing. Needed a smith since that other one got run out."

"'Got run out'?" Lucenta asked. "Just happened, did it?"

The Beetle scowled. "Yes, it did. He and I had come to perfectly reasonable terms, but he tried it on with a Roach girl, and she turned out to have a whole mess of family. Cursed thieves and vagrants, the lot of them. And suddenly the streets are crawling with them! I never saw so many in all the Lowlands as we've got here. And they're always *making* and *mending*. Never in bulk, never actually setting up shop, but every one of them seems to be able to make a botch out of anything, and they'll undercut you for a pastime, the little bastards. They need to get kicked of back to the Empire or the Commonweal or wherever they've come from."

"Wasps and Dragonflies don't want them either," Lucenta noted, as Garrerly poured her a new bowl. With some suspicion she sniffed at it, then tasted. "Now that's better," she agreed. "That's... Wait, that's Collegiate east vinyards somewhere?"

Garrerly grinned. "Oh, my dear Lucenta, you're there. Care to narrow it down?"

She looked at him levelly. "Not really. If it's not Spiderlands vintage, it's hardly worth it, eh?" The offended frown he hastily tried to hide was vastly amusing to her.

"Great lady, there are more here to see you."

Her eyes opened with a start, banishing that circling vision; two men, one bright, one dark. Always in that mind's eye moment she was too late, just as she had been in real life.

"I don't want to see anyone."

It was the old Roach man: Sfayot, his name was. He had been there from the start. He had been close to Salma. That was why she let the man talk to her.

"They have come here just to see you. You do not have to talk to them. You need not even acknowledge them," Sfayot said gently. He was a weathered, leathery Roach-kinden with a white beard, a man who had travelled the hard places of the world, and come out of it with two daughters he would go even further to protect. Roach-kinden had no city, no nation. They lived where they could, wherever they were not driven out. The Wasps enslaved or butchered them; the Commonweal called them thieves and moved them on; the Lowlanders mostly barred the kinden from their cities, and the Beetle and Ant merchants refused to sell to them.

But here they were. The great wave of refugees that the Imperial armies had driven ahead of them had swept up plenty of Roaches, the splintered shards of their clans and families. They were coming to Princep Salma in ones and twos and little groups, looking for their kin, looking for somewhere to belong. And here, amongst the lost and the homeless and the hopeful, they seemed almost to fit.

It helped that many of them had fought alongside Salma's doomed and noble few. It helped that Sfayot had been the guiding hand that kept the noncombatant refugees ahead of the fighting. It helped that Prince Salme Dien, the golden champion of the abandoned, had smiled on Sfayot and his kin. Because Salma was who this was all about. When people came here, his name was on their lips. For all that his light had gone out, somehow his memory seemed to have touched countless people who had never seen or known him.

He had been a nobleman of a distant and insular land. Somehow, though, the war had made him *one of us*.

For her – for the woman who saw those two men fighting whenever she closed her eyes – he had been her love, her beacon. She had danced for him, and lived for him, and shown her vivid colours for him. And now he was gone and she was grey and drab as any Moth. She had been Grief in Chains, and Aagen's Joy, and Prized of Dragons, and now she was just Grief.

And still they wanted to see her, to touch her, to solicit blessings from her that she could not give. They came from every corner of the world, it sometimes seemed, to look on the woman who had inspired their hero. She was all they had left of him.

So she let Sfayot draw back the curtain of the hut his family had thrown up for her, and the curious and the reverent entered in little huddles and stared at her like an exhibit. She knew she was not what they wanted. They wanted the fire and the light and the colour, but she was just the shadow and the twilight after the sun had been put out.

"Is that even her?" Sperra wanted to know.

"I never got much of a look at her," Balkus admitted. "But a lot of these are Salma's people. They lived with her for ages, during the war. I can't see them being fooled."

"But you said she was all bright coloured and glittery." The Fly woman sounded oddly disappointed.

"Well she was," Balkus said defensively. "I mean, when she took on that Wasp, she was burning like you wouldn't believe – too bright to look at." His hands tried and mostly failed to describe the effect of this, almost elbowing a Roach-kinden woman as she hurried by. This part of Princep Salma – of the sprawling camp that was supposed to become Princep Salma – was Roach-town, as far as they could see. The white-haired wandering people were everywhere, in tents, in huts or under lean-tos. The air was lively with their conversation, there was singing and playing from just a few tents away and the ring of hammers on little anvils, the tap-tap-tap of cobblers' hammers, the clatter of looms. The Roach-kinden were people who knew the value of being self-sufficient.

And, at the heart of their community, this site of pilgrimage: come and see the woman a prince loved; the woman who avenged his death.

"Well now she looks like a Moth, all grey," Sperra complained.

"It is because she is grieving."

They both started to see a young Roach girl, surely no more than fifteen, regarding them solemnly.

"She was bright like firelight and the sun on leaves before," she told them.

Balkus squinted. "I know you, you're... You were with that old boy, the Roach chieftain with the beard."

"My father is no chieftain, just a man whose wisdom others respect," the girl told him. "Sfayot, his name is, and mine is Syale. They say you're a war hero."

Sperra snickered at that, and Balkus shot her a glare. "Yeah, I am. A real one. I led the Collegiate mess over at Malkan's Folly."

"But you're not in Collegium."

Balkus opened his mouth for an easy answer, then paused.

"Too much baggage," Sperra answered for him. "We both did our bit, in the war. We came out wanting something different."

Syale nodded but her reply was cut off by a commotion down the tent-lined alleyway. A cluster of Roach-kinden came up, one of them being half-dragged, half-carried. Balkus had a brief glimpse of a bloodied scalp, an arm held tight to the body.

"Fetch a healer," someone snapped, and Syale was off instantly. More than one of the Roaches had weapons in hand: knives and cudgels and triangular blades on lengths of chain. They regarded Balkus suspiciously.

"What happened?" Sperra asked them.

There was a moment when they weren't going to answer, but then one of the women spat out, "The Vekken. He got in their way or looked at them funny, so they beat him, right in sight of everyone."

"And nobody did anything," another added. "All those Beetles and Sarnesh Ants there." She glared at Balkus.

"I cut my ties with Sarn a long time ago," he assured them, but from their expressions it didn't make much difference. There were a lot of Roach-kinden about now, and most of them staring at the two strangers.

"Let me look at him," Sperra said suddenly. The suggestion didn't meet with much enthusiasm, but she pushed her way to the injured man anyway, a woman not much over three feet tall not taking no for an answer. She did have some training as a surgeon, and she was able to at least make the right noises and examine the man's wounds. After that, a couple of Roach healers turned up and took over, but at least the attitude of the crowd towards her – and by extension Balkus – warmed ever so slightly.

"We'll be going," Sperra said to them, after that. "I'm sorry about your friend. I hope he recovers."

Lucenta had put some money behind the bar, and Garrerly had put the word out to those men and women he felt were the aspiring quality of Princep Salma: Beetles, Ants, a few Spiders; traders and artisans he did business with; no Roaches, and precious few of the dispossessed who had first come here to make a new home. Instead, he reached out to those who had followed after, coming only once the ground was broken, scenting a nascent market. His kind of people, basically. The people who were going to run this town, when there was town enough to run.

Artescus was staying away, for obvious reasons. He and his Vekken had already done their bit towards this little piece of theatre, and the taproom was full enough without them. Above and beyond those in whose ears Garrerly had dropped a word, a whole crowd of the better off had turned up, lured by word of mouth. He let his eyes drift over them, seeing who he could name. Many of them were new, and he assessed them by their clothes and their bearing. Some were plainly men of his mind, but others would be idealists lured here by the risible freedoms that the rabble espoused. But that was all to the good. The plan needed some idealists on board just now, for all they'd have to learn better or leave eventually.

His gaze snagged on a couple in the corner: the biggest Sarnesh Ant he had ever seen, in the company of a sharp-faced Fly woman. He didn't know them, and he didn't think they were his kind of people, but they weren't the paupers that thronged the dirt streets of Princep Salma, either.

He got Lucenta's attention and nodded at the pair. "One of your countrymen there; too much to hope that he's with you?"

She frowned, narrow eyed. "None of mine," she confirmed out of the corner of her mouth. "I need to rattle the cage, but you make some enquiries."

Then she was banging a dagger-hilt on the bar to get some quiet, and stepping up on a crate to address them.

"Fellow citizens of Princep Salma," she started, her first lie of the evening. Garrerly wasn't sure whether anyone actually counted as a citizen of this non-city, but as far as citizenship went, Lucenta was very much already spoken for.

"Like me, you've all come here seeking your fortunes," the Sarnesh woman went on. "This place is a grand opportunity for anyone with a bit of initiative to make their own way in the world for once. A state for the stateless, drawn here by the banner of our fallen prince to craft new lives for ourselves." She smiled a perfect smile, and Garrerly couldn't help but nod along. She really had her patter down pat; she sounded just like the dreamers and the wastrels would sound, if only they could put their feelings into worlds.

"But, like me, I'm sure you've all realised that dreams are only going to take us so far. It's not natural for human beings to just *get along*, let's face it. There are always going to be those who envy what we'll build here, and want to make it theirs. I'm sure you've all noticed just how many Vekken there are in Princep Salma these days."

As a matter of fact, there weren't many at all, but everyone was nodding sagely nonetheless. Artescus had perhaps a score of his kinsmen with him, but they had been very busy running about the place and causing trouble. And, of course, because Ants all looked very similar, nobody was in a position to point out that it was the same band every time.

Garrerly Screwser was an accomplished liar, but even he had to admire the sheer mendacity Lucenta could muster at a moment's notice. Here she was, preaching about what they would have to do to keep themselves free, and her orders came straight from Sarn. Those friendly Sarnesh Ants, who had won the war against the Empire; the Sarnesh, who were the Ants that didn't take slaves. The Sarnesh: *our*

Ants.

But everyone forgot that the Sarnesh cared mostly for Sarn. The appearance of a threatened city-state so close had raised more than a few Ant eyebrows over there. Unsurprisingly, the Sarnesh would be happier with a Princep Salma that they could properly influence.

And Artescus, the mailed fist of Vek? That was the joke, of course. Artescus and his people really were renegades, misfits for whom the regimen of Vek was too restricting. They were more than happy to blacken the name of their home in return for pay.

Now Lucenta was talking about leaders and government, about how if they just went about with everyone talking, nobody would listen. They needed some serious, level-headed folk to start organising things; respectable businessmen like Garrerly Screwser, and she named a handful of others of a like mind. Poor, fragile Princep Salma needed to be guided and protected.

There were some frowns, more nods, plenty of uncertain faces, but she was getting through to them.

"The big Sarnesh," one of Garrerly's staff murmured into his ear. "He's called Balkus. He was a Collegiate officer in the war, an important one."

Garrerly's eyebrows went up, reassessing the man. *Trouble*, he'd thought originally, but now he wondered if that could be bartered into *Opportunity*.

And then Lucenta was starting on her next point. "We have a chance to build something special here," she told her audience. "But this place is already getting overrun with a certain type of kinden. Do you want this place to be a stinking campsite forever? Have you *seen* just how many of them there are?" She didn't mention 'Roach-kinden' by name but, from the looks on many faces there, she didn't have to.

Balkus was staring at the Sarnesh woman – not even listening to her words, particularly, but feeling her mind. It was like a closed nut, letting nothing out, not the slightest thought, but it was still like someone prodding him in the head with a finger, impossible to ignore. He remembered how it had been at Malkan's Folly, fighting alongside his former kin. He had got caught up in their Art, the Ant-kinden shared mind. He had been a cog in their machine as he directed the Collegiate soldiers, and while it lasted it had been glorious. And then he had caught up with himself, and felt several different flavours of shame and disgust. He had been running for half his life to escape just that.

And of course there were Sarnesh everywhere these days, loyalists and renegades, and they kept their thoughts to themselves, but none of them could ignore the rest, and Balkus felt it more than most. Seeing this woman up there speaking – of his own kinden, of his own city – was making him think about why he had left home. Soon would come the unwelcome but unavoidable soul-searching: *Should I have stayed?*

He was about to push himself to his feet, but abruptly there was a burly presence at his elbow. A broad-waisted Beetle man was there holding two bowls of wine.

"No need to get up, friend. This round's on the house."

Balkus eyed him narrowly. "You're the house?"

"Garrerly Screwser's the name."

"Screwser, really?" Coming out with that, Balkus realised he'd probably had a bowl of wine too many already, but the words were said and the Beetle seemed to take them in good spirit. Balkus took a bowl from him and passed the other to Sperra, who was listening to the Sarnesh woman. "Thanks."

"Not often a hero walks into my humble establishment," the Beetle remarked, piloting another bowl from a Fly-kinden server.

"Really? Half the people here were in the war, surely."

"But heroes? They say you did more than your share. Balkus, isn't it?"

The big Ant caught himself grinning. "That's me."

"Surprised to find you here. I'd have thought you'd be back in Collegium, enjoying the glory."

Balkus made a dismissive sound. "Look, don't take it the wrong way, but you Collegiates... Not saying I didn't have a fine time there – I held the wall when the Vekken came, did they tell you that? I got plenty gratitude for that one, you can be sure. But... *live* in Collegium? And do what, exactly? I've been a mercenary for years. What would I do in Collegium, guard warehouses?"

"And yet, while I reckon I hear a touch of Helleren to you, you've not gone back there?" Garrerly fished.

"You've a good ear," Balkus allowed.

"Just one of my talents."

"Helleron..." For a moment he searched for a polite way to say it, but then: "Seriously, I never lived in any worse place than Helleron. Helleron's a cold bastard that wants you dead. There's always work there, but... Nobody cares, in Helleron. And I did time on the Silk Road, too, but the Spiders... They play games with your head. And so... here."

"Our budding little city," Garrerly agreed.

"I mean, who knows how this place could turn out. Could be anything. Could be something great."

The Beetle clapped him on the shoulder. "You know, we could use a man like you."

Balkus nodded sagely. "I like to be useful." Hearing himself say the words – the very *Ant* words – he felt one of those sudden painful stabs of yearning for when he had *belonged* somewhere.

"I can see you're moved," Garrerly had more wine, somehow.

"Real potential here, sure," Balkus agreed, and then winced as a spark of pain beneath his ribs coalesced into Sperra knuckling him in the kidneys.

"A word," she said, hooking his collar and dragging him down to her level.

"What?" He glowered at her.

"Have you been listening to this woman?" Sperra demanded.

"What?" He saw the Sarnesh woman was still talking, her audience of Beetles and Spiders and assorted Ants obviously lapping it up. "Why?"

In truth he had been blocking her out: if he paid no attention to the words it was easier to ignore the woman's mind. Now, though...

"If this place is just left to the likes of them it'll never be anything more than a refugee camp," the Sarnesh woman told them all. "We need to take the reins here, if we're going to build. We need leadership, direction. Otherwise the rest of them, so many of them, they'll rise up like a tide. We'll drown in their squalor and their laziness and petty theft. Or else we'll wake up tomorrow to find a Vekken soldier on each corner because *we* didn't act quick enough."

"Vek and... who?" Balkus blinked, feeling slow. "Does she mean... the Roaches?"

Garrerly Screwser eyed him narrowly. "You think the Roaches are going to build anything worth building, war hero?" he asked, still the very model of avuncular. "Them and the Mynans, the escaped Imperial criminals and that rabble from down the Silk Road."

"You're talking about… Salma's people." Balkus felt his thoughts finally come together. "The ones he got together, in the war." He wanted to go on and say, *The ones who fought with him*, but so many of them had died in that glorious charge that Salma had led; the charge that had cut to the heart of the Imperial Seventh Army and wrecked its artillery, so the Sarnesh and the Collegiates could commit their forces. These here at Princep Salma were mostly the noncombatants, whom those valiant, doomed warriors had been seeking to protect. They were why there was a Princep Salma at all.

Balkus lurched to his feel. "You can't just come here and take it off them!" he got out.

Screwser's expression didn't change, except around the eyes. "Perhaps you're not the hero I took you for." A twitch of his fingers reclaimed the bowl from Balkus. "Perhaps this isn't the place for you after all."

"Yeah?" He lurched to his feet, looming, and Screwser's feet took him a step back without his head giving the order. "This isn't your place. It's everyone's place. That's the point of it. That's what they said. That's why I'm even *here*!"

He realised, in the echo of that, that he had been talking louder than anticipated and people were paying attention. He glowered around at Screwser's clientele, at the coolly amused Sarnesh woman.

"You people better watch yourself. This place isn't yours," he told them, somewhat incoherently. He met a lot of different expressions: surprise, alarm, even concern, but mostly a hostility to match his own. Then he was shouldering his way through them and out of that place, because otherwise he felt that he would want to break heads.

Sperra came slinking between elbows and hips to follow him. "Nice work, genius," she said, as soon as they were out.

"What? You said yourself –"

"Balkus, you remember Sten Maker, right?"

He blinked at her. "Well of course."

"And what do you think old Sten would have done, if he'd discovered a bunch of people doing something he didn't approve of."

"Well…"

"Let me prompt you: do you think the answer is, 'march up to them and let them know he was onto them without actually having any plan to stop them'?"

Balkus rubbed at his face. "Oh shut up."

"It was a dream we had." The old Roach man stared up at the night sky. "The prince, the Dragonfly prince, he told us a story of it."

Sfayot sat at the doorway of the Butterfly-kinden's hut, half guard and half beggar. Around him were a fair number of his people, and others too – the detritus of the war that Salma had brought together and given purpose to.

"Perhaps it's not to be," Sfayot added softly.

"You don't know that," said his daughter, Syale, angrily. "This is *our* place. If it's anyone's, it's ours. We gave our blood for it. We all lost people, to buy this place. And now they're going to take it from us."

"They always do." The white-bearded Roach sighed. "You're young, you haven't had it stamped into you. Oh, they'll buy from us; they'll use our labour; they'll let us mend their pots and pans. In the Empire they'll even enslave us," he said it as though it was a great favour. "But not so often. They don't like us as slaves, even. Mostly they just want us somewhere else." He looked about him, meeting the gazes of those who were not his kin. "I'm sorry for those outsiders who have inherited our lot. We thought this place would be different."

"It can be different," Syale insisted, and then Balkus stood up from the middle of the gathering.

"It will be bloody different," he burst out. "I'm going to make it different."

Sfayot looked up at him tiredly. "What is it to you, Ant-kinden?"

"I..." Balkus clenched his fists. "You know what? I want a place to belong, too. I want a place to be *me*. I've been fighting other people's battles for too long."

A Spider-kinden boy stood up too, looking far too young to speak before this many people, though he had ridden with Salma during the war. "The prince would have stood with us." His eyes shone with adoration for their dead hero. "Now we must stand for him, for all he meant to us." His name was Arad, or so Balkus vaguely recalled, and he had a strange accent; his first home must have been some far haunt of the Spiderlands, before the tide of war beached him here.

"We do not fight," Sfayot stated.

"Speak for yourself," Balkus said flatly.

"We fought the Empire," Arad pointed out.

"Prince Salma, he went to Sarn, he went before their court and won their recognition. You think Sarn will listen to any of us here?" Sfayot asked them, exasperated. "Sarn will listen to those Beetle merchants, the ones with money and powerful friends. Why should Sarn or Collegium or *anyone* recognise us?"

Balkus's jaw was set. It was a look that many of his past comrades would have recognised.

The conspirators had met with Artestcus in plain view, like before. Garrerly made sure the word was put around that he and Lucenta were heroically negotiating to get the threatening shadow of Vek to go stand in a corner somewhere and stop bothering them.

"I've got a list of places for your boys to show their faces," the Beetle tapster noted. "People who need a bit of convincing about this idea of a central authority."

Artescus nodded equably. "Do you also have our money?"

"Waiting for you, usual place." Because Garrerly couldn't exactly be seen handing over bulging bags of coin to the Vekken.

"You're going to make the big announcement, Colleague?" The Vekken raised an eyebrow, putting a spin on the word to stress the similarity to *Collegium*, because Garrerly's way of going about things was a very Collegiate thing.

"You don't think it's necessary."

"It's always been a weak way of doing business." Artescus looked to Lucenta for support, but she was shaking her head.

"Who beat whom, when Vek came to Collegium?" she pointed out. "For our kinden, Artescus, it's a nonsense, but others don't have our gifts." She gave them both her best smile. "It's a grand con the rich men of Collegium pull. You should appreciate it. Get the people thinking that they choose their leaders. Means they're responsible, they have *ownership* for what those leaders do. The lying, the cheating, all of it's their fault as much as the liars and the cheats. And so they go along with it; they don't call attention to it; they even cheer it on. You'd better make yourself scarce. Look angry."

Looking angry – showing any particularly strong emotion – wasn't an Ant forte, but Artescus got up so fast he knocked his chair over, and then stalked off, heading to where his men were waiting outside in a black-armoured cluster of blank-faced hostility. On his way out, he almost rammed straight into the big Sarnesh, Balkus.

"Trouble," Garrerly murmured.

"Let me handle it." Lucenta rapped a dagger hilt on the nearest table until she had a modicum of quiet. "Listen to me," she said – not a shout, because she didn't need to – and they listened. "You've all seen the same as me – that Vek is getting interested in us here. And why wouldn't they? We're on Sarn's doorstep. The Vekken'd just love a foothold here." And that made perfect sense, except for the way that Vek was still licking its considerable wounds from being slapped down by the Beetles and their allies. "We're going to need to do something to keep them away. It's like I've been saying all this time. We need authority – most of all we need an authority that will be recognised by Collegium and Sarn. If we just keep squatting here like vagrants then we're going to find a whole lot more Vekken soldiers on our streets one day – and the day after, we'll find Sarnesh ones too, because they won't let that pass. And on that day we'll just be another satellite town of Sarn. You know how it'll go."

"That's all very well," put in Garrerly, "but what's going to make anyone recognise us? You reckon Broadsmark here –" he picked out a Beetle smith from his clientele – "can just present himself to the King of Sarn and say 'hello, I'm calling the shots for Princep Salma'? Who's going to believe him?"

"On his own, with nothing but his word, nobody," Lucenta acknowledged. "That's why we need to do this the proper way. The Collegiate way. We'll have Lots. Cast your stone for whoever you want. We can't exactly have an Assembly of six hundred, but we can have a Council of Thirteen, say, like Helleron."

"Like Helleron?" The big Ant, Balkus, burst out. "You want to start a new city and your model's *Helleron*? Have you ever been there?"

And maybe mentioning Helleron had been a mistake. There were at least a few frowns in the audience. The richest and most powerful might well salivate at the idea of becoming new magnates here, but there were enough who knew that nobody did well in Helleron except the people at the top.

"And you're going to have Lots, are you?" Balkus put his hands on his hips. "Well fine. Lots is for everyone."

"Perhaps you didn't pay much attention over in Collegium,"

Lucenta told him sweetly. "Lots is for citizens, my friend. Not for any vagrant and drifter who comes by on the day."

"But…" Balkus paused, visibly thinking, and Garrerly thought, *Not exactly the most complex tool in the box*. "Everyone here is a – everyone's just come here. Who's a citizen, then?"

Lucenta looked about her, at the modestly affluent, conservative people who had come to drink Garrerly's wine and hear her speak. "You ever hear of a Roach casting a Lot, my friend? I never did."

Balkus scowled. "I'm not your friend."

"You're right," Lucenta agreed smoothly, going right up to him. "I know whose friend you are, though."

"That's right," and probably Balkus would have gone on to name some Collegiate magnates he was in with, but Lucenta didn't give him the chance.

"I've heard about you," she told him, speaking loud for the crowd. "I heard how you fought in the war. You did good work there, they say, leading the Collegiates. But you did Sarn's work."

Balkus's mouth hung open, words drying up.

"I heard how you threw those Beetles into the fray, just like playing chess. Sarn was in your head all through that battle, wasn't it? And now you come here, trying to stop us choosing our leaders, and Sarn's in your head again. You tell a lot of people you're a renegade, my friend, but we both know who your masters are. Sarn doesn't want us choosing for ourselves, any more than Vek. Sarn would rather let us fall apart and then send in a governor and a garrison, make us no more free than some slave-state in the Empire. And so they send some fellow with a war record to sow dissent among us, and I'm looking at the man they sent."

It was, Garrerly had to admit, a masterful piece of falsehood, laced with just enough truth that it rang like the pure metal when tested. This Balkus was no debater. The man was utterly flummoxed by the accusations, and whoever would believe his denials now?

Balkus wasn't exactly sure how things escalated quite so quickly after that. He had a bad feeling that turning up at the makeshift taverna and making words come out of his mouth had not helped. He had tried to shout the Sarnesh woman – Lucenta, apparently – down, but she had one of those voices that carried even when she didn't raise it properly, so that his best battlefield bellow somehow didn't cover it up. And the more he said how much he wasn't with Sarn any more, the less anybody had believed him. Everything he had said, she had turned into a weapon against him. She had one of those minds, too. He wished Stenwold Maker was here to help, and that said something about just how he had been backed into a corner, because the old Beetle War Master was more trouble than anyone else Balkus had ever met.

Anyway, apparently they were going to have Lots. All the people of Princep Salma were going to choose their leaders, who would then go to Sarn and hope to be recognised as the new city's rulers de jure. And they would be recognised, Balkus knew that much. He knew because Lucenta had let one thing slip – or she had shown him deliberately: not a word, but a thought, shared secretly between them. Perhaps she had just wanted him to know how well she had played him.

She was Sarn; that was what he knew. She was what she had accused him of being – a Sarnesh quisling come to make sure that the Ant city's new neighbour turned out right.

Today they had started with the Lots. The taverna was the place, and the hardworking and the hopeful of Princep Salma were turning up to cast their votes.

The game was skewed from the start, of course. Most of those who had come to Princep Salma didn't even know what Lots were – only those who had spent some time in Collegium. Garrerly Screwser's friends heard the word and all queued up dutifully to pop a stone in the box with his name on it. Most of those who had followed Salma to this place came from states where government was what was handed to you, though – and frequently came only in a black and gold colour scheme.

And yet some of them tried. There were Roaches and Mynans and ex-slaves who went to do their bit for participatory rule. Garrerly had a lot of friends, though. A few of the hopefuls got through, but many more found that the streets leading to the taverna were not their friends. People had been stopped, challenged, harassed. The Vekken were out, too, and whilst they made a lot of noise about wanting to stop the Lots, their boots and their fists only seemed to come out for the Roach-kinden and the rest.

"So, then," Balkus decided. "Time to make things right."

Sperra regarded him doubtfully. "I can't help but notice that you've got your armour out."

"Yes." He shrugged the chainmail hauberk more comfortably across his shoulders.

"And your nailbow."

"Oh yes." He hefted the blocky, murderous weapon in his hands.

"And this will help, will it?" Sperra demanded of him. "Shouldn't this sort of thing be the last resort?"

"I'm out of resorts."

"Well that didn't take long. Look, what do you think they're going to say, when you turn up and try to stop them by force? How do you think that's going to look?"

He took a deep breath. "It'll look like we're not going to take it lying down."

"It's 'we', is it?"

Balkus frowned. "Yes. I think it is."

Sperra looked at him for a long time. "You're going to get yourself killed."

"The Empire couldn't do it. Why should these shopkeepers get to?" He hefted his nailbow again and checked the action. "Sfayot!"

The old Roach came out of the Butterfly woman's hut and looked at him miserably.

"I'm going to fight for your people's rights," Balkus explained.

"No good will come of this." Sfayot told him. It wasn't exactly the effusive thanks the Ant had expected. The old man probably had quite a speech prepared, but at that moment the rest arrived.

Nobody had looked for Syale to turn up in a leather cuirass, with a bladed chain in her hands. Nobody had looked for Arad either, here now with a spear and a Wasp shortsword in his belt. There were over a dozen others: Roach youths, a couple of burly Mynan women, a lean Grasshopper with a quarterstaff.

"Oh, what is this?" Sfayot demanded.

"We're going to fight for our home," Syale told her father flatly. And then, with a nod to Balkus, "*You* can help *us*."

And they marched off, the gallant handful. Sperra looked away from their receding backs and met Sfayot's eyes.

"I know men like this Beetle, women like this Ant," the white-bearded Roach said softly. "All my life, I've known them: Dragonflies in the Commonweal; Wasps in the Empire; Beetles and the rest in the Lowlands; Spiders… They are all happy, they all like to think they are good people doing good things in their good cities. And then come my people, wanting them to share just a little, and it turns out they are not good at all. It turns out that if you push at that good outside, they are all sharp points and edges underneath. You get cut. You get cut, if you try to share the world with such people. It is better to move on."

Sperra stared at him. "You know," she said, apropos of nothing, "the Sarnesh tortured me, once."

Sfayot blinked at her.

"Yeah. Balkus was really, really angry. Didn't stop him taking their orders in the war, apparently, but that's war. I guess fighting the Empire comes first."

The old Roach coughed. "*Balkus* was angry?"

"Yes. Not me." She managed a weak smile. "Because I was scared. I was so scared that if I came to their notice, they'd do it again." And he was nodding at that; that, he understood. But then she went on with, "Well, you know what? This time I am getting angry. But I don't have a nailbow like Balkus, and nor am I a complete moron like he is. But I do have an idea of how to turn this ass-backwards situation around."

There were a handful of Beetle-kinden up ahead when Syale went round the corner. They started off grinning, because they had been standing here all day, in this tent- and shack-lined avenue, turning away Roach-kinden.

"You look lost, little one," one of them told her. The others were younger and bigger – engineers and smith's apprentices and artisans, men of their hands, but this one looked like a man whose normal weapons were paper and ink. He had a roll of the former in one hand, levelled at her like a knife.

"I'm coming to cast my thing," she told him. "My stone. Lot."

He nodded. "Perhaps you can find your name on my list."

She smiled brightly; she'd heard about this. "My name's not on any list, Master Beetle."

He frowned at her. "Why then, in all reason, are you sure you are entitled to cast a Lot at all? This is only for citizens of Princep Salma, after all."

"I am a citizen," she said simply. "I was one of the first to stand with the prince. I was one of the first to come here. My father chose where our new city would be built. Nobody is a citizen of this place if I am not."

His smile was distilled condescension. "That's all very well to say, young Roach, but such claims are very easily made. Perhaps you could come back with witnesses."

"I have witnesses," she trilled out, and the rest – waiting within earshot for something like that – trooped around the corner. Their numbers had reached somewhere near forty by then. They blocked the street.

The Beetle with the scroll stared at them, too aghast to be afraid. "What is this?" he demanded.

"This is us coming to cast our things," Balkus snapped at him, nailbow casually visible on his shoulder.

"This is democracy!" the Beetle spat at him, outraged beyond reason. "This is the civilised democracy of Collegium, most enlightened state in the world. This is a pursuit of the rational and the mannered! By coming in *force*, with *weapons*, you only show how creatures like you should not be entitled to a voice in this city."

Syale squared off against him, hands on hips. He was taller by half a head, but he didn't seem so just then.

"You don't get to complain about us shouting," she told him, "if you weren't listening to us from the start. Get your fingers out of your ears and step aside."

They pushed on towards the taverna.

"Hello..." Sperra suddenly realised she could not remember the Butterfly-kinden's name. Or had she been told more than one, from time to time. Too late to go back out to Sfayot and ask. "I..." The woman was not looking at her. Those blank white eyes were staring at the inside of the tent. The woman looked gaunt, Sperra realised, as though she was wasting away.

I..." She had been going to introduce herself, but instead she asked, "What are you looking at?"

For a moment there was no response, but then the face angled towards her slightly. "Two men, one dark, one bright like the sun," whispered the woman who had been Salma's lover.

Sperra could place that soon enough: Salma, golden Salma, had died in a fight with General Malkan of the Seventh Army. The Butterfly had been in time to avenge but not to save him.

"I know you're..." *Sad*, she wanted to say, but that sounded ridiculous, "grieving."

"I am Grief," the woman told her, and when Sperra made an uncertain noise she explained, "I was Grief in Chains when the Empire held my leash. Now I am just Grief."

"Because of the bright man."

"Because of the bright man," Grief echoed.

"Because of Salma."

And something changed in the woman's face. The dull grey of her skin flickered and flared briefly, but not with happy colours: bruises and burns came and went across her face. "Not Salma. When I arrived, he was already dark."

Sperra opened her mouth, worked it a little. "You're grieving for General *Malken?*"

Those pale, featureless eyes met her own, and the feeling behind them hit Sperra like a blow. "He is bright and burning because I *killed* him. We do not kill. That is not the way. I can find my peace with death outside me, but death within... I see them over and over. I see him burn. I see him as *I* burn him."

This wasn't the conversation Sperra had expected to have. "Look, er, Grief. Your people need your help. Right now, they do. Also a very stupid friend of mine who's going to get himself killed."

"I have no people." Grief's voice was bleak. "The Empire took me from them when they raped the Commonweal. They took every treasure, and that was what they saw, when they set eyes on me: a commodity, just another painting or sculpture."

"And then you got free," Sperra prompted, "and then there was Salma. And Salma would want you to —"

"Who are you?" Grief suddenly shrieked at her. "What do you want? Can't you see I'm trying to die?"

Sperra goggled at her.

"That's the place," Balkus declared. He was still gamely trying to pretend that the whole insurrection was his idea, despite the fact that everyone looked to Syale. Up ahead there were a lot of people around the taverna. Most of them didn't look as though they were there to stop

Roach-kinden, but that might change as soon as they saw this many on the way.

Not the enemy, Balkus told himself, amidst thoughts of emptying his nailbow into the sky to scatter them. The crowd there were of many kinden, though Beetles more than the rest; nor were they all affluent would-be magnates. They had come to do their bit for Princep Salma. Most of them probably hadn't even thought about just who was guiding their hands and closing off their choices.

Even so, there was quite a stir when Syale's two-score came marching down on them, armed to the teeth. Some of them got out of the way, others retreated to the taverna itself, which put them right *in* the way. Still others…

Others were scattering, because another mob was coming in at a run. Balkus saw dark armour and skin like coal: a good score of Vekken with swords and crossbows.

Two to one odds is no good if the other side is Ants, Balkus knew well. Still, the Vekken were supposed to be the enemy of everyone, weren't they? Wasn't that what Lucenta had been saying?

Except, now they were here, the mailed fist of Vek didn't seem to be keen on overturning the outbreak of participatory government going on in the taverna. Balkus read their stance and saw uncertainty there. In that moment he understood – the sort of soldier's assessment that didn't require book learning – that they had been summoned because of him and Syale and the rest, which meant they were in cahoots with whoever was inside. He wanted to scream it out at everyone there, to say how they'd been fooled, but the Beetles and the rest of the respectable citizens of Princep were drawing back, clustering about the taverna, ready to defend it from anyone they perceived as a foe. And Syale and the rest were kept out by that just as much as the Vekken. *The enemy of my enemy is my enemy.*

One of the Vekken was a step ahead of the rest, which made him a leader in Balkus's estimation. Even as the pack of them was readying a charge, Balkus pointed his nailbow right at the man's face.

"Go for it," he snapped. "Perhaps you're all good sons and daughters of Vek, ready to die for your cause. But I reckon you came here in someone's coin-purse, and that's a lousy reason to die, believe me."

The lead Vekken met his gaze levelly. "That's quite a weapon you have there, Sarnesh. Is it because you have little else worth pointing?" And that sealed the mercenary theory, because Balkus reckoned that Vekken loyalists didn't make dirty jokes.

He spent an awkward moment trying to think of a witty riposte before saying, "It'll really mess up you and your little best friends before I have to resort to smaller pointy things." Having said it, he wished he hadn't, especially as the 'little best friends' bit sounded like an oddly specific reference to the man's parts. It was odd what you thought about in the moments before the fight.

He saw the Vekken's thoughts in his eyes, or imagined he did: a job to do; the esteem of his colleagues at stake; no ready way to back down. *Bugger.*

"Ready!" he yelled at his ragbag followers. *It always comes down to the shooting and the stabbing. Glad Sperra isn't here to see it.*

But even as the thought came to him, he heard Sperra's high voice shouting at him.

There was another thing Sperra had never known: that Butterfly-kinden lived on air and sunlight. Keeping to this dingy tent, day in, day out, was Grief's way of attempting to starve herself to death. All this time, all those pilgrims who had come in here to gaze worshipfully on the Prince's Lady, the woman who had inspired their saviour, and they had been watching her drawn-out suicide.

"That's the... that's why you're grey now?" she tried. "Like a Moth."

"I have no light in the world," Grief told her, overly cryptically as far as Sperra was concerned.

"Look, you know all these people who come here? They come because you give them hope," she told the Butterfly hotly.

"I cannot give them hope. I have none to give."

"They come here because they believed in Salma – you remember Salma, right? – and he looked after them. For once in their miserable lives they met someone who had power over them who didn't treat them like dirt. You ever listened to them? He was their prince. That *means* something to them. And you're all they have left of him."

"I didn't ask to be."

"If we all got what we asked for then we'd all have a fish," Sperra quoted angrily.

Grief blinked, jolted from her melancholy. "A… what? Why?"

Sperra frowned. "I'm not sure why a fish. It's just what people say over Spiderlands way. I don't even like fish. Look, enough sidetracking. My stupid friend, and a whole lot of people who loved and believed in Salma, they're going to get themselves beaten or killed. I need you to go help."

"Why?"

"Because they'll listen to you. Everyone will." Sperra had no idea if this was true, but she was running out of things to say.

"Leave me alone."

Sperra's eyes narrowed. "Leave you to die?"

"Yes."

"I don't think you want to."

Grief glared at her. "What would you know?"

Sperra's knife thudded into the ground between them.

"Go for it. All yours," Sperra told her.

Grief stared at her.

"Go on. In fact, I'm going to count to ten. That's your chance. Pick up the knife. Open your wrists or stick it in your belly or your eye. However you prefer. Because that's *death*. The blood and the screaming. Not this moping and sighing and making poetic little statements about how miserable you are."

"How dare you?" the Butterfly hissed at her.

"I see my knife's still there, and I forgot to start counting, but I reckon ten's up by now," Sperra said. "So how about you stop letting Salma down."

"I am not —"

"You *are*, because these are his people, and when he died, whose care did he leave them in, precisely? Sarnesh agents and Collegiate merchants? Don't think so. You are all they have of him. That means they need you whether you want them or not. Or will you do the coward's thing, walk away or wither away."

"My people do not fight —"

"Cowardice's got nothing to do with whether you fight or not!" Sperra yelled at her. "I'm a Fly, trust me on that! So what's it to be? Look at it this way: if you get on your feet and come with me, at least I'll stop shouting!"

218

Balkus saw another mob of Roaches and a few others surging unevenly towards the taverna. *Reinforcements!* But they weren't reinforcements. They weren't even armed, most of them, and many were old or children. Sperra was there, buzzing about overhead, and at the front was some Moth woman he thought he should know, was that...?

A quiet was imposing itself across everyone there: the taverna crowd, the Vekken, Balkus's own people, the newcomers. The grey woman was the focus of everyone's attention, and Balkus was probably the last there to realise who she was.

So say something, then. He was waiting for her to speak; everyone was. She just stood there, though, looking thin and downcast, as though she had turned up just to sulk at them all.

A Beetle was coming out of the taverna, arms open in slightly strained welcome: Garrerly Screwser. Behind him, Balkus saw the woman, Lucenta.

"My lady, my lady, this is an honour. You've graced our little venture here, you're giving us your blessing." Screwser was pitching his voice to carry. "Why not come in, cast your stone." He looked a little wildly at the gathered Roaches and the rest, the undesirables at his gates. If he could get the Butterfly away from them though...

"She's not here to vote!" Sperra yelled, her high voice carrying to everyone. "She's here to be voted *for.*"

That seemed news to the grey lady as much as to Garrerly, but it was news a great many people had been awaiting. Screwser was trying to get a word in, but the roar of two hundred throats drowned him out, and the crowd outside the taverna surged inwards a little.

"Hold!" It was Lucenta, calling above the mob. "Of course we would welcome the lady in the council of Princep Salma – she shouldn't even need a vote. We'll give her a seat without the need –" and Balkus had to admire how quickly she was adjusting to circumstances: see a threat; tame a threat.

But Sperra was shouting as well. "She's from the Commonweal! They don't do merchant's councils there! They have Monarchs!"

She's mad, Balkus thought, and Lucenta's mouth was open, her words momentarily stilled, and...

He saw movement amongst the Vekken ranks: a crossbow coming up quietly behind the leader. Pointed at Sperra? Pointed at the Butterfly? Did it matter.

Balkus roared and discharged his nailbow into the air twice, the firepowder boom sowing screams and yells throughout the crowd. He went for the Vekken, and Syale and the rest followed his lead – something that rather surprised him in retrospect. In that moment, the entire mass of people there hovered on the brink of irrevocable violence.

"Do something!" Sperra yelled at Grief, and something there snapped the Butterfly from her gloom enough to cry out, into the thick of that turmoil.

"*Stop!*"

Did Sperra hear the word? No, she felt it; she saw it.

Grief spread her wings. At first they were just a smog-like shadow in the air about her, like a Moth's wings might be. Then colours smouldered and glowed within them, and broke out across her skin like lighting inside clouds. She flashed and flickered, and it seemed to Sperra that the colours were burning their way out of her grey shell like flames devouring a house.

Grief let herself rise into the air over the heads of the crowd. She was brighter and brighter, the last of her grey consumed; her face was full of emotion: fear, rage, loss, *grief.*

"I give you this from Salma!" The words came in the pulsing of her colours, in the trembling of the air. She was blazing now; this was the fire that had roasted General Malkan in his armour, the beacon that had signalled the end of the battle they had named after him.

But nobody burned in that fire: not Lucenta, not Garrerly Screwser and his merchant friends, not the Vekken marauders. Instead, when that light fell on them, it revealed... something. Their true natures, perhaps. Nobody who saw any of them, in that unforgiving light, would ever trust them. Their lies and schemes and petty ambitions were laid bare, stripped of the shadows and masks they had relied on to win people's love.

And still Grief rose, blazing like a new sun, and Sperra realised that all over the nascent city of Princep Salma, all those displaced people, the lost and the homeless, they would be looking towards that signal fire. They would be on their way even now, to see what this sign in the heavens foretold.

And when they arrived here, they would cast their votes, Sperra knew. They would take back their rights from Screwser and the rest. There would be a real Lots, for the real citizens. Rather than a cozy afternoon's voting by a handful of privileged Beetles, the people of Princep Salma would have spoken.

Only days later, the whole episode had virtually passed into myth, Sfayot emerged as the leading light within Grief's new-forged government. She herself remained a figurehead, as grey now as when Sperra had first seen her there. Perhaps she still wanted to die, but the needy adoration of her people would not let her. They were already talking about building her a palace. Some wit had even written to the Monarch of the Commonweal with greetings from a sister ruler.

"They're asking me to take over the defence of this place," Balkus confided in Sperra, one evening some tendays after the event.

"Defence from whom?"

"We're not exactly short of options."

She looked out at the first stars. "You're staying, then?"

"You're not?"

"I didn't say that. I just assumed you'd have got twitchy by now. You do tend to."

Balkus shook his head. "You know what I hate? Other people's rules. Maybe if I'm setting my own rules, it'll be fine."

"That just means everyone gets to hate you."

"I'm in charge of defence. They're supposed to."

Sperra nodded at that; it made as much sense as anything else did. Around them, the ground was already being quartered and re-quartered, the skeleton outlines of streets and buildings being sketched out, a city of the mind; a city of possibilities. What else could it be, built by so many of the displaced and the dispossessed? A city of hope arising out of their grief, like the dawn.

TALES OF THE APT

The new-founded city of Princep Salma is first seen in the novels in *The Sea Watch* and this story stands as something of a prequel for the drama played out there. Hence we see a lot of familiar faces, not only Balkus but his fellow trouble-maker Sperra, Sfayot (from 'Spoils of War' in the collection of that name) and his daughter Syale (later to play her own part in *War Master's Gate*) and even a cameo from Aradocles of *Sea Watch* fame, although nobody has any idea who he is at this point. On this level, it's something of a personal fan service, filling in a little gap in the series history.

Sperra is another character who was only supposed to be a name and possibly a demise in *Empire*, but somehow became a significant player all the way through the series. She does indeed get tortured by the Sarnesh, and she turns up all over the place during the second war. And, to some surprise on my part, she scrapes a halfway happy ending.

I originally wrote the story back in 2014, when there was a suggestion of expanded editions of the novels, each with a relevant bonus story – this would have gone with *Salute the Dark*. Coming back to the story just two years later, it seems remarkably topical and modern: an invasion and disenfranchisement whose villains wield not swords but civic power and a manipulation of the law.

The Peacemongers

When the news came it was still unwelcome, no matter they had all been waiting for it. The words passed through the Dragonfly force like a cold wind. On the fringes, there would be some who would sidle away. Some of the levy would be minded of home and family, until the pull of them would overcome all shame and they would vanish into the trees rather than face what was to come. Yes, they had been given all assurances: *This will not be the way it was before.* Who could blame them for having little faith, though? Nobody had forgotten just how bad last time had been, twelve punishing years of deaths and defeat.

One of the mercenary bands chose that moment to vanish away as well. They were a band of Grasshoppers and noisy Cicadas and even a few Mantids, but they had all lost comrades in the first war. They remembered how their bows and spears and blades had broken on the automotives and the Empire's fierce discipline. When word came that the black and gold column was closing, they became ghosts, lost all substance and were gone.

Of those that stayed, most lost their discipline. It had never been the best quality of Commonweal armies, but the leaders of this host had been trying to instil them with something of the iron of their enemies. With the Wasps close at hand, all that was left was rust. The new-minted soldiers trembled or clumped or ran about or took to the air in brief, undirected hops.

Their leaders regarded them with dismay, listening to the unheeded commands of their subordinates trying to restore a semblance of dignity. Or – not their leaders, not really. The best they had left, in the circumstances, but none of them exactly the picture of Commonweal chivalry.

Dal Arche was a robber prince, a man who had been a soldier and then a brigand and then a counterfeit noble installed amid the protests of all those who were born to the station. He had been given a principality of villains to bring into line, and the proof of his endeavours was that some of those villains were here under arms and notionally serving the Commonweal. And some of them had just now run away, but not so many; not so many more, head for head, than anyone else.

Of his two co-commanders, one was a bona fide princess, born and bred to the position: Princess Minor Elles Rosenn. She wore the glittering mail of last generation's war casualties, but she wore it as though she had atrophied since she put it on. Her mother had been a great, stern warrior and become a great stern corpse under the Empire's crossbows. Rosenn herself had taken more joy in inheriting the family library than the family armour, but here she was, with some hundreds of her people and an understanding of war that erred considerably on the theoretical. And her self-claimed status as a seer, but Dal wasn't factoring that into his tactics.

Last was Janice Blucraff, a short woman, dark and prodigiously heavy set. She had come all the way from far Collegium to advise on matters modern and military, because the only local masters of the trade wore black and gold and nobody had proposed hiring one for the purpose.

When the scouts reported that the column was set to reach them all too soon, the three co-commanders shared helpless glances that all said, *If only* he *was here*, because none of them was supposed to have direction of this host. There had been another, who would surely have a plan for this moment and the right words to say.

"Any volunteers to go front them?" Dal Arche murmured at his fellow non-commanders. It wouldn't do to let the rest of the war host see them divided or uncertain – he remembered enough from the war to know exactly how that felt. His recollection of the Commonweal leadership was hardly glowing.

The other two exchanged glances. "I'd assumed it would be you, Prince Dal," Princess Elles Rosenn put in, swallowing. "I understand you're very used to the company of… Well, all sorts. Your own deputy is a Wasp, is he not?"

Dal's Wasp-kinden partner in crime had indeed been left to hold the fort – pretty much literally – back in Rhael Province while this foolishness was going on. "One Wasp," he said flatly. "One *renegade* Wasp. You understand they don't exactly welcome their deserters with open arms."

"But still... Their manners and ways..." Rosenn said vaguely.

Janice Blucraff, the Beetle-kinden, made a rude noise. Making rude noises about the Commonwealers appeared to be one of her official duties. "You two lovebugs give it over," she growled. "You're too bloodless for this? Then fine. I'll go call out the Wasp leader and tell him how it's done. Only I don't *know* how it's done in this backwoods place, so you'll forgive me if I get it wrong."

"Fine," Dal sighed. "I'll do it. Just... get our people in some sort of order, will you?"

"I would face them," Rosenn declared, now that there was no chance of her having to. "Only, you know who they've sent. You know, in the war... "

"He killed a lot of people in the war, or his forces did," Dal said flatly.

"My mother died charging him. She thought if she could kill him they would leave..."

"That doesn't work with Wasps."

"I *know!*" Her eyes were bright with tears, so perhaps she was being more sincere than he'd given her credit for. "But I saw my mother die there, trying to get to him. I saw her fall beneath their stings. She was almost within a spear's thrust of him. I saw it."

"My dear, you couldn't have been more than nine. You couldn't have been there," Blucraff said brusquely.

"I *saw* it!" Rosenn insisted. "I see things, more and more."

Dal expected the Beetle woman to make another rude noise, but her expression said she was withholding her opinion for once. Rosenn's visions had started right out of the crib, and recently anyone with even a scrap of the old power seemed to be strong with it. What that made Rosenn now was anyone's guess. The old Dragonfly magics of the stories had been sun-bright and inspiring, making impossible heroes out of mere mortal warriors, but they had fallen into shadow long before the Empire came.

"I said I'll do it," Dal repeated firmly, and he went off a ways from the host to be ready, leaving the other two to set things right about the camp.

More and more scouts kept blundering home, giving contradictory and unlikely accounts of the Imperial force's size and composition. Giant warriors, they said; metal engines that belched fire; hundreds of

Wasps; thousands; uncountable numbers.

Dal Arche wished more than anything for loyal friends about him right then; even competent underlings would have done. Mordrec the Wasp was back home, though, and Soul Je was scouting deep past enemy lines, because they had nobody else as good at that game. That left Dal with the wan princess and the bludgeon-natured Beetle, and the turncoat.

"Turncoat! Gaved!" he yelled, without needed to glance about. The skulking shadow of the man would be somewhere within earshot. True to form, someone pitched up by his elbow a moment later: a weathered Wasp-kinden man in a long coat, his neck and jaw withered and shiny with old burns.

"Add me into the balance all you want, they're still going to have more Wasps than you," the turncoat said bitterly.

"You'd rather stay out of sight, is that right?" Dal understood.

"Cursed right I would. What were you saying about deserters and how they don't love them? You realise that goes for me, too?"

"And there's you always saying you're not a deserter, Gaved: that they let you go," Dal observed.

Gaved shook his head. "And there's every other bastard in the world never believing me. Look –"

"Hush your mouth now," Dal told him. "We've got company."

They heard the engines first: two war automotives according to the scouts, and Dal reckoned they could be trusted to count up to two without mishap. One was just a hauler but the other made the vanguard of the column and it was an armoured beast. The plates of its carapace were teased out into spikes at the corners to make crowding round it as unpleasant as possible. Its blunt prow was like a knuckled face with two black holes for eyes and a ram for a nose. It picked its way through the trees on careful legs, tucking them beneath its shell to creep through the gaps, then extending them out to stride on with an unpleasant burst of speed. Behind it came the black and gold, and even Dal had a moment when the fear rose up in him, feeding on all those battlefields that he had run from, and so many others had not.

And they came on – he reckoned there must be a good two hundred, marching in good order in their banded mail, those new weapons sloped across their shoulders. Janice Blucraff had brought a score of snapbows with her and they had been given over to the Thorn

Bug mercenaries, who were the only Apt troops with the war host. The Wasps all had them, and no doubt plenty of experience in using them.

The lead automotive stopped and let out a great hiss of steam, then settled down on its legs. Dal risked a glance back at the host: everyone was at least not visible pissing down their own legs and running away. There was a terrible tension in them, though. He could see all the wide eyes, the twitching muscles and gritted teeth. If the Wasps so much as shouted, half the Commonweal host would take to their heels or to the sky.

Then a man was stepping past the automotive, an older Wasp with metal-grey hair and a close-cut beard stubbling his chin. Gaved started visibly and nodded. *It's him.*

The scar was just as they said: a crooked line that drew the left corner of the man's mouth up into a vicious pugilist's smile. The puckered trail of it ran almost to his eye, tugging at the lower lid to give the man's stare a lop-sided, brink-of-madness quality.

"Colonel Jagoric, I take it," Dal forced himself to say.

Did his mutilated smile twist up another fraction of an inch at his name in a Dragonfly mouth? Here was a man who had more than done his part to crush all resistance to the Imperial advance during the war, a brute and a torturer and a master tactician. He had left the print of his iron-shod boots at plenty of battlefields, fallen fortresses, rebellious villages, and in the collective mind of a beaten people.

And now he looked brightly at the mustered Dragonflies and their allies as if he could not imagine what such a gathering was present for.

"We come in peace," Colonel Jagoric said, holding up a clenched fist for all to see.

The stamping efficiency with which his men formed up behind him did little to support the words. For the man himself, that damnable forced smile masked his thoughts as well as a full-face helm.

The Wasp commander eyed Dal Arche. "You don't look old enough to be Lowre Cean." He didn't butcher the name as much as Dal had expected.

"I'm not." Dal had spent the last year trying to forget he was a prince. Right then, he had to fight to remember that he really *was. I am not this creature's prey, or his inferior.* But of course the back of his mind spoke back: *you're a bandit and a murderer, and that probably makes you this man's close brother.* "He's... engaged on a mission."

Jagoric's eyes were like cold little stones. His voice was low but clear, and it carried. "Is that so? Well, I do hope I won't be waiting too long on the pleasure of his company. As I understand it, we have work to do."

"Perhaps you would join us in the Prince Major's tent, and we can explain the disposition of our forces," Dal invited. The tent was in the midst of their war host, and he was genuinely curious about how trusting the colonel would be.

"I'd be delighted." And it was not trust at all. It was a bloody-minded Imperial assurance that nobody would lay a finger on him.

Or no, not Imperial any more. They had some other word for what they were. It didn't seem to have changed them much.

Jagoric apparently decided that an escort of two would be sufficient to hold off the might of the Commonweal if things went rotten. One of them really was a giant, though, sitting outside the doorway of the tent with her head shoved through the flap to listen, so perhaps the colonel wasn't so foolish after all.

The giant's name was Ma Orvid. She had coal black skin and red eyes, like a monster out of stories. "She's my second of engineers," Jagoric introduced her, by which Dal took it that Orvid picked up and carried the automotives if the ground was too difficult for them, or pulled up trees by the roots when they were in the way.

The other aide he'd brought was a halfbreed youth, too young to have been in the war. He had the features of a Wasp, sharpened to a Mantis aesthetic, and they'd had to re-tailor his uniform to account for the spines that jabbed from his forearms. He seemed twitchy and eager to be somewhere else. "Lieutenant Escon," Jagoric named him. "He's my chief of scouts, so he'll need to hear what you've got to say. Where the pits is Lowre Cean?" When no answer came that instant, he looked about at them narrowly. "I see a girl barely grown; I see a Collegiate; I see a defector and I see you, who I think must be Arche the brigand-lord, am I right?"

"Near enough. We received a delegation from the enemy, inviting us to go talk."

Jagoric froze for two full seconds. Dal almost fancied he heard the buzzing murmur of the man's thoughts chasing down the correct conclusion. "You're not telling me he went to *talk* to them?" Nobody needed to tell him it: their faces did all the work. "I'd heard the Prince Major was a smart man. I'd give a lot to know what led him to *that* piece of tactical genius."

Elles Rosenn took a dangerous step forwards. "The Prince is a man of peace, above all. Some of us are sick of Commonweal blood being shed on Commonweal soil. He went, because if there was even a chance that he could bring about a surrender, he felt honour bound to try it."

"Well that's exactly the problem with honour, now, isn't it?" He blinked. "You said 'is.' So he's still alive, or at least you're holding out the hope of it."

"He lives," Rosenn said flatly. Her divinations had led her to the belief, and Dal sincerely hoped she was right.

"And no doubt they'll trot him out as soon as we come near, and threaten to cut slices of him. He should have known his enemy better. You all should."

"He knew that many of them, most of them, are our kin and our kinden," Rosenn spat at him.

"Not any more." Those pebble eyes cast about the room, calm and callous. "In *here*," a fist against his own chest, "they are like us."

The Imperial Commonweal – all that great swathe taken by men like Jagoric in the Twelve-Year War, had endured a turbulent history. Beaten down by the Wasp armies, its noble houses exterminated, those governors set in charge of it had for the most part been venal and cruel. They had been men who had come to a hostile and subjugated land where they were outnumbered by the native population, and the Empire had taught only one way by which they could maintain their dominance. More, they had come to an old land, a rich land, and they had set about pillaging those riches with rapacious speed.

And then the Emperor Alvdan had died, and the Three Cities had revolted, and suddenly the Imperial Principalities were cut off from the state that bore them, the Wasp rulership abruptly under threat from all sides, terrified that the armies of the free Commonweal would seize their moment to reclaim the conquered lands. Out of that uncertain balance, a new order arose, for there were those amongst the subjugated who had seen the ways of the Wasp and come to love and desire them. More, in the manner of powerful men everywhere, the governors themselves had looked at the old power exercised by Commonweal princes and decided that being mere tributaries to a greater Empire was unsatisfactory. Their numbers were swelled by those fleeing the civil war that consumed the Empire – men who came with their own riches and their own desire for power that fell outside the shadow of the new Empress Seda. Their power structures were shored up by Dragonfly upstarts and minor nobles who were only too happy to wield the whip that kept their own people down.

So endured a curious hybrid state, where the black and gold was slowly adulterated with the bright hedonism of elder days; where every captain or lieutenant made himself a colonel, and every colonel was a prince. In so short a time, the labouring peasantry found that they had exchanged the bloodlines of their old lords not for a military occupation but for a new landed class of Wasps and Dragonflies that was the worst of all worlds.

And still the Commonweal proper made no attempt to take back its lost lands, despite all the tales of cruelty and barbarism from over the border. Nobody in the Empire understood that to the Dragonflies the peace was sacrosanct, sealed by the unbreakable word of their own Monarch. Had matters been different, the Wasps would have broken it in a heartbeat.

But time moves on. The Empire itself had brought its second war into the Lowlands, far enough west to conquer Collegium and threaten Sarn, and then to lose it all until the Beetles and the Ants were raising their engines at the very gates of Capitas. From that brutal end, something new had flowered: the Empress was gone, her supporters dead or scattered; an Assembly ruled where once a single human being's whim swayed all the Empire. The Wasps called themselves a Republic now, and learned new ways of governance from their erstwhile enemies.

Those surviving supporters of the old regime found few friendly ports, but of course there was one place left where the black and gold was still honoured as it had been. Many of the Empress's Red Watch, or others who could not abide what the Empire had become, had fled to the Principalities, to become new-minted tyrants over the enslaved Commonwealers, and to plot their revenge.

The tyrant governor-princes of that land paid only lip service to borders and diplomacy. Amongst them, the old writ of the Wasp-kinden right to conquer ran deep, and they transmitted that same disease to the Dragonflies who had become their task-masters and their peers. They were swift to raid across into the Commonweal. They clashed with the armies of the Three Cities, still weakened from the war. They raided the Empire itself when they could, seeing each slave and each coin as part of their birthright returned.

But the Monarch of the Commonweal's forbearance was waning, for they were no longer the Empire. Even the Empire was no longer the Empire, and soon enough Wasp diplomats were seen at court at Shon Fhor. Proposals were made in respect of the mutual irritation and embarrassment that was the Imperial Principalities.

To the east, so it was said, Imperial armies and Three Cities soldiers were on the march, rolling back the borders. On the western border, men like Lowre Cean had summoned up what forces they could, by right of blood or gold. The Commonweal armies that had marched in their tens of thousands were no more, though. The war bands under arms now were only a shadow of the dead that had carpeted the battlefields of the Twelve-Year War.

"I assume you have a plan?" Jagoric asked. He was sitting on a stump away from the orderly camp his soldiers had thrown up. A Fly-kinden messenger had courteously asked Dal to join him. Why a Fly? Because a man in black and gold would cause less disruption amongst the Commonwealers if he was only four feet tall, no matter what his war record. It had been an interesting piece of tacit diplomacy.

"If we're talking plans I'd better fetch the other two," Dal started, but the Wasp colonel raised a closed hand to stop him.

"I..." He looked away from the gathering gloom of the trees to turn that crooked smile on Dal. "This will no doubt sound odd to a Commonwealer, but I find it very difficult to have these discussions with women." When Dal neither spoke nor moved, he went on. "There have been a lot of changes in the Empire. Including that we are not supposed to call it an Empire, any more." Impossible from his jagged expression to tell what he thought of that. "Most of all, the women. Suddenly they're everywhere. Women artificers, women diplomats, Spider-kinden officers, Beetle women running Consortium factora... I fought against the empress, did you know?"

Dal gave a brief shake of his head.

"Back during the rise of the Traitor Governors. I was never a governor myself, but I fought against her. For whom? Even now I can't tell you. We were none of us fighting *for* anything, save our own power, our own selfish ambition. A whole civil war, and it was motivated by little more than the horror of having a woman on the throne."

"And yet here you are."

"I spent some considerable time in a cell." From his light, philosophical tone Jagoric might even have been remembering those days fondly. "It seemed likely I would be put on the crossed pikes like so many others. In the end, I suspect that it was my war record that saved me. I had a reputation as a man who could get things done, no matter what. I suspect I might have something of the same reputation on your side of the border."

"You're remembered," Dal told him flatly, and then: "Rosenn hates you, for her mother." A heartbeat's pause, looking at that scarred face. "She died charging you – you, personally – at Or Shante." And again. "And it's just one of many, to you, so you don't remember. But for her, it was her mother."

Jagoric shrugged. "What can I say?"

"I don't know. I don't think 'sorry' is going to help."

"And you, Dal Arche? What is your personal grudge?"

"None. Possibly we were in the same battle, you and me, but they were all such bloody meat grinders I don't imagine you being there made any difference." And did that wound the Imperial, that he had been at a massacre and not signed it with his name? Impossible to tell from that crooked expression. "So: plans. The best of our scouts are off past the border to see what surprises are waiting for us. Now your troops are here, there's no reason we can's march in and start work."

"Except for Lowre Cean who, I imagine, will get his throat cut if we start winning."

"Do you care?"

"I had hoped to meet him. There are relatively few Commonwealer nobles who get mentioned by name in the Imperial war records. And I assume *you* care, and we are supposed to be allies now."

Dal grimaced. "I like the old man," he said. "Rosenn practically worships him. If he dies, it'll take a lot of the fight out of our people."

"And I imagine Colonel Sevig knows that."

"Friend of yours? He calls himself Prince-General Sevig now."

"Of course he does. I'm amazed he hasn't declared himself Emperor." The twisting of his scar showed for a moment what happened when Jagoric really smiled. "Oh, yes, Sevig and I are old comrades. We fought on the wrong side together. Nobody told us it was the wrong side at the time, of course." For a moment his grey gaze was fixed on his memories, then he glanced at Dal again. "I should pay him a visit to renew our acquaintance, perhaps. Speaking of plans."

"I'm going to get the others," the Dragonfly told him flatly.

Elles Rosenn was in her tent, although from her haunted expression her mind had been fixed solely on Jagoric's presence. Blucraff, in contrast, Dal found laughing and drinking with the enormous Mole Cricket woman, Ma Orvid. Apparently the language of artifice crossed all borders, and certainly the gregarious Beetle had been short of anyone to talk shop with for some time.

When they had all assembled about Jagoric's tree-stump seat, and the proposal put to them, Rosenn shook her head angrily. "It's out of the question."

"And why might that be?" Jagoric asked mildly.

Dal knew exactly why, but he had thought Rosenn too restrained, too politic, to say it. To give her credit, though, she went straight in with, "Because we cannot trust you."

Jagoric said nothing, just let his maddening fake smile do its work.

"You would be exactly where you can best betray us to the enemy. To your *old friends*," Rosenn went on.

"You think I've come here to shore up the old regime in the Principalities? We all saw how things were when we marched in here, Princess Minor. I could have ordered my men to attack there and then, and guaranteed the safety of this little corner of Empire for the next year in one stroke. Why would I need some more convoluted way of turning on you than that?"

Rosenn let his stony eyes fix her, and told him, "What I think is that you ordered the death of over a thousand prisoners after the battle of Lief. I think that when the people of Hera Eshe rose up during the war you put two hundred of them on your pikes to die in agony over days. I think that when you broke the defenders of Aka Mal, you had to order your troops to rape and brutalise the people there, because by their natural inclination they were not harsh enough for your wishes. I think you watched my mother die, but that is no great matter, against

Adrian Tchaikovsky

the rest."

Dal had never heard such a silence as came after that. It seemed that even the wind ceased to gust, the crickets to play. Jagoric's face was devoid of animation, but that still meant he was smiling.

"You are well informed," he said at last.

"And you are the man your Empire sends to us, now we are *allies*," she hissed.

"I am the man the *Republic* sends, but only because I requested it." He closed his eyes and rubbed at the bridge of his nose for a moment, as though he could banish all those accusations so easily. "I am the man who is your best chance to free Prince Lowre Cean."

"Because the Wasp-prince will welcome you with open arms."

"For precisely that reason."

"We have our own plans."

Jagoric nodded. "One thing I recall from the war is that you Commonwealers love your infiltrations, your assassins and sneakers. I've guessed your plan, I take it?" Seeing the confirmation in their eyes he went on, "You will send your strike team, but they will do far better if I am on the inside to open the doors and to prepare their way."

"No."

"Princess, there is something to this," the Beetle, Blucraff, piped up. "He's right that there are far less complex ways of screwing us over, if he wanted to. And the Empire is definitely assisting the Three Cities troops with the eastern front against the Principalities."

Rosenn was going to dig in, Dal could see. She was going to refuse to countenance the idea, and then maybe Jagoric would go off and do it anyway, and maybe he would betray them and maybe he wouldn't. And, if he went, maybe there would be no rescue attempt for fear of that betrayal. None of this boded well.

But then the princess closed her eyes. "I must take counsel," she said, and walked away without another word. She would go looking for omens and signs, he knew, trying to sieve the future for clues because she didn't know what to do.

Prince-general Sevig was just one of many new-minted lords of the Principalities, but he was a powerful one, supported by a cabal of Wasp expatriates and Dragonflies who had found they enjoyed the authority and licence that wearing the Black and Gold lent them. He had a core of Wasp-kinden as his personal guard, and when he heard that the Commonweal was finally making its move he had raised a formidable levy, equal parts conscripts and gangs of brigands and bandits. His territory had long been a haven for criminals and raiders, who were assured of a safe home to strike from and a place to dispose of their gains. Now at least some of them had rallied to defend their home.

The news found him at an impromptu council of war – he was at his table with a rabble of brigand leaders. Actual talk of tactics had degenerated into feasting, and he'd had some girls brought in – just like old times. And then a timid slave had come up and told him there was someone being held at the gates to his palace, someone who was conjuring with Sevig's name.

What he called a palace had been one of the old Commonwealer castles once. It had fared just as badly as all the others when the war touched it, but the Wasps had since re-edified it using local labour and modern architecture so that the resulting hybrid was spacious inside and siege-worthy outside. Beyond it was a sprawl of a town: some of the original slant-roofed Commonweal dwellings, some blocky Imperial, and a great deal more shacks and sheds and squats and tents. Recent edicts had renamed the place as Sevig's Fist.

There was a moment, only, when he didn't know the Wasp man brought before him, but that twisted visage was hard to mistake. Sevig leant forwards, eyes going wide. "Smiler?"

"Hello, Knuckles," Colonel Jagoric made a great show of looking around him. "They tell me you're a prince now. They must have lowered the entry requirements."

The mood in the hall was uncertain: nobody talked to Sevig like that. In that hush, Sevig momentarily saw himself as an Imperial officer would see him – through his own younger eyes, perhaps – a Wasp got up like a caricature of Dragonfly hedonism, bright with silk and heavy with gold, the banded colours of his uniform almost hidden.

Then his confidence reasserted itself enough that he could laugh, though with an edge to it. "You're old, Smiler. I never thought you'd get old." *Older, balder, fatter,* he noted, with some satisfaction. Jagoric had been whipcord lean back when they had come to these lands the first time around.

"I sometimes feel that most of the world shares your opinion," Jagoric agreed pleasantly. "It's done its best to kill me, on and off."

Sevig leant forwards, feeling the pressure that told him he himself was fatter than he once had been. "How is it you're here, old friend?"

"That depends on who's asking." Jagoric stepped up to the table and leant in, as though it was just the two of them. "Officially I'm here to negotiate your surrender."

That brought a whoop of laughter from all and sundry, but Sevig was waiting for the other shoe to drop. "And unofficially?"

"Unofficially, there's a Dragonfly brat out there who's decided she's my sole and mortal enemy, and if you leave her to me I'll deliver all the rest of them to you, easy as you please."

Sevig left his old friend Smiler to settle in and called a council of war with the more trusted of his underlings. This boiled down to two locals and a former Consortium bean-counter. Of the locals, both were wholly Imperialised as well as anyone could want. Of the Dragonflies, Lorres was a man of smooth good looks and enormous vanity who had spent the latter years of the war hunting down his fellow nobles for the rekef. Sark was just a thug, a man whose sole pleasure came from dominating those weaker than himself and grovelling to those above him. He made an ideal second and Sevig had promoted him to colonel.

"I remember Colonel Jagoric," the Consortium man confirmed, "By reputation, anyway."

"There were a lot of Wasps in the war." Lorres shrugged. "There are a lot of Wasps out there waiting to fight us, too, or that's what it looks like. And now your old friend comes calling."

Sevig gave him a cold look. "He was friend enough when we were fighting the cursed Empress."

"And yet he did not flee her wrath, as you did, and he is not dead, as so many are," Lorres pointed out. "So maybe his loyalties have changed."

"We've all pissed under the bridge since then," Sevig said thoughtfully. "However he might have got around the Empress, we've all outlived her now. Probably they let a lot of people out of the cells once she'd gone."

"So your friend Smiler is currying favour with your new regime."

"Or he's using that as an excuse to make his exit," Sevig countered. "If he brings his men over to our side…"

"Why would he? Why would they go? None of this makes sense,"

Lorres objected.

"Perhaps we can test him," Sevig considered. "You didn't know the man like I did. He put the fear into everyone who went against him, and he won some hard battles against bad odds. If he's for us, I'm loathe to just cast him aside."

"Show him the prisoner," Sark suggested. "Have him put the boot in."

Sevig considered his chief asset, to wit one Prince Major Lowre Cean. A good deal of frustration had already been taken out on the old man. One more boot might be one too many. He looked around at his advisors, face to face, and in his mind that other face hung, with its mocking scar.

What to do…? What to do…?

"I imagine they told you who we've got," Sevig cast over his shoulder as they descended. There were cells under what remained of the castle – oh the Commonweal might make itself out to be light and splendour, but when they had a need to stick someone in a windowless pit, their ancient architects hadn't let them down. Behind him, Jagoric took the worn stairs with care. At the back, Sark had a lantern that sent their shadows ahead to loom and dance across the close walls.

"They told me, but I wasn't sure that I believed them," Jagoric replied. "The man who did for the Sixth Army, stuck in a hole in the ground."

"The Sixth Army! The clear-up after that was a mess and a half," Sevig agreed almost fondly. "You were there when we broke them after that?"

"I held the right flank. I used incendiaries." A chuckle: *such times we had.* "I don't think they'd ever seen firebombs before."

Sevig let the keys ring in his hand, to let the prisoner know he had visitors. The pit might be Commonweal but the door was Imperial, thus it came with a lock. With a flourish he had it open, and beckoned Sark to bring the lantern close to reveal the occupant.

Prince Lowre Cean was an old man, even for a Commonwealer. He had been tougher than Sevig expected, too: close-mouthed under the crude sort of interrogation they had the kit for here; possessed of remarkable willpower. Frustration, and a kind of incredulity at just how much iron there was in the prisoner, had led to certain excesses. The prince was not in a good way.

"I see you've kept to your old habits, Knuckles," Jagoric observed, pushing forwards a little to see the mottled bruising that made up most of Lowre Cean's visible skin. One of the prince's eyes was swollen shut and there was a dried crust of blood about his mouth. The other eye was sharp, though, flicking from Sevig's known cruelties to the unknown of Jagoric.

Then it knew him, that eye. They saw it widen. Jagoric had the most famous smile in the Twelve-Year War.

"You're sure he'll live long enough for you to make an example of him?" the owner of that smile said softly.

Sevig grunted, shrugged.

"What's it to be? Put him on the battlements with some crossed pikes and see if they love him enough to take their war home with them?" Jagoric pressed.

"Haven't decided. You'd like that, though, would you?" Sevig had taken a step back.

"They're a sentimental lot, these 'Wealers." Jagoric was very still.

"Why don't you take a closer look, maybe give him a kick yourself, for the Sixth?" But Sevig's tone had changed, as had the set of Jagoric's shoulders.

"What's up, Knuckles?" Jagoric turned, and by that time Sevig had the lantern and it was Sark blocking up the corridor, with a couple of Wasp soldiers descending to back him up.

"I don't trust you, Smiler," Sevig said. "I never did. You were always too clever, and you were never shy of letting everyone know it. Well this time I'll be the clever one. Maybe you are just my old friend, but if so you won't mind keeping the old man company until I've dealt with the vermin at my gates. But I don't think you are. I think you came to free him."

"This is you being the clever one, is it?"

"Just get in the cell," Sevig told him. "This will all be over soon."

Jagoric sighed and spread open hands. Sevig was already starting back but, even after all this time, Sark was a moment too slow in remembering what that meant in a Wasp. The crackle and flash of Jagoric's sting caught him about the face and chest and knocked him flat, and then Jagoric was going for Sevig, and the two soldiers were pushing past to go for Jagoric. Stingshot seared briefly about the walls and then they had wrestled him to the ground, struggling to get his hands under control.

"Alive!" Sevig shouted. "Keep him alive!" Sentimental for his old friend? No: one more hostage, because he needed all the help he could get.

Only afterwards, when Jagoric had been bound and beaten and thrown into the pit with Lowre Cean, did Sevig consider how close he had come to dying, and the thought brought him out in a cold sweat.

Soon after that, a lean Grasshopper-kinden archer slunk into the Commonweal camp and gave a terse account of what had happened. His name was Soul Je, and he had been a comrade of Dal Arche since long before the man was made a prince.

"That went about as well as I'd thought," was Dal's considered opinion at the end of it. "And all this came from his man, Escon, the half-breed?"

Soul nodded. "Got a good pair of sneaking feet, that one."

"Who'd have thought Jagoric was a mind-linker," Blucraff considered. "I'll bet he kept that quiet most of his life. I hear the Wasps were still putting them on crossed pikes not so long ago. Makes you wonder if he didn't have a few others of his kind to hand, back when he was winning battles. Must make it a whole lot easier to fix your tactics if you've got a few people you can command with a thought."

"So where does it get us? What was the point of it? Assuming it's true, and it's not all some new betrayal," Rosenn complained. "And if he hasn't turned coat, why did he even offer?"

Soul shrugged. "The half-breed believed what he told me," he said simply. "As for why?" And another shrug, as though the Grasshopper never really bothered himself about why people did things.

"So what now?" Dal asked. "What's he given you?"

"A good idea of exactly how to get in, and how to get to the cells," Soul explained, adding "If he's not sold us down the river," with a nod to Elles Rosenn.

"You reckon you can get inside their walls?"

"Been planning that since before the Wasps turned up," the Grasshopper confirmed.

Dal hesitated on the point of speaking, the silence building as he wrestled with himself; as Rosenn and Blucraff watched him. At last,

Soul Je took the responsibility from him.

"I'll do it," he confirmed. "The old man's done right, by us. You, me, Mordrec, we've been living well. When did we ever have luck we didn't pay for?"

Dal Arche nodded. *I wish I was a brigand again. None of this orders and responsibility nonsense.* "Who will you take?"

"The half-breed; The turncoat, Gaved." Soul Je sucked at his teeth. "Could use another. Think about it."

"Out of the question," Rosenn snapped. "We'll need you in the battle."

I doubt it. Dal had never led men into any kind of fight that wasn't about running away the moment things went wrong. The idea of actually attacking a large armed force *on purpose* seemed insane.

"Prince Dal, you forget your place," Rosenn cautioned him.

He gave her a bleak look, because he felt as if he'd been forgetting his place ever since some fool gave him a province to rule.

"Princess," Janice Blucraff spoke up diplomatically. "I'm not sure we need so many voices shouting orders, on our side. The Wasps have their officers, and our people will follow you more readily than they will Prince Dal." A little lacking in tact, but at least she hadn't come right out and said that while Dal had the title and the mandate, nobody would ever mistake him for nobility.

"Well," Elles Rosenn cut the air angrily with one hand. "You want to go play bandit one more time."

"I want to rescue Prince Lowre," Dal put in. Even as he said it, he wasn't quite sure it was the real reason. Rosenn's words had an uncomfortable ring of truth to them.

"Do you know me, Prince Lowre?"

The old Dragonfly forced open the one eye that would. The cell was lightless: even the keen eyes of his kinden could not pierce the dark there. He was sharing his cell, though: he could feel another body there, knees and elbows stealing what little space there was.

How he ached! Sevig's men had been brutal with him: fear of the force that had marched against them; contempt for what they saw as his weakness; perhaps just force of habit, with some. But he had known what he was doing, when he had gone alone to invite Sevig to surrender. He had known what would come of it.

"I'd say that I came to rescue you, but I don't think I was ever that optimistic. Although I'd thought being one of the Prince-General's old friends might count for a little more," the voice went on.

Lowre's cracked lips moved. He tried for words, but managed just a hoarse little sound.

"I suppose he's grown used to not trusting Wasps," continued his unseen fellow-prisoner. "You know, I thought a lot about this moment. Meeting you face to face. The great Lowre Cean, scourge of the Sixth."

Lowre closed his useless eye again and put all his efforts into moving lips and tongue. "A pleasure," his voice was like the ghost of a breeze, but in the cell's confines it had no competition.

"Here, let me..." And then there were fingers fumbling at him, digging painfully at his bruises no matter how light they tried to be. They tracked down one arm and found the hand there, and Lowre cried out as they encountered his two broken fingers.

Still, the other man was firm, drawing his hand up, forcing him to move to save the twisting of his joints. He touched something, his intact fingers hooking at it automatically: a face, a stranger's face. He touched stubble, dry old skin, a mouth. A scar.

The man had let him go then, but he plotted out that scar intently, fingertip by fingertip, until he knew its topography; until he could have drawn it out on a map as though it were a river valley.

"Is it..." What did he feel, then? Probably he should have felt fear, anger, hatred, all of those energetic young emotions. He just felt hurt and tired and old. For a moment he couldn't even remember the name, though he remembered the man. "General Jagoric."

"You promote me, but yes."

The dark pushed in from all around them and brought a silence with it as Lowre Cean digested that. There was a curiosity in him, but it was such a worn-out onion-skin of a thing that for a long time it couldn't move him. He felt Jagoric shift in the dark and wondered what response the man actually expected.

"What do you want?" Peevish, an old man's complaint.

"I want to get you out of here."

"The thieves have fallen out over their treasure, is that it?" Lowre rasped out.

"I —" A pause, perhaps for Jagoric to work out what he actually meant. "I'm not a local. I came here with a relief column from the

Republic. I'm fighting for the Commonweal."

Something like vomiting seized Lowre, with that. He retched and he coughed and every spasm of it sent agonies through him, and only after he had stopped did either of them identify it as laughter. Jagoric started on some arch comment, but Lowre wasn't listening. He forced himself up until he was sitting, back to the wall, with a long gasp of pain. Jagoric, the scar-faced butcher, was back in the Commonweal; Jagoric, the man who had taken his principality from him – these very lands that even now sat under Wasp rule; Jagoric, whose famous scar had become the face of the war for so many who had lost everything.

"I don't believe you," he got out. "I don't believe *in* you. I'm dreaming you." Another racking laugh. "I knew I shouldn't have gone back."

"You want to know –?"

"I don't *care*," Lowre said, starting off bitter but running out of energy even for that. "I had made my peace. I turned my back on the war. I had no lands, I had no family, just the last few segments of a long, long life, hollowed out into husks. I had my pets and I had my guests and that was all I was fit for. I didn't *want* to be the prince any more. I didn't want to think about the war." He stopped, fighting for breath, and then, "What, you think I was all those years cursing your name? I hadn't even *thought* about you until now."

He let his voice trail away, listening to the other man's breathing. "Don't tell you you've been all that time thinking about an old man like me."

"When I was in prison, I had a lot of time to think," Jagoric said. "I thought of old battles, won and lost. We clashed more than once, Prince Lowre. The Commonweal never had another man like you. If it had, the war might have gone very differently."

Lowre hacked up some phlegm that was blood-salty in his mouth. "I don't do that noble-adversaries business. That's a Wasp thing. Sorry to disappoint. I don't feel like catching up on old times."

"That's not why I'm here. And it's not to finish the job, if that's what you're thinking."

"It might be the kindest thing you could do."

"Don't *say* that!" For just a moment, Jagoric's dry façade cracked. He leant very close, banging heads awkwardly and then his lips at Lowre's ear. "There is a band of men entering this fortress even now.

They are coming here to rescue you. Hopefully me as well, but it's you they want to save. I am speaking to my man there, mind to mind. They're coming *right now*. And there are your warriors, and my soldiers – they're mounting the assault as we speak. We brought a ramming automotive that'll make short work of the gates. I have snapbowmen and engineers and the Light Airborne. They're coming for you."

"Not the most reassuring thing I ever heard," Lowre whispered. He let the next pause drag on for a very long time, mostly because speaking or not speaking was just about the only control he could exercise over his circumstances right then. "All right, Wasp. Here I am, a captive audience. Why are you here? What's so important?"

Getting in hadn't been easy, but the four of them were working very well together, and each of them knew his business. Dal and Soul Je had been sneaking about various parts of the world together for years, barely needing more than a look and a hand signal to coordinate their work. The Wasp half-breed, Escon, had a calm, patient manner to him, and probably he'd been in the Pioneers and done all manner of bad and clandestine things in his time. He was content to follow Soul's lead, rather than trying to take charge, and that was a pleasant surprise. And Gaved, of course: Gaved was one of life's great survivors. He could practically skulk standing in plain sight. Dal didn't like him, but he reckoned the man had just enough personal honour to stand fast until things turned bad. And if things turned bad, then having Gaved to hand probably wasn't going to help one way or another.

They had left three dead sentries behind them, and someone was going to pick up on that sooner or later. On the other hand, Elles Rosenn and her merry band were on the march, and that was hopefully commanding a great deal of the defenders' attention. Certainly the bulk of the fighting men that Sevig had amassed were already outside the walls. Waiting to be besieged wasn't the Imperial way. Dal had a rough idea of numbers, and Seving probably had more spears to put in the field. At the same time, a great many of those were the old Commonweal levy – peasants forced into mobs and thrown at the enemy without training or hope. *Ah yes, that brings back memories.* Dal had come out of that mess with honed skills and an appreciation of just how useful it was to bring a bow to a spear fight. Most of his contemporaries hadn't come out of it at all.

Dal had killed one sentry with a quick knifing but the other two had been shot from the ground by Soul Je, who was the best archer Dal had ever met when allowed to take his time over it. The bodies had been stowed out of sight, and now the four of them were creeping through the hybrid architecture of Sevig's palace as dawn began to light the place up. Not the ideal time for it, but who knew how long Lowre Cean would last?

And, of course, Sevig would come for his prisoner before long. He would want to try and use the old man as a shield.

All along the border there were skirmishes and battles. The Commonweal was finally trying to close its old wounds. The Wasps and the others to the east and south were trying to rid themselves of a constant irritation. What would become of these lands once the Wasp princes and the Dragonfly generals were cast out? Would they go back to being compliant subjects of the Monarch? Would they ask to join the Republic, or declare themselves independent of all? Dal couldn't imagine, save that in his experience such things were fine for the history books, which never had no speak about the suffering and the hardship of ordinary folk.

His own staggering hypocrisy, in playing any part in this mess, was not lost on him.

Escon and Soul had a brief conference, the half-breed outlining the route down to the cell, setting out the hazards and the terrain in a scout's economic language. Up ahead, a band of half a dozen warriors – Wasps and Dragonflies both – passed hurriedly across their view. Somewhere, someone was screaming. Not Lowre or Jagoric, apparently, but it set Dal's teeth on edge. One of Sevig's people was letting out his pre-battle frustrations on his slaves, perhaps.

Then Escon stopped, one of his eyes losing focus and straying slightly, which was a strangeness Dal had not got used to: Jagoric was talking.

"They're coming," the half-breed stated flatly, echoing the words in his head, and then: "We need to hurry."

Lowre Cean sat and stared into the darkness, after all the words had been said. Something was expected from him, and in his more diplomatic moments he would have known what it was. Right now, though, beaten and bloody and crammed into this cell with this smiling warmonger of recent history, the words would not come. In the end, because the silence was becoming intolerable, he managed, "What do you want from me?"

"I don't know. What have you got?" Jagoric gave a faint chuckle.

"Colonel..." Lowre took a deep breath. "I could go there. I could limp back down that road, the battles and the dead and the loss of everything that I was. I could list for you all my fellow nobles who died in battles you brought to us. I could admit with shame the countless men and women who died under my banner without my ever knowing who they were. And when all of that was raw and bleeding between us, we could work out whether what you have just said takes the edges off it or not. Whether it makes anything better." To his astonishment he found that he was getting angry, as unexpected at his age as a sudden rush of lust. "So you're sorry, is that it?"

"No, that's not what I mean at all. Or – I wanted to show you *why*. I wanted you to know why I – why *we* did what we did."

"You wanted me to understand?" Lowre felt that anger still burning in him, wanted to be let out.

"I thought..." For the first time Jagoric sounded baffled.

"You thought I was sitting in a ruined castle all this time agonising over all the terrible things that you and yours had done to me," Lowre finished for him.

The following silence was sufficient admission.

Lowre took a deep breath, despite the pain it caused him. "Colonel, I lost so very much in the war – my lands, my friends, my son – that if I sat brooding over that wound I would have bled out years ago. I moved on. I moved on to other pastimes that would keep my mind from the past. So I will not go back over those bad years with you for old time's sake. And you do not have the right to make me. I am not interested in stabbing at myself just to make you feel better." By then he had his feelings under control, his habitual reserve back in place. "But thank you for the information. On an intellectual level it was interesting."

Jagoric had nothing to say to that, and the silence came back, but this time it was Lowre's silence, and he felt comfortable with it. He thought over Jagoric's confession, couched in guarded terms that exposed the man to a minimum of censure. He had spoken about 'actions' and 'events' without ever ripping open the terms to expose the bloodied meat within. He never said sorry, or made any actual admission of guilt. He had hovered about the subject, but never quite landed.

Then they heard the scrape of metal and the scuff of boots, and Lowre understood that either Sevig wanted entertaining, or the assault was underway.

"They're coming," Jagoric hissed: a fact obvious to both of them, save that it wasn't Lowre he was talking to.

Light danced about the door's edges as a lantern came close. They heard the staccato rattle of the key in the lock and then the prisoners were hunching away from the glare. Hands seized them, hauling the two of them upright.

"Well, Prince Cean, your friends are here. Yours as well, Colonel," Sevig's voice brayed out. "They seem very keen to get in, despite the welcome party I got ready for them. I do hope they're not planning to rescue you, because we both know that's not going to happen. But I thought I'd take you to the wall top so everyone can get a good look at you."

"This isn't about me," Lowre mumbled, and then Sevig was shaking him, dragging closer to hear, hauling the words out of him again. He felt tired to death. Speaking to Jagoric had beaten him down far more than the fists of Sevig's people.

"What he means, Prince-general," Jagoric spoke up, "is that they're here for you. Whether Lowre Cean lives or dies, your rule here is under sentence of death. But if you surrender, if you let us go –" and Sevig backhanded him, then slammed him into the wall, grinding his head against the stone.

"We are *not* surrendering!" the Prince-general shouted, deafening in the enclosed space. "Bring them up! Bring them out!"

The prisoners were manhandled out. Lowre saw Jagoric's face: cut lip and bloody cheek. The scar stood out livid against his skin and his eyes were bright, like a mad thing's. "Sevig," he spat through flecked lips, "Knuckles, listen to me. Run away. Run to your fellow little tyrants. Run where nobody knows you. Because if they don't get you here, then the Empire will get you coming the other way!"

At the top of the steps, Sevig rounded on him. "What *Empire?* You and your kind ruined the Empire. You destroyed it!"

"My kind?" And, though his cut-up face accentuated it, the smile was real. "Oh, you flatter me."

Something like thunder made the stone beneath their feet dance, and Jagoric said, "That'll be our ramming engine. You're behind schedule if you want to make a speech from the walls, Knuckles."

And Lowre was aware of a burning smell. One of the guards cried out, stumbling back, and Jagoric got a shoulder into another's chest, lurching towards Sevig. His hands were free – raw and red and still trailing smoke from where he had seared through his bonds and his own skin. Sevig fell back, calling for aid, his own sting spitting from his fingers.

Lowre leant against the wall and watched, too worn down even for encouraging words.

There were more guards coming, and Jagoric was trying to sting Sevig and failing – his self-inflicted injuries bottled up his Art so that nothing came out but flickers and sparks. One of the guards tried to get a sword in him, and Jagoric went down on one knee trying to avoid it, his face a grim mask of concentration.

Then Sevig was back with them, and Lowre saw fighting ahead. A Wasp in pirated Dragonfly armour dropped with an arrow through his throat, and then another knocked into Sevig, stingshot scattering off his mail. The two of them collapsed in a tangle of limbs and Lowre saw a fierce struggle in the next chamber.

One figure bolted through, treading heavily on Sevig as he did. A bolt of gold fire caught the guard who was trying to impale Jagoric, though not before his blade had gone in at least once. Of all people, it was the turncoat Gaved who ended up crouching by Lowre, breathing heavily and shaking his head.

"This was a stupid plan," he hissed.

"You shouldn't have come," Lowre said mildly.

"Funny, that's exactly what I said." Then one of Sevig's men piled him away and the two Wasps went down, punching and kicking at each other, each fighting to control his enemy's hands.

That left Sevig. Past the prince-general's shoulder Lowre had a glimpse of Dal Arche, a prince dressed like a brigand and trying to aim his bow. He was in a forest of elbows and knees and blades, though, impossible for any man to make the shot. Then he was ducking the swing of a blade and the tide of the fighting carried him out of sight.

Lowre just watched. Something beautiful was coming, out of this mess of a skirmish. The inevitability of its approach was a marvel just for his eyes.

Sevig had a hand at Jagoric's throat, forcing the man against the wall. Jagoric's hands fought his grip, still trying to sting but he had nothing left in him. His face was purple, the scar stark white.

"Game's up, Smiler," the prince-governer snapped. His other palm jabbed at Lowre. "But the old man first, since you seem to care. Old man. Old man, *look* at me!" because Lowre could barely spare him any attention at all, so wondrous was the sight of what was coming.

He had thought he wanted to die. When they sent him on this fool's mission, to reclaim the lands he had been trying so hard to forget, he had realised he could not survive another war, even a small one. It was as he had said to Jagoric: to open those old wounds would be the end of him. But this: this gave him hope. This was some small piece of the old, old days. This was magic.

The blade came down in a silver flash, perfect and polished, and lopped Sevig's hand off at the wrist. It spun away and took his killing Art with it.

Jagoric lurched away as the prince-governor clutched at the stump, mouth open in a scream that Lowre barely heard. The world had contracted to that single figure: a Dragonfly in gleaming opalescent mail who had walked through the fighting in the next chamber as though each move had been arranged with her in advance.

"Who are you?" Sevig demanded, but Elles Rosenn was not interested in talking to him, and she drove her red sword past his flapping lips and made an end of him.

His dying cry broke the defenders, who were abruptly fleeing through every door. Only a couple had died: a battle of men who preferred arrows and stings shrunk down to one small room. Dal Arche had a seared arm and a broken bow, and there was a Wasp half-breed there nursing a gashed leg.

Jagoric was sitting, his back to the wall and the tunic over his shoulder darkening with red. He was looking up at Elles Rosenn; she was looking down at him.

"Now let's not do anything hasty," Gaved murmured, and then clamped his mouth shut, obviously deciding that Wasp solidarity only went so far.

"How are you even here?" Dal Arche's voice broke in. His Grasshopper second was picking at his wound and he winced, but wouldn't let go. "You're supposed to be leading the assault! You complained about *me* –!"

Rosenn did not look at him. "The Collegiate and the Wasps have clever ways of making war that don't involve throwing our people into the fire. Just like the Empire's ways back in the war. So I followed you, step for step, and I waited for the moment I had seen, when I could do most good."

Dal's face was so bewildered that Lowre couldn't help a painful smile.

Jagoric nodded weakly. "And what now, may I ask? Or have you still got one more Wasp to kill?"

In the taut silence that followed, Lowre let himself recall the Wasp's words to him in their shared cell.

We thought we were right, he had said. *They told us we were right, from the first moment they told us anything. We were the Wasps. We were born with the right to make the world our own. We were progress; we were superior. We believed it. It meant no matter what we did, we were right.*

And then, later, after the Republic and the Assembly, it all went wrong. All that rightness *just fell away. There were Collegiates and Spiders and Ants everywhere you went, and they remembered everything differently.*

Many of us didn't care, even then. Many of us told more and more elaborate lies of why we had been right, and why we'd lost, and we believed those lies because it was easier.

And one day I was arguing with some fat, pompous Collegiate woman, and she was giving me facts and figures and what she *thought, and… she was talking about* my *battles. She didn't know who I was, and she was telling me about those victories of mine, how many dead and how many tortured and how many starved because I'd razed their grain stores to teach them a lesson. And I was denying and denying and then something broke in me, and I remembered it.*

And it was true, every word of it. I'd done all those things, and we hadn't been right. We'd just been stronger, and now we'd lost the war to the Lowlands, nobody could pretend those were the same things.

And so Colonel Jagoric had broken under the sight of his own atrocities through someone else's eyes, and he had come here to hunt out an old enemy and show how much he had changed. For what reason? Because it would make good any part of what he had done, or because absolution would ease the pain of self-knowledge?

Lowre looked at him now, at the point of Rosenn's blade, wounded and at bay, and still somehow unrepentant. "Colonel," he rasped out, "you had a lot to say to me, before, about your purpose in coming here."

"Yes?" And there was hope in the Wasp's voice, that the sought-for forgiveness was about to be dispensed.

"Tell her," Lowre suggested. "Don't tell me. I'm too old and my life has already run its course. Elles Rosenn is the future. Tell her about her dead mother and her wounded people and what you think of it now. And then let her decide what she will do. "

Jagoric's eyes met Rosenn's truly, and at last his certainty was cracked and he was struggling to find words, and his scar no longer looked like a smile.

Like "A Time for Grief", this is something of a greatest hits, with plenty of old faces making a showing. We finally get a little closure on all the Twelve-year War business of the previous collection. The last holdout of Imperial power is being obliterated by an unlikely alliance of Commonweal and the Wasps' new post-Empire state. Of course Dal Arche, Soul Je and Gaved are in the thick of it, along with poor Lowre Cean, while Mordrec is apparently playing prince regent back at the ranch. In a sense, this story is about a happy ending for the Commonweal, however piecemeal and fought over.

This is also a story that changed considerably in the telling, because initially it was going to be about the redemption of an anti-hero. Jagoric would have come in and saved the day, and represented a new leaf in the history of the Empire. In the end, I decided that was too convenient, but also simply not very palatable. I didn't want to round up with a story where the entire heartache and blood of the Twelve-year War was reduced to a lesson for the moral betterment of the conquerors, as though the Wasps learning the true meaning of Christmas would be somehow worth all those others left dead in their wake. And so, in contrast to the ending I originally envisaged, we have this cliffhanger. Will Jagoric's halting self-knowledge be enough to earn forgiveness or will be pay for his crimes? He doesn't get to decide. The choice can only be his victim's.

About the Author

Adrian Tchaikovsky was born in Woodhall Spa, Lincolnshire before heading off to Reading to study psychology and zoology. He subsequently ended up in law and has worked as a legal executive in both Reading and Leeds, where he now lives. Married, he is a keen live role-player and has trained in stage-fighting and historical combat. He maintains a keen interest in history and the biological sciences especially entomology.

Adrian is the author of the acclaimed ten-book Shadows of the Apt series starting with *Empire in Black and Gold* published by Tor UK. His other works for Tor UK include standalone novels *Guns of the Dawn* and *Children of Time* and the new series Echoes of the Fall starting with The Tiger and the Wolf. His SF novel, *Children of Time*, won the Arthur C Clarke Award and he has been shortlisted for the David Gemmell Legend Award and the British Fantasy Award.

TALES OF THE APT

Adrian Tchaikovsky

Tales of the Apt is a companion series to the best-selling decalogy *Shadows of the Apt* (Tor UK) by 2016 Arthur C. Clarke Award winning author Adrian Tchaikovsky.

Tales gathers together short stories from disparate places and supplements them with a wealth of new material written especially for the series. Together, they combine to provide a different perspective, an alternative history that parallels and unfolds alongside the familiar one, filling in the gaps and revealing intriguing backstories for established characters. A must read for any fan of the *Shadows of the Apt* books, where epic fantasy meets steampunk and so much more.

"The whole Shadows of the Apt series has been one of the most original creations in modern fantasy"
— *Upcoming4.me*

"Tchaikovsky makes a good and enjoyable mix between a medieval-looking world and the presence of technology" – *Starburst Magazine*

Spoils of War
A Time for Grief
For Love of Distant Shores
The Scent of Tears

Available now from NewCon Press: **www.newconpress.co.uk**

LEGENDS

Stories in honour of
DAVID GEMMELL

Joe Abercrombie
James Barclay
Storm Constantine
Jonathan Green
Tanith Lee
Juliet E McKenna
Anne Nicholls
Stan Nicholls
Gaie Sebold
Jan Siegel
Adrian Tchaikovsky
Sandra Unerman
Ian Whates

Cover art by Dominic Harman

Legends is an anthology of all original stories written to honour the memory of one of Britain's greatest fantasy authors. Determined warriors, hideous creatures, wicked sorceries, tricksy villains and cunning lovers abound as fantasy's finest imaginations do their best… and their worst.

Produced in cooperation with the David Gemmell Awards, every copy sold raises money to support the awards.

Read the origins of James Barclays' famed *Ravens* mercenary band, enter Adrian Tchaikovsky's Realm of the Apt, follow warriors bent on vengeance and others seeking redemption, weep for the fallen, pity the lost, and cheer for the victors. Steel yourself, throw caution to the wind, and dare to enter the realm of ***Legends***.

Also from NewCon Press

London Centric – Edited by Ian Whates

Future Tales of London. **Neal Asher, Mike Carey, Geoff Ryman, Aliette de Bodard, Dave Hutchinson, Aliya Whiteley, Stewart Hotston** and more. Militant A.I.s, virtual realities, augmented realities and alternative realities; a city where murderers stalk the streets, where drug lords rule from the shadows, and where large sections of the population are locked in time stasis, but where tea is still sipped in cafés on the corner and the past still resonates with the future...

Ivory's Story – Eugen Bacon

In the streets of Sydney a killer stalks the night, slaughtering and mutilating innocents. The victims seem unconnected, yet Investigating Officer Ivory Tembo is convinced the killings are sar from random. The case soon leads Ivory into places she never imagined. In order to stop the killings and save the life of the man she loves, she must reach deep into her past, uncover secrets of her heritage, break a demon's curse, and somehow unify two worlds.

Dark Harvest – Cat Sparks

Award-winning author Cat Sparks writes science fiction with a distinct Australian flavour – stories steeped in the desperate anarchy of Mad Max futures, redolent with scorching sun and the harshness of desert sands, but her narratives reach deeper than that. In her tales of ordinary people adapting to post-apocalyptic futures, she casts a light on what it means to be human; the good and the bad, the noble and the shameful.

Frequencies of Existence – Andrew Hook

Andrew Hook sees the world through a different lens. He takes often mundane things and coaxes the reader to find strangeness, beauty, and horror in their form; he colours the world in surreal shades and leads the reader down discomforting paths where nothing is quite as it should be. *Frequencies of Existence* features twenty-four of his finest stories, including four that are original to this collection.

www.newconpress.co.uk